The Memory Hunters

THE MEMORY HUNTERS

Mia Tsai

an imprint of Kensington Publishing Corp.
erewhonbooks.com

EREWHON BOOKS are published by:

Kensington Publishing Corp.
900 Third Avenue
New York, NY 10022

erewhonbooks.com

ISBN 978-1-64566-208-2 (hardcover)

First Erewhon hardcover printing: August 2025

10 9 8 7 6 5 4 3 2 1

Printed in the United States of America

Library of Congress Control Number: 2024944353

Electronic edition: ISBN 978-1-64566-212-9 (ebook)

Edited by Viengsamai Fetters
Interior design by Leah Marsh
Interior images courtesy of Hein Nouwens/Shutterstock

The authorized representative in the EU for product safety and compliance
is eucomply OU, Parnu mnt 139b-14, Apt 123
Tallinn, Berlin 11317, hello@eucompliancepartner.com

To the ones who don't know and will never know their grandparents' names;
to every person who cannot draw a family tree;
to those who need someone like Key:
This book is yours.

The Memory Hunters

ONE

Connection is power. We can be strong on our own, but we are the most whole when the chain of knowledge is unbroken from generation to generation. We are each of us an ecosystem. We are all of us an ecology.

—Aurissa Strade, senior hunter for the Museum of Human Memory, academy commencement speech

MEMORY DIVING IS DIFFERENT FOR EVERYONE. THAT WAS THE FIRST lesson Key's mother taught her, and one she internalized long before she attended the academy. From the beginning, diving had been righteous and holy, suffused with an expansive joyfulness, and that had not changed since she was a child.

Key stared at the fungi at her feet, her mouth watering on reflex. The mushrooms had proliferated overnight after the storm. Squat, bone-white cups had matured unnaturally fast in the sodden ground, pushing aside leaf litter as they formed in a tight cluster beneath the shade of a sprawling bull magnolia veined with ghost orchids. Drops of red guttation oozed from the sides of the cups and collected in the bottoms, thus giving the mushroom its name: the blood chalice.

Key kneeled beside the chalices—a set of them? a troop of them?—two small, rectangular tabs of rice paper held between thumb and forefinger, each tab sized to fit on her tongue. She bowed her head, her lips moving in whispered prayers to the ancestors. The saints would guide her in her search for memories and protect her during her dive. She ended with a prayer to Saint Aurissa, her grandmother, to ensure she would find a missing piece of information that could be used to mend what the Decade of Storms destroyed over two hundred years ago.

Calm settled upon her as she finished. The ancestors had heard. Key knew this in her gut, believed it as surely as she believed that the moon would rise or the rivers would flood. She lifted her head and blotted sweat from her face with a sleeve, swept an errant, salt-stiff curl behind her ear, and dipped the corners of the papers into one of the cups, soaking in a drop of juice. She repeated the motion, visiting each cup until the tabs were as saturated as the air around her.

"Storm's coming." Vale, Key's guardian, emerged wraith-like from behind the ruins of a three-story house. It was the largest building in the compound and the most well preserved, though half the roof was missing and much of the floor had been torn down to the joists, exposing a cellar below. The stacked-stone chimney stood tall, however, and it was that structure which had alerted Key to the house's existence, the skeletal finger of it beckoning to her through verdant canopy as she'd surveyed the forest from a rickety, abandoned fire tower several miles away.

"We should be going now that you've got the samples." Vale went to her rucksack, which she'd left on the wide front porch of the house along with her moon guitar, and withdrew a slim packet of antifungal powder and an empty water pouch. There was enough to kill off the nascent mycelial network, as well as other networks, just in case. The Institute of Human Memory held the copyright to their version of the chalice, and they abhorred sharing. "The stream by the water mill is running high. Won't take long to finish up."

Key stood, dead magnolia leaves crackling beneath her boots, and shook her head. "Specimens, not samples. I thought I could dive here quickly, just to see if there's anything interesting. The porch is a good spot."

"I said, storm's coming. And we're late. The curator's gonna kill me if I don't get you back soon. She's probably worried sick."

"We might as well delay the inevitable, then." Key smiled cheerfully, but faltered as she met Vale's eyes, as black as mountain rutile in the golden tan of her face. "Vale, it'll only take a minute. You let me dive at Bonnie's Holler."

"That was before you wanted to take this detour," Vale said. "Now it's after. That minute might cost us catching the train back to the city. Which puts us back another day, on top of the six days we're already behind. They probably think you're dead and I'm at fault."

"It's just one day. We can say the last storm kept us." That wouldn't be a lie. The storm had caught them out, the sky's mood changing on the turn of a strong wind. Quicksilver clouds formed into a hard squall line, and the only thing they could do was shelter in place and pray to the ancestors that they wouldn't get flipped out of their hammocks.

Vale's lips pressed into a frown, sealing her mouth shut.

"You can sing me out in half time," Key offered. "I just want to know more."

"You always do."

Vale's gaze shifted, and Key followed it to the magnolia's low, gnarled branches, several of them stretching away from the trunk in shallow arches until they knelt on the ground, their leaves mantling overhead like wings. The tree was old, likely untouched by anything but wind and rain for at least a hundred years, and had been growing unchecked until its conical form was the same height as the house beside it.

"How could I not want to know more about all this?" Key joined Vale on the porch, pinching the tabs lightly in one hand as she picked up her mat, still tied in a roll. "An unmarked compound half eaten by the woods, still standing, large enough for several families at least? No deep history except for what tales the locals tell? It's a mystery!"

The only information Key could glean from speaking to people in town—to be fair, it was Vale who had opened the channels of communication on account of her ability to establish a quick rapport with rural people—was that a hunter from the Museum of Human Memory had come by within the last five years. And it wasn't the first or even second time a big city like Asheburg had turned its attention to a tiny place like Crystal Grove, despite it being far from Asheburg's legal reach. Notable, that. The museum's protocols emphasized careful documentation, yet Key had found no mention of Crystal Grove nor records of hunters coming to the area during her extensive research for this exploratory trip.

"It's not like milk. The tab won't spoil if you leave it out for a day."

"It might." Key paused. "Can you unroll this for me?"

Vale cast her a disapproving glare. "I didn't say you could dive."

"But you didn't say no. What about quarter time instead of half?" Key softened her voice, using the gentle, soothing tone she often took with her penitents at the temple. "Please? Imagine if I found something marvelous. A missing link to the past. A light to illuminate the path behind us so those following won't stumble. Kiana Strade and Valerian IV, heroes of history."

"Don't you temple voice me!"

Key sighed, dropping the act. "You'll get a raise?"

"If I don't get fired," Vale retorted.

"You won't get fired. I won't allow it."

"Last I checked," Vale said, "Dr. Wilcroft was in charge, not you."

"Last I checked, my grandmother's name was engraved on the wall at the Museum of Human Memory. My family's foundation helps support the institute. You work with me, which means you're connected to the head resifix, as well as a city councillor. Firing you reflects poorly on the museum and the institute, and the papers love a scandal, which we all want to avoid. Therefore, you won't get fired."

Vale's jaw flexed.

"Also, I already prayed about it."

"You told the saints?"

"Yep, all paid up on the prayergram."

"Blood in the mouth, Key."

"Watch your language, they're still listening. And—" Key cocked her head and cupped a hand around her ear. She wasn't above a little mischief to get what she wanted, not when the ancestors had already granted their blessing. "What's that? They're telling me you won't get fired."

Finally, Vale reached out and pulled on the knot of the cord to unravel it. "Fine."

Key grinned. "You're the best!"

"Quarter time," Vale replied curtly, taking the mat from Key. She unrolled it with a snap and laid it on the floor of the porch, then retrieved a mycoleather case and two pouches from her rucksack. Inside the case were several pricking needles, extra rice paper, disinfecting wipes, a pen, and small, laminated cards specially designed to store tabs. Without a word, Vale held out a card, into which Key placed one of the tabs. Vale marked it with the date, site name, and site number, checked off some boxes, and then sealed it into the pouch labeled SPECIMENS.

Key kept her hand outstretched, waiting for Vale to tear open a package of wipes. The brief coolness of the alcohol was welcome in the humidity rising from the forest floor.

Vale brought out a pricking needle and a fresh tab of rice paper. "See me."

"You are seen," Key replied automatically.

Vale pressed the needle against a calloused fingertip. "Hear me."

"You are heard." Key winced at the pop of her skin, the small shock of pain. Blood strained out of the pinprick, expanding into a deep crimson drop.

Vale trapped it on the paper. "Remember me."

"You are remembered."

Key squeezed the tip of her finger as Vale slipped the paper into a laminated card and labeled it. The rest of the words formed in Key's mind, the ones that would have been spoken next in the temple. *Sanctify me.*

And Key, favored of the ancestors, would bow her head, tracing her finger in a circle over her petitioner's forehead before tracing a circle over her own. *You are sanctified.*

Key checked her finger and, finding it suitably clotted, lowered herself to the mat, lying on her back, allowing her arms to rest at her sides. "What's the codeword?"

Vale frowned, thinking. "Cochineal."

"Cochineal," Key repeated, visualizing the word, then drawing it in the air. When she woke, she would need to speak it to prove she was still whole in mind and not drowning in a stranger's memories.

"Quarter time," Vale reminded her. She lifted herself onto her tiptoes in a stretch, then walked out of Key's line of sight. A few seconds later, she heard muffled thumps as Vale began kicking over the blood chalices.

Key closed her eyes, then placed the tab on her tongue. Bitterness and spice filled her mouth, and her salivary glands went into overdrive, sending an ache into her jaw. She swallowed, her face creasing with displeasure, and waited for the concentrated fluid to trigger the dive.

One breath in, one breath out. Washes of color and light covered the insides of her eyelids. Key imagined her body disintegrating into the dirt, her tender flesh falling off the bone. Another breath in and out, sinking backward through time

until it's less diving and more expanding. Less
floating in the depths of space and more becoming its
uncontainable wholeness.

Key solidifies the idea of herself before she begins traveling, reminds herself of who she is. Despite her shortened dive, she takes time to do it right. There is no memory diver, no memory hunter, who is not secure in themselves the way a mountain is secure against rain. The further she goes, the more she needs to force herself into the memory to parse it, and if she doesn't hold fast to who she is, her psyche will fray and fall apart.

She's in luck. Often there are no memories at all, and Key remains suspended in the dive until Vale recalls her. In the dark, memories begin to glow, twisting and flapping like streamers in the wind. Key catches the tail of a particularly bright one, tasting pepper, salt, butter. It will yield, then. She follows it, knowing instinctively when she has passed fifty years, a hundred. It's a short distance, like walking from one room to another.

The next fifty carries with it the discomfort of clothing that is too tight. Fragments branch from the main memory, flashing like pale, ephemeral fireflies, each of them linked with threads as slender and fine as hyphae. If Vale had agreed to a full dive, Key could explore the echoes of remembered laughter or the glimpses of faces, hoping for something more profound. But she can only traverse the strongest path with the time she has.

The last memory dive dead-ended abruptly at a hundred fifty years, holding only annoyance over the flat humming of a fluorescent light. Too many of the souvenirs the other hunters bring back contain the hook of an earworm or the scent of extinct flowers.

Those memories would feed the penitents at the temple, but not the museum.

Key needs something better, something special. Something worthy of the Strade name.

At two hundred years, the memories are of floods and hurricanes, disaster after disaster. The streamer thickens and strengthens, cording like rope, and Key steels herself to pass through the emotional gauntlet. The time period after the Decade of Storms is rife with tragedy, and though Key has seen enough of it to be conditioned, she isn't unaffected.

Key trains her focus on the period before the Decade. As one of the few blessed by the ancestors, she has the ability to go that far, or further, unlike the other hunters at the museum, senior hunter and head curator excepted. She drops another ten years back, certain she'll find something. Key splays her senses out, searching for the invisible limit of her ability. She descends through a nebula of light, where a woman is crying. There is mud between her toes, and the silence outside is too loud.

Another ten years go by. Key slows, her progress dwindling to single digits. The strongest hunters can see two hundred thirty years into the past without their minds fracturing, and Key isn't there yet. She forges on, safe under the saints' protection. A man slams his fist on a table mid-argument. Howling winds rattle warped glass windows. The taste of metal coats Key's mouth as she senses a strong memory and pushes herself into it, changing her shape to fit it. One of the techniques she'd learned at the academy was to find a focus and grow from there. A hand is clutching a mug. Red clay, white paint, handmade. Bumps of glaze have gathered and hardened on the handle.

She looks from her hand to a wooden table, her eyes following the swirl of a large knot. The motion carries with it a sense of déjà vu. Her fingers flatten against the side of the cup as she scrapes her tongue against her teeth. No amount of sugar or prayer can hide the tang of blood, and the more she thinks about it, the more nauseated she becomes.

Chair legs bark across the hardwood floor. Her grandfather drops a spoonful of powder into her mug, pours steaming water into it, stirs as the heat transfers through the ceramic and scalds her fingertips. She pulls her hand away.

"Drink," he says.

"I've had so much and nothing's happened," she replies.

He pushes the cup toward her. "You need more. The blessing only is given after the full sacrament is taken. This is the last. You have been seen and heard and remembered. Now, you will be consecrated."

"Can't we do it later?" She'd rather be outside shoveling snow than here beneath her grandfather's hooded, wild-rimmed eyes.

"You cannot take from the chalice later."

A pure note shivers through her, and her vision blurs. She has a vague sense of being outside her body. The note turns into a familiar melody—a hymn from the temple, sung to her since she was a baby in a sling on her mother's chest. It threads through the bits of her, stitching her together, tightening, forcing her to break out of her shape. She isn't done, though. She can't leave. She's going to gag and force down the concoction, and that night she will fall ill. She

took a deep breath as she surfaced from the dive, waiting for fresh oxygen to spark recognition of herself. Beside her, a voice was lifted in song. But the memory held on like a burr, digging deeper as she attempted to shed the image of a small kitchen, the snowfall outside muting the colors of the stained-glass panel hanging in front of the window. Her mouth buzzed with a sour, coppery aftertaste, and pressed all along her skin was the scent of wet humus and the trilling of birdsong.

A phantom teaspoon clinked twice against the side of a mug. *Drink again*, her grandfather said.

The song restarted. The singer's voice caught silver and barbed between her ribs, reeling her through layers of the memory. The image splintered as she ascended, parts of it left behind, spinning away like seed pods on the breeze.

She opened her eyes to the burn of daylight, her senses heaving. The glory of infinite connection dimmed, and with it went the euphoria of the dive. Above her, sun and sky and tree leaves showed through the broken roof of a covered porch. The scent of earth persisted, as did the sourness on her tongue. She blinked as a woman leaned into her field of vision. She was beautiful, her monolid eyes intense and black, set in a youthful, delicate face with lightly tanned skin and a rosebud mouth.

Vale.

"Who are you?" Vale said.

There was a second of disorientation as the memory laid itself stubbornly over her, as if she were looking through a film negative. Her temples throbbed as she fought past the image of the kitchen in haloed triplicate, her hand grasping for the mug and getting only the spongy surface of her mat.

"Who are you?" Vale repeated, her eyes narrowing.

She took another deep breath and finally, the remnants of the memory dissolved until only fine strands of it were left, caught on her like spider silk. She sat up, fully grounded now, and lifted a hand to her head. "I'm Key. Hunter."

"Who am I?"

"Vale." Her tongue was thick and foreign in her mouth. "Valerian IV. Guardian."

"What's our word?"

Key scrubbed her wrist across her cheek, searching for the knowledge, her thoughts sluggish.

"Key?" Vale's tone lifted in warning.

Alarm flogged her heartbeat. She needed the codeword before it was too late. "A bug, or something. Color. Pink."

Vale tensed, her arm blurring with speed. Before Key could finish gasping, Vale had a slender knife to her neck, her face so close they could share breaths. "Who are you?" she demanded.

"No, no! I got it! Cochineal."

Vale exhaled and withdrew, putting a hand to her chest, relief spreading over her face as she sat heavily on the floor. "Don't scare me like that."

"Don't scare *me* like that!" Key retorted, still feeling the residual coolness of Vale's blade as a spectral kiss. She swallowed, sending a silent thank-you to the saints.

"You're usually faster to recover. Are you okay?"

She held Vale's eyes, unwavering as she tamped down her fear. Vale was her protector, but according to the academy, Key might need protection from herself. "I'm okay. Not used to quarter time, I guess. Like being roused too early from a nap."

Vale returned her knife to its sheath. Key rose to her feet as wind swept past her, tugging at the fine curls on the back of her neck. She closed her eyes to savor it better, and as she did, the image of an old three-story house, its gray-painted sides furred with unseasonable snow, projected itself on her eyelids. The magnolia in the yard bore tightly furled white buds, and inside the kitchen's garden window hung a stained-glass panel.

Key's eyes popped open. She scrambled off the porch, ignoring Vale's exclamation, and sprinted down the remains of the front walk until she had gained enough distance to get a better view. The magnolia here was much bigger now, and what was left of the kitchen had collapsed inward, deflating much the same way the other buildings in the compound had, pierced as they were by time and nature. But Key could imagine the outlines of the wall, the orientation of the furniture inside.

You have been consecrated. That was what the old man had said: consecrated, not sanctified. Everything else in the recitation had been the same. If she included the iconography of the magnolia in the stained glass, it could only mean that she had found an early version of the temple's main recitation.

She drew a long, slow breath, gratitude swelling within her. After too long spent finding nothing, the ancestors had guided her to a memory that fell directly into her research specialty at the museum. It could not be more perfect.

"Thank you, Gramma," Key whispered, putting a hand to her chest. There was no way she could leave. Whatever the curator did, she and Vale would have to bear it. "Vale," Key called. "We have to stay."

"No."

"But—"

Vale swept her arm to the side, indicating the area of freshly turned dirt where she had trampled the mushroom and doused it with the antifungal solution. Pieces of rust-stained mushroom poked up like teeth, their ivory sides already pitted brown with rot. "Storm's coming and we're behind schedule. I gave you the quarter time you asked for, and more besides."

"I need to journal."

"Do it later."

Key frowned, her hands twitching for want of ink and pen, but it was true: Vale had relented and was unlikely to budge further. Besides, Vale was the expert when they were this far from the cities, and it wasn't wise to keep arguing with someone who'd spent most of her life half feral, raised on the cruel shore and new barrier islands of the southern sea.

Instead, Key set her desire aside. The blessings of the ancestors were permanent and would not wane the way the seasons once did. She'd come back, for certain. "You're right," she said as she returned to the front porch. She glanced quickly into the doorway, scanning for anything useful to bring back to give to the blood chalices in the museum's lab, but was met only with trash from squatters. She picked up her mat and rolled it up. "I can journal on the train."

She paused as Vale began checking her weapons. "Are you . . . expecting someone?"

Vale settled a hand on the pommel of the butterfly swords scabbarded at her side. "Yep. Well, I wasn't before, but now I am. Been waiting on 'em since the station."

"You let them track us this far and didn't say anything?" Key glared as she tied the knot.

"If you'd listened to me, we'd be gone already, and we wouldn't have a problem." Vale shrugged.

"Vale! I had a feeling!"

"And so did I." She grinned, her previously taciturn demeanor melting away into wild beauty. Vale took the mat from Key and attached it to the top of a frame backpack. "I wouldn't worry too much. These fools are from the city, or close to it. Don't know who trained 'em, but they had no idea how to hunker down against a storm as big as we got. Their camp got washed out. Here."

Key accepted her staff, the bamboo smooth and solid beneath her palm, a tangible comfort. "When did you have time to spy on them?"

From the fringes of Key's hearing came the faint, hollow

crunches of magnolia leaves being stepped on, which she wouldn't have noticed if Vale hadn't called attention to it.

"Quiet, now," Vale murmured, not answering the question. She bounced on her toes, loosening up, honing her radiant smile into something predatory and keen. "Get in the house and stay there. Put your back to the corner nearest us."

Apprehension tightened in her gut.

"They'll come through the hole in the wall to your left. Bring 'em to the front door." Vale pulled on a pair of thin mycoleather gloves. "Go."

Key slipped around the frame of the front door, edging toward the corner Vale had indicated, gripping her staff in her hands. Through a broken window, she caught a flash of motion. She peered at it, straining her eyes. It could have been the stirring of the magnolia from the strengthening breeze, or it could be something else. She couldn't tell.

Her gut tightened further despite the reassurances she gave herself. She might have hated combat training at the academy, but she knew how to use her staff. And she had Vale here. Vale wouldn't let anyone hurt her.

Key amended herself. Vale wouldn't let anyone hurt her *and live*.

From outside, Vale called, "Come on out, friends. I'll make it quick for you."

There was only the rustling of leaves.

Key could picture it now: Vale with her hands on her hips, drawn up to her full height of five foot nothing, a taunting smile on her face. Though she was slight, she was two hundred pounds of fight in a hundred-pound body, and whatever she lacked in size, she made up for with her capacity for violence.

"No nearer," Vale said. "I can hear you fine from where you are. How goes, friend?"

A man's voice answered. "Steady, now. We're travelers."

"You know that's a damned lie."

Key risked a peek through one of the house's front windows. About twenty yards off, close to the puzzle cairn Vale had built to entrap unbound spirits, there stood a man, his hands raised. Something about him looked oddly familiar. But then the world spun, and she was forced to close her eyes briefly, riding out the residual effects of her dive. Sweetness and grit filled her mouth, the tidal pull of the memory licking at her. The stronger ones left more behind, which meant she needed to work harder to remain herself, or risk succumbing to the visions.

She opened her eyes to ground herself, rubbing her thumb against the smooth surface of her staff, and willed the memory away.

"Just looking for some shelter, like you," the man said.

Key heard Vale's derisive snort. "Second warning, friend. No further. Stay out there until me and mine leave, and there won't be any trouble."

"Ah, hell. Sorry. She's too valuable."

Black market memory hunters. Shit. Key clenched her teeth, regretting her decision to argue with Vale. The chalices might be unusable, but there was a living, breathing treasure trove of memories standing inside a ruined house, clutching a staff. All they needed was a single drop of her blood to unlock every secret residing in her.

Movement from the left caught her eye again, and this time it was accompanied by the rattle of magnolia leaves underfoot. A woman dressed in camouflage hiking gear came striding through the broken part of the wall—and promptly tripped over a wire Vale had set, crashing onto the ruined floorboards. They gave way with a wet, dull crack, depositing her in the darkness between two joists.

Key didn't bother waiting to see whether the woman could get out of the cellar. Her heart gave a wrenching twist and about sprang out of her chest, and she raced to keep up, exiting the house through the front door as Vale had instructed—only to freeze as she saw the man, also in a camouflage jacket, his lank brown hair in a ponytail, a sword dangling off his belt. He was pale and lean, and not all the shadows in his deep-set eyes were caused by age.

A memory stirred and shook itself free.

Vale spoke from her position to Key's left. "If you want to help your buddy, you'll stay put and let us go in peace." She flicked a glance at Key. "Keep away from the door."

Key scuttled to the right, her head whirling with visions. She swayed, her heartbeat a thrum in her ears as she flashed back to an afternoon at the temple a few months ago. A petitioner from beyond the city limits had brought an offering for Key, wanting her to speak his family history. He was new, a fresh convert. Key remembered the fear in his eyes as she pricked his finger with a needle and squeezed a drop of blood into the divining pool, its still waters hiding tangles of mycelium.

"Make good choices," Vale said blandly to the man. "We aren't worth your trouble."

"I think *she's* worth quite a bit," the man replied, jerking his head at Key. "We've been told about you, Miss Strade. I've never met one of you before. You and your memories, that'll get us set for life."

"What?" Vale drawled, her accent showing through. "You ain't heard of me?"

The man gave her a once-over. "No."

"That's too bad, then. Funny how you knew her name when I didn't say nothin'. You tell me how you knew who she was, and I promise to call down your saints when I collect the blood price."

The voices of the ancestors rose, clamoring, demanding she speak. Key could not deny them. "A family member of yours came to the temple in the spring," she said, lifting her hand to point at him. She took a step forward, then another, the memory solidifying. "Perhaps your brother, or cousin. He wanted to know what his grandfather looked like as a young man. I saw him through his grandmother's eyes as I drew the portrait. You're his exact image."

"Shut up," the man in the camouflage jacket said.

"Your family's been going to the same lake for generations. You and your grandfather have the same birthmark. A strawberry patch." Key tapped her finger on her chest, over her heart. The man stopped short. "Your grandfather had a scar through his eyebrow. A childhood injury gained from falling on the corner of a table. Their house smelled like tallow in the winter."

Key dropped the pitch of her voice, planing it smooth until it was benign and comforting. The situation could still be turned, though the probability was low. "Isn't that what we all want, to be seen and remembered? To know what it was like for our ancestors? Now your family has something that can't be taken by storms."

"I don't want to be remembered by *you*." The man spat at the ground. "You stole his blood. You and your family and that museum. All you're good for is what you'll fetch on the market."

"Enough talk." Vale's voice was low and level, a bad sign. "I'm advising you to run."

"I won't be running, little girl. *I'll* be collecting the blood price and leaving with her."

Key winced. That had been the absolute worst thing to say to Vale.

Footsteps thumped; Vale spun around. "Key!"

The woman who had fallen staggered through the doorway, a knife in hand, and threw herself at Key. She stumbled back, but it was too late. The tip of the blade caught the sleeve of her shirt, snagging in a crease and ripping it open. Pain shot up her arm as her skin parted.

Vale blurred forward, and the woman cried out, the knife gone from a hand now bent at an unnatural angle. In the next second, Vale had the woman on her knees.

"Key?" Vale hefted the woman's knife, testing its balance, then nestled the flat of it against the skin of the woman's neck. "You okay?"

She looked at her arm. Medium brown flesh gapped open, weeping beads of blood into the unbleached bamboo linen of her shirt.

"That was stupid as hell," Vale said to the woman. "I wasn't even done talkin' yet. Who sent you?"

The woman jerked to her feet, but Vale was prepared. She grabbed her hair, the movement casual, and hauled her back, flicking the tip of the knife over the woman's cheek. Her skin split, a mirror of the wound on Key's elbow.

"I won't ask again." Vale leaned in close, her lips by the

woman's ear. She went as still and crystalline as morning dew. "Who sent you?"

"Don't say anything," the man said, his voice tight with warning.

"Arvensis," the woman replied.

Arvensis. A morning glory, often called bindweed, invasive and tough to get rid of. An apt name, Key thought, for a black market hunter, someone who preyed upon legitimate hunters and flourished in the cracks of society.

"Let me go, please." The woman cast a pleading gaze at Key. "Tell her to let me go."

"My ma taught me to be polite, so thank you for the information. Now I invoke guardian law, since I'm registered and I bet my life both of you ain't." A glint appeared in Vale's night-dark eyes as she settled her gaze on the man in the jacket. "Two things. First, I'm twenty-four. Second, it'll be both of your lives on top of the blood price."

Vale steadied the woman, then drove the knife into her throat.

Key cringed hard, dropping her staff, and scrambled off the porch.

"You little bitch!" the man yelled, drawing his sword.

Vale uncoiled, her butterfly swords in her hands, meeting him with a clash of metal. It would be over in seconds; very few could stand against a guardian trained at the academy, and even fewer could stand against someone as quick and vicious as Vale. The man hollered, dropping his sword, his hand dangling uselessly. Vale flowed through, elbowing him in the jaw, and when his head snapped back, she bulled forward, sending him sprawling.

She put a knee on his hand and her sword to his throat. "Correction," she snarled, baring her teeth, her profile made more terrifying by freckles of blood. "I'm a *country* bitch. Give me your name, fucker, so you can be remembered."

The man spat at Vale.

Without looking up, Vale said, "Key. This one's yours by right. Take the blood price."

"Make it quick after I'm done." Key's voice was soft with resignation. When she turned toward their packs, the memory of the house as it used to be came to her so strong as to mute everything but the sound of her grandfather's voice. *You will be consecrated.*

"Key."

She gasped in a breath, startling, then stepped back onto the porch to get the supplies she needed. "I'm going."

Belatedly, the wound in Key's arm began throbbing. She dug around in her rucksack for a mycelium pad, affixing the lightly scratchy material to her skin with adhesive, then took a spare tab from Vale's pack before walking back to the wounded man. Her shoulders were heavy. "Hold him, Vale."

"No," the man moaned as Vale rose. She anchored a foot against his cheek and took his hand, lifting it and cutting the tip of his middle finger open. He flinched and writhed under Vale's weight. "No," he moaned again as Key lowered her head.

"You are seen," she said, touching the tab to his finger. In a split second the paper was glutted and limp with blood. "You are heard. You are remembered."

Vale was true to her word, grunting as she yanked her sword across the man's neck. Key bore witness as was the correct thing to do, every muscle in her body tensed as she forced herself to watch. Later, workers in the Department of Public History would prepare his blood for a dive and take the measure of his life. A few of his memories might be worth saving. A few of his memories might be worth giving.

When he was still, Key drew a circle on her forehead and said, "You are sanctified."

"One more for the city," Vale said, standing. "Let's clean up fast and head back."

Two Years Ago

THE WESTERN WALL OF THE MUSEUM OF HUMAN MEMORY rises four stories up and is composed of bare mountainside, hewn mostly vertical. By whose hands, Key doesn't know. Workers from somewhere, their names likely lost, purposely unremembered as menial labor often is. The dark gray ruggedness of the rock makes it stand out all the more against the serenity of the museum's atrium: whitewashed walls; a high ceiling from which colorful hand-embroidered banners hang; long, cushioned benches for footsore patrons to sit; and a large central display where the growth stages of the blood chalice are depicted in models of molded phenol resin.

Key stands on wide, polished sandstone tiles in the middle of the museum's atrium and looks up past layers of compressed time to a large slab of smooth black granite set in the wall, into which names are chiseled. She starts reading from the top of the list. Poria Strade, Key's great-grandaunt, a former head curator and the founder of the Institute of Human Memory; Walter Huffeler-Wright, a member of the wealthy Huffeler family from the city-state of Spruceton, where he established a second museum; Orden Payne, a legendary figure of Asheburg high society, former director of the museum, and a great-uncle by marriage; and all the way down until she gets to the last name.

Aurissa Strade. Key's grandmother. Senior hunter for the Museum of Human Memory. Missing as of sixteen years ago, presumed dead after ten of those years had passed.

Key's been looking up there all her life. She's been in and out of the museum ever since she was a baby. It's as much a temple to her as the real temple over which her mother presides. Key remembers being four years old and holding her grandmother's hand, walking proudly alongside her to attend the ceremony where Aurissa's name would be unveiled on the plaque. After that, they'd gone to view the newly opened Strade Collection, a permanent exhibit on the fourth floor filled with the artifacts and memories discovered by her family over multiple generations, made possible by donations from the Strade Foundation.

Four is too young to feel called to something, but it's the truth nonetheless. Key has prepared to be here since the moment she got her acceptance to Asheburg Academy. All her hard work over the last nine years has been in service to this moment: today, her first day on the job as an associate memory hunter at the museum.

Far to her left, the elevator bell rings. Seconds later, the echo of high heels on the floor comes to her ears. Key turns her head. Dr. Genevieve Wilcroft, current head curator and Key's mentor, steps out from the hallway where the elevators are located and directly into a blade of sunlight on the floor, her shadow cutting across it as she strides toward Key.

Key is unsurprised to see her. Despite the early hour, well before the museum is set to open and well before Key's expected arrival time, Genevieve has a statement outfit on. Her entire wardrobe is a statement, as Key knows after a year spent interning for her. She's never seen Genevieve in anything approaching casual, no matter the hour or situation.

Genevieve is a commanding presence in a pristine white pantsuit, her cravat tied crisply around her neck. Honey-blond hair sits at her nape in a chignon, her signature look, and dark red rubies, likely mined from Ashe's Ridge, refract bloodied light over her neck. Her inky black stilettos, as severe and pointed as the personality she curates, strike the floor in a martial tempo. The shoes are unsuitable for the weather. The forecast predicts storms again, which would drive most people to waterproofed boots, but Genevieve is not the type of woman to let man, ancestor, or nature inconvenience her.

"Early on your first day?" Genevieve says once she's close enough. Her voice is low for a woman, and melodic. Key thinks of it as mesmerizing. Captivating, even, hooking Key from the start, the line of her fascination tightening with each lecture Genevieve had given at the academy. Genevieve is a beautiful woman. It's not hard for Key to maintain attention when her mentor speaks. "Who let you in?"

"One of the security guards who comes to temple all the time," Key responds. "Lenny."

"I suppose you are the least threatening to the museum. I appreciate the enthusiasm, as always. Though I thought you might give yourself a little leeway after last night's soiree. How late did it run?"

Genevieve is one to talk about leeway. She must have gotten in right after sunrise. "Past midnight, and on a Saintsday, no less." Key gets a twinge of embarrassment. She lifts a hand to grab the end of one of the fresh braids cascading from her head—six hours spent in the chair and not a single minute less—then puts it down, reprimanding herself for breaking control in front of Genevieve. Key is a museum hunter now, not a young student or a starstruck, wide-eyed temple neophyte. "I had to excuse myself early, and no amount of explanation would get our guests to understand. It isn't a difficult concept."

"I'm sure they've never had places to be on Firstday morning." The smile Genevieve directs at Key is small, brief. A pull of the lips and nothing more. Key understands. Genevieve comes from a respectable family, but not so respectable that all the family members can forsake a regular job. The Wilcrofts live well as long as they keep working. This isn't the case for Key's family, nor for the other families with houses on the mountain, like the Paynes and the Mewborns. To have someone like Key in Genevieve's employ and not the other way around, someone who doesn't need the income and would never need the income, is a constant reminder of Genevieve's and her family's class limitations. As it is also a reminder of how far Genevieve has risen. She's the first Wilcroft to be head curator and the first person unconnected to high society to hold the position.

That Genevieve is comfortable enough to express her sentiment is a testament to how well they know each other. Key is grateful for the relationship she's forged with Genevieve over the last couple of years. It's made the transition from academy advisee to intern to employee much smoother. And, Key hopes, one day, she'll be where Genevieve is. She returns her eyes to the slab of black granite, high above. *Poria Strade*, she reads. *Aurissa Strade.*

"Praying to your ancestors?" Genevieve asks.

"Manifesting," Key replies softly.

"I see." This time, Genevieve's smile is genuine. "A word of advice, Kiana. I know you want my job. But you can't manifest it. You have to fight me for it."

Key, surprised and a little bewildered, turns toward Genevieve. "Fight for it, do you mean?"

"No. You want this job, you fight me for it."

"I'm afraid I still don't understand."

"This is not easy work, and neither is this an easy place to work. You show me with your tenacity and strength of will and conviction that you deserve my position. You sacrifice whatever you deem necessary for the good of the museum, for the institute's mission. You do my job better than I do. You do my job in spite of what I do." Genevieve's emerald eyes glint beneath the overhead lights. There's an intensity in them, a flame that grants Genevieve a second, third, fourth wind when all the other employees at the museum are long past done, when all the vehicles of research or funding have stalled and been given up for dead. But Genevieve has never believed in the permanence of death, not as a student of history and not as one of the finest hunters in Asheburg, one who has wrested knowledge and memory from death's clutches.

Genevieve gets what she wants. She's a living arrow shot unerringly at a target. "Then and only then, Kiana, do you get my job."

"I understand." Again, Key does. Because she is that arrow, too, and unlike Genevieve, the hands on the bow belong to her ancestors.

TWO

To be seen, to be heard, to be remembered—isn't that what we all want? To have our existence validated and affirmed by our elders and our communities? What higher service can we mediums perform than to grant the comfort of being known?

—Journal of Resifix Janea Strade, year unknown,
personal collection of Resifix Lanelle Strade

KEY LEANED DOWN, THE FLOOR OF THE TRAIN SHUDDERING GENtly beneath her feet, and used the eraser of her pencil to scratch at the raised constellation of mosquito bites scattered between her ankle and calf. Each bite was evidence of her hubris in thinking she could roll her pants up to get relief from the heat.

"Don't scratch," Vale said from the window seat beside her. "You'll bleed." She sat at an angle, leaning half against the wall of the car and half against the seat, creating room for the moon guitar cradled in her arms. For the past hour she'd been humming secular folk songs from her home village, raising soft twangs from the instrument with her right hand as her left slid over high, triangular frets, the music barely audible over the noise of the helper engine laboring behind their car. Daylight poured in from the window, spilling over a face scrubbed clean and an elegant throat unmarred by splashes of blood. Between her relaxed mood and beautiful singing, Vale looked like a carefree, innocent young girl, with no indication that she'd brutally taken two lives the day before.

Discomfited, Key scratched harder. "What's this song?"

"It's a southern love song." Vale bent a note, then released it, the string springing free beneath her finger.

After two years and many hours spent on the train together, Key knew Vale's entire repertoire by heart. "It doesn't sound like the other songs from your hometown."

"Because it's not. It's from Burdock's. An old lay about two lovers, one from his village, one from his sister village that was lost in a storm."

"I don't think I've ever heard you sing it before."

"Just learned it not too long ago, that's why." Vale coaxed a plaintive moan from the string. "It's real sad. The girl waits for her betrothed to arrive, but he never does because he's probably been taken by the sea, and she sits and waits as the stars change in the sky. It's also a navigation song."

Intrigued, Key said, "Do the ethnomusicologists know it? You know we're putting that folk song exhibit together for next season. This would fit in perfectly."

Vale eyed her, then wrapped her hand around her guitar's neck, muffling the sound abruptly. "Not everything belongs in a museum and not everything needs a museum. They don't know it 'cause it ain't for them to have. I'm the only one Burdock's taught it to, and he's only begun teaching me these songs in the last few years. He'd kill me if I taught it to anyone else."

"Not even Cal?" Calamus, one of the other guardians at the museum whose focus lay in ethnomusicology, was guardian to Jing, Vale's boyfriend. He was also Key's close friend and a musician who often traded songs with Vale.

"Burdock said no one else, and I'm gonna abide by it. You know how he is. You'd do the same if Dr. Wilcroft asked."

Key elected not to push any longer. Vale's mentor, Burdock, was as close as a brother to her, and if there was one person Vale could be counted on to stay loyal to, it was the man who'd scouted her for the academy, brought her up, took her in, and taught her everything he knew. And Vale was right: Genevieve engendered the same loyalty in Key.

She poked at her mosquito bites again, this time using the point of her pencil.

"Just get the camphor rub."

"No, it reeks, and I can't get it out of my clothes."

A hint of a smile played around Vale's mouth. "Put enough of that on, and even your fans won't wanna be near you. You'd love that."

"Hush!" Key glanced around, taking a quick survey of the people scattered throughout the passenger car with them. Some were asleep while others were lucid dreaming from the memory tabs they'd purchased for the ride; others, reading or contemplating the passing scenery. No one had heard Vale, or if they had, they were smart enough to pretend they hadn't.

"You could always tell me to handle them." At this, Vale grinned.

"Vale, no!"

"Vale, yes," she countered.

"I want them to feel safe with me, not afraid!"

Vale shrugged. "They'll feel safe with you and afraid of me and will think twice about asking you for shit they could have just prayed on themselves. I'll teach 'em how to respect your time."

"You're not allowed to hurt my penitents."

Vale shrugged again. "Suit yourself. Would solve your problem faster for you."

"Don't call it a problem."

"Fine. I'll lay on hands. Call it holy work."

"It's called responsibility." Key did wish, not for the first time, that she could accept Vale's offer. The typical weeklong expedition didn't allow Key to fully take off the mantle of being Kiana Strade, scion of her house, daughter and heir of Lanelle Strade. But after two weeks—two weeks of being alone, unburdened, and unbothered in the southern forests, bent completely to the mission of retrieving memories—she never wanted to feel the weight of her mother's expectations on her shoulders again, much less the whole city's.

"Being a welcome mat is responsibility?"

"It's part of what my gift entails." But Key was sure her gift was meant to be shared with as many people as possible through her work at the museum and not as a concierge service at the temple.

Vale tilted her head, her eyes narrowing. Then the moment of hardness passed, and her features softened. "What do you *want*, Key?"

To voice it would be blasphemy. "Can you imagine what people would say if I did what I wanted?"

The headlines alone would be murder. Add in morning radio and the gossip rags, which already ran on a diet of pure speculation . . .

"Can you stop imagining what people would say?" Vale settled back against the window and grunted.

That was the problem. Her mother was the head resifix of the city. Her father, Mershon, was a city councillor, and the two of them together symbolized everything about Asheburg: money and power, the temple and the state, intimately connected. Growing up at the edge of her parents' spotlight meant Key had always been visible and always had to watch herself in public. While other young children learned their letters and numbers, Key learned image management and public speaking. Other children had sports coaches; she had an etiquette consultant. After a few blunders during her teenage years—and a headline her father had killed—she no longer wanted to be in the top three reasons why newsstands sold out of papers.

Key shoved the rudder of the conversation roughly to the side, confident Vale would tack with her. Though quiet and taciturn on the outside, Vale had a mind constantly jumping from river rock to river rock, and abrupt turns in conversation never seemed to bother her. "Of all the things to survive over two hundred years of climate chaos," Key said in a half whisper, "it had to be an entirely useless insect. Mosquitoes are the real thieves. Think the babies will have my memories?"

Vale snorted. "Not unless the ancestors grant them the same blessing they gave you. Holy mosquitoes?"

"It could happen." There was, to Key's knowledge, no record of how memory diving developed or came to be, only that it had appeared as if by magic before the Decade of Storms. Usage of the blood chalice had been widespread, but the hallucinations granted by the mushroom, for those who were not blessed like Key, were only of recent memories. For Key, the vast disparity in ability was evidence enough that a miracle had occurred. "Some of the saints were entomologists. They could work through the mosquitoes that bit me."

"Ento-whatogists?"

"People who study bugs."

"Gross. And then what? You take 'em to temple and sanctify them? Let them buzz ancestral names into your ear so you can put their mama and their mama's mama in the Book of Saints?" Vale drew a tiny circle on her forehead, pantomiming a resifix at temple, her lips pursing, eyes closing, head bowing. Her voice rose, high and reedy. "Bzz bzz *bzz.*"

Key laughed, unable to help herself. "I could. Maybe I should found a museum and create exhibits about their lives." She looked down at the journal article from *Conscious Anthropology* that she'd brought as pleasure reading and decided she wasn't going to finish annotating it after all. "You could call me a blessed mosquito too."

Vale drew her fingers up the neck of her guitar; it whined in response. "I can't tell if it's all those people in your head what's making you weird, or if it's just you turning yourself in circles again. You're too pretty to be a mosquito. The memories aren't always tied to where you found them, and the folks you're finding memories of died generations ago. There's been time for the families to anchor their spirits. What would Dr. Wilcroft say to you, if she were here?"

Key answered without hesitation. "She'd say, 'Is it thievery if the house you are taking from is empty? Is it robbing if the people have abandoned their homes?'"

"That's too good of an impression, damn. She'd probably also tell you to stop thinking about what that day-rate hunter said yesterday."

The dead one, whose blood lay trapped in Vale's rucksack, soon to be property of the city. The specter of his grandfather had stalked Key through fitful dreams, interspersed with a clinking teaspoon and someone moaning *no, no*.

She'd seen dead bodies before in her work at the temple, but they were laid peacefully in state, ready to be cremated, with no hint of what had happened to them in life. She had also seen violence in dives, but that was not the same as standing and watching a human being die, the body choking and twitching, witnessing the exact moment the spirit departed in an obscene kind of intimacy.

But Vale was right, and she had taken the correct action. The man's life was forfeit by law.

Guardian law, much like the museum's right to knowledge, had been written long ago and ratified by all the city-states up and down the Spine. Key had thought, perhaps erroneously, that it would still be the law once she left the confines of each city. But in Crystal Grove, a small town beyond the outstretched fingers of the big cities and the lands surrounding them, did guardian law hold?

For that matter, did the museum's reach extend there?

A silly question. That's what Genevieve would say about it. Just as Key could be a resifix everywhere, so could the museum operate everywhere. Anywhere there was knowledge to be found, made use of, archived, was where the museum needed to be. And Key was a representative of the museum.

She could not, however, shake the sight of Vale's blade ripping through the man's throat, or the sound of his heels scraping against the dirt as he died in a pool of his own blood. She closed her eyes, nausea sweeping through her.

"Key." Calloused fingertips pressed gently against her forehead, her temples. "Are you okay?"

She opened her eyes to Vale's concerned look, and heat rose into her cheeks at Vale's nearness. She hoped Vale wouldn't notice the change. Vale was attuned to Key's state of being, as any good guardian ought to be, but sometimes the awareness bordered on the supernatural. There were times, like now, when Key thought that awareness was a detriment, not a benefit.

"Key?"

"I'm okay." What was Key about to say? The man's and woman's deaths, despite them being black market hunters, were not consequences she had foreseen when she'd set her heart on being an anthropologist, though in theory, she'd known death was a possibility. She had the best guardian, after all, and Vale had not gotten to that station under the belief that life was sacred. "He didn't want the blood price taken."

Vale drew a breath but pulled back. "It's not what he wanted that mattered. You know guardian law."

The law stated that Vale could not attack, only defend, and if either she or Key were provoked, she could only respond with proportionate force. Whether or not Vale had done so was the question. The blood price, adapted from hunter culture by the Spinal cities, was legal proof for registered hunters and guardians that a threat existed. "You really thought they'd kill me?"

"I thought they'd try." Vale scooted forward in her seat to wedge a toe beneath the shell of her guitar case, lifting it toward her. "Listen. You worry about the hunting, and I'll worry about the guardianing."

Key's lips tightened. "Guarding."

"You know what I meant. You do what you do, and I do what I do, same as always. Their lives were forfeit when you got blooded."

"Doesn't that bother you?"

Vale stowed her guitar, replying without looking. "The black market hunters are getting bolder. Heard they picked up a museum hunter in one of the cities up north. Left the guardian cold and unremembered in the woods. Still haven't found the hunter, not the body, at least. Memories are probably already on the market. I don't want that to be us. And they knew who you were. Followed us all that way just for you. So, should it bother me that these two are dead and we are not?"

"I didn't hear about that." The fact that the hunters knew her, too, was troubling.

"You gotta listen to the long waves more often. The shorts don't tell you anything useful."

"I like the programs." When she could, Key tuned in every night for her favorite radio plays.

"Like I said, nothing useful." Vale passed her guitar over. "Can you put this up for me?"

Key unfolded herself from her seat, wincing at her stiff, sore knees, and stepped into the aisle to stretch before tucking her pencil behind her ear. Outside, the scenery was changing, the forest of hickory, birch, and sweet gum yielding to plots of giant bamboo tended by workers harvesting young shoots, their backs rounded like beetle carapaces. Before long, they'd be in the city, and the peace she'd found with Vale would disappear, snatched from them as swiftly as a flash flood plucking a house from its roots.

"Don't twist yourself up over the thief thing," Vale said as Key stood on tiptoes, adding a few inches to her five-foot-eight frame, then rearranged the luggage in the overhead rack. "You at least did him a favor by promising to remember him."

"That's true," Key allowed, though he hadn't wanted her to remember him. She used the top of her boot to scratch her leg, but it was inadequate. She bent over, clawing at her calf.

"Camphor rub is in the outside pocket of my rucksack."

Key groaned, but straightened. She retrieved the camphor rub, balancing like an awkward stork as she applied it to her bites, then shoved it back into Vale's rucksack and took a seat once more.

"Yep, that'll clear the sinuses," Vale said, laughing.

"Shut up," Key grumbled, the inside of her nose prickling. "You should declare guardian law on all mosquitoes, how about that?"

"Guardian law doesn't apply to bugs."

"It should." She had crushed her papers under her by accident. Key shifted her weight, yanking the sheaf out, then drew her journal from her rucksack and opened it to the latest page she'd been working on, where a detailed drawing of the compound with the magnolia tree was taking shape opposite a thorough accounting of where and when the dive was taken. She folded the article and stuck it between the leaves of the journal.

"That the site we were at?" Vale craned her neck to get a better look at Key's sketch. "I don't remember it like that."

"From the past." Key glanced around again. Was that older man the next row over staring too intently at his book? She recognized his face. "They were talking about a ritual, but it was different—like the one in the temple, maybe an early version. I saw snow, and a lot of it. Enough to shovel. The last records we have of snow that deep are two hundred thirty-five or more years back—up to two hundred forty-two, to be precise, and that was when the almanacs were no longer able to boast about their 80 percent accuracy, which—"

Vale stared at her, blank-faced. "Key. I failed history."

"Um," Key said, having received the highest marks in the academy in every subject but combat, survival skills, and herbalism. Those three had gone to Vale, where they'd done a valiant job of pulling her average over the minimum necessary to keep her scholarship. Key revised herself. "The ancestors guided me to this memory for a reason. I need to go back. Think about what else I could find, what I could reconstruct if I could stay for a month!"

"A month!" Vale barked a laugh. "Your ma is already going to kill me. You're fucked too. If you think you'll ever be let out again after this—"

"You told me to stop stressing, and now I'm telling *you* to stop stressing—"

"How can I when you don't listen to me?"

"I listen!" If the worst did happen, Vale would likely spend hours in a tight-lipped state of emergency, making contingency plans and budgeting for when she'd be living hand to mouth. Ridiculous behavior, and needless. Key would of course immediately hire her friend back on as a personal guardian.

Vale glared. "You're too important to pull this shit. So for the love of the ancestors, both yours and mine, stop pushing everyone's patience with you."

"And now you sound like Burdock."

"Of course I sound like Burdock," Vale shot back. "Where do you think I got this speech from?"

Key set her jaw. Her patience with how others treated her—like a rare, expensive orchid under glass, to be looked at but not touched—had worn through long ago. But Vale was Key's only ally, the only one who fully understood the pressure Key was under, the only one who knew how far and to what ends Key would go to throw off the trappings of the temple. It would be a bad idea to alienate her. "I think this dive might be it. Call it a gut feeling."

Vale leveled dark eyes at Key.

"Why are you looking at me like that?"

"Every time you get a gut feeling, someone's unhappy about it."

"Why else are you looking at me like that?"

"Just wondering how you feel after going that far back. Two hundred and thirty-what years?"

"I'm great. Could do it again and go deeper."

"Whoa, take the bit out your mouth. That's too dangerous."

Key gave Vale an incredulous look. "Are you *cautioning* me? You?"

"It's my job!"

"I'll be fine." Key gestured to her journal, and a note of enthusiasm brightened her voice. "Just imagine. If I got solid evidence? This could be a huge joint endeavor with the temple and the museum and even the city council signed on. I can piece together a thorough history of the people who used to live in that compound. Maybe even find their descendants! That's worth a dissertation at least, right? Like Genevieve."

Dr. Genevieve Wilcroft had built her doctorate and

postdoc on the memories of an undiscovered village, and the reconstruction and subsequent exhibit were what got her the position of head curator. "And a job," Key continued. "An extremely demanding, my-work-is-my-life, oh-no-I'm-out-of-town-for-two-months kind of job? I could get my name on the wall!"

"Is this about your ego, or is this about getting away?"

Key shook her head rapidly, eluding the question. "We'll need to write a proposal to get council funds."

"Uh, won't you just invite everyone over for dinner?"

"No," Key said, though that was precisely how she meant to do it. She had the tools at her disposal; why wouldn't she use them? "It needs to be official. Oh, and I can petition for a crew."

"The senior hunter can't get a crew. What makes you think you'll get one?"

"Jing has gotten a crew before," Key said.

"Once, and only after Dr. Wilcroft made him run an obstacle course, jump through hoops, perform several blood sacrifices while dancing naked under the full moon in sight of the ancestors, and promise his firstborn before she started the paperwork. The crew ended up being two whole people." Vale shifted, leaning against the window of the train as it clattered over the bridge spanning the New River. The banks were lined with weeping willows, each bent toward the murky water, their shy leaves flirting with the surface. Every so often, there was a long scar in the greenery where trees lay splintered and toppled, a claw mark left by a storm.

"I have a good feeling about it," Key said. "The saints have spoken it to me."

"The saints talk too much," Vale muttered.

THE TRAIN TRUNDLED over the last bridge before Asheburg Main Station, the waterfall of Ashe's Peak coming into sight as they rounded the bend. Key's spirits lifted briefly as she glimpsed the Garnet House's pale gray walls partway up the mountain. A bath would rid her of the sweaty waxiness sitting on her skin. She couldn't wait.

Vale deadpanned, "Thinking about conditioner already?"

Key tugged at a curl in her ponytail. "Look at this mess. Yes."

Vale grinned as she ticked off a list on her fingers. "Plus a ridiculously large bed with at least three pillows, morning coffee on the loggia, a five-course meal cooked by your butler, and Dr. Wilcroft gushing over your latest discovery."

"My butler doesn't cook," she said, ignoring Vale's snort, but glad regardless to tease out one last smile before the supply of them was locked away. "My cook cooks. And protest it if you like, but you're going to use all the hot water at my house, and you hate wet shoes. You hate having to wear the same clothes day in and day out. And you want to spend time with Jing."

"That much hot water is disgusting and it's my duty to use it all. I do hate wet shoes and I do love my fancy dress. As for Jing, if I can pry you off him, I'll get my time."

Key said, skeptical, "Shouldn't it be the other way around?"

"You're aiming for a salvage crew. You're gonna—what's that expression you Asheburgians use?—chew on his brain? Why would you do that? Brains aren't even chewy. And you can get sick from eating them and die. City people, ugh."

"Vale," Key said.

"Yeah, sorry, but it's true. Make sure you invite Jing over for dinner at the very least. You know how he is." Vale pursed her lips in thought. "Might have to go drinking with Cal tonight."

"Aren't you still banned from the Toadstool?"

"That wasn't my fault. I didn't start nothin'."

"No, you finished."

"Damn right I did." Vale lifted her chin, her nostrils flaring.

The front door of the car opened, and a stately, well-dressed older woman entered. Before Key could think to duck her head, the woman zeroed in on her, a light appearing in her eyes as she proceeded down the aisle, hands flitting from seat back to seat back, the charm bracelets on her arms tinkling as she did so. She took no haste, giving Key time to study her features: dark brown skin, burnished at the cheekbones from smiling; crow's feet at the corners of her eyes; a dignified, wide-tipped nose, just shy of hawkish; stone-gray hair springing away from her head in tight twists and coils.

Key's enthusiasm drained away, replaced by the heaviness of realization. Rumor of her presence must have crept to the front of the train. So much for escaping being noticed. "Ms. Floretta Noble," Key said, her voice dipping into a serious tone, one befitting her station. She stood. "It has been too long. You are seen."

Vale got to her feet, and several passengers twisted in their seats, their eyes zeroing in on Key, including the older man she'd recognized.

Floretta smiled and came to a stop, lifting a hand to

trace a circle over her forehead. "I rejoice. What a pleasant surprise to find you here, Miss Strade." Her voice was rich mahogany, the timbre pulling the memories to the fore of Key's mind. Floretta had inherited the sound and cadence of the Noble women. But all Key could think of was Floretta as a child, her hair in tight braids with ladybug clips on the ends, big-eyed and adorable, one chubby finger pointed at the stained glass set into the temple doors.

"I'm returning from the field, Ms. Noble."

"In the last car on the train? How . . . quaint."

Ah. Because a Strade should have been riding in first class instead of lowering herself to economy, despite economy offering social comfort for Vale and relative anonymity for Key. "You are gracious to come visit."

"Nonsense, of course. It makes me feel better, knowing you're here. With the ones who need you most." Floretta glanced at Vale.

Key motioned subtly at Vale not to move or take offense and hoped it would be enough. "I am happy to have given you that ease, Ms. Noble." She inclined her head, doing her best to close off the conversation before Floretta sat and began giving her opinion—especially about Key's appointed guardian. Vale would not be averse to challenging an elderly woman on a train. Key, on the other hand, had only so much time remaining before she would be back in the city and lost in a thicket of people, trying not to give all of herself away.

She reined in her frustration. Showing her emotions would result in Floretta staying longer. "Would you like a blessing?"

"Oh, I don't know—" Floretta began.

"And you, Earnest?" Key addressed the older man. He was stout, with an olive cast to his lightly tanned skin and short, sandy hair thinning into a tonsure. His family was modest and devout, his ancestors written into the book two generations ago. Key never forgot a face or a name, but sometimes it took a minute to fetch the information.

"Yes, Miss Strade."

"Key has not offered anyone else a blessing so far," Vale broke in. "You two are lucky."

Floretta cut her eyes at Vale before looking back to Key. "I appreciate the generosity."

Key warred between kicking Vale in the shin for being rude or hugging her for being perceptive and settled for doing nothing. "I speak as the voice of the ancestors. Floretta Noble, you are seen."

"I rejoice in your sight."

"Floretta Noble, you are heard."

"My voice among many."

"Floretta Noble, you are remembered."

"I shall not want more."

As one, she and Floretta bowed toward each other, drawing circles on their foreheads. Floretta left, her perfume trailing heavy behind her. Key motioned for Earnest to approach. "A blessing for you too, right?"

"Yes, Miss Strade, and thank you very much." Earnest lowered his head for the benediction.

"I look forward to seeing you at the next service," Key said once she finished. She wrestled her sagging smile back into place. The blessed, she reminded herself, were always grateful to do the work.

"You are seen," Vale said firmly.

Earnest didn't move. "I just wanted to ask one thing—"

The front door of the car clattered open again, letting the conductor in on a swell of sound. "Asheburg Main Station!" he called. "Transfer here for the Cardinal River Line. Asheburg Main Station is next. Please watch your step."

Earnest frowned but turned to retrieve his belongings. Key exhaled, then squinted through the far window on the approach. The track split, and the train yawed left past the rail yard, where cargo and passenger cars sat exhausted and glazed with heat. Soon, they would be called back to service, much like herself.

Key leaned into the aisle for a better vantage point to gauge the number of passengers on the platform. Asheburg was the most populous of the city-states dotting the mountain range known as the Spine, and as a result, it served as a transportation hub, and the station was never empty. But there was an unusually large group on the platform, a fruiting body of people growing from the caution line all the way to the row of tab vending machines beside the ticket window.

"That's a lot of people for a weekday," she murmured as she counted, then glanced back at Vale. "Shouldn't they be at work?"

Vale got to her feet, her hands touching first the knife at her side, then the scabbarded swords. She spoke without looking at Key. "They're here because I sent a gram ahead."

Anger stabbed through her, anxiety rising in its wake, followed by the urge to throw open the back door and jump into the furnace of the helper engine coupled to the car. "Vale! No! I wanted to—"

“I had to.” Vale braced one arm against the back of the chair as the train’s brakes squealed. “We’re over a week late. We’ll have to deal with it.”

Key crimped her lips shut, catching the uncharitable words, and instead reached up to wrap a hand around the slats of the overhead rack, her knuckles tightening until they cracked. “I just wanted some time.”

“I gave you time.” There was a brief softening in the set of Vale’s shoulders. “More than I should’ve.”

“You know I hate making a scene,” Key said from behind her teeth. A thin coil of resentment snaked through her gut, hot and venomous. Vale was not the one who couldn’t go out alone; Vale was not the one who would be asked for blessings at any time of any day and viewed poorly if she refused. Vale could speak harshly, use her hands with direct intent, and walk away from situations that made her uncomfortable.

“I do,” Vale replied, motioning for the other passengers to disembark first.

It seemed to Key that the crowd held its breath as she got her and Vale’s belongings down from the rack, the anticipation building like a cumulonimbus cloud, billowing up and flattening against the barrier of the windows. Outside, Floretta had a ring of people around her, many of them glancing at the train with eagerness in their faces.

Key swallowed a mouthful of saliva and wiped a palm on her shirt. She had to get away from this spectacle, find an excuse to leave the city for long periods without raising concern. The museum was her—

Faintly, a teaspoon clinked.

Her head shot up, eyes wide.

"Ready?" Vale straightened her clothes under her rucksack.

Key gathered herself and glared, swinging her own rucksack on. "You didn't have to."

"I didn't have a choice." Vale hefted Key's staff, then handed it over. "Not if I want to keep this job."

Vale exited first as she always did, her head swiveling from left to right as she assessed the surroundings. The crowd rippled and bent like grass in the wind, a murmur going up when Vale gave the all clear. Key breathed out, her stomach trembling, and gripped her staff close, leaning on it to help her stand tall the way she had been taught. She drew up her fortitude, still shaking, then prayed for the strength and wisdom of her foremothers.

She disembarked into the scouring heat of midday, the bright sunlight summoning moisture from the ground underneath the tracks. Vale held out a hand to assist, and as Key stepped down, the helper engine let out a whistle, heralding her with a hiss and an impressive puff of steam. It blew toward Key, enshrouding her. Someone in the crowd gasped.

Of course. The ancestors would ensure an appropriate entrance.

Key wished she could fold the steam around her like a cloak and float away unnoticed, but it dissipated in a second, the veil of it tearing away at the exact moment she began walking forward.

"Ancestors be praised!" shouted someone in the crowd. "Resifix Kiana has returned!"

The anticipation broke, and motion flowed through the crowd like a wave as people bowed and traced circles over their foreheads. *See me, see me*, they whispered, their words falling as a silvery wash of rain.

"You are seen." Key put on a practiced half smile and nodded her thanks, returning the gesture. Two paces ahead, Vale forged a path through bodies, creating a bubble of space that shut seamlessly behind them. Key kept up her litany as she followed on Vale's heels, ignoring the fingers brushing her shoulders and her arms, glad for the rucksack covering most of her back. But it didn't cover her bottom, and when the inevitable touch came, Key stifled a yelp, sucking in a breath instead.

Vale whirled, one butterfly sword out of its scabbard. The metallic *thwack* of her strike lanced through the air at the same time as the man's startled squawk of pain. The crowd froze, the people in it gaping at both Vale and the offender.

"Touch her again," Vale growled, "and you will be short a hand."

"It was just a joke!" the young man protested weakly.

"Do you see me laughing?" Vale did not hiss, yet the air vibrated with menace.

Key spun slowly toward him, narrowing her eyes, riffling through her memories for the man's name. If not for the crowd, she'd let Vale handle things, but the situation was now as much performance as it was discipline. "Kyler Turrel. Son of Myla Turrel, daughter of Leslianne Turrel. You are seen."

"I—" Kyler's eyes darted between Vale and Key. "I rejoice in your sight."

"And in the sight of the ancestors." She pointed at him. "Your disrespect is noted and witnessed. Is this the behavior you want the saints to see?"

"They're not here," Kyler said, rubbing his hand, glaring sullenly at Vale.

A memory appeared, strong and clear, refuting his words. She closed her eyes and tilted her head back as if listening to the sky. "Best keep your silver shined," Key murmured, letting the accent in the memory seep into her voice. "That's what your uncle used to say to you. 'Because your momma is quick with a switch. Learned it from *her* momma.'"

She opened her eyes and stared at Kyler, who dropped his gaze to his shoes. "Do you still think the saints aren't here? Your grandmother witnesses your shame through me. All that discipline, and you haven't learned."

"I'm sorry," he mumbled.

"You're only sorry because I hit you," Vale said.

Key took a step forward and stood uncomfortably close to Kyler. "Take time to pray. If you are truly sorry, your saints will know. If not, then stay away from anything that looks like a switch. Leslianne always liked to hear the stick whistle."

Kyler leaned away. "You don't mean that."

Key swept an arm through the air, motioning to the crowd. "Hear me!"

"You are heard!" the crowd chorused.

"And so it will be in the eyes of the ancestors." A warm, pleasing voice broke in, the cadence of it deliberate, measured.

A shiver ricocheted down her spine. She'd know that voice anywhere.

The crowd parted to reveal a statuesque woman with medium brown skin a match for Key's, and wise brown eyes.

Her black hair, threaded through with gray, was braided back in elaborate cornrows on her head. Dangling from her ears were large silver hoops studded with rubies, and surrounding her were three disciples, as well as Jing and his guardian, Calamus.

Key genuflected immediately, the movement mirrored by the rest of the people on the platform, and raised her hand to her forehead, two fingers tracing a circle.

Her mother would expect no less.

THREE

The blood chalice, *C. diabolum*, and the needle orchid, *A. caliceum*, once were commonly found in the mature conifer forests along the Spine, growing in the damp soil and leaf litter beneath pine trees. *A. caliceum* is mycoheterotrophic and parasitizes *C. diabolum* exclusively. *C. diabolum* guttation contains psilocybin, and *A. caliceum* is believed to have antifungal properties. In the last hundred years, both species have largely disappeared from their habitat, a consequence of overharvesting and changing climate patterns.

—Jethro Gorley, *Mushrooms of the Spinal Forests*

"RISE, KIANA," HER MOTHER SAID, "AND WALK WITH ME."

Key planted the end of her staff against the platform and stood, the crowd around her following suit a second later. Behind her, the conductor's shout of "All aboard!" rolled over them right before the bell began clanging. The crowd shifted again, straining against itself as it divided, the passengers making for the doors, the faithful closing up the vacant spaces.

She fell into step with her mother, who remained silent but for the whisper of her robes as she turned for the pedestrian bridge connecting Asheburg Main Station to the row of inclines abutting the slope of Ashe's Peak. Two of the four cable cars were in service, counterbalancing each other as they crept up and down the mountainside. Key's mother paid for two fares at the ticket window, then waited in line beside a display of travel brochures as a liveried attendant helped guide an incline car into the bay. After letting the passengers out, the attendant bowed to both Key and her mother and led them toward the empty car.

Key entered first. The incline carriage was designed like a small streetcar, with windows all around to take advantage of the spectacular view during the climb. A varnished wooden bench lined the inside; the walls were painted a fading red. Overhead was a recessed ceiling, gilded and embossed and set with soft lights. Key had always thought it a design mismatch, outmoded and out of place, better suited to the inside of city hall than a cable car.

Lanelle turned in the doorway to face the others, holding up a hand. "No. This is a private car."

Vale took a step forward. "I go where Key goes."

Lanelle did not budge. "I said it was a private car, Valerian. Both of you can stand being separated for a few minutes after two weeks together." Lanelle nodded at the attendant, who yanked on the handle of the door, slamming it shut in front of Vale's face.

The bell shrilled to signal their ascent. Lanelle remained standing, curling a manicured hand around one of the poles in the car. With a jerk and a rattle, the car began moving, leaving Vale, Jing, Cal, and her mother's coterie behind.

Key sat on the far end of the car next to the corner, laying her staff beside her, turning her face away from Lanelle and toward the city. Without the pressure of performance, anger and frustration took flight in her gut; wingbeats pulsed in her ears. What she wanted was an unremarkable journey home, a short presentation to Genevieve, and a long, hot bath in her own room. With a single telegram, Vale had struck those possibilities down.

"You cannot blame Vale for this."

Her mother was right; Key could not. She'd do it anyway. "You don't need to defend her."

"There's nothing to defend. She did the right thing." Lanelle approached and took a seat catty-corner from Key, close enough for their knees to touch, her back to the vista unfurling beneath them.

Key looked at the scenery to find a measure of calm. The rivers were wide and brown and glutted with rainfall, rushing white-tipped past muddy banks where industrial buildings clung, expelling wastewater downriver. The waterfall, also thickened with rain, thundered past hydroelectric generators built on shelves of granite and schist. Below, the residential sector was a broken quilt of sloped red-and-ocher roofs, and wide avenues crisscrossed with streetcar tracks sliced through the city in a grid. At night, the fungi growing on the curbs and in the streetlights would illuminate the roads with foxfire.

"I know, but . . ." She could not throw a temper tantrum here. She'd need to reframe things and appeal to the part of her mother who appreciated Key's hard work. "I wanted to be thorough. I would have sent word when I was done, you know I would."

"Kiki. Before anything else, I'm glad you're home safe." Lanelle reached out, pulling Key in for a warm hug. Key sighed and hugged her mother back, some of her anger fleeing at the scent of coconut and the feel of her mother's familiar, solid form. "We are all glad. Your safety is critical, and Vale was only doing what she's been trained to do."

Key opened her mouth.

"She's your guardian, not your friend," Lanelle said. "You would do well to remember that. What's this?" She pulled back, fingering the torn edge of Key's sleeve.

"Nothing." What Key needed was a friend, not a guardian. She was friendly to others and vice versa, but aside from Vale and Calamus, there were few people in the city she could trust to be a friend. Her role prevented it. Trust flowed toward Key the way rivers flowed toward the sea, and rivers did not reverse direction.

"Just a small cut. I'm fine."

"Doesn't it seem like a strange place to get a cut?"

A simple question without a simple answer. "There was a mishap."

"A mishap," her mother repeated, raising a brow. "Kiki."

"It isn't anything for you to worry about, and I am happy to share the details with you after my meeting with Genevieve."

A smile lifted the corners of Lanelle's mouth. "Are you planning to disclose what happened to you at that meeting? Yes? I suppose I will come with you, then."

"Mama!"

"Don't. I haven't seen you in two weeks and until yesterday, we all thought something terrible had happened to you."

"I had Vale with me the whole time."

"Your guardian might be one of the best, but she isn't infallible. She is a single person, and a small one at that." Lanelle ran her thumb lightly over the mycelium bandage still affixed to Key's elbow. "And lest you think I'm being unfair to her, I know it's you who pressured her into staying later."

"It wasn't all me." That was a neutral tone, wasn't it? It was difficult to be level when her mother was eyeing her, her head held at a certain angle, a mannerism Key was sure was universal to all parents. Under that stern look, Key was a little girl again. "We had a storm to deal with."

"And that's how you got your wound?"

Key grimaced inwardly, calculating whether she would rather get an earful in private, or if she'd rather be speared by her mother's glare while in front of her boss. She glanced out the windows of the incline, gauging the distance to the top. They were more than halfway up. She could get ahead of it, downplay it. "Black market hunters. It isn't serious."

Lanelle's eyes went wide before they narrowed. "What happened to the hunters?"

Key couldn't suppress her shudder. They hadn't buried or burned the bodies before they left. Instead, she and Vale hauled them into the shade of another magnolia beside the stream and left the corpses to the deer and pigs. "Vale declared guardian law."

"The blood price?"

"Taken."

"I want to know who hurt you."

"She is unremembered." Key did her best not to think again about how Vale had opened the woman's throat, the raw sound of it, the woman's delayed reaction. "I promised to remember the other. They're the city's now."

Lanelle grunted. "Kiki, you should be careful—"

"I know!" The anger returned, tinged with defensiveness. "You've said as much."

"I meant that you need to have a care for the others around you. You being late isn't without consequences."

"I'm very sorry I'm a week late, Mama," Key said. "And I'll apologize to Genevieve when I see her."

"I know you and Genevieve are close, but never forget she is now your boss, not just your mentor. And she is certainly not a friend. You should expect her to remember those facts even when you do not."

"Genevieve is—" Key started to say, but the look on her mother's face stopped her from continuing.

"You owe Vale an apology too. You can't drag her into your plans and expect her to go along with them all the time."

"She's my guardian. Isn't that part of the job description?"

"This hardheadedness of yours comes straight from your grandmother," Lanelle muttered, then put a finger to the bridge of her nose. "Kiki, you need to consider how this affects you both."

"I did, and I told Vale she wasn't going to get fired and that I'd take care of it, whatever happens. I was going to come back and make my report, but Vale sent a gram to you and we had all this."

Lanelle scoffed. "What makes you think she would send a gram to me? It's Genevieve who told me, not Vale."

"Same thing," Key grumbled.

"Perhaps, but you need to fix your attitude when it comes to Vale. She made the correct choice. And she might need some help managing you. Two guardians might work."

"No one needs two guardians!" Key could imagine the headlines on the sheets—UNPRECEDENTED: UNCONTROLLABLE KIANA STRADE GIVEN SECOND GUARDIAN.

"You will if you want to go afield again. I'll speak to

Genevieve about it and offer some candidates. Cordelia has recently finished a contract. You two have worked together in the past. I think she'd do well."

Cordelia—named Rocket at the academy—would do well if she weren't Key's ex-girlfriend. "I don't want her, and I don't need two guardians. It'll send the wrong message."

Lanelle's nostrils flared. "I think it will send precisely the right message. You are important."

"I think my work at the museum is important."

"Your work at the museum is a conceit."

Key drew in a long, slow breath, counting backward from five. She had known this. Lanelle's opinion of her work had never been secret. Yet it hurt to hear it spoken aloud.

"I've tolerated it because it's been harmless so far. You've been happy and occupied for the last two years and everything has been running smoothly at the temple. But you are a target for black market hunters, whether they know who you are or not. You're safest at the temple, where you belong. You have been blessed. To do any other work is a waste of your gifts."

The incline shuddered as it slowed, coming to a stop at the upper station.

Lanelle's expression softened, a look of pain crossing her features. "My time at temple is coming to an end, Kiki. I've held out as long as I can. You need to claim your place."

Before she could ask what her mother meant, another attendant met them on the platform, opening the door and stepping aside. Lanelle's features smoothed as she put her public face on and prepared to exit the car. "Let's wait for the others before proceeding to the museum."

Key closed her eyes briefly, slackening her mouth and jaw, her cheeks, and her forehead before deploying her trademark half smile. She gathered her staff close and got to her feet, then adjusted her clothes under her rucksack. The ancestors would not suffer dishevelment. “Yes, ma’am.”

One Year Ago

KEY MEANDERS AROUND GENEVIEVE'S OFFICE WHILE HER REPORT is being read, looking over the spines of the books on Genevieve's shelves, admiring the knickknacks she's accrued in her years as one of the foremost memory hunters in Asheburg. Some, like the blown-glass blood chalices, are gifts of appreciation from the city's arts and humanities council; others, pieces of memorabilia, like the framed title page of Genevieve's first article published as the main author. A few of the pieces sitting on her shelves are mysteries to Key, like the four flattish, rounded stones stacked in a pile.

She hasn't managed to ask Genevieve about them yet, knowing if she pries too hard and too often that Genevieve will shut her shell tight. The woman is allergic to what she sees as fawning and adulation. Her past achievements, Key's heard her say, are in the past, and the only reason to linger there is academic in nature.

There's a small storage closet where the rest of her keepsakes are, along with filing cabinets and magazine racks. These are more personal in nature, things that have strong emotional resonance but are of little import in the grander view of public history.

Key glances at Genevieve when she flips a page in the report. Try as Key might to pretend she's fine, she's incredibly nervous about what Genevieve will say once she's done. Over the last year, Key and Vale have assisted on research trips, first with Jing and Cal until they were satisfied Key had a good understanding of how to comport herself when afield, then with Tags and Ina, and finally, Amity and Dhonia. This is the first time Key has written a proposal for a solo trip of her own, and she's not sure if Genevieve will say yes.

Key comes to a stop in front of the antique revolver Genevieve keeps on the shelf above her prized chaise longue. Though Key knows the revolver is old—steel is too precious to be spent on creating new firearms when it's needed for trains—it has been well maintained, its silvery-gray surface free of rust, gleaming in the warm light coming from Genevieve's green glass desk lamp. The wooden handle begs to be touched. Beside the revolver's stand is a single, perfect round, and next to that is a tattered box, inside which Genevieve has amassed a collection of shells and casings and cartridges of various sizes.

Maybe today is the day, Key thinks, to ask Genevieve about the gun.

"I've just finished," Genevieve announces. Key turns around, her anxiety aflutter, and goes to one of the wingback chairs in front of Genevieve's desk, her shoes swooshing across the carpet. "You've done your work well, as expected."

"Thank you." Really, it's the time spent with Genevieve that has been the biggest benefit to Key. She has read every one of Genevieve's research proposals she could find. Key waits to hear the rest, not willing to celebrate prematurely.

"You've addressed the budgetary concerns as well as some of the concerns raised by your parents," Genevieve continues. "As much as I'd enjoy cutting the kite strings and allowing you to venture out, your safety remains foremost on my mind." She sighs, a rare look of weariness crossing the flawless features of her face, and leans back in her office chair. "You didn't provide much detail about your departure, only its expense. Tell me about your plans."

"Vale and I are planning to take the earliest train out to Glennford City as possible," Key says. "It departs at six in the morning, sharp. I can have my driver pre-buy tickets and then drop Vale and me off at the station. We can get a private car and reduce the chances of me being recognized. I considered leaving on the last train the night before because there are fewer commuters, but there's no express, which means extra connections."

"We don't have the budget for a private car," Genevieve says, wry. "Unless you plan to fund that yourself. Remember that the museum's expenses are public information."

"Economy, then."

"All right," Genevieve says. She turns to the second page of Key's report. "You say here that you plan to use local resources to best determine a place to begin exploring. Which resources? A library? Local government officials? A guide?"

"Oh." Key fights the urge to clear her throat. "I saw Jing and Cal ease into conversation when I was assisting them. They just talked to people. I was planning to do the same."

"You'll get better results if you approach local officials and tell them you're with the Museum of Human Memory. They'll understand how important you are, and because of that, it will be easier to make demands of them. Many officials are pleased to provide you with a free guide, as well as the shield of authority when you begin excavating around someone's house."

"That's not how Jing and Cal did it," Key replies. "They got good results, so I'm inclined to follow their lead."

Genevieve raises an eyebrow. "Jing often cites local historians and city officials in his field reports."

"Oh," Key says again, and this time, she does clear her throat. She hasn't meant to expose Jing as a liar. "I may not always realize the importance of who Jing talks to, I suppose. I've still got much to learn."

"That you do, and I can't facilitate your development if you're limited to the city and its surrounding department. And I'm not inclined to keep you in Asheburg by dint of who you are. There are no glaring omissions in this report, and it's as well written as I could ask for from an associate hunter."

Key finds herself holding her breath.

Genevieve graces her with a smile. "Congratulations, Kiana. I'll sign off on this trip and send a request to get you and Valerian a per diem. Then we can schedule an official departure date."

Key breaks all the rules she's been taught about how she should act and leaps from her seat, jumping for joy, pumping a fist. "Thank you, Genevieve! I really mean it. Thank you so much. I never thought I'd be able to go into the field by myself, even if it's to a safe place."

Amusement crinkles the corners of Genevieve's eyes. "I look forward to your reports when you return."

Genevieve stands and comes around her desk, then offers her hand for a firm shake before going over to the chaise longue and draping herself gracefully onto its tufted velvet upholstery. She sighs once more, toes off her high heels, settles in, and closes her eyes. "I saw you looking at the revolver again," she murmurs as she relaxes. "Go on. Ask."

"Where did you find it?" Key's glad she doesn't have to sneak up on the subject.

"Oh, it was such a long time ago that I've forgotten where precisely, but it was in the southeast. I wasn't even on a dig. I was passing through a small town, more a village, and I saw it sticking out of a junk box at a thrift stall. The parts still moved, so I thought I'd buy it for novelty's sake." She pauses, chuckling. "The vendor must have thought he was the best con artist in the world. He threw in the box of ammunition out of pity, I'll bet. He said it and the revolver had been salvaged from a house that had flooded during the Decade, so neither the gun nor the ammunition would work. I took it anyway."

Key observes once again the pristine condition of the revolver. "You cleaned it, though. Where did you learn?"

A brief smile. "When we got back, I tried taking specimens off the handle. There was barely anything. I dove and came out with fragments of memories. Sensations, like dreams half remembered. What you see there is the result."

Key notes how Genevieve has tacitly admitted to the strength of her diving skill. One day, maybe soon, Key will match her, then exceed her. "Do you know how to use it?"

The smile widens, and a hint of mischief dances around Genevieve's mouth. Key blinks, struck by the change in her mentor's demeanor. Genevieve is so often serious that Key forgets there must exist other sides of her, that's she's only thirty-eight and still young. "I do. As it turns out, the latest owner of that revolver was not only a collector, but a skilled marksman."

"You learned from the memory?" Key tries to imagine how difficult that would have been. She'd learned wood joinery from Lenny's great-grandfather, a carpenter, but those memories had been multisensory, robust and full, and not patchy wisps of ghostly sensation.

"Yes. Thankfully, his kinesthetic memory was the strongest, though that isn't saying much. It took me some time to pick up the mechanics."

"I don't recall you ever writing about it."

"Some things don't need to be written." Genevieve's smile remains. She lifts her arm and forms her hand into the shape of a gun, aims it at something Key can't see. "Some things should be held in confidence, don't you think? How exciting to have a secret skill. How special."

Genevieve pulls the imaginary trigger, her hand jerking back with recoil, and lets her arm fall back to the chaise longue. "Bullseye."

FOUR

Reintegration is essential to a diver's health and the best tool for prevention a guardian has. If the guardian fails to initiate reintegration at the correct time, the diver will suffer. There are few actions that can be taken by the time a diver manifests aspects of a strong memory or rogue personality.

—*The Guardian's Text: An Historical View of Current-Day Practices for Supporting Memory Divers,* 1st ed. (first printing)

THE MUSEUM OF HUMAN MEMORY WAS LOCATED IN THE ARTS district built partway up Ashe's Peak, situated alongside columned buildings and the marble houses of the rich. The sharply angled roof was visible from any place on the main thoroughfare, serving as a landmark for those navigating the area. Its architecture, combined with the shale and limestone cladding that mimicked the striations found in Spinal geology, gave it the look of a thrust fault, as if the mountain had cracked open and gifted Asheburg a fully formed structure.

Key gazed at the tall banks of windows as she walked across the flagstones of the expansive front entry, holding the roil of her emotions behind teeth clamped tightly shut. Vale stalked beside her, tension clear in the hard lines of her shoulders and the punctuated thud of each deliberate footstep. She kept herself facing forward, though Key had already caught her looking back to where Jing and Cal walked, the pair flanked by her mother's coterie.

She should have given Vale more grace. But why should she give others grace when none was afforded to her? The idea simmered in her even as she told herself that arriving to a crowd wasn't Vale's idea of relaxing either. In a perfect world, they'd have been met at the station by Jing and Cal, and Vale would have had a happier reunion with her boyfriend.

In a perfect world, Vale would likely say, they would have arrived on time.

The pneumatic glass doors of the museum yawned open at their approach, revealing the light-soaked atrium. Milling around was a decent crowd of museumgoers for a weekday. Their voices, smeared into a low murmur by the space, were indistinct save for an errant shriek or two from a toddler.

As was her custom when she entered the museum, Key set her eyes on the black granite slab set into the western wall, seeking her grandmother's name.

The group turned right toward the Institute of Human Memory's welcome desk, away from the stanchions and red ropes leading to the museum's admissions windows. The receptionist startled as Key neared, leaping up so suddenly that he sent a cup of pens and pencils flying. The crack and clatter of the items hitting the floor echoed across the hall, mixing with the busy tones of an announcer over the radio and the squeals of children from across the atrium.

"Resifix Lanelle! Miss Key! I mean—" He stumbled over his words as he dropped to his knees, trying and failing to grab writing implements as they rolled out of reach.

"Alec, it's okay," Jing said. "Relax. Is that the Mountaineers game? Who's winning?"

"Hi, Jing!" Alec exclaimed, popping his head up over the edge of the front desk. He spilled his handful of pens and pencils onto the desk, then shot a hand out to turn the volume dial down on the radio. "Yes—but Spruceton is winning. Mountaineers are two points behind and they're in the grip of the fourth quarter struggle—"

"Damn," Jing muttered.

"I'm sorry, I didn't mean to go on a ramble, hi Calamus and—and Miss—" Alec paused, gulping, when Vale turned her eyes on him. His ruddy cheeks grew ruddier. Poor thing, Key thought, terrified and turned on and hopelessly in love from the moment he'd met Vale. "Miss Vale. Should I, um, call Dr. Wilcroft?"

"If you would be so kind," Lanelle replied, to which Alec gave the tightest of nods. He scurried back to his station, his eyes darting around and landing on Vale before he pressed a button on a control panel.

"Dr. Wilcroft, I'm so sorry to bother you," he said. "But, um . . . the Strades are here to see you. And Miss Vale. And Jing and Cal."

There was dead air for a few seconds before the intercom crackled. "Send them down."

"All of them? I'm sorry, Dr. Wilcroft, but Resifix Lanelle is here too and, uh . . ."

The intercom crackled again. "She is always welcome. I'll be waiting."

"Okay. Okay." Alec took a deep breath. His gaze darted around and landed on Vale before he ducked his head, like he was avoiding eye contact with a potential predator.

"Those of you not going to see the curator, would you be interested in hearing about our most recent exhibits? There's some literature by the ticket window."

Alec continued his speech, and Key's group broke off toward the bank of elevators to their right. As they approached, Jing and Cal came up alongside Key, each of them wearing a smile. "Managed to say hi to Vale, but not to you," Jing said, his smile going roguishly lopsided. He swept his forelock of impeccably styled black hair back into place. "So, hi."

"Hi." Key supposed Jing was handsome in a pretty, symmetric way; that was probably why Vale liked him. He had an easy charisma and breezy nature that put everyone at ease, even Vale, which Key counted as a small miracle. Objectively speaking, his features were youthful and pleasing to the eye, with cut-glass cheekbones and soulful, dark brown eyes that could be melancholy and haunted in one moment and sparkling with mischief in the next.

She smiled at Cal while Vale poked the down button. "Hey, Cal."

"Hey, Key." Calamus's resonant baritone voice was a pleasure to hear, and his singing even more so. Whereas Jing was supple and wiry and an unassuming height, his tan skin evoking the warmth of early autumn, Cal was a thick and looming sort of tall, the pin-tight curls of his black hair kept close to his scalp, his deep brown skin glowing with the robustness of summer. His sweet, earnest face and placid nature had drawn Key instantly at their initial meeting, and they had been fast friends since.

Jing slung an arm around Vale, who grunted, staggering with the unexpected weight before bracing herself to hold him.

"Are you okay?" Key asked. "You look tired."

"I feel tired," Jing replied, poking the side of his head with two fingers. "Picked up some demons on the last dive. Nothing a little reintegration won't fix, right?"

Key couldn't suppress her shudder. "The clinic isn't a day spa, Jing."

He pointed at her. "To *you*." He grinned, then pecked Vale on the cheek before straightening.

"Was it that bad?" Key looked to Cal, who nodded. "You really want the memories of your last day wiped?"

"Three," Jing mouthed cheerfully, holding up the appropriate number of fingers, though the deep shadows beneath his eyes belied his tone. "Can't wait. I love not having intrusive memories and hallucinations. You should try reintegration sometime. It's healthy for you, like taking a tonic."

"No thanks." Key shuddered again. "It sounds terrible." She knew what reintegration entailed, in theory: A hunter would be strapped to a bed and force-fed guttation created from their most recent blood specimen, which would have been taken before the dive yielding the intrusive memory. The concentrated level of genetic material in the guttation, twenty-five times the standard strength according to the suggestion listed in the guardian handbook, would trigger an automatic dive for those with heightened sensitivity and drown the hunter in their own memories, leaving the hunter to relive them until the mind was rewritten. Everyone at the academy was supposed to be reintegrated once for experience, but Key had excused herself from it, citing her religious duties.

"Speaking of drinks, ready for dinner tomorrow?" The elevator doors opened, allowing the group to pack in. "Because I know Cal is."

"Dinner?" Key's brows climbed up her forehead, but she put them back into place and assumed a pleasant demeanor. She caught her mother's eye, doing her best not to glare. The blessed did not glare at their mothers.

"Your welcome home dinner," Lanelle explained. "It's on short notice, so the guest list is slim, I'm afraid."

"No, it's perfect," Key said with false warmth, smiling to sell it. She'd seen her mother and Genevieve do the same thing countless times. "I appreciate the thoughtfulness in keeping it limited."

"I knew you'd like it. It's not a formal dinner, but a little dressing up would give the evening just the right touch."

Vale snorted rudely. Key shellacked her expression onto her face—of all the people! Vale loved to dress up—but noted how Lanelle's eyes narrowed. Key changed the subject. "Jing, do you have any plans for tonight? I'd like to chew on your brain, if that's okay."

"Can we do it tomorrow? I'm not sure how long the reintegration will take, and I like to relax after." He gave Vale a look. She rolled her eyes, but the corner of her mouth turned up.

Key deliberately did not think about what relaxing could mean, especially with Vale. "All right, tomorrow then. After dinner."

"You'll owe me."

"Aren't you already getting free dinner at my house?"

"Via invitation," Jing replied. "So this is extra."

"Saints," Key muttered, ignoring Vale's I-told-you-so expression. "What do you want?"

"A ride back to my place when I'm done with the reintegration, and the rest of the day off for your guardian."

Key pursed her lips, thinking. She'd have to send a gram to her driver and suffer tonight's family meal without Vale's companionship, but it was an acceptable price to pay for Jing's expertise. "Mama? Is that acceptable?"

"I dislike the bartering, but yes," Lanelle replied.

The elevator stopped, the doors opening to a plain white hallway lit in golden incandescence.

Dr. Wilcroft—or "just Genevieve, please" to everyone but Vale, who refused to use her given name—had her modest office on the first basement floor, sharing the level with the assistant director, the assistant curators, the volunteer coordinator, the docents, and other personnel belonging to the Institute of Human Memory. The floors beneath the museum's atrium were a complicated warren of hallways, barely marked, but two years spent at the institute meant Key could navigate the labyrinthine underground twists like a bird migrating home. That hadn't been the case when she and Vale first started. More often than not, they'd gotten lost, finding themselves in the armory when they meant to access the mycology lab, or the therapy suites instead of the archives.

Genevieve's office door stood open, revealing one of two wingback chairs and a swath of nondescript gray office carpet. "Come in," she called.

"Don't take too long," Jing said to Vale, plopping himself onto one of the benches beside the door. Cal joined him a second later.

"No guarantees," Vale murmured, then entered Genevieve's office first, forever the vanguard.

"Resifix Lanelle." Genevieve put her pen down and pushed herself away from her desk, standing. She was striking in a silver wrap blouse with a matching skirt that ended slightly beneath her knees. As she came around her desk to shake Lanelle's hand, Genevieve's black stilettos thumped, muffled, on the carpeted floor.

"You are seen," Lanelle said.

"I rejoice in your sight. What brings you to the museum?"

"I have some concerns about my daughter's management and have suggestions on how to improve her current situation."

Genevieve didn't react. "I would be delighted to hear them once Kiana and Valerian have finished their debrief."

"I will await you outside, then." Lanelle stepped out of the doorway and went to take a seat on the bench.

"I appreciate it." Genevieve glanced at Vale. "Close the door, Valerian." She then turned to Key.

There had been a time, years ago, when Key would get hot-cheeked and flustered at the sound of Genevieve's alluring voice, or find her notebook of great interest after a lingering stare. Whether she was agitated because of Genevieve's looks or her accomplishments, Key couldn't say. Perhaps it was a little of both.

Genevieve had been the top of her class at the academy, recruited straight to the museum after graduation. At twenty-five, she and her former guardian, Burdock III, uncovered a historical raised field system with flood protection that led directly to new riverside community gardens. She had become senior hunter by the time she was twenty-eight and ascended to head curator before she was thirty, the youngest ever to hold the position, buoyed by the success of her exhibit about an undiscovered southern village. The memory tabs she collected about the villagers' daily lives had been vivid and detailed; the exhibit, the year's unequivocal award winner.

"Kiana, Valerian, I'm so grateful you're both safe. Please sit."

Key set her staff against the back of one of the chairs and hooked a thumb under the strap of her rucksack, calling the memory she'd found to the tip of her tongue, ready to argue her case to Genevieve. But in the moment before she could take the rucksack off, the world shivered apart, shearing into separate layers. Nausea struck as the interior of the kitchen took shape in lines of neon green, afterimages forming without sun. She gasped as the mug, transparent, was set on the equally transparent table.

"You are consecrated," her grandfather says.

Key's knees buckled. She grabbed for something, anything, her vision slipping sideways, losing focus. She heard Vale's soft exclamation right before steady hands caught her, guiding her to the seat.

"Are you okay?"

She grounded herself in Vale's voice, real and immediate and always with her. Also real was the upholstery of the chair, its tightly woven cloth, its uncomfortably stiff cushion. Key breathed in through her nose, exhaled through her mouth. She opened her eyes, willing away the scene, forcing herself to see what she knew was there: Genevieve's broad desk, papers piled neatly atop it; the chaise longue in the corner, adorned with a worn pillow; a tall bookshelf holding its assorted memorabilia, including the antique revolver in its display case, the single round still beside it.

Vale put a palm to Key's forehead, bending close. "Key?"

"I'm okay, I'm okay." The scene reorganized itself, falling securely into place. She took Vale's hand, drawing it away, giving it a squeeze of reassurance. "I just need some rest."

Vale grunted, holding Key's eyes with her own for a second too long before squeezing back and retreating, shrugging off her rucksack and guitar case, arranging their belongings at their feet. "That much is true."

"I won't keep you long, then." Genevieve's voice was colored burnt orange with worry. "You can write the report—"

"I want to talk about it." Key scooted forward on the chair, reaching over to grab Vale's rucksack, unbuckling the flap and pulling open the drawstring. "Because I think I got something really important. We found a well-preserved abandoned compound several miles southeast of the Crystal Grove station, which I estimated to be at least two hundred years old. As it turned out, I was off by several decades."

"Kiana," Genevieve said.

She withdrew the bag of specimens and placed it on Genevieve's desk, excitement fluttering in her belly. Of all people, Genevieve would understand. "The site is rich with memories. I was able to dive over two hundred thirty years back. It yielded—this will be of interest to both the museum and the temple, I think—a ritual that seems to be the predecessor of the current responsorial rite. A blessing that was given to one of the faithful, except instead of being sanctified, the person was consecrated. I think that's a fascinating change of language and I'd like to find out more about this precursor."

"Kiana," Genevieve said again, walking toward her desk to stand beside it.

"Haven't we always wondered when and how our ancestors began speaking to us?" Key imbued her next words with a breathy enthusiasm. "We've never had any solid answers. I know my choice of research specialization could be trendier or less niche. I know the subject isn't a publishing darling and that your name and reputation are attached to mine. But I believe I have something of real substance. This is a sign from the ancestors. I'm meant to be researching this. I have to go back."

Key wasn't sure what she expected, but it wasn't a heavy, rocky silence.

She shored up the conviction in her voice. "I have the specimens here for verification."

Genevieve blew out a breath. "Kiana, I'm not sure this is as big a discovery as you think it is, but two hundred thirty years is no small feat. That's beyond what anyone else at the museum can do, except for Jing and me. I'm impressed."

"Thank you," Key replied, pleased at the praise, but stung at the dismissal. No matter. She was practiced at thinking on her feet. "It was a whole compound," she continued. "Even if the ritual itself turns out to be nothing, though I think it won't, this was a settlement. There's a lot to uncover about the daily lives of these people, who they were, what they ate and how they interacted with the world, their family structures, whose ancestors they are. I'd follow your blueprint from your doctoral project. If I can go back—"

"You said Crystal Grove?" Genevieve's brows furrowed. "Where is that? I don't recall giving you authorization to go there."

"No, but I felt, after my initial survey of the local population in the general area where I was given clearance to go, that it was within my purview to do so. There seems to be a discrepancy in our records regarding the village, or the people there have misremembered. I think that it's far more likely our records are incorrect and that we may need an audit of the—"

"You think you found a precursor to the responsorial?"

"Yes," Key said, excitement rising. "There's quite an interesting language change. It's only a single word, but—"

"It's only a single word. Variations occur commonly; you know that, Kiana."

"But there have been no recorded variations of the responsorial in temple history that far back," she argued. "I'm sure of it. I've known the history of the temple since I was a child."

"I'm aware," Genevieve said, a touch dry. "But just because there is nothing recorded does not mean a variation or two, or three, didn't exist. Ritualistic customs commonly have regional variants. Take the epics from the shore communities, for example."

Vale mumbled, "They're called lays, not epics. And they don't have variations because they're not allowed to have them."

Genevieve glanced at Vale, who did not make eye contact. "So you've said before, but, again, none of our ethnomusicologists can prove either of your claims." She turned back to Key, clearly finished with Vale. "Kiana, I know it's in your nature and training to find significance in every memory you uncover. But you mustn't let your temple experience bleed into the work here. I highly doubt there's anything significant."

Key's forehead wrinkled. "But my research specialty—"

"Is making you biased. You're jumping to conclusions too swiftly for someone with your experience and knowledge. I'll personally verify your specimens and give you an evaluation. I can't promise you more than that."

"What?" Key blinked. An evaluation was the bare minimum, and she never got the bare minimum. "Why?"

"Because I can't reward your tardiness or your rules-flouting by giving you everything you've asked for without proof. The potential impact of your discovery is not an excuse for being late. Neither is it acceptable to disregard authority on the strength of a whim. We have rules and regulations here for a reason, Kiana. Our legitimacy is predicated upon following said rules. Without them, we cannot maintain the trust of the population."

Key protested. "I just found something both the temple and the museum can use and you don't think that's justification?"

Genevieve narrowed her eyes, her gaze intensifying until Key wilted and shut her mouth.

With a soft sigh, Genevieve half sat on the edge of her desk, folding her arms over her chest, one long leg braced against the floor. The hem of her skirt rode up, and Key couldn't help but look at the elegance of Genevieve's leg and ankle and the fineness of her bones.

"You tell me what I should do when the daughter of the city's head resifix—who is waiting outside my door, need I remind you—and a city councillor goes missing for a week," she said, her voice weary. "When we're fielding enough grams to disrupt not only the director's day, but his secretary's, the assistants', and mine as well, and dodging reporters itching to print headlines saying I'm responsible for the blessed one's death. It's been hard enough getting the funding we need from the council, and bad publicity won't help. I am not jeopardizing the livelihoods of the people working here for your gut feelings."

"Okay, I'm sorry," Key said. "But—"

"No. Take the loss. I am being more than generous in offering to evaluate your finds personally." Bright anger glimmered in Genevieve's eyes. "This isn't the first time you've pulled a stunt like this, only the most egregious. Your actions warrant more punishment, not less."

Key lowered her head. "I'm . . . sorry. I won't do it again."

"And you, Valerian," Genevieve went on. She turned her stare on Vale, her emerald drop earrings swinging with the motion. "Why didn't you push Kiana to return? You are an extension of me when afield. You carry my responsibilities, and more besides. We chose you because we thought you were capable."

Key watched Vale's jaw flare and broke in, hoping to avoid disaster. "I wanted to stay longer. It's not Vale's fault."

"Noted." Genevieve kept looking at Vale. "You cannot capitulate to your hunter's every wish. You're too permissive."

Though Key couldn't see Vale's flush—she rarely showed color in her cheeks except after hard physical exertion—there was a distinct glow radiating from her, like the heat shimmer over a stretch of sunbaked granite.

"I'm not," Vale muttered. "I told her as soon as we went off course that we'd be late."

Genevieve's mouth flattened. "That isn't enough."

"She did hurry me along." Key gestured to herself. "It's all my fault and none of hers."

"And your wound? The tear in your sleeve is too neat. What happened?"

"There were black market hunters," Vale replied tightly. "They tracked us to the site. Two of them. They're dead. Key took the blood price. Show her, Key."

Key picked up the specimen bag and opened it, emptying it onto Genevieve's desk. Genevieve, without so much as a glance, pushed the specimens aside.

"But we wouldn't have encountered them," Vale continued, keeping her eyes trained on Genevieve, "if we hadn't taken the detour to start with."

Key couldn't stop her reaction this time. "Vale!" she exclaimed quietly through gritted teeth.

"I see. Did you tell Kiana you were being tracked?"

"No." Vale dropped her eyes to the floor, her fingers digging into her thighs. "They were green. I thought it'd be best to avoid them. I didn't want to burden her with it."

"I think it's pertinent knowledge, don't you?"

Vale clicked her mouth shut and said nothing further, her demeanor souring.

The discussion was turning, and it wasn't in a direction Key liked. "Genevieve, I promise I won't be late again. I was foolish not to consider how my decision would impact others, and I regret my actions. I'm willing to face the consequences."

"Are you? Good. I've had plenty of time to decide what sort of disciplinary action to take." Genevieve studied Key intently, as cold as marble and as unyielding, a statue draped in silver.

Vale shut her eyes, her hands curling into fists upon her knees.

"You are both prohibited from fieldwork pending disciplinary review and will have your pay suspended for a week, effective immediately." Key gasped, but before she could protest—prohibited from fieldwork!—Genevieve stood, forcing Key to crane her neck up. "Once the week is over, both your salaries will be set to one pay grade lower. You will be placed under the supervision of the senior hunter and guardian until you can demonstrate responsibility and reliability."

Key opened her mouth, concern rising like floodwaters over the unfairness of Genevieve's punishment, especially for Vale. For all Vale's ferocity in battle, she would never speak up for herself in front of Genevieve, which meant it fell to Key. "When you say effective immediately, do you mean this pay period, or the next?"

"I mean immediately, Kiana. I'm freezing payments to both of you as soon as we're done here."

"You can't!"

"Don't presume you can tell me what to do," Genevieve said levelly. "The privileges and personal oversight I granted you can be revoked at any time. You are my protégé and well regarded in the community, but you are still an employee of this museum. If you'd like to remain one, you'll accept this with grace."

Key recoiled, aghast. To her left, Vale began breathing faster, opening her eyes. "Dr. Wilcroft, I really need the money."

"She does," Key said. "Vale supports her family with this money—"

Vale rounded on her with a snarl. "Don't tell her my business!"

"I'm sorry, but that's not fair to you when you've got all those people relying on you—"

"Enough." Genevieve cracked the word like a whip. "This is supposed to be a lesson, given you didn't pay attention to your warning from last time. Valerian's family will have to do without for the time being."

Key held still for what felt like an eternity before Vale unlocked her jaw to speak. Emotions raced across her face before she looked at Genevieve, pleading. "Dr. Wilcroft, please. Suspend the next pay period instead. I'll deal with it. But I need the money to land for this one."

Genevieve shook her head. "Learn your lesson first."

Vale sucked in a breath, eyes blazing.

"Hey," Key said, reaching out, touching Vale's shoulder. Anything to keep her short fuse from reaching the payload. "Don't worry about it, I'll spot you the money. I'll take care of you."

Vale shoved Key's hand off, standing so abruptly that the chair surged back, its legs leaving skid marks in the carpet. "I don't need you to take care of me!"

"Vale, that's not what I meant—" With a sinking heart,

Key watched Vale snatch up her belongings one by one and storm wordlessly to the door, wrenching it open.

Jing's voice was audible from the hall. "Vale? What's wr—"

Vale yanked on the handle, slamming the door shut. It rattled in its strike plate as if afraid, the sound a chittering of teeth.

Eight Years Ago

Vale accompanies Burdock to a warehouse on the East Shore, a shabby industrial district that sits level with the river but has none of the flood protections of other, better-funded parts of the city. Overhead, the weathered steel length of the East Shore Bridge connects the area to Asheburg Main Station's loading docks. The streets here are dingy and littered with cigarettes, and liquid pools in the potholes around poorly maintained streetcar rails. Vale isn't sure if the liquid is water or something else, but it's probably something else. Rainbow sheen floats atop the puddles, catching the light of the foxfire streetlamps. It's constantly wet in Asheburg, which after two years of living in the city still manages to surprise her. Back home, it's drought season, the salt season, and every year it's a race to see who wins: nature's lust for death, or the community's will to live.

"It smells," Vale says as she trundles behind Burdock, whose long legs carry him swiftly through the half dark, his hands in the pockets of his jacket giving nothing away about his mood.

"The river is polluted." Burdock and Vale fall in with other people all going the same way. He says no more, as is typical for him. Vale wants to ask the next questions: Who polluted it? What's it polluted with? It's important to know, especially where she comes from, where rising water and storms pull remnants of the past out of the ocean and crash them ashore. There's a difference between the smell of bloated death and something once contained, now a contaminant. Sometimes, it doesn't have a smell at all, and people will burn in the floodwater. It's hard not to curse the ancestors whose deeds, it's said, led to so much destruction, hard not to think of the earth as vengeful when many of its gifts are poisoned.

There's no time to ask. Burdock approaches a stone-shouldered woman with a scar bisecting her left eyebrow, obviously standing sentinel in front of an open, nondescript door. Noise floats out from within, voices chattering, like songbirds before a thunderstorm. There's a line of rough-and-tumble folks to Vale's right, but Burdock avoids it altogether.

"Burdock," the guard says, nodding at him. He nods back. "Guest?"

"Valerian IV. Not eligible."

The guard scans Vale up and down. Vale bears the heat of judgment, knowing her uniform is too short, too stained for pride. "Academy? Starting her early, are you?"

Vale puffs up, hot. "I'm sixteen."

"You're a child," the guard replies. "Thin as a rail."

Burdock says, "She's the rail I'll use to beat someone's ass in the future. She's off-limits today."

The guard scowls, but steps aside. "Get her the right color."

They enter the warehouse, and Vale is immediately swamped with sound, enveloping her like the late summer humidity of the southern coast. People press in from all sides, jostling her hard enough to make her stumble, and high above are giant lights radiating heat. Spotlight beams concentrate on something in the center of the room. It's almost impossible to stay with Burdock in his black jacket and black pants and black boots, his black hair tied neatly at the base of his neck. Vale tries her best to focus, but there's an overwhelming urge to *move*, to run wildly about, to shuck her skin and free the thousands of electrical currents building beneath it so they can seek ground somewhere.

Burdock snags her by the wrist and folds her under his wing, guiding her to a bar where more people are clustered. He shrugs off his jacket and lays it on the counter, then drags the sleeve of his shirt up, enough to bare half his forearm. A man behind the bar takes a paintbrush and stripes Burdock's arm in green. Burdock gestures for Vale to do the same. Her wrist is swamped in the too-large sleeve of the academy shirt one of the janitors salvaged for her a year ago. She tugs her sleeve up, rolls it, tucks it. A streak of red, brighter than blood, goes on her skin.

Burdock gives her an assessing look, as if he can see the chaos roiling inside her, then says, "Upstairs. This way."

As they go, they pass a few familiar faces. Vale recognizes them belatedly as part-time instructors at the school, people who drop in to take over a class when a faculty member can't make it, or who run training hours on non-lesson days. These, Burdock greets with a short nod. Everyone in the crowd seems to know Burdock. He cuts through, sometimes shaking hands, sometimes clasping forearms, sometimes laughing and clapping shoulders, and as Vale steps along in his slipstream, a small fish trailing a large fish, she notes the way some people look at him, their eyes hooded, faces firming with an emotion Vale can't name.

"What is this place?" Vale asks once they're on the catwalks running over the space, at enough of a distance from the crowd that she can hear her own thoughts again. She's noticed that everyone has a streak of color on their arm, even those who don't look much like fighters. Cigarette smoke drifts up past their feet. Vale's no stranger to heights, having climbed her share of magnolias and oaks to get away from her siblings; this, too, is calming. She leans against the flimsy railing and peers at where the spotlights are focused. They illuminate a cordoned-off area in the shape of a ring, elevated, the floor of it reflecting an under-steeped yellow.

"It's a lot of things." Burdock leans his arms against the railing as well. He glances around, likely counting the number of people also on the catwalks and assessing available exits. The paint has dried on his skin. Vale's suddenly aware of the paint on hers, itchy and tight. "A place for information. A social club. A place to test yourself and anyone who challenges you."

"You fight people here?"

"I've done it, yeah. You won't, not today. But you will. I brought you because this is the world you'll need to prepare for, and it's best you start early."

"I thought I was already preparing." What else was she doing at the academy but trying and failing to stuff her sieve of a brain full of geography and history and music and psychology?

"No. Those students are rich kids who'll end up as glorified bodyguards. You, Vale, you're a guardian. And it's here where you start toughening up." He points to a corner with a few tall tables. People are sliding what look like tab folders across the surfaces, waxed cards skittering from one hand to another. "Deals made there. And there"—he gestures—"info brokers. Radio operators. Anything worth knowing, you'll learn from them."

Burdock points to each section of the warehouse, breaking down the space for Vale. "Betting, over there. You can make decent cash at events like these. Medic's by the ring, talking to the ref. Only one rule you need to know: No fighting outside the ring. See those flags? White flag means fight to first surrender. Black flag means to the death."

Vale turns wide eyes on her mentor. "Death?" Below them, two people separate from the crowd, moving toward the ring, where the referee has appeared in the middle. "If they're all guardians here, wouldn't that . . . not make sense?"

"It's not all guardians. There are hunters here too, and managers, and scouts. People want to see who they're contracting and what that guardian's made of. Ain't no better place to learn about others than here. If you do things right, nobody here will best you."

"Because of your training." Vale thinks training is torture sometimes, that Burdock must get a sick sense of joy from beating the shit out of her at any time of day. He says it's good for her. That it'll keep her on her toes, that she gets more combat hours than any other student in the school. He's right, but he also doesn't have to make it hurt so much.

"Because you're a survivor. Your instinct is to live, to win. My task is to temper you so you have the strength and clarity of mind to use that instinct. To get it sharper. Sharpest. You'll need it." Burdock finally looks at her. "Never forget where you're from, little sister. We're drifters, me and you. We know what it's like to lose."

Burdock points to two guardians standing on opposite sides of the ring, one a woman, the other a man. "Almost time," he says. The woman is of medium height, lightly built, her blond hair plaited close to her scalp. A sword and dagger hang from her hips. The man across from her has a foot on her easy, with broad shoulders and pants that cling to a muscled rear and impressive thighs, and he's also armed with a sword and dagger.

The referee raises a black flag.

Burdock winces. "Someone's overconfident." At Vale's confused look, Burdock adds, "There's a chance that man can beat Laurus. But I wouldn't bet against her."

Vale's eyes go so wide that she feels her skin straining. She stares, shocked, at the woman in the ring, who is calmly donning black gloves. The spotlights glint off the plates embedded in the mycoleather.

Now Vale remembers her. Laurus is a legend in guardian circles, a role model who could be relied on to do anything to protect her hunter. She'd fought for him. Killed for him. Nursed him through illness and injury. And then, when the weight of rogue memories was too much to bear and he became unstable and violent, when there was no hope of reintegrating him, she ended him. At the academy's special recognition ceremony last year, Laurus had seemed anything but honored, her face pale and drawn through the affair, like she was being haunted.

Laurus should not be hiding her light here. She should be on adventures with a new hunter, finding memories, writing her mythos instead of fighting in a death match in an underground ring. Aghast, Vale asks, "What *happened* to her?"

Burdock says grimly, "Don't look away."

The bell rings. Laurus is beautiful savagery; she's poetic brutality. Vale's helped butcher animals, but that's clinical work, devoid of emotion. Laurus is rage channeled keen into the edge of her sword. Vale can't help it; she shies as Laurus spears the challenger's throat through with her knife. It's dead silent in the warehouse, so Vale can hear the sound of cartilage tearing.

The bell rings again. Burdock seizes Vale's head and wrenches it up, forcing her to watch the man collapsing to the floor of the ring, his neck pulsing ruin. The warehouse erupts in cheers as Laurus shakes the blood off her knife, face impassive.

Vale, trembling, casts her eyes to the side, afraid to move, her head squeezed painfully between Burdock's palms. His mouth opens and shuts, but his words are drowned out by the crowd. She already knows what he's said, though. She's trained with him long enough to feel his disappointment worming up acidic behind her sternum. They'll need to do this again. Over and over until she's internalized the violence, same as everything else he teaches her.

FIVE

There are few regions across the continent as diverse in medicinal plants as the Spine. For centuries, beginning well before the Decade of Storms, the Spinal peoples have foraged for and farmed medicinal plants. To honor that tradition and to assist guardians with the identification and preparation of these plants in the field, each new guardian is given a plant name.

—*The Guardian's Text: An Historical View of Current-Day Practices for Supporting Memory Divers,* 1st ed. (first printing)

THE DOORS TO THE ACADEMY'S TRAINING GYM HAD BEEN propped open, allowing afternoon sunlight and a strengthening breeze to sweep the interior clean of musty scents. Vale came in like the desert wind, hot and brittle with anger, throwing herself onto one of the benches lining the wall to remove her boots before stepping onto the mats that had cushioned at least ten thousand of her falls.

Burdock's office was on the other side of the gym, directly across from the entrance, the largest one in the row, befitting his status as the top advanced combat instructor. The door was closed but the light was on, a warm glow visible through wavy glass, marred in one spot by his distorted silhouette. Vale struck out toward the office, striding past the pairs of students training with bamboo weapons, the staccato rhythms of engagement as familiar to her as her own heartbeat. Key could have her temple and her pool and her supplicants; Vale would take the gym and baptize herself in sweat and combat.

She ignored the sparring matches in progress, though her presence didn't go unnoticed as she stalked by, her proverbial tail lashing. Students paused to observe, several of them whispering to themselves and darting furtive, wide-eyed looks at her. Vale understood why once she glared at the mirrors on the wall to her right.

Her reflection glared back, her demeanor bristly and cantankerous. Her hair was poking out from her braid; she hadn't had the time nor the inclination to coax it back into sleek order. She looked like a travel-worn alley cat, grimy with mud and clay and blood, hungry and scrappy and ready to do violence.

Obviously, her self-imposed cooling-off period hadn't worked. Vale had taken the long way to the academy to save herself the fare from the incline and to stop by the bank, but during the walk her mind filled up with arithmetic, the pluses and minuses of her calculations mutable and slippery until she gave up figuring. What she knew was a missed pay period and a transfer of almost all her funds to her family meant there could be no food nor travel expenses, and the new shirt she'd been carefully saving for, the one in the seconds bin at the tailor's, could no longer be hers. She'd have to make do with her old one, the material so worn it could have been mistaken for a gauzy rag.

It was the right thing to do—the only thing to do. Her duty to her family came first. It was the whole reason she'd become a guardian. But a selfish part of her mourned the loss. Key could have ten shirts if she wanted; all she had to do was ask. Why couldn't Vale have something new, or even someone else's castoffs? Anyone's. She was the sixth of seven children and was used to hand-me-downs and was no slouch with a sewing kit.

A shout of recognition made Vale lift her head. A stocky woman with curly, bright copper hair pulled into a pouf waved to her, a fencing mask in one gloved hand, a needle-thin sword in the other. Vale scowled back, not breaking stride. Of course Rocket would be here instead of anywhere else.

"Vale!" Rocket hustled up, matching Vale step for step. She switched her foil to her left hand and tucked her mask under her left arm. Her hair, darkened to auburn with sweat, clung to her pale, freckled skin, the strands of it framing her face with thin, curvy snakes. "Welcome back. See you at the party tomorrow, yeah?"

Vale stopped and faced her, surprise lancing through the anger. "How do you know?"

Rocket grinned, showing off even, white teeth. "Resifix Lanelle hand-delivered an invitation to me last night. It's a little last-minute, but no one says no to Key's mom."

"So you're going to be there?"

Rocket snorted a laugh. "Um, yes? That's why I said I'd see you there. Pay attention, Valerian."

Her hackles went up and her anger rekindled, evaporating whatever residual surprise was left. *Pay attention, Valerian* had been the favorite phrase of every teacher at the academy except Burdock—and as a classmate, Rocket knew it.

"Besides," Rocket continued, "I figured I'd take the

opportunity to scout out terms of a new contract. I just got my registration renewed and my new suit's back from the tailor too. Now I have a chance to use it."

"A new contract?" Vale's unique contract with Key was through the museum and wasn't slated to end for another several years. The terms covered Key's safety while working at the museum and nothing else, although there was a clause giving Key the flexibility to expand the definition of "working." If she needed protection going to and from the museum, Vale could be tasked with it. If she felt her safety was at risk at the temple, Vale could be called upon to accompany her.

As a result, they spent more time together than the job demanded. Since there was nothing else to do, Vale didn't put up a fuss over it, except for that time a year ago when Key finally convinced her to move into the Strade mansion. Vale still lived mostly out of her meager travel bag just in case and could be found bunking at the academy half the time.

"Yeah. Isn't yours ending?"

Vale furrowed her brows. "What? No. Who said that?"

Rocket's mouth pursed into a tiny, perfect O. "Whoops! No one, exactly. It was . . ." Her light brown eyes shifted away from Vale. ". . . sort of the impression that I got. Since you got Key back a week late. And you know you and Key's mom have never gotten along."

Vale scowled but didn't refute the statement. In contrast, Rocket and Lanelle got along wonderfully.

"I thought since I got a personal invitation and Genevieve is kind of a hard-ass . . ." Rocket shrugged. "I wouldn't worry too much if I were you! The second people get wind that you're free, you'll have offers coming at you from all sides."

What Rocket didn't know was that Vale had already turned down multiple offers for shorter-term, riskier contracts when she was off duty, but she had no faith that her handlers would give her necessary critical information, and neither was her family guaranteed a payout in case she died. She would do her family no good if she were dead. "My contract isn't up."

"My bad. Maybe they just haven't told you yet?"

"My contract isn't up," Vale repeated, because unlike Key, she was no good with words.

"It might be soon," Rocket said, and offered her a taunting grin.

Vale unslung her guitar case, then shrugged off her rucksack. It hit the mat with an echoing thump. "You wanna challenge me? 'Cause you're acting like it."

"Hold on," Rocket said, lifting a hand. "This isn't a challenge."

"Best do it now before I get really pissed. I got lots of things to be mad about and no outlet, and you're looking like a good target."

Rocket eyed her but took a step back regardless. "You get mad over too much."

"Don't push me then." A pause. "Bitch."

"I wasn't pushing."

"Telling me I won't have a job counts as what, then? You're acting real bold for someone who's gonna get her ass kicked." Vale's emotions finally coalesced into one big, darkened cloud, which began to rotate and churn.

"It was a friendly conversation between two colleagues—"

Vale punched Rocket square in the nose.

Rocket yelped, her free hand covering her face, and staggered backward. Vale closed the distance, yanking the fencing mask free from the crook of Rocket's elbow, rearing back. With a shout, she brought the mask down hard in an overhand strike, crashing it into the left side of Rocket's face.

Vale unleashed a backhand, the muscles in her torso and arm tensing and contracting. But before it could connect, Rocket recovered, her fighting spirit sparking in her eyes, and blocked Vale's arm with her forearm, her height and weight giving her the advantage as she set her feet and shoved herself forward.

Undeterred, Vale dropped the mask and pushed back, bracing her right arm against Rocket's to create a space between them. She snaked her left hand through it and clamped down on Rocket's windpipe, right below her jaw, and with her thumb and forefinger, pinched the glands there. Rocket gagged, her body contracting, the foil clattering to the floor.

She heard a door opening to her right. Burdock roared her name.

Vale flinched, but didn't let up. "Run your mouth again, I dare you," she said through gritted teeth. There was no hint of apology on Rocket's face.

Footsteps approached at a run. Vale released Rocket and sprang back just in time to avoid the whistling blow Burdock had aimed at her. She pivoted, but he was faster. Even knowing what to expect, the speed of his attack took her breath away. Burdock's practice sword flashed into existence, the flat of it cracking across her cheek a split second later.

Vale reeled, tripping over her rucksack, the world juddering before her eyes from the force of the hit.

But she kept her feet.

"Pick your weapon," Burdock growled, the challenge clear in his near-black eyes, so similar to Vale's own that they'd been mistaken for siblings upon her arrival at the academy. "You wanna push someone around, you do it to someone who can take it."

Vale grinned at the implication, though her face was throbbing and on fire. "Sword. Don't make me break my guitar."

"Rocket." Burdock indicated Vale's belongings with a flick of his sword. "Be a dear and move those out of the way, then get Vale a sword."

Vale pretended not to see the nasty smile on Rocket's face and focused only on Burdock. Every skirmish, every sparring session with him required her to push herself. She was at a disadvantage in every category against him: strength, speed, reach, experience. Burdock had almost a foot on her and eighty pounds at least, and a tenacious, vicious streak that almost matched her own. Almost.

She welcomed the odds. This was what she wanted, what she needed. Tunnel vision, the satisfaction of a hit, the chance to let her venom out. Being slammed to the mat over and over until pain and exhaustion could do for her what she could not.

Vale stuck out a hand for the practice sword, her bicep tightening when the weight of it dropped into her palm.

Burdock's sword blurred, and Vale caught it with her own. The first touch was hers, a perfectly placed parry-riposte that landed the tip of her weapon directly over

Burdock's heart. The next was his, and the one after that, and the one after that.

"Sloppy," he said as she circled him, residual pain ricocheting through her torso.

"It's not even real," she replied, changing her stance. Their swords clashed, and sharp pain bloomed in Vale's side. She gasped, dropping her sword, and in her moment of weakness, Burdock swept her leg, depositing her onto the mat.

He stood over her, one thick black eyebrow cocked, a beam of sunlight from the high windows illuminating the ruggedness of his face.

Vale sucked in a breath and rolled, grabbing her sword in the process, bouncing to her feet. Then Burdock extended his arm, the movement so quick she could not react. Her sword went flying.

His blade continued in its trajectory and came to a stop a hair away from her throat. In a real fight, she'd be dead.

But this wasn't a real fight, and she was already moving.

Vale knocked the tip of the sword away and lunged for Burdock's neck. There was the sound of a slap, and her hand rebounded, her skin stinging. Vale found herself at a disadvantage again, a large hand closing around her throat. It was her turn to gag and choke, but as she did, her fingers twitched toward the knife sheathed at her waist.

Burdock tossed his sword away and tightened his hold. "Stop."

Vale hissed and brought her left hand to her neck, digging at his vise grip with her fingertips.

"So be it." Burdock heaved, pitching her to the mat so hard she should have split the boards beneath. "Was that worth it, little sister?" he asked as she struggled upright, her diaphragm spasming. He seized her throat again and bent her back. "You ready to talk?"

Vale closed her eyes. Blue sparks danced in the darkness, lifting the weight from her shoulders. There it was: the calm she sought, like a shaft of sunlight piercing through clouds, holy and pure.

She dropped her arms to her sides.

Burdock let her go. "Show me your hands."

She did as she was told. Light gleamed off the short blade of her dagger.

Burdock threw his head back and laughed. "Lock me down next time and you'll do better." There was a flash as he sheathed his own knife. "Get your ass in my office. Rocket, a word."

Vale picked up her things and trudged away, smiling to herself at Rocket's cry of "She hit me!"

"Are you a guardian or not?" Burdock scoffed loudly.

"She fights dirty. Look at my face."

"She fights to win, which you ought to know by now." Burdock continued speaking, though Vale couldn't make out the words the farther away she got. She entered his office and glanced around, taking in the familiar map on the wall with its collection of multicolored pins and constellations of pinholes, the stacks of papers piled atop the desk beside a knot board and a coil of thin jute rope. She put her rucksack on one of the chairs and leaned her guitar against a free patch of wall.

Burdock came in a minute later and closed the door behind him, then drew the curtain across the window overlooking the gym. In the absence of daylight, the office seemed sickly, the wan yellow ceiling light struggling against the shadows. His old office hadn't a curtain nor a walk-in closet, and Vale had been lucky that she'd been small and had no issue sleeping in its cramped confines. When Burdock got promoted to advanced combat instructor, the first thing he'd done, unsurprisingly, was to increase his privacy measures by installing a curtain over the window and a peephole in the door.

"Was beating her with her helmet necessary?"

Vale knew the answer was supposed to be no, but she was also a terrible liar. "Yes."

He closed his eyes, drew in a breath, and folded in his lips, probably holding back the scolding he thought she deserved. Eventually, he said, "Vale."

"I warned her!"

"That's not what I was going to talk to you about."

"Rocket's been invited to Key's party tomorrow and she thinks I'm out of a job. I should have knocked her out for that."

"Vale!"

"She could've walked. I listened to you and I give people chances not to engage and they never take them. What's the point in offering?"

Burdock used a finger to smooth out the crease between his eyebrows. "For probable cause later. Are you mad because you think your job is at risk, or are you mad because Rocket is Key's ex, you've never liked each other, and you perceive her as a threat?"

Vale had never liked Rocket because Rocket hadn't an ounce of nice in her and not because she was Key's ex-girlfriend. Vale also didn't understand what had drawn Key to Rocket to start with. "She's not a threat."

"If you say so. Just one question, then. Would you have stabbed me?"

"What?" She gave him an incredulous look. "No!"

"Considering how many times we've fought each other, the answer should be yes."

"Would you stab me?" Vale already knew the answer. "I hope you don't stab me."

"Same."

Burdock opened his arms for a hug. She threw herself at him in relief, exhaling, finally relaxing against him. Ancestors, she hurt.

"I'm glad you're safe," Burdock said. He pulled back, lifting his fingers to her cheek for a second before stepping away. "Are you okay?"

"I'm fine." Vale touched her throat and made a face. "Nothing you haven't done to me before. You didn't even hit me that hard."

"No, I meant your situation with the museum." Naturally.

Vale eyed him. "How'd you know?"

"Key sent a gram as soon as you left."

"That all fit on one gram?"

He chuckled quietly. "She sent six. Consider me debriefed. She also said you'd be coming here."

Vale frowned. "I didn't come directly here."

"She said you'd likely go to the bank first. Please tell me you left enough for yourself to make it to the next pay period."

The unruly stack of papers on Burdock's desk was suddenly very interesting. Vale studied the top sheet, engrossed. There were too many numbers, and all of them were unreasonably large. She changed her focus to the knot board; she fiddled with each of the ropes. "I'm good. I'm still friends with the kitchen staff. There's always leftovers."

Burdock looked up as if asking for help, exasperation clear on his face. "You cannot be scrounging in the kitchens after hours! You don't even go here anymore."

Vale could have told him from past experience that the ceiling tiles held no ancestral spirits whatsoever and therefore wouldn't grant his prayer. "I don't want to talk about it. I did what I had to." She unfastened the belt holding the scabbarded butterfly swords. "Here. Said I'd give these back. I can't die owing you."

He shook his head, but a smile stretched over his tanned face regardless. It transformed his usual sternness into handsomeness—or would-be handsomeness, if not for his crooked nose. Ten years ago, his nose had been straighter. Vale had contributed to its crookedness only once as an academy student when she'd taken issue with his tone during detention. A mistake. The trouncing she'd received in return had been thorough, brutal, and demoralizing. She'd had bruises on bruises and a shoulder that popped weird for two weeks. In retrospect, she probably shouldn't have hit him with a staff mid-lecture.

"You owe me nothing," he said, reaching for the swords. He strode toward the back of the office, where a storage room door was open, and beckoned for her to follow.

She did, entering a small room that was more an armory

than anything else, stuffed from floor to ceiling with real weapons. This, Vale thought, was the closest she'd ever get to paradise. She cast her gaze around, her heart leaping at the swords in their racks, the staves propped up in the corner, the pile of brass knuckles atop a cabinet. Displayed on the wall within easy reach was Burdock's personal weapon, a beautiful wooden spear with a curved blade sharp enough and fine enough to cut a man and not have him realize until it was too late.

Her eyes came to a rest on a scabbarded sword leaning against the wall, its grip wrapped with black mycoleather, its guard and pommel worked in silver. That hadn't been here during her previous check-in. Though plain, it seemed well-made, like many of the pieces Burdock owned, some of which were priced beyond what Vale could afford—and she did enviably for herself at the museum. Or would, if she could keep all her money.

Irritation flared. Whatever joy the weapons granted was gone too soon, replaced by the worry of not being able to provide for her family. She was the unequivocal breadwinner, the result of a long-term investment that had only begun paying dividends in the last two years. The first time she wired money home, she'd almost cried. A paycheck like hers was substantial for one person, but not when it paid bills for eight. Her money kept her family afloat during disasters and helped ward off late fees and overdrafts. Two weeks was too long to go without the extra funds.

Burdock examined the butterfly swords and, finding their condition satisfactory, stowed them in a footlocker. "You get any use out of these?"

Vale snapped to attention. "Huh?"

He chuckled, indicating the new sword with his head. "Like that one? Came in with some others. And no, you can't touch it."

"Damn," she muttered. "What'd you ask?"

"Whether you got any use out of the butterflies."

Vale nodded. "Once." A reminder to ask Burdock an important question sparked bright in her mind. Pleased with herself at remembering, Vale added, "Has anyone been talking about Key on the radio lately?"

Burdock tilted his head, clearly not following. "She's 97.9's daily favorite."

"No, I meant on the . . . you know. Long waves." Vale tried to abide by the rule of not mentioning black market ham radio stations, but it wasn't a topic that came up often between her and Burdock. She did listen to the long waves for weather forecasts along the Spine and the coastal areas, as well as the latest guardian reports, but turned the radio off when the talk show hosts began debating conspiracy theories about why hurricanes struck where they did. What was there to debate when there wasn't a single thing to be done to stop a storm? It didn't matter who you were or how hard you believed when the skies darkened. Only things that mattered were getting people out safely and figuring out how to rebuild.

"That station?" Burdock sucked air through his teeth. "No, at least not directly. I'm sure they'd use a code word for her anyway. I don't know what it is. What happened?"

Vale relayed the situation, watching as Burdock's eyebrows drew closer together and the furrow between them deepened. "I didn't say nothing to Key about it, but it's weird. Right? It's weird. We also got a name for the leader. A weed of some kind. Like the black market hunters are making fun of the academy."

Burdock settled his weight against the edge of his desk and tapped his knuckles gently against his mouth. "Got anything more specific than a weed?"

"Arvensis."

At that, Burdock's eyes widened. "You sure?"

It was always strange to Vale that she couldn't do mental math without wanting to scream, yet she could remember the names, descriptions, and uses of hundreds of medicinal plants from the southern coasts and the Spine as if they were members of her family. "Yeah, I'm sure. You got contacts. You heard of him?"

He shrugged. "Only a little. Don't know much. I wouldn't trust me with the black market stuff either. I don't listen in as much as you think, and I don't know the code they use."

"What about the fight ring?"

"That's for everybody, legitimate or not." A pause. "Key always goes out under an alias, doesn't she? Ana Shrieve?" After Vale's *mmhmm* of assent, he continued, "That's concerning."

"So you agree it's not normal, being stalked like this. I don't know how they'd know her name. We don't tell anyone except Dr. Wilcroft and some folks at the museum. And you, unofficially."

"Word must have gotten out somehow," Burdock said. "Well, at least those two won't trouble you again, blood price or no. How'd the butterflies treat you?"

"They're fun." Vale patted the knife at her side, dissatisfied with Burdock's inability to help. "But I still like these better."

"And you'd like that sword even better, I bet." Burdock glanced at it.

Suitably diverted, Vale said, "You're right, I would."

"Didn't I just say you couldn't touch it?"

"What?" Vale gave Burdock an empty look. "I don't remember that."

"Sure, you don't." A pause. "You ready to talk about your situation yet?"

"Didn't we just talk about it? What's there to talk about?"

"You being grounded for a week and getting your check pulled."

Burdock always shot true when it came to her, his vision never obscured by any smokescreen, real or figurative. They were too similar, he'd explained once while helping her nurse a black eye, too alike in their wants, their angers. He'd recognized the emotions in her, sussed out their purity and quality when he'd first scouted her.

The anger came back, burning like firewater down her throat. "I tried my best. If Key wants to do something, she'll do it. Tell her no, and she'll say the saints put her up to it and do it anyway. I don't know what Dr. Wilcroft wants me to do. Knock Key out, hogtie her, and drag her home?"

"If that's what it takes, yes."

"First, she's way bigger than I am so that would be really hard—"

Burdock snorted a laugh.

"And second, how is she supposed to trust me if I'm ordering her around? Key's not a dog or a horse that I can tell what to do. She's a person with her own thoughts and feelings, even if the rest of this city doesn't think so. I'm not ordering her around like everyone else. She hates that."

"Maybe," Burdock said, reaching across his desk, closing his ledger book. "But you're her guardian, and there are times when you know better than she does. I'll wager most of the time, you do."

"She's got a direct line to the ancestors."

"And? That's supposed to make you know nothing? You ain't stupid, Vale, quit acting like you are."

"She got something good this time, she swears it. Dropped more than two hundred and thirty years back, probably closer to two hundred and forty."

Burdock straightened, sending her a curiously intense look. "How many exactly?"

Vale shrugged. "Dunno, I don't do numbers. Far enough to match Dr. Wilcroft, probably."

"Two hundred thirty-seven," Burdock said, his voice hushing.

Her eyebrows drew together. "What?"

"That's how far Gen could go, back then." A fleeting look of sorrow crossed his face before being replaced with that strange intensity. "Tell me more."

"All I know is that it's about the temple's responsorial rite. Some snow too. And then I got chewed out about being late. But if I'd made Key turn back before the last dive, she wouldn't have found something important. She was real excited about it. She has roughly three things to be excited about in her life, and this is one of them. I'm supposed to know my hunter, right? And I know Key enough to know how much she wanted to stay." Vale also knew Key enough to clock the two times she'd blanked out. For anyone else, it wouldn't merit alarm, only a watchful concern. For Key . . .

"Very moving," Burdock replied. "You still tell her no and get her back on time."

"Now you sound like Dr. Wilcroft." Vale harrumphed. "I can't believe you're taking her side on this."

Burdock raised both brows and tilted his head, which was a warning sign. "There are no sides. You knew when you were hired that this wasn't an ordinary guardianship. That's why you're paid the way you are. Gen and I don't talk anymore, but she has a point. Report in on time. You can always come back later."

"That's the thing, though! She doesn't want to come back later. She wants to stay and finish. I don't want to make her come home and have her be mad at me."

Burdock rolled his eyes. "Let her be mad. You're the guardian. She should defer to you."

"Did Dr. Wilcroft defer to *you*?" Vale threw the challenge at his feet, then winced at the expression on his face. "Sorry."

"Be glad Key isn't Gen, though she takes after her." There was silence after, as if Burdock meant to say something else but was withholding it. "Key's here in the city, and that's a credit to you and how much Key trusts you. No one could tell Gen what to do, not even me."

Vale scowled, feeling mulish. "Still sounds like you're taking sides."

"Little sister, if you want to finish this on the mat instead of being cussed in here, you should just say so."

Vale scowled deeper as Burdock leveled a look at her.

"What have we said about feelings, Valerian?"

"Don't patronize me!" She crossed her arms and bored her gaze into the floor, which was offending her.

Burdock leaned against a patch of bare wall with an affected casualness. "Offer's open."

"No thanks." She might be slow, but not that slow. Finally, Vale worked up her nerve, her mouth puckering like she'd eaten something tart. "I just don't want to let my family down. I need this job. If Key doesn't want to work with me . . ."

Burdock said nothing.

"She's my friend." It came out easier than Vale had anticipated, which was worrisome in a city as shockingly cutthroat as Asheburg. Death was ever present on the coasts where she grew up, wheeling vulturelike over their lives. Storms could spin off the ocean and come howling ashore, and if the village did not evacuate in time, there would be no good choices left to be made, nowhere safe from the fury of sustained 180-mile-an-hour winds and the destruction of a thirty-foot surge. Vale, her family, and her community had stood shrunken with loss and grief over and over, but at least they had grieved for their missing and dead. Here, in Asheburg, an inland city protected by its distance from the sea and sheltered in spirit by its temple, grief was more theoretical than practical. Something that people knew was the natural progression of bereavement but had few real, observed rituals. People were remembered after their passing but were spoken to by the resifixes, summoned from the beyond for opinions and wisdom, as if death were a minor inconvenience and the dead were simply neighbors gone on vacation, just a telegram away.

Vale hadn't come to Asheburg to make friends, and she hadn't come to Asheburg to harden herself to violence and loss. Before Key, no one in the city had cared about Vale except for Burdock. Key had been the first person to make it past Vale's prickliness, the first to look past Vale's shabby, country-bumpkin appearance and bad head for numbers, the first to see Vale as a real person. Without her inroads, there would be no friendship with Cal or long nights with Jing.

And really, that's what made staying with Key worth it. Vale was indebted, and she had to repay it.

Being a friend made Vale's role more difficult, though Jing and Cal made friendship and guardianship look easy. She ought to ask Jing for tips. "It's weird, okay? She's Kiana Strade. Comes from a rich and powerful and blessed family. And I'm . . . me."

Burdock sighed. Like Vale, he was from the southern villages, and had originally come to the academy on scholarship. The other students and teachers were monied folks, or from good families in the city. "Caring for Key means you do your job the way Gen says to. You're Key's guardian. You are the best the academy's turned out in a long time. I saw that in you when I scouted you. So did Gen when she selected you at graduation."

"We've done fine the last two years without me bossing her around."

"Have you, though?" Burdock sounded unconvinced. "If so, quit and be a supportive friend. Rocket can take your place. You could get a job anywhere else with your skills. Black market would pay a lot for you."

Vale dug in, her jaw jutting out. He wasn't wrong, but she wasn't about to throw her lot in with criminals and ne'er-do-wells. "I *need* this job. I made promises to my family and I'm gonna keep them."

"Then be the last word with Key. That's all. She's nice. She'll understand, even if you have to be firm with her." Burdock sighed. "You don't want to be like Ginseng II. Key won't get mad at you. Maybe a little frustrated, but she'll find something big again, guaranteed. Talent like that strikes true more often than not."

"Personal experience, huh? Like with Dr. Wilcroft? Say, how come you don't tell more stories of the two of you?"

"What's there to know? We used to work together. That's it."

Vale gave him a skeptical look. "You were guardian to the head curator of the Museum of Human Memory. You were there for her biggest discoveries. You think 'we used to work together' is going to cut it for me?"

"Yep."

"Nope." It was common knowledge that Dr. Wilcroft, before her doctorate and meteoric ascension, had been accompanied by an equally talented, equally young guardian: Burdock III. "You never gave me a straight answer on what happened with you and Dr. Wilcroft. She's over there at the museum making tons, and you're here in early retirement with a closet of death, teaching kids how to beat each other with sticks and getting scraps. What gives?"

"I'm fine where I am," Burdock replied.

"You always say that. Just because Dr. Wilcroft doesn't go afield anymore doesn't mean she doesn't need someone. She'll need help diving into Key's sample."

"Specimen. Didn't you learn anything? And she didn't and doesn't need me. That's the end of this discussion."

"What have we said about feelings, Burdock?" Vale showed teeth in what she hoped was a sweet smile.

Burdock's expression didn't change. "End of discussion, little sister. As for Key, don't worry too much about her. I'd say you're more fussed about it than she is because you're worried you're going to lose your job. I'm telling you your job is secure. If Gen were serious, she'd have fired you instead of putting you on probation, but she needs to show everyone that Key doesn't get special treatment because of who she is. Just shepherd Key along in a timelier fashion and it'll all go smooth. You're the guardian, not her."

"You make it sound easy."

"Because it is. Now, will you stop stalling and go to Key's house already?"

"I'm supposed to go to Jing's." But she didn't have the desire to do it, especially after a reintegration. He'd forget the deal he struck with Key, and Vale could clean up in the locker room showers, maybe wheedle Burdock into letting her sleep on the floor of his office.

"You don't sound real excited about it. Also, if you're thinking about dodging folks for the next couple of days, stop. You can't miss the party."

She hadn't gotten there yet, but she let Burdock think she had. "Says who?"

"The one in the room with a brain." Burdock smirked.

"It's because you beat it out of me," Vale retorted.

Burdock smirked harder. "Do you need a bribe? I saw you eyeballing the new sword."

"You'd let me have that?"

"Yeah, you can borrow it." He waited a beat. "If you go to Jing's tonight and the party tomorrow."

Vale thrust a finger at Burdock and glared. "Deal." She could already imagine the weight of the sword in her hand, see in her mind's eye the smooth, unmarred finish of the blade, hear the grind of a stone against it and the faint, echoing ring of the steel after each pass. She could take it and pretend she was going back to Jing and Cal's apartment.

"You better not be thinking of taking the sword and lying to my face. See Jing or not tonight, that's up to you, but you skip the party, and next thing you know, Key will get back together with Rocket and you'll be the third wheel."

Vale's face grew hot all over. "She wouldn't."

He shrugged. "Don't the two of you have adjoining bedrooms?"

Her face grew hotter. For such an expensive house, the walls were surprisingly thin. "I hate you. Fine. I'll go."

"You don't hate me. Come see what else you might need for your next assignment, whenever you get it." He went back into his armory. "New shipment came in, like I said."

Vale marveled again at the lethal density of weapons in the closet. "What'd you get?"

"Some new daggers, a new stiletto and tac knife, and a trench knife. They threw that one in for free, all praise to the ancestors. My wallet shed a tear."

She oohed with excitement, already feeling better. "Trench knife! I want it."

"Where on earth," Burdock replied, exasperated once again, "are you going to be that you'd want a trench knife?"

She shrugged. "I don't know, but they seem fun."

"I am begging you. Bring something that makes sense."

"Trench knife makes sense if I get in a bar fight," she mumbled.

"How many bar fights are you getting into?"

"None. Sadly. I can start one, though."

"I have failed as a teacher." Burdock pinched the bridge of his nose. "Don't start nothing you can't finish."

"I'd be able to finish better than the last time." She sniffed. "If I had a pair of those."

"Finish outside the bar, not in it." Burdock straightened. "You're as impossible as ever. Take the stiletto. It's lightweight and less situational."

"Okay, okay." She had to admit that Burdock had the right idea. Being out in the wilderness with extra weight was a bigger problem than not having trench knives, and it wasn't as if there were bars in the swamps and forests. "Can I have one of those shiny knuckles too?"

"And gloves, and new armor, and a pony?"

"No," Vale replied blithely. "Just the sword, the knucks, and the stiletto."

He sighed in a put-upon manner, then handed over the weapons, pulling out his notebook to log their absence. "Take good care of my stuff."

"I will," Vale promised. "And I'll lead the favored of the ancestors around on a leash and thwack her on the nose if she gets ideas. Thanks, Burdock. For the stuff and the talk."

"Anytime. You'd better get yourself showered and changed so you can look presentable."

"What for? She doesn't care what I look like."

"For Jing," Burdock said, shaking his head. "You know, the boyfriend you supposedly like and can't wait to spend time with? Don't you want to look nice?"

Vale deflated. "Oh yeah. Him." More like Jing couldn't wait to get into the clinic once she'd assured him she was okay.

"Now scram," Burdock said, shooing her out of the closet and toward the office door. "Have a nice evening instead of sneaking into the dorms to find a room."

"I wasn't—"

"Oh, quit. Close the door on the way out, and leave Rocket alone, okay?"

"No promises," Vale replied.

SIX

ABSTRACT

Building puzzle cairns is a cultural practice that has been, up until recently, confined to the southern coastlands and swamps. Although the reasons for building these primitive yet clever constructions are not entirely clear, current research suggests the cairns are part of a syncretistic folk religion among shore communities, who are often called, derogatorily, drifters. Indeed, the predominant understanding is that the displaced believe puzzle cairns will entrap the spirits of wandering ancestors who have not been bound after death, thus protecting against possession. As of this writing, increasing numbers of cairns have been sighted in more urban areas, suggesting the practice is no longer contained and is moving north. This article examines theories on the cultural migration of puzzle cairns, their commercialization, and the way in which they may be a symbol of changing Spinal modernity.

—Doudle, Alonso. "Not Just a Pile of Rocks: Puzzle Cairns in Spinal Cultural Practice." ***Pathfinder: The Journal of Ethnogeography*** **8 no. 2 (winter 247): 258–271.**

"Whoa," Jing said upon opening the door to the apartment he shared with Cal. Vale hardly had time to appreciate his lean, bare arms and the apron wrapped around him before his eyes zeroed in on her face. "Didn't know you had to fight someone to get here. You won, right? Of course you did."

Vale didn't bother responding and looked beyond Jing

into the living room, where the earthy tones of the plush sofa and overstuffed armchairs gave the modest space a sense of coziness. The scent of coconut curry and lemongrass floated out, and Vale's stomach growled in response.

"Is that Vale?" came Cal's voice from farther inside.

"Yeah," Jing called over his shoulder. He stepped backward, allowing Vale in. She dropped her rucksack and guitar by the door and bent over, tugging off her boots, then whacked them a couple of times against the wall in the hallway to rid them of dried mud.

When she straightened, Cal was in the entryway with a glass of water. His eyes widened as he looked at her. "Vale, what happened? Are you okay?"

She took the glass from him and drained half of it. "I'm fine. It was Burdock."

"You're *purple*," Cal said.

Jing appraised her, one eyebrow lifted. "Did you deserve it?"

"Yeah," she replied, and shoved aside the irritation. Jing of all people should have been concerned about her, even if she'd told him a dozen times not to worry over how Burdock dealt with her cussedness. But she couldn't expect Jing to show he cared when she'd warned him away from it.

Key would never have asked if Vale deserved it. Sourly, Vale said, "But now Rocket's gonna think twice before she says something stupid to my face."

"You beat up Key's ex?" Jing laughed, then sobered. "Over Key, or something else?"

"Why would I need Key as an excuse when Rocket's bitchy ass is enough?" Vale scowled, then winced as her face throbbed.

"I think we have some arnica gel in the medicine cabinet." Cal gestured in the direction of the bathroom. "Want me to get it?"

"No, not right now." She could take care of her swelling after she got cleaned up. She sucked down the rest of the water in the glass, and by the time she was done, Jing had disappeared.

"He's in the kitchen," Cal explained. "It's his turn to cook tonight."

"It's not fair!" To Vale's left, Jing poked his head around the corner where the kitchen stood. "I had a reintegration! I don't remember saying yes. I should be excused."

"Don't let the chicken burn," Cal told Jing succinctly before turning back to Vale. "We have this argument every single time," he said in an undertone. "He says he forgets, but he's lying."

"How can you tell?" Her brows pinched together so hard that she felt her ears move. "I thought he was supposed to be a good—"

"Cal better not be telling you I'm lying about forgetting! I can't remember anything from the last few days!"

Cal rolled his eyes, then said over his shoulder, "You've cooked after reintegrations before. I know those are in your memories."

"I don't know what you're talking a— Shit, the chicken!" Jing darted back into the kitchen.

Sudden exhaustion washed over Vale, but she smiled nonetheless. There was something comforting about how Jing and Cal spoke to each other that reminded her of family gatherings at home, especially when her parents were bickering affectionately. A little strange to associate her parents with her friends, perhaps, but that's how she felt about it: Jing and Cal's home, and the warmth between them that suffused the entirety of the apartment, drew her in as surely as a moth to a flame, bringing her back no matter her arguments with Jing or last-second commitments to Key. There wasn't any other place like this in Asheburg. Not Burdock's office, not Key's house. The only other time she enjoyed this type of relaxed back-and-forth was when she was afield with Key, setting up camp or doing the washing, or sitting side by side in Key's hammock on a rare night without clouds, their skins sticky with heat, their eyes turned up to the stars as Key told stories about old, forgotten constellations.

"You should go wash up," Cal said to her, reaching out and taking the glass. "You still have a clean change of clothes in Jing's top drawer."

Vale's brows furrowed again. "How do you know that?"

"I did Jing's laundry after you stayed over the last time."

"Of course you did his laundry." Jing's wheedling powers always worked on Cal.

"He does mine too. Actually, I think he does more of the laundry than I do." Cal shrugged.

Jing doing Cal's laundry was shock enough, but hearing Cal admit Jing did more than his share of laundry was liable to make her knees fail. He never exceeded expectations, only met them, and that was his life's philosophy. "He does more of the laundry? Not fifty percent exactly? Or forty-seven-point-six or something because you're taller and your shirts are bigger?"

"Oh, we did away with that ticky-tack figuring a while ago," Cal explained. "How do you calculate the value of what I do for him, or him for me? It's easier and less stressful to just do things for each other. It'll all iron smooth in the end."

"What's he do for you that's so special?"

"Jing would never forgive me if I said." Cal smiled. "Let me keep his reputation intact, all right?"

Vale pursed her lips. "How can I get that smooth-iron deal for me?"

"Don't put up with his shit?"

Easier said than done. "There's gotta be more. I already don't put up with his shit."

Cal looked as if he was going to say something, then hesitated.

"You said 'what you do for him.' You mean like . . ." Whereas Key spoke freely about her life and the things bothering her, Jing kept parts of himself cordoned off, accessible only with an entry fee. "He tells you what he wants out of his head, doesn't he?"

The corner of Cal's mouth lifted in a wry smile. "Yes."

If there was one person who knew what Jing's nightmares were about, it would be Cal. Jing hadn't once told Vale any of his bad memories, and she couldn't decide whether it meant he was trying to protect her or didn't want to bother her. Neither, probably, when she didn't have any memories or troubles of her own to give in return. "I bet you'd want reintegration too."

"Not really," he said. "I haven't lived through what he has. The memories don't rear up outta nowhere and ruin my day. I've never dropped a dish or disassociated or hallucinated because of them. He's said the bad ones lay themselves over what he's seeing and hearing, like suddenly there's a shadow puppet show on a screen and he's forced to watch. I don't blame him for wanting to forget all the time."

"Does he . . ." Vale frowned, thinking of Key in Dr. Wilcroft's office and how she'd gone stiff and gasped at nothing. Her teachers at the academy had described multiple telltale behaviors for when hunters experienced intrusive memories but cautioned against hypervigilance. "Kind of go blank?"

"He talks to people who aren't there," Cal replied. "He . . . argues back, sometimes, before he gets a hold of himself. He tried to hide, once. The blanking out, that's less of a thing for him. My first hunter, though, she was prone to that. Why do you ask? Something wrong with Key?"

"Key found a memory really far back." Vale pressed her lips together briefly. "She's blanked out, spooked at stuff that isn't there. But she's as tired as I am, probably more tired, and those are the same things that can happen if you're exhausted."

Cal nodded in acquiescence. "True. Or it could be something. Only time will tell. Key's strong, though. I don't expect her to get stuck under a memory."

But she could. There was a tug on Vale's heart, and she almost turned toward the door. "I should be watching her."

"No," Jing broke in, leaning around the corner, pointing a bamboo kitchen spoon at her, "you should be here with me. No work. I bargained with her for you."

Vale frowned at Jing's choice of words, like she was an object and he was willing to trade work or money for her. He probably hadn't meant it like that, and she ought to be pleased he was willing to strike deals for her time and attention. "You remember that?"

"Cal debriefed me, so I know essentially what happened. Dinner's almost ready. You gonna wash up?"

Vale nodded, reaching for her sword belt and undoing the buckle. She deposited it beside her rucksack.

"Arnica gel is in the second drawer down, next to the sink," Jing added.

She padded off toward Jing's bedroom after first snagging a fresh towel from the linen closet. His bedroom was the smaller of the two in the apartment, with not much more than a simple double bed draped in light-gray cotton sheets. It was always somewhat of a surprise to go from the living room to Jing's bedroom; clearly, the grounded, unassuming aesthetic of the living room had been guided by Cal and Cal alone. The whole bedroom was unremarkable except for a bamboo chest of drawers on the left side, a small stack of diving manuals atop it, and a tall wooden wardrobe in the far corner. The walls, like the rest of the apartment's, were painted a plain white, and the floors were old hardwoods, scuffed and scratched in many places.

Vale opened the top drawer of the chest and retrieved a worn pair of too-short pants and one of Jing's old shirts, the collar of it torn in multiple places. It had enough structural integrity for her, however, since she wasn't doing anything other than sitting on the sofa or sleeping. The pants were a little tight around the middle—she'd outgrown this pair years ago but kept them just in case—but she could probably alter the waist with an hour or two of work and turn it into a pair of shorts.

Finding time to do the alterations was the trickiest part. Back at the academy, she'd had plenty of time to catch up on mending during the breaks, which were long enough for most of the students to return home but not long enough for her to justify buying a round-trip ticket for a handful of days with half her family. These days, her time was taken up by Key and Jing.

Vale winced as she stripped herself of her clothes. Her body ached, and she inspected herself in the mirror over Jing's bureau, rotating each shoulder and stretching her arms forward and back to check for sharp pains. Burdock had probably popped something out of alignment in her back when he threw her to the floor. Later on, if Jing wasn't too tired, she ought to ask him to massage her soreness away.

That done, she wrapped her towel around herself and went to the bathroom to take a shower. The hot water at Jing's house was not unlimited the way it was at Key's, and Vale would have at most fifteen minutes before the tank was used up. She allowed herself a brief moment to sulk. Her room at Key's had an adjoining private bathroom and a tub that could have fit her and all her siblings in if they squeezed.

The water began warming, and Vale gritted her teeth and got in the shower, the call of cleanliness overcoming the distaste for cold water. She'd gotten soft after living in the city for ten years. The dorm showers would always have hot water, and there were no flood lines on the academy walls from an angry ocean. Vale had hardly even gotten mud in her shoes, and they had holes in them. Back home, during bad storms, the electricity would go out and the water would quit running, and maybe the outside water would invite itself in, and she'd have to share two bathtubs of water with eight other people until things could be fixed. Having clean water at all was a blessing.

She soaped and scrubbed, shampooed her hair twice to make sure all the dirt was out, and just as the water temperature began dropping, she finished. She stepped out, drying herself off as best she could, and wrapped her hair in the towel before getting the arnica gel and applying it to her bruised, puffy face. The swelling would go down by tomorrow, but she'd still look like she got caught in an alley.

Vale sighed. She was going to need Key's makeup help to look presentable for the party.

She slipped into her fresh clothes, hung her towel on a rack, and exited the bathroom on a puff of steam. The scent of curry and lemongrass grew stronger, and added to it now was the smell of fresh jasmine rice. Vale approached the dining table, where Jing and Cal were already in quiet conversation over their bowls. The latest edition of the guardian handbook sat crookedly to Cal's side; it was likely he'd been refreshing his knowledge ahead of the exam required for registration renewal. A third place at the table had been set, but nothing awaited her.

"Jing, you didn't fix her a bowl?" Cal shook his head.

"No, she can fix one herself. She's grown." Jing didn't bother looking up from his food. "Right, Vale?"

It would have been considerate of him to have a bowl of food ready for her, but she was too tired to be upset about it. She reminded herself of how annoyed she got if anyone tried to help her, Jing included. "Right. I can fix my own. Besides, Jing has a hard time guessing how much I'm going to eat, so this works out just fine."

"Everyone's happy," Jing said to Cal, who shook his head again.

Vale brought her bowl to the kitchen and scooped rice out of the pot for herself, then returned to the table and began serving herself the semi-burned chicken. She garnished her bowl with cilantro and took a few slices of pickled radish for herself, then lifted her spoon to her mouth.

She stopped, her hunger dissipating as she remembered the afternoon's events.

Cal paused in the middle of speaking and looked at her. "Something wrong? Jing's cooking not to taste?"

"It's not my cooking!"

Jing was decent enough in the kitchen, despite the burning, and Vale had eaten this dish enough times over the last year to know what to expect. It wasn't gourmet, but food was food, and Vale was not picky. "No, it's not the cooking," Vale said, reassuring. She set her spoon carefully back in the bowl, laying it so it wouldn't tip and fall out. "I just . . . I'm not hungry."

"That can't be possible," Jing said. "You haven't had a moment to yourself, much less time to eat since you got back."

"I could have picked something up and you wouldn't know." Vale set her jaw.

Cal added, "You never spend money on food if you can help it."

"What's wrong, Vale?" Concern settled over Jing's features, his dark brown eyes warming with worry. She was suddenly absurdly grateful that he'd asked, despite his own exhaustion. She fought the compulsion to dump the full bucket of her troubles over him.

"You're among friends," Cal said. "And you've had a lot going on."

She spoke, halting, doing her best to be as careful as Key. "Do you ever . . . not listen to what Cal tells you to do?"

"All the time," Jing replied, the corner of his mouth tipping up, mischievous.

"No, I mean when you're afield. Do you ever disagree with what Cal says?"

"Why would he?" Cal's face twisted into an expression of puzzlement. "I'm the one in charge when we're out."

"Yeah," Jing said. "Whatever Cal says, I do. It's not worth fighting. Whatever I'm looking for, it'll still be there when I get back. He's got our best interests at heart and has a finer sense of danger. Why? Does Key fight you?"

Vale dropped her eyes to her bowl. "She doesn't fight me exactly, but she insists on getting her way. Like staying late. That was her idea, and it was either I go along with it, or she'd leave me and go off by herself. So I went along with it."

Jing tsked. "Unwise of her. Clearly, as you're in this situation now. You need to have a talk with her."

"Isn't that your job as senior hunter?"

"You're her guardian, and you see her more than I do."

Cal glanced at Jing, then at her. "What's this really about, Vale?"

Silence swelled between them; Vale felt her reluctance ratcheting up in tandem with the tension. Finally: "It's Dr. Wilcroft. I'm okay. I already sent what I had back home."

"Hey, at least you can eat for free at Key's house, right?" Cal likely meant his words to be optimistic, but the sudden reminder that she'd been living off the Strades' largesse sat sour on her stomach.

"Vale, if you need money, you know you only need to ask for it." Jing extended his hand across the table until his fingers touched hers.

That was the difficult part, the asking. And Jing wouldn't give her anything if she didn't ask first. Pride hardened her resolve. "No, I'll be okay."

"You sure?" Cal put his bowl and spoon down and made to push away from the table. "Because I can spot you—"

"No!" Then, softer: "No, thank you. I'll get through it."

"You'll get through it better if you have food in you." Cal sat back down, the bamboo-and-wicker chair creaking as his weight settled against it. "Please eat, even if you're not hungry."

"I told Key to meet us back at the museum tomorrow, so instead of going to her house, you can go straight to bed after dinner," Jing said. "Saints, I'll follow you there. I'm exhausted."

Vale nodded, then took up her spoon to shove food in her mouth. "It's good," she mumbled as she ate, the flavor profile muted like a song heard in the distance. She finished her bowl with workmanlike discipline, her mind racing. She could handle a pay period. If she was cautious and had a plan and kept her activities limited to places she could walk, she'd be fine. She could even get her mending done.

Cal waved her off as she picked up her empty bowl. "I got the dishes. You get ready for bed. You look like you're going to pass out."

"Thanks," Vale said, realizing she was leaning heavily against the table. In short order, her teeth were brushed and she was folding back the covers on Jing's bed. He came in after she had them pulled up to her chin, gave her a quick smile, and turned off the light switch. The mattress bent as he added his weight to it.

She reached for his hand under the covers, found it, and interlaced her fingers with his. "You okay?"

"Shouldn't I be asking you that?" he murmured, wiggling against the mattress in a move Vale often likened to a crab burying itself in sand.

"Thought I'd beat you to it."

"Mm. So you did." He sounded subdued.

"You gonna answer?"

There was silence for a moment, broken only by the faint sounds of Cal puttering around in the kitchen, singing to himself as he washed the dishes. "I'm okay. I'm always okay after a reintegration."

"You keep saying that."

"Because it's true."

Vale thought of Key and how she'd frozen in Genevieve's office, shock on her face. "Do you really not feel any different?"

Jing lifted a shoulder in a shrug, the sheets rustling against his sleep shirt. "People think there should be a hole where my time's disappeared to, but it's not like that. More like getting blackout drunk. A sense that something small is missing, like a signal got dropped for a second, or the static between stations. I'm used to it now. Long as I see Cal first thing, I know I'll be okay. And from what he says, the alternative is always worse."

"You trust him with everything?"

"Yeah."

"You trust him with your life." A statement, not a question. It should have gone without saying, but Vale put it out regardless.

"Of course." Jing freed his hand from hers and slid it under her pillow, probably to find the cool side of it. "Doesn't Key trust you with hers?"

For a second, Vale almost told him about Key's lapses. He might not remember what happened to him, but he could add valuable perspective. But her throat grew tight, trapping the words within. Jing would counsel her to take Key for reintegration. Key would be unhappy about it, and if she were just Vale's friend, Vale would find someone else to do the job. But Vale was the only one equipped for the job, the only one who held the scales of Key's life, balancing it against her sanity. "Of course," Vale said finally.

"I'm sensing a question."

"How do you and Cal stay friends though he's your guardian?"

"Vale, I'm too tired to answer that and you must be so tired that you're asking."

"Do you think he could do it? Kill you if it gets bad?"

Jing let out a snort of pure irritation and rolled away. "Go to sleep, Vale."

A little part of her recoiled at the dismissal, shrinking back as if touched by fire. She didn't want to be the cause of friction or an argument, not when she had her guard down, not now when she had more thoughts and feelings than she knew what to do with. "I'm sorry. I don't want to—"

"What are you sorry for? I'm not mad, I'm just tired."

"Okay." She wiggled closer and pressed a kiss to his shoulder, breathing him in, unsure whether it was the right move. "I . . ." *Love you.* She paused, waiting for what came next.

"Don't give me something I can't give back," Jing murmured, rolling back toward her and kissing her on the cheek.

Vale accepted it, as she always did. She'd stopped being hurt by things he said months ago, devoting herself to conditioning her heart the same way she'd condition her body against pain. His was a cold calculation created by his upbringing on the far west of the continent, past the Spine, past the Wastelands, leftward on the map until land became sea. She interpreted his statement instead to mean he didn't want to get serious just yet, and when he was ready, he'd give her what she was willing to give him.

She sighed and sank into the mattress. As she was drifting away, Jing spoke, his voice soft and slurred, the consonants worn down by grains of sleep.

"He could, and I'd want him to."

SEVEN

Met Burdock's family for the first time. I never thought he could be shy, but in front of his family, he was. I knew he wanted to show me that kissing tree he keeps talking about, but I got distracted by the shrines, the puzzle cairns, and the village priestess. She's asking for my help in recovering memories. It's an incredible opportunity to further my studies and my work at the museum. No one else has this level of access to these rural areas. Rather than be excited for me, Burdock is upset that our vacation is now, in his words, a combination work trip and village hazing.

—Journal of Genevieve Wilcroft,
senior hunter for the Museum of Human Memory

KEY HAD WORKED THROUGH THE TOP FILE OF HER PAPERWORK pile when she heard the elevator at the end of the hall ding. She caught the cadence of Jing and Cal's footsteps, the sounds floating through the propped-open doors of the archive. Key stretched her ears, listening for Vale's soft tread, but got nothing.

Jing and Cal entered the archive, each bearing a respectable stack of brown accordion folders in their hands. Vale was not with them. Perhaps, Key thought, Vale had abandoned her post for the day since money was no longer a motivator. It wasn't as if they had parted on good terms yesterday, and Vale's anger could be banked overnight and brought back to life the next morning.

She'd missed Vale and her refreshing directness last night, both during dinner, where Key listened with half an ear to her mother, father, and the coterie talking about temple politics in southeast Asheburg, and after dinner, where one of the coterie, Zerua, tried to corner her by the passionfruit mousses and Key had to excuse herself as quickly as possible and retreat to her room. But Vale's presence, or lack of it, had no bearing on what Key's task was for the day, and she sealed her question away for a better, more appropriate time.

Key looked pointedly at the clock on the wall above the doors, its black minute hand nowhere near the top of the hour.

Cal raised both eyebrows as he used his foot to nudge one of the doorstops out of its position. "Don't say it."

She didn't think she could get in more trouble than she already was, and Jing and Cal weren't petty enough to tattle, so she said, "You're late."

"Called it." Jing shut both doors, then approached and dropped his stack onto the large main table.

"I told you not to say it." Cal placed his stack on the table beside Jing's, swung his dulcimer case gently off his shoulder, and hung it by its strap on the back of a chair. From a pocket on the dulcimer case, he fished out a wanderer's notebook, then laid it on the table.

"Be more specific next time," Key suggested.

Jing snorted a laugh. "Back to being the star student so soon? C'mon, Key. I can't be the only one flouting the rules around here." He pushed both stacks over to Key, then took a seat.

Key checked an item on her list against the accession record, sliding her finger down the rows until she was satisfied she hadn't made a mistake. It was easy work, but it was also easy to create errors, and she'd made too many mistakes in her first months at the museum to allow herself shoddy recordkeeping. Genevieve was upset enough. "Are those all yours?"

"Mostly," Cal replied. "Couple from Amity and Dhonia. They came and went while you were gone. Dropped off their records, resupplied, and headed out east again."

Key put down her pen. "They don't let things get backlogged and they normally wouldn't let you touch their files. What's in it for you, Jing?"

He grinned and tipped his chair backward, balancing on two of its legs. "Not sure yet, but you never know when a favor will come in handy, right? Dhonia's got connections west of the Spine. Might be worth something. Meanwhile, these are indeed all for you. I'd say good luck, but I have faith in your work and your work ethic."

Key reached for the topmost folder on the nearest stack and pulled it off, then unwound the thin red yarn holding it closed. She peeked inside. "This is your most recent one!"

"Yeah, and I had a reintegration, so now it's your job."

That much was true. Museum regulations kept hunters from handling their own records post-reintegration so as not to trigger any other memories. Sometimes, though, Key wondered if Jing underwent reintegration just to avoid having to file his own documents. "Remind me not to get into trouble again."

"Now, why would I do that? I get to boss you around if you do."

"Jing, quit it," Cal said, leaning over the table to pluck a pencil out of one of the cups stationed in the center. "If we all work on this together, it'll go faster. We might even beat Vale."

"Speaking of," Key said, "where is she?"

"Decided to walk," Jing replied.

"All the way from your place?"

"Well, we took the trolley to the incline together. Then she said she'd walk. Said the exercise would be good for her and she didn't want to pay fares."

"Wait." Key sat forward, narrowing her eyes. "She walked because she didn't want to pay for the incline?"

Jing paused. "Yeah?"

"And neither of you lent her the fare?"

"She doesn't want our help. Or any help."

Vale would be more willing to accept help from Jing, Key was convinced, if it wasn't expected of her to repay said help in full later. "So she's coming late because she's walking up the switchbacks to get here while you two rode the incline?"

"Cal offered four times and she said no." Jing shrugged. "No means no means no means no." He looked at her then, his gaze clear and piercing. "You're one to talk about being late."

Key pressed her lips together. "Point conceded."

"Good. I like winning." Jing waved vaguely at the pile of documentation in front of Key. "Saints, how'd you manage to find extra work already?"

"I needed to research something," Key said, cross-checking an accession record in Genevieve's handwriting against one of her travel journals. The geographic area was correct, but yet again, there was no mention of Crystal Grove.

Jing cast his eyes around the table, finally arriving at Key's list. His brows furrowed as he picked it up, reading over her keywords. "Crystal Grove?"

"Yes. I was checking to see if we have any records of that here, though I don't recall any. But the people I spoke to there were sure museum hunters had visited several years ago, and a number of years before that." Key exhaled and straightened, wincing as muscles held tense were forced to move. "Didn't you go down there a couple of years ago? Right around when Vale and I first started here."

Jing handed her paper back, his head tilting in thought. "Did I? I don't know, did we, Cal?"

"Hm?" Cal looked up from his wanderer's notebook.

"Did we go to a place called Crystal Grove a couple of years ago? About when Key and Vale started working here."

"We went to the southeastern hills, but I don't think we went there specifically. Didn't find anything much."

Key frowned, picking up the stack of records, paging through them until she found what had caught her attention: the southeastern hills. She had specifically focused on that area because, in her research, only a few hunters had gone: her grandmother, Genevieve, and Jing. Nothing remarkable had been recorded. Small wonder, then, Key thought, that Genevieve was reluctant to approve Key's travel request.

"Maybe a different museum's hunters went there?" Jing suggested. "Like Spruceton. You know how they are. I'm not sure how they keep things running over there, and that's coming from me. The contingent from the Spruceton museum had Genevieve in fits at the last colloquium."

"I did just read about less-than-optimal recordkeeping in *Annals of Diving Practice*," Key said, ignoring Jing's eyeroll and Cal's quiet laugh. "It's a possibility, but Crystal Grove isn't near any old urban centers, so they'd be less interested in the area."

"Well, whatever question you're trying to answer, you're going to need to put the brakes on it. Because"—Jing patted his stack of accordion folders—"time to get to work. No more stalling."

Key offered a conciliatory half smile. "I'll take your file, and maybe you can sort through one of Amity's while I'm getting yours squared away."

"Oh, no," Jing said, "no foisting this off on me. I said these were *all* for you. And besides, I'm supposed to be your supervisor."

"Is that what Genevieve said?" Key tried to keep her tone light. Jing's work, when he did put effort into it, was excellent, but he relied on the registrars to maintain order in the catalog. Key, on the other hand, knew each process down to the microscopic level. Everything Key had internalized beyond her classes at the academy had come about as a result of Genevieve's keen sense of pedagogy and close mentorship. This many years into their relationship, Key knew Genevieve's workflows by heart, from how she set up a dive site to the order in which she cataloged items. The first week she'd interned with Genevieve, back when Key was a student, Genevieve had introduced her to a new cataloging system, redesigned by Genevieve herself. By the end of the internship, Genevieve was ready to turn over caretaking to Key.

"It's what she told me she told you. Don't try to spin your way out of this." Jing stood, then turned to Cal. "Wanna get a drink at the automat?"

"No, I'd like to stay sitting," Cal replied. "But a pop sounds good."

"Okay." Jing pushed his chair in, exited the archive, and sauntered out of sight, hands in his pockets.

Key sighed and turned her attention back to the mess before her. She'd need to clean up before she could start on the two dozen or so folders, her own included. A short distance away from her were blank intake forms meant for copying information, and at some point during the day, her job would be to copy and make corrections to the top sheet of each file, give each sheet a new accession number, and put the copy in the outbox for the catalogers.

She almost reached for her own folder, driven by the desire to look at her research notes and journal, though she remembered everything she'd written. *You will be consecrated*, the man had said. The ancestors had guided her to that memory for a reason, and she was called to find out what it was instead of doing another hunter's paperwork.

Immediately, several memories appeared in her mind of elders snickering at the impatience of youth.

She closed her eyes and lowered her head a fraction in prayer. Message received. She would be patient and see her punishment through. She deserved it, and doubly so since Vale had been disciplined as well. Key set herself to putting away what she'd taken out, then to sorting the piles, sending some folders to one side of the table for reshelving and some to the other side for indexing.

It often seemed that time existed outside the archive when she was working inside it, flowing past the way it did when she was diving. Being several stories deep in the mountain meant there were no windows and only artificial light, which was excellent for security and climate control but also lent the space a capsule-like quality. As she went from shelf to shelf, sliding folders into their rightful places, Key zeroed in on her task and only her task, her mind slowly freeing itself from the grip of extraneous thoughts, entering a meditative state. She heard Jing return, followed by the sound of a deck of cards being shuffled. A conversation sprouted, blossomed, receded.

Key wedged an accordion folder onto a shelf, one of the last of her stack, muscling aside other folders as she did so. Strains of guitar and dulcimer came to her, muted through the stacks. "No," Key heard Vale say. "It goes like this."

Cal responded, his baritone voice slightly muffled. "What'd you call it again? 'The Cypress Knees'? I know it as 'A Maid and a Lad.'" A melody followed, picked as nimbly as a goat leaping up a mountainside. "It's a little different, but mostly the same."

Key hauled another accordion folder off the floor and forged deeper into the stacks, her eyes scanning the reference numbers marked on each one. Vale and Cal's conversation faded, replaced with the soft sound of her shoes against linoleum. The scent of old paper strengthened.

She paused at the end of the stacks, recalling when she'd begun working at the museum. One of her first tasks as Genevieve's intern had been to reorganize the archives according to the new cataloging system, which involved an enormous shelf shift that resulted in Key leapfrogging her way over folders for days. Later, after she'd become Genevieve's de facto assistant and had to assemble the materials needed to create a new exhibit, she'd used Genevieve's dissertation and doctoral project as a guide, following the path laid from the initial dive to opening day. The final exhibit proposal included a reconstruction of a lost village that had lain beneath the waves of the southern coast. The fieldwork had been completed when Genevieve had been partnered with her former guardian, Burdock, but despite his name being listed next to hers on the index sheet, all the writing and sketches were Genevieve's. The only indication of his involvement was his blocky all-capitals handwriting on the master tabs from the dive site, proclaiming who took the specimens, where, and when.

Key squinted at a label on a folder, not truly seeing it. She had no assigned guardian when she'd been Genevieve's assistant, and Burdock's absence—like he'd been erased from the record—hadn't raised any questions then. But now, after being partnered with Vale for two years and watching the other curators consult Cal on ethnomusicology, Key understood how much a guardian could contribute to research, both in finding dive sites and analyzing the data. Burdock had graduated in the top three at the academy and was well known as an outdoorsman and fighter. His skills and knowledge of the southern coast would have been instrumental in locating the dive site. It was, therefore, neither a coincidence nor an oversight that he was missing from the folder.

Genevieve had never given Key the details of why she and Burdock no longer worked together, and Key had never pressed. As far as Key could tell, Genevieve remained fond of him. And it wasn't as if she no longer needed a guardian. She still took an assistant with her when she went to conferences in the other Spinal cities.

Maybe Vale knew since she was so close to Burdock. Key turned for the main area, the sound of Vale humming growing louder on the approach. As she neared the end of the stacks, Cal and Vale came into view. Cal had one large hand practically wrapped around a pencil as he scribbled in his wanderer's notebook, taking dictation from Vale, who looked on, her voice lingering on a note.

A teaspoon clinked.

Key paused mid-step, her vision swimming, and put a hand out to steady herself, her fingers first striking the dry paper of an accordion file before slipping past and landing on the cold metal of the shelf. Without warning, the image of the kitchen leapt forward, pasting itself over Vale, Cal, and their instruments, disorienting her and forcing her to close her eyes. Around her, the world tilted and jerked, rattling her head as if it were a piece of dropped silverware. She breathed through her nostrils, fear lifting her heartbeat on a rising tide. An intrusive memory this long after a dive?

She recalled her extensive training at the academy. It was rare but not unheard of to experience the tail ends of strong memories more than a day after. She anchored herself as best she could, helpless as the scene from the dive replayed itself. The mug on the table. The intensity in her grandfather's eyes. The gritty, cakey feel of the stuff her grandfather had put into the tea, which hadn't fully dissolved.

"Key." Jing spoke her name quietly but firmly. "You good?"

It was so unexpected, so jarring, that it made her head snap up, the memory disappearing, leaving only the stacks of the archive, Jing's hand on her shoulder, and Vale and Cal looking on, concerned.

"I'm all right," she said, straightening. That marked the second intrusive memory in the last couple days, which would be more than enough cause to send her to be reintegrated. She risked a glance at Vale, then stared at the size and shape of the reddish-purple welt rising from her cheekbone.

"What?" Vale finally snapped.

"Your face," Key said, hurrying out of the stacks toward Vale. Disquieted, Key extended a hand. "What happened?"

Vale hunched into herself, turning her head away, speaking to the table. "I'm fine."

"That does not look fine."

"Well, it is."

There was only one person Vale would allow to touch her that way, and it was Burdock. Key inhaled deeply, bypassing the wariness, the concern, the anger, and the protectiveness, then exhaled, looking for her calm. It had fled, and to saints knew where.

She borrowed some from Cal, grabbing on to it to ensure it'd stay. "This was Burdock, wasn't it?"

"I deserved it," Vale said.

Not unless she was about to harm him, Key almost retorted, and gripped her calm tighter. "I doubt it." She looked at Jing and Cal. "Aren't you two worried?"

"Vale said she's fine," Jing replied, a little sharply. "And from what she told us, she instigated the fight against someone else, so in addition to being fine, she's also right: She did deserve it."

Jing defending Vale meant that Key was in a precarious situation. She'd have to discuss what happened without Jing around. "I'll bring some makeup for you later," she said to Vale.

"Okay." Vale's tone indicated the end of the discussion.

"You sure you're okay, Key?" Cal asked.

"I'm good. Just a bit preoccupied. I need to talk to Genevieve."

"About what?"

"Crystal Grove," Key replied. "And some of her other research."

"You sure you want to do that?" Jing joined the group, his eyebrow arching with skepticism. "If I were you, I'd go to ground for a while."

"Why, Jing, are you giving me advice?" Key put her best public appearance smile on. "What do I owe you?"

He turned to look at Vale. Key looked, too, at the set of Vale's mouth and the tightness around her eyes. Her shoulders were tense beneath the oversized button-down shirt hanging over her thin frame, its sleeves cuffed at the elbow. The shirt was likely Jing's. Key glanced back to him, and for a second, as their gazes connected, his eyes crinkled with smugness.

Key had asked what was owed, not who. But it was best to confront Jing over his treatment of Vale elsewhere, without Vale around. Vale, as Key well knew, took poorly to being protected. "We aren't doing this."

"Forget I ever said anything, then. Do what you want. Would you rather talk about your mother's party tonight?" Jing flashed her a smile, but it didn't touch his eyes. "I know Cal's looking forward to celebrating."

"Those mushroom tartlets your chef makes?" Cal sighed, a wistful expression settling over his features. "It's really too bad Garth is out of my age range. I'd ask him to marry me."

Jing turned, disbelief coloring his voice. "What?"

"I said it. I'd ask him to marry me. Ain't like I'm waiting on anyone." Cal leveled a look at Jing. "A man that cooks well is worth it. Maybe he's not the one, but we could grow to love each other. I'd court him for that recipe alone."

"*Court* him?"

"Yeah." Key caught the sparkle of mischief in Cal's eyes. "I could serenade him. 'A Maid and a Lad,' but I'd change the words. What do you think?"

"No." Jing was curt. "You've got me already."

Vale frowned. "Uh, I'm sitting right here?"

"You've got Vale." Cal sniffed. "Let your third wheel go off and find a man of his own."

Key looked back and forth between Jing and Cal. "Upset, Jing?"

"What do I have to be upset about?" Jing laughed.

"You sound upset."

"He's upset because Cal likes Garth's cooking better," Vale chimed in. "C'mon, Jing. Let Cal have some fun."

"He has plenty of fun!"

"You know what I mean. Cal would be an amazing partner for the right person. He's strong and nice and talented and handsome. And is wasted on you." Vale punctuated the end of her little speech with a grin, revealing a row of semi-crooked teeth, which Key found endearing and alluring.

"Thanks, friend." Cal held up a hand, and Vale high-fived it.

"I agree with Vale," Key said. Cal saluted her. "Don't be selfish. Share the glory of Cal with the rest of the world."

"The glory?" Cal sat straighter. "Key, have I ever told you how much I like you?"

Vale propped her chin on a hand, thoughtful. "Hmm, men who can cook. I know some guys at the kitchen. Might be I could fix you up with one."

"Vale!" Jing exclaimed.

She turned her head slowly, her eyes boring into Jing. "Yes? Do you not want your best friend to find someone the way you found someone?"

Jing spluttered. "Yes, but he's already—"

"Already what?" Vale stared harder.

"Nothing. Forget it." As quickly as the changing of the wind, Jing's expression turned pleasant. "You're right. Cal should go meet someone. Get married. Put down roots. Leave all this."

Cal's eyebrows rose. "You serious?"

"As the grave."

Cal's eyebrows rose further, his expression going from surprise to warning. "You lying to me?"

"Why would I lie to you? I want you to be as happy as I am. Happier." Jing stuck his hands in his pockets. "Saints, something about the archives always makes me hungry. I think I'm gonna get a snack from the automat. Vale, come with? My treat."

Vale's eyes darted between Jing and Cal. "Yeah, sure." She rose to her feet, still glancing at Cal. Jing offered Vale an elbow, then exited at such a pace that the tips of Vale's shoes snagged against the carpet.

Key waited a few seconds before saying, "That was a little strange."

"Yeah."

She looked over at him, concerned at his subdued tone. "Cal, are you okay?"

"He didn't answer my question." Cal's chin was lowered and his shoulders were slumped, and pressed against his lap were his hands, curled into each other. "And he's not . . ."

Key elected not to state the obvious and finished the sentence for him in her head: *happy*. "That's just how he is. He's like air, you can't catch him."

"I didn't know." He took a breath. "I mean, I do know. Have known exactly who he is. Watched him do to others what he does to Vale. I thought the best I could do was . . ."

A sudden pang went through her, like a dessert fork struck against a glass before a speech. Key knew for certain what was happening, as if the ancestors themselves had gathered around her and whispered the truth in her ear. She had seen that exact look in her memories dozens of times through dozens of eyes over multiple generations. Rarely did unrequited love result in anything but regret and heartbreak.

Oh, Cal, she almost said. Instead, she took Vale's still-warm seat, then reached for his hands. His fingers unclenched beneath hers; she gave them a light squeeze. She would need to choose her words carefully, saints guide her. "Are you upset because you thought Jing might fight for you and then didn't, or are you upset because you thought you couldn't have him before now?"

Cal froze, his eyes on hers, their near-black depths carrying shock. "How did you—"

"I'm a resifix," she replied with a small smile, releasing one of his hands so she could tap her temple with a finger. "I've been on thousands of dives. I've got more memories in my head than any other hunter in this city. And I don't forget what I've seen. There are plenty of ancestors who went through what you're feeling now."

"Was it—"

"Obvious? Only to me, most likely." Key gave Cal another squeeze. "And only because I know you. I won't say anything if you don't want me to, but I also think the road you're on will only get harder to walk."

He shook his head. "Please don't. It's not just Jing, but Vale too. More Vale than Jing. I don't . . . She wants to be happy with him."

"But she isn't." There was a finality to her words, a truth that weighed heavier for being spoken aloud. Key wasn't sure whether Vale could be happy in Asheburg—she was happy when she was afield and alone with Key—and the moments of sunshine that had occurred so often in the beginning of her relationship with Jing were now few and far between.

"You said so yourself about him," Cal said. "He's the way he is, and Vale hasn't figured out how to ask him to do more."

"I see. But if she figures it out and he decides to commit—can you be happy if they're happy?"

"I can." Resolution firmed Cal's voice, but Key's heart sank regardless. She didn't think Cal had it in him to be jealous and hoped his warmth toward Vale wouldn't spoil and rot. Good outcomes in these cases were a rarity, and that was a fact. "Vale's like a sister to me. I want her to be happy."

"Okay." Key let go of his hands. "But don't push either of them toward that end. They both respond disproportionately to force. Also, don't be married to sacrifice. If it comes to an end naturally, take your chance."

Cal said nothing for several breaths. Then, finally, he heaved a loud sigh, dragged his hand across his face, and said, "Thanks, Key."

"You're welcome." Warmth and affection rose in her; she smiled at the glow in Cal's cheeks, the closest he could get to a blush. Cal was as wonderful as Vale had said, and compared to the people surrounding Key, being in his presence was a balm. "You should be happy too, no qualifiers. I won't say a word about this. It'll be like you came to me at temple."

Cal cleared his throat, then reached for his dulcimer case and wanderer's notebook. "You're all done, right? We should pack up and go get Vale before she causes damage. She thinks if you hit the automat enough times, it should give you a snack. Plus, you have a party to get ready for."

"How could I forget?" Key pulled over Vale's guitar case and set the instrument inside. "Seems like our only joy tonight is going to be those mushroom tartlets."

A faint thump came to Key's ears.

Cal chuckled. "Time to go rescue a machine."

Two Weeks Ago

KEY WAITS FOR HER DRIVER TO OPEN THE DOOR AND EXITS THE car into overcast daylight, the soles of her shoes scraping quietly against the large flagstones of the museum's courtyard, where Jing, Cal, and Vale await her, their travel gear arrayed around them. Her driver hands over her rucksack and staff. He's a longtime employee of the Strades and has been part of the household for so long that Key sees him as an uncle. She thanks him, then takes her things and approaches the others.

"This is a sight I didn't think I'd see," Key says, coming to a stop in front of Jing. He's sitting with his back up against the wall, casual, one knee up, the other leg laid long beside Cal's. Vale is on his other side. "The only person who's gotten to work earlier than I in the last two years has been Genevieve."

"I don't intend to make a habit of it, so you can throw this statistic out and keep your streak going." Jing pushes himself to standing, then holds a hand out for Vale.

"I told them you'd be here this early on a travel day." Vale accepts Jing's help, rolling easily and lightly to her feet, then drops a quick kiss on Jing's cheek. She casts an amused look at Cal. "You believe me now?"

"Yeah, yeah," Cal says, hauling his dulcimer case up and settling the strap across his broad body. He then saunters to the front doors and knocks on the glass to summon Alec.

Inside, without patrons, the atrium's ceiling seems higher, the room larger, grander. That's always part of the wonder of the museum to Key, that the presence of people can change the living quality of the space, as if the museum's personality depends on who is in it at any given time.

"Is that Ina?" Jing says, his voice pitched so it won't carry. He indicates a woman in front of the blood chalice models, her back to them. She's one of two people already in the atrium, which is yet another surprise to Key. Being beaten to the museum by Jing is singular enough, but to have this many precede her is a professional embarrassment.

"And Tags." Cal looks at the other person in the atrium: Tagetes, Ina's guardian, is currently some distance away from Ina, as if observing her.

Cal gives Jing a meaningful look.

"I'm not on the clock yet," Jing mutters. "Leave me be."

"Something's off," Vale says quietly.

Key stares at Ina. Vale's correct. The body language is wrong.

"They're not expected back in until tomorrow, and Tags is always punctual. Never early, never late, only ever on time," Cal says, divesting himself of his travel gear. Vale follows suit.

"Why are you always right about everything?" Jing lets out an exasperated sigh and starts toward the center of the atrium, his steps brisk, stringing out the group's formation. "Hey, Tags!"

"Jing," Tags replies as the group nears. "Hey, all."

At close range, Key sees the shadows gathered under Tags's heavy-lidded hazel eyes, as well as a listless haggardness to their square-jawed face, over which grows what has to be several days' worth of shadow. Their clothes are rumpled, and in the white of one eye, a small cluster of capillaries blooms crimson.

"You're early," Cal says, clasping Tags's hand briefly. "Something the matter?"

Tags cuts a glance at Ina, who is now running her hands over the blood chalices, her brows furrowed in concentration. "I think it'd be better if you asked her. She responds to Pleasance."

"Pleasance," Vale calls out. "How are you?"

Ina turns to face the group, and Vale, who has stepped up beside Key, instantly goes on alert, the air around her sharpening. Cal mirrors her, and the two guardians lock in on Ina like hounds on a scent.

"Hello," Ina says, her normally contralto voice high and soft and breathy. "Thank you for asking. I'm all right, but a little tired. And you?"

Key blinks, taken aback. Ina is well known for her big personality and uncanny nose for office gossip. She's outgoing and, like all the other hunters, has a knack for names and faces, and she should have greeted Vale like a colleague and not like a seldom-seen neighbor.

Tags indicates Ina with a tilt of their head as if to say, *You understand now*. "I'd love to catch up, but we've got an appointment downstairs. Just stopped to admire the chalices, is all."

"These sculptures are exquisite. I've only worked with clay and marble. This material is new to me, and mighty fine." Ina molds a hand over the top of one of the resin chalices.

"Sculptor," Tags says simply.

Key's skin tightens, and her scalp prickles. Ina is a good hunter with a solid range, but it's rare for someone with her diving talent to learn a new skill this quickly from a memory.

Ina hasn't just learned a skill.

"You want any company?" On any other day, this would be an innocent question, but Key hears the subtext behind Cal's words: *Do you need help subduing her?*

There is only one destination for Ina, one ending. Tags is herding her to the medical floor for reintegration. Key darts her eyes between Cal, Vale, and Tags, sees the calculations being done. Cal's face is neutral, but Vale's is grim.

"Wouldn't mind a little," Tags says, smiling again. "'Preciate it."

"Excellent," Jing says brightly. He approaches Ina and slings an arm over her shoulders like they're best friends—and, to Jing in that moment, they are. "Pleasance, right? The material you're looking at is a phenol resin, which is poured, not sculpted. Well, injected, in this case. Cutting-edge stuff. Can't even buy it yet. We've been developing it downstairs. You want to see how it works?"

Ina's brows furrow as she concentrates. Uncertainly passes over her face. "I'm not quite sure . . ."

"I'll give you a personal tour. I'm Jing, by the way." Jing continues, turning for Alec and the elevators down to the institute. Ina turns with him.

Key keeps silent, following Tags and Ina, watching Jing work to ground Ina so she won't get agitated and lash out.

Vale separates from the group to confer with Alec, who nods, then speaks inaudibly into the intercom.

Suddenly, Ina shoves Jing away hard enough to make him stumble. Immediately, Tags and Cal spring into action, reaching for Ina. Tags grabs for her first, but she slaps their hand out of the air, then twists with a catlike grace and sidesteps Cal.

"Don't touch me!" she shouts. Her body language changes again, like she's an entirely different person. She dodges Tags, then lashes out with a punch to their jaw that sends them staggering before whirling to put distance between herself and Cal. "Get—"

Key gasps as Vale's running tackle sends both women hard to the floor. Vale scrambles to her knees and grips Ina's wrist, wrenching it behind the larger woman to control her arm. Ina half rises on her free hand, but Vale jerks Ina's arm up, dropping her back to the floor.

Ina issues a thin cry of pain. "You're hurting me!"

"Come with us gentle, and I won't hurt you more." A knife materializes in Vale's right hand, flashing as quick as a shooting star. She levers the point against Ina's jaw. "Or you can fight. Either way, you're doctor-bound."

"Ina." Tags crouches in front of her, seeking her eyes. "Listen. Come back." They begin singing softly, their voice a light, reedy tenor.

"Shut up!" Ina wriggles, thrashing against the floor. Her neck skids over the edge of Vale's knife. Vale pulls away, air hissing between her teeth, and in that moment, Ina breaks free, getting both feet and a hand beneath her. She barrels forward, headbutting Tags. They topple with a shout.

Cal crushes Ina between thick arms, but not before she

grabs the handle of Tags's belt knife. She slashes backward wildly. Cal flings himself away from her, pivots, then resets, and for a moment, Key thinks that's the end of it: Ina is surrounded by three guardians in a standoff, and help is on the way.

Vale, fearless, darts in low for a takedown. It's too fast for Key to follow. All she knows is that Tags shouts for Vale to stop, *stop*, but Vale doesn't listen. Both women hit the floor again. The knife in Ina's hand falls and is swept out of reach. Vale's hand streaks silver toward Ina's throat.

"Valerian!" Jing's voice thunders through the atrium. "*Stand down!*"

Vale stops, her eyes wild.

Cal shoulders Vale aside and grapples Ina into submission.

"Jing," Vale starts.

"No. You aren't her guardian. Not your call to make when Tags is right here."

"Tags?" Ina, as she should have been, but lost and desperate. "Tags, help me. Help me, please—I need a reintegration. I don't know what's happening anymore. I'm so tired, I don't know why Cal's hurting me, help, please."

"Help is coming," Cal says, unruffled, soothing. "Hold out just a little longer for us."

The elevator chimes, disembodied and hollow. The sound of a gurney being wheeled out follows, accompanied by multiple pairs of feet hurrying toward them. In short order, Ina is administered a sedative and maneuvered onto the gurney with wrists and ankles secured, then is whisked away, Tags trotting beside her.

Vale, stony, sheathes her knife.

"Hard work, but good," Cal mutters.

"Good?" Key's adrenaline is up, her breath stolen by Vale's sudden violence, her lack of hesitation. What if Key had been in Ina's place? Would Vale reach so easily for violence then? "That was good? Ina could have—"

"Yes," Cal says. "She could have, if not for Jing."

Key looks at Jing. He shrugs once, then turns for the elevators. Vale remains silent, meeting Key's gaze as unblinking as a cat before following Jing, her hair swaying in its ponytail, the movement accentuated by the fluttering of a thin purple ribbon tied around the base.

EIGHT

Of the Strades, what else is there to do but declare their contributions to Asheburg and the world at large priceless? One need only look at Aurissa Strade, who rediscovered vacuum tube radios, as an example among many. The Garnet House, designed for the Strades by the famed architect Timothy Hunt Morris, is visible from Asheburg Main Station. No tours of the property are available.

—"Asheburg, Jewel of the Spine," a travel brochure

VALE WOUND A BRIGHT PINK RIBBON AROUND THE END OF HER braid, where it joined half a dozen others, each a different color. She observed her reflection in the vanity mirror, pleased. There were things she regretted spending money on, but ribbons were not one of them, and the sheer joy they gave her made the purchases worth every last coin. She was self-indulgent in this arena only, holding nothing for herself except her duty, telling herself things like validation or personal desire were as distant as the roll of thunder from ten miles away.

She touched the frog closure holding the high collar of her dress together, rubbing her forefinger over the satiny threads. The dress she wore was beautiful, a midnight-blue marvel that draped over her frame with a grace she lacked. It had been gifted to her by Terry, the Strades' exclusive tailor, who upon their first meeting had loudly and vociferously declared her his muse before bursting into frenetic activity. Within minutes she was stripped to her undergarments in front of a mirror, grinning from ear to ear as he drew furiously and yelled at his assistants to bring bolts of fabric. Key, relegated to the background, had groaned and settled herself into an armchair to wait.

It was also Vale's only dress and had seen its share of duty over the last two years. By now, the Strade family and their circle of acquaintances expected her to wear it to formal events.

She gritted her teeth as she thought about dinner, a wave of prickly heat rolling from sternum to stomach. She knew what the routine was: stay silent unless spoken to; hold tightly to her pride and pretend she couldn't hear the whispers and laughter; bend her neck demurely and sing what was asked of her. Vale glanced out the window, noting the orange disk of the sun as it began its slide into a fluffy, darkening bed of clouds. The storm had caught up with them, then. Though the day had begun overcast, the afternoon was clear and cheerful, as if the sky were trying to lull the earth into complacency. But Vale had felt in her gut—not her gut, precisely, she just *knew*—that a storm front was coming, and a strong one that would last through the night and possibly through the next day.

It wasn't too late to run. She could leave now in fresh gear and be hunkered down at the academy before the wind could scour people off the streets.

Her eyes went to the reflection of the scabbarded sword propped up in the corner by the door, its plainness at odds with the lilac-and-champagne damask wallpaper and the intricate carved molding in the room. With a sigh, she picked up the last ribbon in her collection and tied its lacy mustard-yellow length around the base of her braid. Then she got up, the dress moving like liquid night around her. Vale looked at herself again, frowning at her unpierced ears, then at her cosmetic-less face, the reddish-purple welt diminished in size thanks to the arnica, but still garish against her skin tone.

She'd need Key's makeup skills. That meant talking to Key, the idea of which set her stomach curdling. Vale didn't particularly want to do that, not when she was about as collected as the frayed end of a rope and every glimpse of Key reminded Vale acutely of the emptiness of her bank account. Vale had avoided notice this afternoon by slipping into one of the servant entrances and rushing to her room, but dinner was fast approaching and instead of hiding, she was trussing herself up for the spit. Stupid.

Well, at least Rocket couldn't hide either. Vale's lips curled into a smirk.

There came a knock on the door. "Vale?"

She froze, going as still as a fawn with a predator nearby, and held her breath.

"I know you're in there," Key called. "I heard you running your bath earlier. May I come in?"

Vale cursed whoever in the Strade family had decided to be frugal with the wall budget when their house was built.

"Vale?"

"Let me unlock it," she responded, going to the door and turning the bolt. She pushed down the lever, allowing the door to open a crack, then backed away, her dress fluttering around her legs.

"I've been thinking about what I wanted to say," Key began as the door swung open. "I brought—" She sighed. "Oh, Vale."

Vale's eyes went wide at the sight of Key, her anger and anxiety evaporating, replaced by a gentle heat in her cheeks and ears. Key's broad, muscled shoulders and hourglass figure were accentuated perfectly by a sleeveless cream-to-red ombre jumpsuit cinched at the waist with a wide belt. From there, loose material tapered into cuffed hems that encircled Key's ankles. Casual, elegant sandals completed the outfit. The jumpsuit had a slit neckline going partway down Key's sternum, and Vale could see a hint of—

No. That was disrespectful. Key was a holy figure. But she also had a body type to make Vale sigh with envy. She herself was possessed of as many curves as a fence and was leaner than a weasel.

"What?" Vale managed.

Key took a step into the room. She'd put on subtle makeup, lining her eyes to make them look larger and brighter; gold shimmer accentuated the warm brown of her skin, its color enriched by the sun. Her halo of curls, freed from its ponytail, had been pinned back on one side, leaving a sweep of hair in front to frame her lovely face. She held an envelope in her left hand; her other was curled around the handle of a makeup case. Over one arm lay a garment with the same cream-and-red coloring as her outfit.

Vale reminded herself to breathe. Key stared at her, and Vale had to fight from shriveling up inside. She would not in her lifetime achieve the effortless grace Key possessed, would always feel shabby and uncouth in comparison. Vale had to work for it. Key had been born into it.

"Your—" Key started.

"I know," Vale finished. She cleared her throat, self-consciousness eating at her. Two years ago, she'd overheard a party guest remark on how it took a certain level of class to bring out the full beauty of Terry's designs. She wrenched her eyes away from Key, who stood still. "I'm hopeless."

"No, it's not that!" Key entered, shutting the door behind her. Her pant legs swished as she approached, transferring her case to her left hand, reaching her right hand toward Vale's face.

Vale flinched and jerked back, covering her left cheek with her fingers.

"May I see?" Key's voice was soft. She didn't move.

Reluctantly, Vale nodded and let her hand drop.

Key laid the garment, envelope, and case on the end of the bed, then came back, leaning down until their faces were inches apart. Vale clenched her hands into fists, not knowing what to do or where to look. It would be odd to keep her eyes trained on Key's cheekbone, and anywhere below her neck was going to be a problem. Some people—Key—were unfairly aesthetically pleasing, and if she weren't careful, Vale would cross the line into creepiness.

She settled on Key's part, the shining curls of her hair well defined through judicious application of conditioner and cream. The scent of Key's hair products rose, heady and addicting.

Key touched Vale's cheek with light, tender fingertips, tracing the outline of the welt. "I'll be careful," she murmured, straightening. Her fingers stayed on Vale's face, sliding down her jaw until they met the point of her chin. Vale shivered. "So, the other person deserved it, did they?"

"She did," Vale mumbled.

Key laughed, breaking contact. "I can cover it up, but you'll still look puffy."

"You can leave it, for all I care." Vale fidgeted as Key returned to the bed.

"I think it'll work better if you come sit." Key toed off her sandals, then sat on the edge of the bed and scooted toward the middle. She patted the spot next to her.

Vale eyed her, wary.

"I completely understand you being upset with me," Key said. "I was being unfair to you. I came to apologize."

"I'm okay."

"No, you're not, you've got a welt on your face. That's my fault."

"It was Burdock who hit me," Vale pointed out.

"And if I'd been more considerate, that wouldn't have happened. He shouldn't hit you in the face, regardless." A light flashed in Key's dark brown eyes.

"I did deserve it," Vale admitted.

Key's reply was sharper than Vale expected, and full of bite. "You don't deserve to be hit in the face." She closed her mouth with a click, paused, and took a breath. "I know that's not what you want to hear, especially not about Burdock. So I'll keep my silence. That wasn't the point of me coming to see you, anyway." She patted the bed again.

Vale clambered on, holding her dress carefully to avoid ripping it, and sat on the pristine white-and-ivory matelassé coverlet beside Key. She shuffled around, straightening the material beneath her as she stretched out her legs. Despite her best efforts to preserve space between herself and Key, Vale wound up hip to hip with her, the lines of their arms and legs pressing together as the mattress, soft with down, yielded to their weight.

Key didn't seem to mind, and truthfully, Vale didn't think she would. This was no different from the time Vale's hammock anchor snapped and she had to sleep with Key, or the time Key had kept her warm with a blanket and her own body after Vale took an accidental fall into a freezing mountain stream and had no spare clothes. The two of them were used to operating in shared space; it was Vale who was off-balance and acting weird.

"Terry had this delivered to me." Key held up the garment partway, displaying a dress with a structured cap-sleeved bodice and a plunging slit neckline. "He told me to tell you he made it extra flowy, just for you."

Vale tensed. Up close, the dress was more gorgeous, the subtle embroidery surrounding the neckline becoming apparent. Terry and his assistants must have worked on it for weeks. Desire gripped her stomach. She almost—almost—reached for it. "I can't."

"He knew you'd say that—well, we both did—and you can consider this payment for inspiring him."

"Oh, no," Vale said.

"Oh, yes. I know you won't believe it, but his business is booming, and it's because of you. If it makes you feel better, he made what I'm wearing as a thank-you, too, and he'd like us to show up at dinner as a matched set. We'd create the new standard for classiness."

Vale unscrunched her hand from the skirt of her dress. Damn, she'd put wrinkles in it. "I'm good with what I have."

"You know what I find funny?" Key lowered the bodice.

"What?"

"You're dating the best liar in the city and you haven't picked anything up from him."

Vale bristled. "What's funny about that?"

Key laughed, a short sound. "Nothing. Terry says there's a garrote wire sewn into the piping here and the right pocket has a hidden slit so you can reach your knives. Get dressed already." She dropped the bodice into Vale's lap.

"Right now?"

"Yes? And then I'll do your hair and makeup."

"Fine." Vale slithered off the bed with a rustle of fabric, trailing the dress behind her. "I'll wear it just this once. Because I don't want to make Terry sad."

"What about me?" Key gave her a bright smile.

Vale's spirit lifted like a kite on a breeze. She yanked it to the ground ruthlessly and scowled instead. "What about you?"

"I'd be sad if you didn't wear it. Don't make me sad, Vale."

"I'll—" She clutched the dress tightly to her chest. Of course she didn't want to make Key sad. "I'll make you sad if I want to." She glared at the plain envelope as Key let out a loud snort. "What's that?"

"Get dressed and I'll tell you."

"Fine," Vale snapped. She dragged the stool of the vanity over to the tall armoire at the side of the room, put the dress on it, and turned her back on Key. She reached behind herself, speaking as she undid her dress, cool air caressing her skin as the top slid down her body. "What's in the envelope?"

"Your paycheck."

Vale straightened. "Dr. Wilcroft changed her mind?"

"No. I withdrew the cash from my account. Think of it as an advance."

Shame ignited, burning acidic in her chest. Vale whipped around, half out of her dress. "Key!"

Key met her eyes, composed and steady. This was the look she got when she was prepared for debate, and Vale didn't like the fact that it was being turned on her. "I thought about this. I spent half of last night trying to figure out how best to ease your troubles in a way that wouldn't get you upset with me. But you don't respond kindly to a soft touch. So: When's Dina supposed to have her baby?"

"That's not—"

"Tuition is due for Bo, isn't it?"

"Key—"

She went on, ticking her points off on her fingers. "Last month you told me a hurricane ripped the roof off the corner of your parents' house and collapsed a wall. They've been staying with your brother Trey since, but will move in with Dina once the baby arrives so they can help out around the house. Elsie has been trying to pitch in on rebuilding efforts, but she has her own job and family to worry about, with the addition of your brothers Roland's and Claude's families because they've both been away since summer harvest started. We both know your family needs this paycheck and that Genevieve was wrong to dock your pay. It's my fault we were late to start with, my fault we were caught out by black market hunters, and if your family is extra needy, it's my fault too. Will you take your money or what?"

Pride entered the field, reinforcing shame. "You don't have to look out for me. I don't want your money."

"You're right." Key got to her feet, taking up the envelope, and approached. "I don't have to look out for you. I want to."

"I'm not someone who needs looking out for."

"Oh, Vale," Key said quietly, holding the envelope in front of her. "You need it more than you know."

"And you're gonna be the one to do it? Burdock and Jing do fine."

"Burdock hits you in the *face*," Key retorted, "and the only person Jing puts above himself is Cal."

She was wrong, but Vale figured she didn't want to know that Jing preferred lying on his back in bed. Stung by the words regardless, Vale threw back, "Don't you look out for enough? Half the city and that?"

"I don't do that because I want to, and you know it. Stop hissing at me because your pride is bruised. This isn't my money. It's yours because it's owed you. You earned it. Whether it comes from me or Genevieve, it doesn't matter."

Vale kept her gaze trained on the envelope instead of Key's face. "It does matter."

"Can you please not be stubborn, just this once? I don't need this nearly as much as you and your family do. Pay me back later." Key took three steps to the vanity and dropped the envelope on the surface with a loud thwack. "I'm going to leave it right here. You can take it or leave it."

Key was right; Vale was being an ass. Any person in their right mind would take the money. It was agonizing, receiving the help, but her personal misgivings wouldn't pay for Dina's midwife, or the house repair, or the groceries, or the bills.

Eventually, she nodded once, her swallowed pride going down like a too-large pill, then turned back around and stepped out of her dress. She pulled the armoire door open with a hollow thunk, revealing her old uniform from the academy, a mostly empty closet organizer, and a single, lonely hanger. She slipped her dress carefully onto it and shook it out before closing the door and reaching for the new one.

She ought to thank Key, but Vale wouldn't be in this predicament if not for her. Vale pondered as she put the new dress on, suppressing a moan at the luxurious feel of satin against her skin. What would it be like to have this all the time? It was unfathomable.

She got her arms into the sleeves, then did up the dress halfway before running into trouble. "Um . . . Key? Can you . . . help with the back?"

"Got it." A moment later, Key's fingers were on her, the spots of pressure thrumming with aching, heightened awareness even through the layered material of the bodice. "Vale, I'm sorry, but it's not closing. I don't think you can wear a bra with this."

Fire caught in Vale's cheeks, spreading down her neck so quickly that she thought she might be having an allergic reaction. "Really?"

"Don't worry, I brought tape just in case. Want me to unhook you?"

She couldn't bring herself to move. "Okay."

A brief touch. Vale shuddered, closing her eyes at the strength of her body's reaction, unable to control the goose bumps cascading over her skin like waves rippling over a pond. She'd thought herself inured to this. The first few months with Key were torture, her body tightening as if jolted with electricity every time Key brushed against her arm or put a hand on her knee, her stomach fluttering if Key stepped into a beam of sunshine just so. Before Jing, the figure in Vale's dreams had brown eyes and skin and a slender, soft hand, and spent long moments staring at Vale's lips.

Vale had to control herself. Exhaustion and stress must have weakened her defenses.

There was a soft gasp from behind her.

"Thanks," Vale managed, trying not to cringe at the state of her body. She pushed the shoulder straps of her bra off, letting the garment tumble to the floor. "I'm ready for the tape."

The next minute or two was spent in painful silence, with Key handing over strips of tape and Vale affixing them to the inside of the bodice, then removing the backs and letting them flutter to the floor like confetti. Finally, Vale got herself into the bodice, smoothing it up her body to settle everything in place.

"I'll get the hooks for you," Key said. "I don't know why, but Terry uses the smallest hooks in existence and they're impossible to get on your own, sometimes."

"It's to keep the closure invisible," Vale answered, though Key should have already known. Vale pulled her braid to the side, baring the back of her neck, bracing herself for Key's touch. At first she conducted herself well, but at the sound of Key's whispered oath and the stirring of breath against skin, Vale lost all composure. Shiver upon shiver ran through her until they collected in her stomach, winching it down tight and robbing her of breath.

She gulped for air when Key stepped away, her shoulders heaving in an embarrassing show.

"Let's see it," Key said.

Vale spun, the dress swirling in red and cream around her. The negative feelings disappeared in a flash of pure joy, and she couldn't help but grin and twirl a second time.

Key put a hand to her face, shock written across her features. "Ancestors, Vale."

Her grin fell, and with it, her mood. "Is it that bad?"

"Not at all. Why would you think that?" Key frowned at her, and Vale got the distinct impression Key was saying something additional in her head. "Come, sit at the vanity. I had an idea before, but now I know exactly what to do." She tilted her head and pointed at Vale's hair.

Vale brought the stool to the vanity and set it as far away from the envelope as she could without insulting Key. "I'm hopeless."

Key inhaled, held it, then let it out. "I heard you the first time, and no, you aren't. You weren't taught, that's all. There's a difference. Here." She began pulling ribbons off.

Vale watched as ribbon after ribbon was placed on the table, her disappointment growing with each length of bright color. "Can you leave them, or put them back?"

"Not all at once. Some of the colors would do better with another outfit."

That was Key, always diplomatic. Key's mother would have called it garish. "You can just say they're ugly."

"Far from it." Key smiled, combing out Vale's hair with her fingers, shaking the simple plait free. Vale barely kept herself from reacting to it. "They're very you. They're a choice you made. It's just this choice doesn't match the occasion. It doesn't mean you can't use all these ribbons together at another time." Key's fingers worked as she spoke, twisting Vale's hair until, magically, Vale had a braid ringing her head and a bun at the nape of her neck. Key went to a vase of wildflowers on the nightstand, selecting a few and stripping off leaves. She returned, winding the stems through Vale's hair, arranging the flowers carefully.

"There." Key stepped back, beaming. "A bit of makeup and you'll knock Jing on his rear."

"I can do that without putting on makeup." Jing was weaker on his left side, and Vale could rattle off at least five ways of penetrating his guard and laying him out, with or without weapons.

Key rolled her eyes and retrieved her makeup case, taking out a small container of lipstick, several brushes, and more compacts than Vale thought were necessary for someone with a face her size. She closed her eyes and tilted her face up, expectant. "Hey," she said, switching subjects. "You know that Rocket's going to be at dinner, right?"

"What?"

Vale risked a peek despite the brush feathering over her forehead and cheeks. Key's eyebrows were drawn together, the space between them creased with displeasure. "Yeah. Your ma invited her. Fair warning, but she's got one of these too." Vale pointed at her face.

Key folded her lips in, doing an admirable impression of Burdock. Mercifully, one of the spirits took pity on Vale and kept Key from delivering the lecture. "I see. Like I said before, I'm sure she deserved it." She went back to work, and Vale closed her eyes again.

Under her breath, Key muttered, "I don't know what I ever saw in her."

Vale exhaled with relief. "So if your mother tries to offer you a contract with Rocket?"

"Don't move, I'm applying your eyeliner." Key worked for a few seconds without talking. "I won't accept it, if that's what you're afraid of. We have a rapport. A relationship. You can open your eyes now." She wiped her hands on a handkerchief stowed in the makeup case, then unscrewed the lid of the lipstick and rubbed her finger in the cosmetic.

Vale parted her lips, reluctant to speak.

Key applied the makeup with an expert hand, her head canting from one side to the other as she scrutinized her work, her finger lingering on Vale's lower lip. "You're my guardian," she said softly. "You, and no one else."

Vale tried not to pay attention to the velvet pull of her lip against Key's finger, or how Key was looking at her with a mix of sympathy and some other emotion. Concern, maybe. It was hard to tell. "Both Dr. Wilcroft and Burdock think I should boss you around more."

Key remained silent. She applied a second layer as Vale forced herself to breathe evenly, heat gathering again as Key leaned close and nudged her chin up with a knuckle, turning her face left and right. Vale couldn't resist watching Key's lush mouth as she said, "I want you because you don't boss me around. Because you treat me like a friend, not an asset."

The thin wall of anxiety in Vale cracked in two, then crumbled. "*As* a friend. Not like a friend." It was a small distinction, but a necessary one.

"As a friend. Yes." Key smiled tightly as she eyed the leftover lipstick on her finger, then tapped it into her lips. "We should go. The dinner bell's about to ring." She wiped off the rest on the handkerchief just as a tinkling chime sounded from beyond the door. "Oh, I need my shoes. You too."

Vale stood and picked up the envelope, hefting its weight in her hand. "Give me a second to put this away." She strode to her rucksack to stow the money securely. "Okay, I'm—Key?"

Key was sitting on the bed, one sandal dangling from a limp hand, staring unfocused into the distance.

"Hey, Key." No response. "Shit." Vale scurried over, taking in Key's slackened jaw, the haze in her eyes. The dinner bell rang again, but this time it was a jangle, mirroring Vale's alarm. She'd believed—wanted to believe—that Key's brief seconds of blanking out earlier in the day had been caused by exhaustion and nothing more. *Time will tell*, Cal had said. And time was telling.

Vale's training clicked into place, pushing aside everything else.

She kneeled in front of Key, grasping her hand tight as a means of checking in. Key did nothing.

"Key," Vale said firmly, but she didn't respond. There was no ice or water; so much for those strategies.

Vale removed the sandal, placing it on the floor. Softly, she began singing Key's recall song.

Halfway through the stanza, Key sat straight, blinking, her eyes focusing. "What . . . ?"

If Vale bit her lip, she'd undo Key's work with the lipstick. She squeezed Key's hand instead, her mind going to Ina, to the worst-case scenario, while the rest of her wilted and sank. Vale was in a disadvantageous position and her weapons were at least three long strides away. The lavish room had little in the way of improvisational weaponry, but Key's throat was within reach.

Vale took in a long breath through the nose, sighed it out. "Who are you?"

"I'm . . ." Realization crept across Key's face, followed by pain. "Vale, I didn't . . . Please don't."

Vale relaxed her muscles, but she couldn't relent. This was the heart of her job, the essence of what it meant to be a guardian. Friend or not, preference or not, Vale needed to keep Burdock's and Dr. Wilcroft's words close. She had already demonstrated her mettle. It would be easy to do it again. "You should have told me. Who are you?"

Key closed her eyes, turning her head away. "Kiana Strade, hunter. I didn't think it was— I don't think it's serious."

"It's not your decision to make anymore." Vale was supposed to protect Key from others, but more importantly, Vale was supposed to protect Key from herself. "Who am I?"

Key made a quiet noise in her throat. "Valerian IV. Guardian. The best in our class."

"Yeah. I was. Where are we?"

"Garnet House. It's sunset. We have a dinner to attend."

The bell rang once more, anger in its tone. Vale stood, hardening her heart even as Key clung to her hand and looked up, her brown eyes liquid.

"Vale, please don't."

She kept her grip on Key's hand. "As your guardian, I have to force you to go."

"You know I hate it. Please."

She observed Key, whose face had gone tight with fear. Vale willed herself to be ruthless, ignoring Key's attempts to free herself. Vale hadn't spared a thought for Ina. She'd read the situation and reacted. She could do that here too. "You've never done it, so how can you know you hate it?"

"You'll—" Key swallowed. "You'll make me sad."

"I know." After the procedure, Key wouldn't remember any of this, wouldn't know that it had happened. "But I have no choice. You need a reintegration."

NINE

Prior to the refinement and standardization of the reintegration process, blood integration, now an obsolete technique, was used as a last resort before neutralization to restore hunters subsumed by rogue memories or personalities. This risky practice had a success rate of only 12 percent. As of this printing, there is a petition before the Asheburg city council to make blood integration illegal.

—*The Guardian's Text: A Historical View of Current-Day Practices for Supporting Memory Hunters,* 5th ed.

KEY'S MIND REELED, STUMBLING FROM ONE BRANCH OF thought to another. Nausea swelled into a bubble in the back of her throat, and, like all the times before, she prayed it wouldn't pop. Vale was gorgeous in her dress, and Key didn't want to ruin it.

Saints help her. She drew a breath, her insides rattling much the same way glasses would rattle atop the drink cart on the train. "We have to go to dinner," she said, and commanded the wild tremors within her to stay put instead of traveling to Vale like a signal down a telegraph wire.

Vale's eyes, soft until a moment ago, hardened into black mirrors. Gone, too, was her vulnerability, its appearance as rare and unpredictable as the flowering of the ghost orchid, which only made it more precious to Key. "We don't have time to go to dinner. Storm's coming fast. If we don't leave now, we'll be trapped here until it blows over tomorrow." Vale let go and reached up, plucking a flower out of her hair.

"No!" Before she could think, Key was on her feet and in Vale's space.

Vale slid aside, fluid as water, her hand flashing out. The feather-light press of her thumb on Key's pharynx was enough of a warning.

Key stilled.

"You're unstable," Vale said.

"No," Key replied, quiet. "I just didn't want you to take the flowers out."

Vale's voice was flat when she spoke. "Why?"

Because for a single second, Vale had looked as beautiful as Key knew her to be, and Key wanted to hold on to that. She wanted to hold on to the blush tinting Vale's cheeks, her open, unguarded look, with lips parted and ready. Key wanted to hold on to those things in the same desperate way she wanted to hold on to the ritual in the house beneath the magnolia, because they were important.

Reintegration would have her forget all of it.

Vale dropped her hand and stepped back, the lines of her body tense. "Okay. You didn't want me to ruin your work."

"No, you looked pretty!" It didn't matter. The brief opportunity afforded to Key to say anything, do something, was gone, the tendrils of electric charge that had built between them leading not to a kiss but to a vicious, destructive lightning strike.

One by one, Vale removed the flowers from her hair. "Distraction."

"What?"

"Things hunters will do when they don't want to listen to their guardians. Number one: distraction."

"Did that come straight from *The Guardian's Text*?"

"Yes." Vale threw a meaningful look at Key as she worked another blossom free. "We're leaving now. You need help."

"I'm not skipping dinner."

"You don't even *want* this dinner!"

"True," Key said. She had to keep the conversation going. Delaying meant Vale would be less able to force her back to the museum, and given an extra day's time, Key might be able to convince her not to initiate reintegration. "But I don't have a choice. My mother is expecting us."

Vale's mouth turned down at the corners. "Delaying."

"The guests are here and the dinner bell has rung already! What should I do, tell everyone to go home?"

"Now you're deflecting. Tell them the storm is gonna be bad, which isn't a lie, and they should go home early. Your ma will understand when I tell her the real reason."

"You *can't*!" Sweat broke out over Key's back. "A resifix doesn't need reintegration—"

"Bullshit! You literally made that up!"

"There's no precedent for it! No one has done it! We're supposed to be reservoirs of memory for our penitents. What would it say to others if the blessed of the ancestors needed reintegration?"

"That you're human? That your brain needs to be able to forget the way everyone else's does? Tell me you want to keep all the bad memories. Every embarrassment, every sad thing, every beating a parent gives their child. Go on."

Key refused to validate her. "It's my duty to keep the memories."

"It's your duty to suffer? Is that what the saints tell you?"

They'd never said anything because Key had never dared to ask. "My mother has never needed reintegration."

"Then your mother's as full of it as you are." Vale glared as she marched over to Key and grabbed her wrist.

"She's never—" Key tried to wrench herself free, but Vale only tightened her grip. "What if we talk about it after dinner? As soon as the last guest leaves, I promise, I *promise* we'll have the discussion then. Right now, we have company."

"I can't risk it. Are you hearing yourself? How many of these fits did you have without me?"

They weren't fits, not exactly. "I'm okay enough to go to dinner. Promise."

"Answer my question, Key."

"I didn't have any."

"You're lying to me too?"

"I'm not!" Key gave up struggling; Vale was going to leave imprints in her arm otherwise. "They weren't . . . fits. More like visions, phantom people, phantom sounds. The memory is strong, but I'll make it through dinner. I'll stay me. And then we'll talk."

"It can't wait, are you even listening?" Vale pressed her lips together. "Didn't you just apologize for being unfair to me? Was that another shoe situation?"

"Of course not!" Key's cheeks flared, shame piling onto shame. The first time they'd met, Key had been horrified at the state of Vale's clothing, especially her shoes, and had taken her to a fancy store, insisting on paying. When Vale selected the cheapest pair available, Key bought her the best the store had to offer instead.

"I don't even know why I'm arguing with you." Vale loosened her grip, her face softening. "I should just knock you out and hogtie you and haul you to medical."

"What?" Key's mouth stayed open with disbelief. "I'm not Ina!"

Vale squared herself up. "Keep going and you will be. I don't get why you're so scared. People do it all the time! Jing does it all the time! He's been fine after every reintegration. He's happy to do it."

"I'm not *people*. I'm not Jing."

"Yeah, you aren't. Cal doesn't have to tell Jing to go, he just does it himself."

"How do I explain this?" Key shook her head, more to rid herself of the sudden overlay of a kitchen table and white-glazed mug on the damask wallpaper of Vale's room than anything else.

"You already did to Dr. Wilcroft, and she told you to leave it alone."

"The memory is important, I know it. The ancestors know it. They brought me to Crystal Grove and showed me directly to the memory. They want me to go deeper. I have to go back for more specimens, but if I don't remember anything, I can't go back."

"Honestly, no offense to the ancestors, it's not worth it if it does this to you. The saints will have to be disappointed. We're leaving now. The easy way, or the hard way." Vale's nostrils flared. "You need help and I need this job. You gave me six reasons why. Or are you going to give me one of those fat envelopes every two weeks, forever?"

Someone knocked on the door, then immediately opened it. Jing swept into the room, Cal behind him.

"Vale, you're going to be fashionably late to—" He paused. Key noted that his gaze landed on her first before traveling to Vale, where it lingered. "Aren't you a vision?"

"Are we interrupting something?" Cal shut the door behind him. "Key, Vale, are you two okay?"

Vale let go of Key's hand and spoke, her words tumbling out of her mouth. "I need to take Key for a reintegration now, but she's unstable and refusing to go. We don't have until tomorrow or even late tonight because that storm will be on us and then we won't be able to leave at all."

Key was not about to demonstrate her so-called instability for Cal. She held herself back, only barely. "I said I'd discuss it after dinner, which I can't skip because it's being thrown in my honor. I'm fine."

"You are *not* fine." Vale turned to Cal. "You saw her in the archive earlier today. You were right. Key's been having intrusions since we got back. Maybe even before. She just had one a minute ago. I have to get her to the clinic."

"Wait, you *knew*?" Key's ribs expanded with breath. "You knew and you discussed it with Cal?!"

"Vale had valid concerns and came to me for a consultation," Cal said in a soothing, calm tone. "I did what any senior colleague would do and advised her on what might happen. I understand you don't like the procedure, and you're concerned about your mother's event. But it's just dinner. That's forgivable. Waiting on reintegration isn't the same. I agree with Vale."

A guardian's position, as she expected. Key addressed Jing, where she might have more of a chance. "Jing, you've been through this. Don't you think I'd know if I weren't okay?"

"I told you," Vale said to Cal, urgency in her voice. "She's checking off every box on the list."

Jing held up both hands. "Nope, I'm not getting involved. Your ma sent me to fetch you, and as far as I'm concerned, job's done."

"Yes, and I'm ready to go to dinner." Key returned to the bed, sat, and began strapping her sandals back on. "You know how she is when people are late."

"Yes, so Cal and I will be on time, and you and Vale will go to the museum. Damn, I said I wasn't getting involved."

Key yanked on her sandal with more force than necessary. "The memory is important! I can't lose it. I went almost two hundred forty years back and saw a ritual that's probably a precursor to our responsorial here. I've never seen anything like it. Isn't that fascinating? Don't you want to know how we got started doing this? Don't you care about our work?"

Jing tilted his head, wry. "I care during business hours. I'm not a priestess and I'm not part of your temple. If you want to dig up the origins of your practice, be my guest. Sounds blasphemous."

"This is about responsorial rites only, not faith," Key shot back. She stood and began pacing. "There was a compound with a magnolia tree—a mug of strange tea—and the grandfather said, 'You will be consecrated,' but I didn't get a full dive; I wanted half, but I got a quarter. I need more time. More resources. If Vale and I hadn't gotten our wings clipped, then I'd be petitioning for a crew to go back there."

Jing and Cal exchanged a worried look.

"What?" Key cut her eyes at both men. When neither answered, she asked again, louder. "What?"

"Nothing," Jing said.

"Liar!"

Cal, at least, had enough grace to hang his head.

Vale snapped her words through gritted teeth. "Key, stop. You're scaring us."

"You think I'm Ina," Key volleyed back. "I'm not. I can control myself."

Finally, Jing folded his arms across his chest, obscuring the fine embroidery on his low-collared jacket, and sighed. "I can't go against either guardian here, and you know that. Vale's the expert. She wouldn't lie or send you to reintegration without good reason. You should listen to her. Besides, reintegration means no hallucinations. It's healthy for you. Like a tonic."

Key's stomach sank. "You said that to me yesterday."

"Oh, did I?" Jing shrugged. "They're good words. See? I'm not missing much after reintegration." He grinned, showing off his teeth. "I'm totally fine. Cal catches me up on the important bits, and I take it from there." He kept his eyes on her as he continued. "How long until the storm hits, Vale?"

Key leaned forward, sensing a change in Jing's strategy.

"Less time than a dinner party would take," Vale replied, wary. "Why?"

"Radio said the first band wouldn't be too bad. I think we can make it through dinner, provided Key can stay herself. She has a point in that she can't duck out of Lanelle's event. She has appearances to keep up."

"Jing!" Vale exclaimed. "She has to go now!"

"Thank you," Key said to Jing. "You understand."

"Just because I understand doesn't mean I'm sympathetic." Jing broke eye contact briefly to glance at Vale. "But if it gets everyone's goals met, I'm there. We should go before the real threat to us comes through that door. Sorry, Vale. But I'd rather not face Key's mother."

"Coward," Vale muttered.

Jing laughed and strode over to her, planting a kiss on the top of her head. Then he gestured to Vale's moon guitar, propped up in the corner. "Bring that with you. Mr. Strade always asks you to play, and Key will probably need the grounding."

"I was going to anyway," Vale said nastily.

"Oh, and Cal brought his lap dulcimer, so the two of you can play together. Maybe that new song you taught him!"

Vale stared at him, the irritation in her eyes a reflection of the thunderheads building outside the window.

"Have I ever mentioned that you're hot when you're angry?" Jing's mouth pulled into a lopsided smile. "And you were already looking radiant in your new dress."

Vale lunged, but Jing danced out of the way, straight into Cal's arms.

"Okay, we're leaving now," Cal said, towing Jing toward the door. "Before Vale stabs you."

"You know I'd let her, and I'd ask her for more." Jing blew Vale a kiss as he was manhandled out. "You've got two minutes to be downstairs or else I'm telling Lanelle to send Rocket. I think she wants a rematch with Vale."

"Take Key with you." Vale pivoted, and then it was Key being pushed out of the room. "Make sure she doesn't escape. You're both on watch duty. I need a minute."

"What, did you forget something?" Jing called from the hallway.

Cal offered Key his elbow, wordless and grave.

"A knife," Vale said bluntly, her eyes boring into Key. "Just in case."

KEY SIPPED AT a glass of sugarcane wine as she stood in the loggia overlooking the courtyard garden, rolling the liquid over her tongue before swallowing. It was an excellent dessert wine, but tonight, she could only register that it was sweet. The other flavors at dinner had been forced into their generic roles as well, the tastes and textures losing subtlety under the burden of her anxiety.

A wet wind whipped past, snagging in the loose material of her jumpsuit, setting it to flapping. Overhead, the front line of the storm had eaten the moon and the stars, and it wouldn't be long before she'd be forced inside. The loggia had doors at either end, each leading to a staircase and other wings of the house; she could be away and into the western wing in seconds. As a child, she'd played plenty of hide-and-seek, and she considered herself adept at escaping notice.

She risked a glance behind her through the open double doors of the formal dining room. She was being watched, as she had been all throughout dinner. Jing sat casually with his chair angled toward the door, a lone monument at the table, finishing the last of his dessert as the kitchen staff swirled around him. He caught her eye and tilted his head, lifting his own glass to her before tipping its contents into his mouth.

He had been unusually attentive throughout the meal, chiming in on the discussion of the upcoming Institute of Human Memory fundraiser when Key faltered, deftly yielding the floor to Calamus when the topic of the museum's folk song exhibit was broached. Jing's maneuvering kept Key's focus drawn tight, his steady hands on the string anchoring her, his well-timed questions keeping her from flying off.

It wasn't being done out of friendship, she suspected. Maybe it was a favor to Vale, whose facility with high-society dinner parties began and ended with recognizing the parts of a place setting. Or maybe it was because he had already planned on having a nice evening and needed Key's participation in order to prolong his enjoyment of the food.

Rocket entered the doorframe, striding purposefully toward the loggia, the stocky athleticism of her body well accentuated by her gray suit and pristine white shirt, the inky curlicues of a tattoo peeking out from beneath her open collar. Her bright red hair was parted deeply to the right, allowing the curls and ringlets to cascade down the side of her head and spill onto a broad shoulder. She had on minimal makeup, just enough liner to bring out her hazel eyes and some shadow to intensify them. Her swollen nose and left cheekbone ruined a look that would have, but for extenuating circumstances, sent Key into a certain state.

"Cordelia," Key said.

"Please," Rocket replied. "Your mother isn't here. You know I'd rather you use the academy name."

"All right." Key allowed a small smile as Rocket stopped in front of her. Though it had been years since they'd broken up, repeated exposure to each other at society functions kept their relationship cordial. "Are you leaving?"

"Excited to be rid of me so soon?" Rocket smiled back.

"I'd have you stay longer but for the weather." Key leaned in, mirroring Rocket's stance, and they kissed each other on the cheek. "You shouldn't delay. Vale's been warning of a big storm."

"Convenient to have your little drifter weather witch beside you all the time."

Key's mouth tightened at the offense. She was instantly reminded of why she had ended things with Rocket. "Speak ill of Vale again, and that contract you've been angling for will disappear."

"I mean," Rocket said hastily, "she has an uncanny sense for storms, better than the weather forecasters. Has she ever been wrong?"

"No." As if to prove a point, the wind swirled through Rocket's hair, sending it into her face, then grabbed hold of the edge of Rocket's suit jacket and yanked, revealing a flowered lining. "Good night. Take care, Rocket."

"You too, Key. You know how to find me." Rocket smoothed the hair out of her face, then reached into an inner pocket, withdrawing her visiting card, pressing it into Key's hand. She left, Jing's faint smirk following her through the dining room before returning to Key.

Vale's moonbeam voice floated out from the parlor on a high note, accompanied by the twang of her guitar and the metallic strum of Cal's dulcimer. Key didn't recognize the words, though the melody was familiar. She turned back to the garden, unable to drink the rest of her wine. She gauged the distance to the grass below as spring coils of tension wound through her stomach and up the back of her throat.

Soon. They'd come for her soon.

"Kiki, turn on some lights out here."

Key startled and let out a small shriek, fumbling her glass. Wine sloshed over the rim and onto her jumpsuit as she grabbed the bowl of it with both hands. "Blood in the mouth!" she growled. She turned from her spot beside a column to see her mother emerging, backlit, from the double doors.

Lanelle squinted through the darkness as she approached. "What's wrong with you? You've been jumpy all night."

Key figured her mother would be jumpy too if three of her friends were conspiring to haul her away for forced memory erasure, but only said, "I'm just tired. I haven't had much rest."

Lanelle joined her, offering her the cocktail napkin from her own glass. Key took it gratefully, setting her glass on the railing, then dabbing at the spots on her jumpsuit.

"Terry has outdone himself," Lanelle said. "Though I would have preferred not to have you and Valerian match. It's beyond his station to editorialize on your relationship."

"I doubt that was his intention. We're helping him tease his next collection. And he wanted to be kind to Vale."

Lanelle didn't respond. Key assumed she was thinking about previous kindnesses that had been bestowed on Vale and whether they were merited. After a moment, Lanelle said, "Come inside before you catch a cold. The forecasters are warning of a bigger storm than anticipated."

A burst of chill wind blew crosswise, and Key was greeted with a nose full of ozone, mingled with her mother's coconut-oil-and-hibiscus scent. "I can't say I'm surprised. Vale called it."

"Sometimes I wonder if that girl should have been a meteorologist at the weather service."

"Guardians make more money."

Lanelle snorted. "Meteorologists don't make enough. Speaking of storms, in a way, I'm glad you're home for a week. It gives us time to talk without you begging Genevieve for another assignment and running for the woods." There was a pause.

"Just say it, Mama."

"You wouldn't be in these situations if you were at the temple."

"I don't want to be at the temple." Key picked up her glass just to have something to do. "I've done it all my life. I want to build a career at the museum, like Gramma."

Lanelle's brown eyes were soft as she said, "You have a divine gift."

"One the ancestors are telling me should be used for the museum. What I found the other day—I truly believe the saints guided me there. Protected me as I went. I saw a version of the responsorial from before the Decade of Storms." Key saw the change in her mother's expression, but went on nonetheless. "Have you ever heard of a variation where people say 'you've been consecrated' instead of 'you've been sanctified'?"

Lanelle thought for a moment. "Yes, actually. But it's from an apocryphal text. The group with that variation was a splinter group, a fringe sect whose practice eventually died out because they became militant about conversion."

"Apocryphal text? You taught me temple history yourself and never mentioned any of this."

"It wasn't necessary for you to know at the time. However, if you succeed me as head resifix," Lanelle said, "I could then teach you all I know. Such as what it means to lead the temple and the demands it places on you."

"You've already told me. My life isn't my own."

"That is so." Lanelle's slight smile carried a tinge of sadness, enhanced by the warm half shadows from the light in the dining room. "I won't get deep into the particulars tonight, especially since you're still recovering after a tiring journey. Once you've rested and the storm has passed, you need to come back to the high temple with me. It would be best to explain while there."

A fit of anger seized Key, but she diffused it until it was simply a snappish tone. "Why is everyone telling me what I need to do? What if I need to do something for myself?"

"You've spent the last two years doing something for yourself," Lanelle replied. "I know what it's like not being able to do what you want, and I did my best to protect your time."

"I wanted more."

"I know, Kiki. But another phase of your life is beginning, like it or not. I'm planning on talking to Genevieve about your position soon."

"You can't do that," Key responded automatically. "Ma, I'm not a child who needs to be told where to sit and how to act."

"You aren't?" Lanelle's eyes crinkled with amusement. "Be a grown woman, then, and come back to the temple."

"That's not the work I want to do." Key forced herself to look into her mother's eyes. When she was little, she fancied herself braver and more courageous than anyone else in the city because she could win a staring contest with her mother. "I've done enough of it."

"Baby, you've hardly started."

Key ignored the dismissiveness and continued. "I want my head to be filled with the memories I create myself. Instead, my head is filled with names and faces and dates, with memories and emotions of people who no longer exist. But what if—" Here was an opportunity, and Key seized it. "What if it's too much? What happens if I'm holding too much?"

"You go down to the meditation pool and spend time there, watched over by the ancestors. Once you're a full initiate, you'll be allowed access."

The memory of Ina on the museum floor, Vale's knife to her neck, shot to the forefront of Key's mind. "What if I need more than meditation?"

"You won't."

"What has the temple figured out that the institute hasn't? How is it that you, or Zerua, or Sima don't need a guardian?"

"We are not governed by the institute's restrictions. Not all divers need guardians. But more importantly, we have faith," Lanelle declared. "That is not something Genevieve believes should live in the museum or anything associated with it, despite her work, however different she claims it to be, being a type of faith itself."

Key, troubled by her mother's criticism, said, "You think Genevieve is a hypocrite?"

"I believe her devotion to science and history above all else to be unprincipled."

"Unprincipled? But the museum operates on the strictest principles. That's why we're a leader in research and conservation."

"Unethical, then."

"How so, when it would be unethical to keep memories and artifacts in places where they're guaranteed to be lost or improperly maintained?"

"People come to us willingly. We don't take the information from them. And we reunite that information with them more often than the museum does. Our goal is to impart the wisdom of the ancestors, not preserve history." Lanelle gave an exasperated shake of her head. "I didn't come to argue with you, Kiki. I came to convince you to go to the temple with me so I could show you something important."

Dubious, Key said, "Do I really need to be at the temple to do that?"

Lanelle fell silent, and for a minute, Key thought it was the end of the discussion. Then her mother heaved a loud sigh, set her wineglass to her lips, and drained it in one large gulp. "Turn on the lights, Kiki."

Key did so, eyeing her mother speculatively, then returned. "What was that for?"

"You wanted to know if we needed to be at the temple. I suppose for this, we don't have to be." Lanelle pushed the loose sleeve of her dress up, baring her arm to the shoulder. Thin bangles clinked against each other as she tilted her arm, turning it until the light caught the inside of her bicep. There, growing a soft cream against her medium brown skin, was a branching tangle of filaments about an inch in diameter.

Chills sheeted over Key, pulling her skin tight from head to toe. She gasped, the sound of it like the cut of a knife. "Mama, what is this?" She put her thumb on the area and rubbed, but nothing came off. She rubbed harder, bending closer to her mother's arm, tears springing to her eyes. "Mama, *what is this*?"

Lanelle covered Key's hand with one of hers. "Stop. It's threaded into the layers of my skin and won't come off. The needle orchid has antifungal properties and I take an extract of it every day, but the efficacy decreases eventually."

"How can you be so calm about this? If it's showing in one spot—the mycelium would have to be throughout—" She choked, cutting herself off. Throughout her body. The fungus would be growing and entangling itself with her mother's major organs, spreading along her blood vessels, feeding off her mother's muscle and fascia and bone.

"Yes. It's systemic."

Key braced herself against a stone column, her legs weak. There was no breath left in her. "Does it have to do with—" She swallowed, sickened. "Is it the blood chalice?"

"It's complicated." Lanelle cupped the side of Key's face, and despite herself, she flinched away. "There is a solution to this. But you need to come to the temple with me. I said to you that I won't be resifix forever, Kiki. You need to finish your initiation, then take my place. You need to understand everything that—"

Lanelle's expression hardened, and she stepped away from Key. "Valerian. This is a private conversation."

"No," Key groaned. "Not now."

"I'm sorry to bother you," Vale said, not looking at all sorry. Behind her stood Jing and Cal. "Something has come up at the museum, and Key needs to come with us."

Lanelle didn't look convinced. "Did Genevieve send a telegram?"

"No," Jing said, "but she did give Cal and me instructions before we left the museum. I didn't want to disrupt Key's dinner party, so I held it in confidence as long as I could. You understand how that is, naturally." If Key didn't know he was lying, she would believe that the expression of contrition on his face was genuine. "I'm afraid it can't wait. Mrs. Strade, on behalf of the head curator, who is probably still in her office, and Calamus, who is an ardent fan of your chef—"

"Those mushroom tartlets are inspired," Cal interrupted quickly.

"I apologize for spiriting your daughter away."

Key turned her head slowly to the three of them. She spoke in a low tone even though the prickling sensation crawling up her spine was telling her to run. "I thought we were supposed to discuss this after dinner?"

"We've discussed it," Vale said. "And it's after dinner. Let's go, Key."

"You didn't discuss it with me." She dug her heels in. Reintegration would have her forget the house under the magnolia, and Vale, and now her mother's infection. No. "I didn't agree to this."

Lanelle sighed. "That sounds exactly like Genevieve, that workaholic. She probably doesn't know there's a storm."

"It won't take long," Jing said. "I promise. She needs us for some paperwork regarding Key and Vale's research, and the faster it gets done, the better. It's the last thing Key needs to do, and then she's all yours. I promise. No more interference."

Lanelle paused, then drew a breath. "Very well, fine. If it's official, then I can't stop you. For safety's sake, I'll have someone drive you there and back."

"That's very generous of you, Mrs. Strade." Cal smiled. It was difficult to stay grumpy with sunshine like his, and Key noted with concern that her mother wasn't immune. "We heard the radio earlier, and Vale has been forecasting doom and gloom, so we appreciate the offer."

"I'm not going," Key said, leveraging herself up by using the column. "I need to be here, at home."

"You've got an order," Vale countered. "Not just from Dr. Wilcroft, but from the senior hunter."

Lanelle stepped closer to Key, putting herself in front as if she were a shield. "What's really going on between you all?"

Jing was the picture of innocence. "Exactly as I said, Mrs. Strade. We'll be out and back before you can even miss us."

Cal came forward, sidestepping Lanelle, and offered Key his elbow again. "C'mon, Key. It'll be good to have this all taken care of, and then we won't have to deal with it next time we head out."

She refused him, leaning away and over the railing, panic welling up. "You don't understand. This isn't about what you think it is. I need to be home, I need to be with my *mother*, she's—"

"Kiana!" Lanelle's voice was thunder itself, even cowing Vale, who ducked her head. "Say nothing. I will still be here when you come back. Then we'll go to the temple."

Key tensed so hard she thought she would shatter into pieces. Her heartbeat pulsed in her ears, and a wave of dizziness caught her.

"Kiki." Familiar arms enclosed her, and she found herself pulled into a coconut-oil-and-hibiscus embrace. The bangles jingled against themselves, each a little chime. "Go on. I'll be here, and when you come back, we'll have that talk."

"I won't forget," Key said hoarsely, then vowed it again to herself. *I promise I won't forget.*

Cal took Key's hand, and Vale the other, and together, the two guardians led Key away step by wooden step. "Be safe," Lanelle called once they exited the loggia.

"We will," Vale called back.

Three Weeks Ago

THE MUSEUM OF HUMAN MEMORY

From: Key
To: Dr. Genevieve Wilcroft
Subject: Interesting journal articles?

Genevieve,

I was just at the library and saw the latest journals on the librarian's desk. Thought I'd send you the ones I felt were most interesting, plus a book review relevant to collections development. Partial citations below.

- Fontseré, Lillie. "Dialectical Curatorial Methods: Toward A(n)Other-Focused Education," _Experimental Museology_
  - It took a moment to parse what she meant—sometimes I wonder whether other anthropologists can write in plain speech so someone like Vale

can understand them; certainly that would help to better make their cases—but I think Dr. Fontseré makes a good point that the writing in current interpretive signage and finding aids could lead our patrons to their conclusions less obviously and encourage analytical thinking and, most importantly, reflection.

- Burdett, Elyas. "Examining the Exhumed," _Annals of Diving Practice_
  - This one is about discrepancies in recordkeeping in multiple museums in Spruceton, Moon Valley, and Ridgeville. I don't think we have those discrepancies here because of your strong stance on properly documenting provenance. Dr. Burdett stops just shy of accusing the various staffs of negligence. He cites a new book titled _Provenance and Ethics in Collection Development_ that was just reviewed in _Archivist Monthly_. I pulled the review to take a look. It's very positive.

- Elgisson, Wylie. "Curatorial Overreach at the Spruceton Museum of Human Memory," _Current Ethnography_
  - I'm sensing that there's something personal behind this article, but

Elgisson does make a solid argument that the voice of the curatorial staff in the excerpts is othering, verges on propaganda, and leaves little room for a patron to interpret information. This is a good companion piece to the Fontseré, despite the article feeling much like it was originally two separate pieces sewn together. The part that's jarring is in regard to curatorial attitude overall, where he accuses curators and researchers of being condescending and even infantilizing toward the communities they study. I normally would disagree strongly, but the evidence he provides does have a distasteful flavor to it. Surely, he argues, the communities studied should have a hand in the interpretation, presentation, and preservation of their own artifacts. The idea has merit. Why not go further and teach them our methods?

- Dustimer, E. Clayton. "Ancestral Binding Practices in the Southern Spine and Wetlands," _Frontiers of Migration_
  - This is related to your work on the Chamuna reconstruction.

Hope these are helpful!

OFFICE OF THE HEAD CURATOR
MUSEUM OF HUMAN MEMORY

From: Dr. Genevieve Wilcroft
To: Kiana Strade
Subject: Re: Interesting journal articles?

Kiana–

Lillie's main focus is to bring more patrons to the museum and increase their time spent in exhibits. Her director is on vacation more than he is in the office and therefore only uses metrics as a means of evaluation. This article serves to fulfill her publishing obligations.

From what I hear, Dr. Burdett is a stickler for protocol. The museums mentioned would benefit from an audit.

Mr. Elgisson is a disgruntled former employee at Spruceton, relegated to publishing in low-regard, editorially weak journals such as _Current Ethnography_. Elgisson's research is not robust. He eschews objectivity and editorializes constantly. As for who is best equipped to handle artifacts, I want to caution you about taking seriously the writings of researchers who study hostile populations and erroneously project their ethical standards onto us. The institute and museum are the leaders in the field of memory diving and preservation and there is no better place to ensure the longevity of memories than here, where they can be properly stored and protected. Perhaps the next time a hurricane smashes a village into kindling and we lose both lives and valuable history, Mr. Elgisson will reevaluate his views.

I'll look at the Dustimer piece.

All best,
Genevieve

TEN

RACK AND RUIN
WEATHER SERVICE MISSES THE CALL
A Dread Gale Destroys Fairlee, Hundreds Feared Dead.

CHIPBURN.—A hurricane previously forecasted to come ashore on St. Adelwick spun west and made landfall in Fairlee on Saintsday evening, bringing a deadly twenty-foot storm surge and massive flooding for miles along the Copper River. The rice harvest has been scattered in all directions, and the mills and silos are beyond repair. The fierce winds and furious water swept over the village with little advance warning, toppling homes, tearing up the railroad lines, and downing wires across the area, cutting off communication. The damage has yet to be reckoned, but great loss of property and life are expected.

—Asheburg Gazette

VALE BROUGHT OUT A PRICKING NEEDLE AND A FRESH TAB OF rice paper. "See me."

"You are seen," Key replied automatically.

Vale pressed the needle against a calloused fingertip. "Hear me."

"You are heard." Key winced at the pop of her skin, the small shock of pain. Blood strained out of the pinprick, expanding into a deep crimson drop.

Remember me. She waited for Vale to say it; Vale *had*

said it. Blank silence greeted her, as if the signal had been dropped on the radio. *Remember me.* "Vale?"

There was nothing but the invisible wall of arrested thought.

Key inhaled. She peeled her tongue off the roof of her stale mouth, forced apart the glue holding her lips together. "Vale . . . ? Remember me?"

She became aware of the lengthening of her breaths and the weight of a thin blanket on her as she unsealed her eyelids. Disorientation seized her, burning away the cobwebs of sleep. She was supposed to be standing on the porch of an old, dilapidated house beside a specimen bull magnolia, preparing for a dive. She was instead on her back in a windowless room with an off-white ceiling, its unremarkable expanse broken by a single brass lamp whose jaundiced incandescence was too weak to reach the corners. She turned her head, tried to move stiff arms and legs—and met with resistance around her wrists and ankles.

Key yanked harder, her breath coming in sharp bursts, a wave of panic crashing through her, raising sweat on her upper lip and goose bumps over her skin. There was a night-stand to her left with a glass of water on it; next to that was a silver pole hung with a mostly empty bag of clear fluid, a tube extending like an umbilical cord from it to the needle taped to her left inner elbow. On her upper right arm was a fresh-looking bandage.

"Ah, you're up. Deep breath, Key."

A shadow fell over her, and she looked up to see Jing, impeccably dressed in a fine black jacket with mother-of-pearl buttons and a short, notched collar. Anger and shock jolted through her, followed by the creak of leather as she tried in vain to move. "What happened to me? Where's Vale?"

"Stepped out of the room for a second. She'll be back, don't worry."

The glibness of Jing's delivery coupled with her half-slurred speech only incensed her further. "Why are you here?" she demanded.

Jing tsked. "Rude. I'm doing a favor for my girlfriend."

"Where's Cal?"

"Was I ever this inquisitive after . . . ?" Jing furrowed his brows, thinking. "He's with Vale. They went down to the automat."

"Why?"

"Because sometimes you need a little sugar after being reintegrated, and the automat has soda pop. Boy, you're cranky when you wake up."

"I'm only cranky because I don't know what's happening! Reintegrated?" But it made sense in a rancid, horrific way. She was adrift in a starless ocean with no navigator, no idea of what day it was, what time it was. Her only certainty was in how she felt. Key gripped her anger tightly; the confusion would be no help here. "I'd never have asked for that."

"Well, okay, you didn't. It was Vale."

Key tugged at her restraints again, voicing a frustrated exhale. "She wouldn't. She knows how I feel."

He shrugged. "Believe whatever you want, doesn't matter to me. I'm just filling in for a minute, which is all it'll take for me to have this chat with you. Relax, you're not getting out of those cuffs unless someone takes them off."

"Then take them off," Key ground out.

"I'll let Vale deal with it, how about that?" Jing left her bedside to get a chair, plunking it down by her head. "All right, about that talk. Consider this a gift to someone who's never wronged me."

"You don't do gifts." Key narrowed her eyes.

"This direct talk is refreshing, Key. Bet if you did it more often, you'd have fewer people bothering you off-hours. Let's not call it a gift, then. A bit of advice from a senior colleague to a junior colleague."

"You do altruism now?" Jing wouldn't stir himself to do something nice for Vale if she didn't do something first. And he certainly wouldn't help Key out of the goodness of his heart if there wasn't something in it for him.

"I dabble in it from time to time." Jing leaned forward and planted his elbows on his knees, letting his hands dangle. "They'll be back soon; I'll get to it. Do you remember what I said to you shortly after we met? The first train ride we had together."

Key frowned and thought, her mouth pursing. Anxiety and fear gnawed at her—what *day* was it?—but she focused her anger, using it to stuff the other emotions into a box. "To be careful?"

The way Jing looked at her made the back of her neck prickle with alarm. He was serious, his dark brown eyes piercing. "I told you to be careful of Genevieve and her mission."

"To restore what was lost to us as a civilization?"

"That's the museum's mission." Irritation swept over Jing's face. "You need to listen. Be careful of Genevieve's mission. Right now, she's in lockstep with everyone else. The museum, the institute, the temple, the council."

Key didn't like where this was headed. "Seems like she's doing perfectly."

"I wouldn't expect anything less from her. She's unearthed a ton of information since she ascended to head curator." Jing's mouth quirked up. "She brings in the practical and the imaginative. Meaning," he said, pausing, holding up his hand to stop Key from talking. "Meaning that she not only provides us with useful, beneficial information, but she keeps a certain narrative alive. A dream of a narrative. A cultivated definition of who and what we were in the past."

"Isn't that what she's supposed to do? You support her. Don't you ascribe to this narrative?"

"I am carefully neutral about it." Jing made a slight movement of his head. "I'm about me, everyone knows that. Long as I don't get in her way, she'll keep me on. I'm not from here, after all. I'm aware of what pays the bills. I'm aware of what your general belief systems are. We want to think we're gifted, or blessed, or have come from good stock. The problem is, for us? When we dive?"

He scoffed. "We will see things no one else will. Remember that, Key. When they use it against you, make you question what you've lived, just remember that we've seen it, not them."

Key swallowed, discomfited by the turn Jing had taken. "Are you . . . okay?"

"Don't ask me, ask it of yourself. I'm fine, and plan to always be fine. You, on the other hand—there are expectations of you in this city. You can do what I do, but better. With talent like that, you're bound to come across unsettling things. If you haven't yet, you've been lucky."

"Cal says you've seen things that would give people nightmares."

"Yeah, that's true. It's true." Jing sighed. "And that's why I wake up where you are right now, liberally and often."

It was a sobering thought, that Jing would prefer this to his retrieved memories, that he would sacrifice his own as collateral for peace. "Doesn't that bother you?"

"Which part, the reintegration or the nightmare fuel? You can work it out, I'm sure."

"Doesn't it bother Cal to have you reset so often?"

"If it does," Jing replied, "all he has to do is think of what I might be like if I didn't get reintegrated."

Key looked at him, unwavering. "Don't you think that's running away? Anything you don't like, anything that makes you the smallest bit uncomfortable, you can ask to have erased."

"What you call running away, I call wisdom. You have to change your mindset about it. It's the best thing that can happen to you, if you let it." Jing tapped his head. "And you should. Because what we can go through is a very horrible, very personal hell, and one you may end up living if you aren't more careful. So here's my advice."

"I thought all of this was advice from a senior colleague to his junior."

"Just the preamble. Dive deep. Look for the truth, however subjective that is. But don't tell anyone but Vale how deep you can go or what you've found."

"What about you and Cal?"

"Not even us, if it's dangerous. It's better to compartmentalize that way. If you need to keep it from Vale, keep it from Vale."

"You want me to hide what I find? Isn't that lying? What if I can't contextualize the memory, but Genevieve can?"

"The past is the past, Key. And in many cases, it should stay that way. It's nothing but trouble to pass judgment on the living based on their ghosts. This city of yours looks backward while walking forward and calls itself blessed to do so."

Key remained silent.

"Don't bring any of this back to the curator." Jing regarded her, his eyes clear and cold.

"You don't trust her?"

She watched the emotions chase themselves over Jing's features. "She would like to preserve the status quo," he said eventually. "I don't trust her to turn her entire world over, to go against the temple and the council and all the work she's done at the museum, to publicize something we've uncovered. She likes where she is. She likes her power. And she doesn't care about others the way you think she does."

"Why are you telling me this?"

"Because you would try." Jing smiled, grim. "Because you're righteous and blessed and you've never been told no. You believe hard, and once you find something that lights a fire in you, you won't let it burn out."

"I don't understand." What was missing from her memories? What was Jing implying? What was so important that he was convinced she'd take action? "If it's so bad, what's stopping you from turning it all over yourself? Whatever it is you've uncovered?"

"Now, why would I go through all that for people who only know how to take? Be reasonable. The system works for me right now." He shrugged. "And until it stops doing that, there's no need for me to give it a push. A world-shattering revelation to you is just a Fourthday afternoon to me unless you do something to get me involved. I really don't want you to get yourself into that trouble. Whatever happens, though, know that I believe you, and I believe in your convictions. Cal too. You know I trust his gut more than I trust mine. There you go. Talk over. Back to the regular broadcast Jing."

"What if I'm intrigued by the special broadcast Jing?"

"You'll have to remain intrigued. It's part of my mystique."

"Does Vale get to see special broadcast Jing?"

He laughed, a short and decidedly unhumorous sound. "She especially does not get to see special broadcast Jing. She's fun, and we're fun together, and I'd like to keep it that way."

"That's not fair to her. You know how she feels about you."

"Do I?"

"She deserves better from you."

"Does she? You have suggestions? Should I treat her as well as you do?"

Key narrowed her eyes. She cared for Vale as a person, not a score sheet. "You—"

"Nuh-uh." Jing held up his pointer finger. "No."

The lights flickered and dimmed, crackling as the current running through them waned. Key looked up, alarmed. "What's going on?"

"Storm outside. Vale says it's a bad one. Wind must have hit something."

There was a series of three soft taps on the door.

Jing levered himself out of the chair with a hearty sigh,

then opened the door to allow Cal and Vale in. Next to the door was an intercom; he pushed a large button on it and held it down for several seconds.

"Key!" Vale plowed past Cal and shoved two sweaty glass bottles at Jing before hustling over to Key's bedside, her evening gown flowing around her. She grabbed onto the bed rail, and Key's mouth dropped open at the sight of the scandalous cut of the neckline. Ancestors, it was practically to Vale's stomach. Heat rolled up Key's neck.

"Who am I?"

"Valerian IV," Key replied immediately, unable to take her eyes off Vale. Saints, she was stunning, even with the swelling on the left side of her face. "Guardian. What are you *wearing*?"

Vale's red-tinted lips went tight before Key could add a compliment. Key groaned inwardly. Anything short of effusive praise for Vale would be perceived as an insult.

Vale went on, curt. "Nothing. Who are you?"

"Kiana Strade, hunter. That's not nothing. That's beauti—"

"Do you know where you are?"

Key's attention went momentarily to Jing, who had popped the cap off one of the bottles. It hissed at the violation. "I must be at the institute. In the med wing."

Vale sagged with visible relief and began undoing Key's restraints. "Thank the spirits you're okay."

Key flexed her fingers and toes as her hands and feet were freed, then propped herself up on arms that felt about as sturdy as matchsticks, doing her best to avoid being stuck further with the IV needle. "One of those sodas is for me, I presume?"

Vale got a hand on her back and pushed, helping. "Yes. Jing said you'd need it."

There was another clink and hiss as Cal pried off the cap with a bottle opener before giving it to Vale.

Footsteps sounded in the hall, and a moment later, a sturdy, middle-aged man of unimpressive height with a dark, well-trimmed beard strode into the room, a clipboard tucked under his arm. "Good, patient's awake. Lucid?"

"Yes," Vale said.

He brought out the clipboard and wrote something on it.

"Thanks for taking the extra time to do this for us, Dr. Arman," Cal said. "You really didn't have to come back in, and during a storm too."

"No, no, it's fine, I was on call. Besides, Genevieve is still here and might not go home tonight." He barked a laugh. "As long as I don't beat her at her own game, I'm doing okay. Key, we'll get the rest of the protocol finished and you can head home."

Vale turned to Cal. "Kit, please."

Key swallowed. "Kit?"

"Yeah. You told me the pocket in this dress is . . ." Vale dropped her eyes to the bed. "Never mind. Cal's pocket was bigger. Cal?"

"Here," he said, bringing out a familiar mycoleather case.

"Thanks." Vale opened the case, withdrawing the needle, the pen, a tab, a wipe, and a card. She scribbled on the card label, her penmanship uneven and malformed as a result of learning cursive later than her peers. Finally, she tore open the package of wipes and cleaned the tip of Key's pointer finger. "See me."

Compelled, Key answered, "You are seen."

"Hear me."

"You are heard." Key curled her lip at the sting of the needle.

Vale touched the tab to the ruby-red drop welling from Key's finger. "Remember me."

"You are remembered."

From across the room, Jing shook his head. "Of course you'd use a responsorial as an anchor."

"You don't?" Key put her soda on the nightstand, then flung the blanket off herself, stopping at the sight of her finery. She looked from her trousers to Vale's dress, her questions once again ready to burst the dam. Why did they match? How much time had passed between her last recorded mind state and now? What sort of memory was it that necessitated a reintegration? What happened to her? What *happened* to her?

Jing snorted. "No. Why would we? We just do a codeword."

Key squeezed the tip of her finger. "You're supposed to have an anchor."

"You'll find," Jing said as he passed his soda to Cal, "that in this profession, not every corner is a necessary one. Don't tell Genevieve, Dr. Arman."

Dr. Arman cocked one silver-threaded eyebrow, amusement written across the brown-skinned planes of his face.

"Ready to go home?" Vale picked up the soda and held it out. "Wait. Jing, why do *you* need a soda?"

He smirked. "I wanted one and didn't want to get it myself. Dr. Arman, is Key done with the IV?"

Dr. Arman angled his way past Cal and Vale to inspect the bag. "Eh, sure. That should be enough. One second." He set down his clipboard and opened the drawer of the nightstand, taking out an adhesive mycelium bandage and a set of fresh latex gloves. He donned the gloves and then, with sure hands, clamped the IV line, removed the tape on Key's elbow, pulled out the needle, and bandaged the site.

"You're all set," he said to Key. "Vale, if you give the specimen to me, I'll get it to the registrar. Be free!"

Key gave Dr. Arman a smile as she swung her legs off the side of the bed, testing her weight against solid ground before standing. Cal offered his arm, and Key leaned on him gratefully as the group left the room. Jing led the way, setting a brisk pace through nondescript hallways until they reached the main artery of the medical floor. Dr. Arman split from the group at that point, heading toward the nearest stairwell to the archives.

"Vale, will you tell me what's happening?" Key let go of Cal and dropped back until she was side by side with Vale. "I'm still really confused."

"Later." Vale stared straight ahead. "I want to get back first."

"At least tell me what day it is."

"Vale, it's okay," Cal said. "She's allowed to know that. It'll help her be less upset. Key, it's Sixthday, waning third."

She stopped short. "So I lost two days?" Key exhaled, closing her eyes, thinking back. It could not have been two days between diving at the magnolia house and waking up in the clinic. It didn't feel like two days. It should have felt like two days. Whatever hole the reintegration had created had been sewn shut by an expert hand, the seam invisible.

"Yes," Vale replied.

"What else happened?"

"Not that much." But Vale kept looking straight ahead.

That couldn't be true. Even if Key didn't know that Vale's mother had, in Vale's words, whooped the lies outta her mouth, it didn't make logical sense. Vale wouldn't call for a reintegration unless something was drastically wrong.

"I'm going to see Genevieve," Key said abruptly. If Vale was going to be dodgy about answers, then she might as well get them from her mentor. "I bet she'll welcome the excuse to stop working. Jing, did you say something about a car?"

"Yep," he called from up ahead, where he was poking the up button for the elevator. "Your mother offered."

Does she know about my reintegration? Key straightened, her resolve firming. "Jing, why don't you take Vale and Cal and send a gram to my mother to let her know we're returning soon. I'm going to convince Genevieve to go home before she gets trapped here."

"No, I'd rather go with you," Vale said.

"I won't be but a minute." Key forced herself to smile at Vale. The elevator doors yawned open, and the group shuffled in. Key got to the panel first, hitting the buttons for subfloor one and the lobby. "And, be honest: Do you really want to see Genevieve?"

Vale's instant scowl gave her away.

Key laughed, the moment of levity a bright spark in the darkness.

"I should still go with you," Vale muttered.

"I'm just going to nag Genevieve to stop working. You don't need to watch me embarrass her. I'll meet you all outside the front?"

"Only if you find some bricks to put in Vale's pockets." Jing grinned, signaling that it was a joke, but he wasn't wrong. The wind had wings and claws in Asheburg, and it wouldn't hesitate to pluck Vale up and bear her away. Even Key had experienced moments of terrifying weightlessness during particularly bad storms. "Vale, sugar, sweetness, remember that I would hold on to you."

"We'll wait inside the front doors," Cal said, and it wasn't lost on Key how he slotted himself between Jing and Vale. They were in an enclosed space, after all. "And I'd hold on to you too, Vale."

"Thanks," she said, sarcastic. Her face was sullen as she addressed Key. "Don't take too long. You're probably exhausted, and you should be resting at home."

It was true. The energy she'd garnered from the soda was dissipating, and each sluggish step she took burned through more of it. Key lifted her hand in brief farewell as she exited the elevator, drew a deep breath, and set out for Genevieve's office.

The door was closed. From behind it, Key heard the muted clacking of the typewriter. She raised a fist, rapping her knuckles against the door in brusque, staccato knocks.

A few moments later, Genevieve opened the door, barefoot. It was clear that she was at the end of a long workday; her hair was escaping its customary chignon in tufts; she was down to shirtsleeves, which had been uncuffed and rolled to her elbow; and her pants were rumpled. A pair of silver-and-garnet earrings in the shape of the blood chalice rested on her desk, and to the right of the furniture, a pair of red pumps lay toppled over.

"Kiana," she said, her voice subdued. Even without her heels, Genevieve remained imposing, despite Key being a full two inches taller and broader in the shoulders. "I trust you're well?"

"Yes, thank you. I'm well." Bulling into the situation would get her nowhere. Key summoned another smile and laced her words with warmth. "The storm is getting worse. Dr. Arman thinks you're going to spend the night on your chaise again, and I'm here to prove him wrong."

"I'm planning to leave in a minute. Thank you for checking in." Genevieve smiled in return, though it didn't touch the top half of her face. "Was there anything else you needed?"

"Might I come in?" Key asked in lieu of an answer. Genevieve might have given the impression she was about to go, but "in a minute" in Asheburg could be anywhere from an actual minute to an hour, several days, or years.

Genevieve lifted an eyebrow. "What's the issue? I thought you were well."

Key inhaled, held it, blew it out. "I just had some questions. About my reintegration."

Genevieve hmmed, but retreated from the door. "That's something I can't comment directly on, but all right."

Key entered and shut the door behind her, taking a few seconds to gather her thoughts. "Genevieve, I've always done good work for you, right?"

"Undoubtedly so." Genevieve walked over to her chaise longue and plopped onto it with a sigh. Lamplight gleamed off the surface of the revolver on the shelf behind her head. "Why do you ask?"

"My dives on record all have significant finds. I'm a reliable hunter for the museum."

"You are, but I'm not understanding what you're getting at. What's the real question?"

Key spoke without hesitation. "What memory caused my reintegration?"

There was a tangible pause from Genevieve. "That's against protocol. You know I can't tell you that information."

"Then can you tell me who you're assigning my file to?"

Genevieve's green eyes flashed as she tilted her head. "No. You don't need to trouble yourself with the file going forward. It's a matter of confidence anyway."

"It was important enough to get me reintegrated. I never need reintegration." Key stepped forward. "I've done this work for you for two years. What was so strong that it needed to happen? What am I missing?"

Genevieve frowned. "Kiana, you know better than most that the significance of a memory is not measured along the same scale as the strength of a memory. Plenty of strong memories are emotionally important to us but historically insignificant."

"I'm secure in my identity. I've always been able to separate me from the memories I'm diving into, no matter how strong they are."

"The weakest memory is, more often than not, the most significant one." Genevieve continued, her tone hardening. "And the strong ones are best left to reintegration before they cause you to hallucinate, or worse. You've been through all of this in the academy; you don't need me to explain it to you."

Key scowled, taking a line from Vale's book. "You're right, I don't. But I want to know what got me reintegrated. What if I found something significant?"

"The significance of it is not worth your mind, or worse, your life."

Key rubbed her thumb and forefinger together until her skin creaked, recalling again the transition between the magnolia house and the clinic. It was too smooth. "I've never brought you anything insignificant or throwaway, Genevieve. Why would this be my first time?"

"Why wouldn't this be your first time?" Genevieve countered. "Kiana, I know you're proud of your record. *I'm* proud of your record. But that doesn't mean that you can't find duds. They won't feel like duds because of how emotional they are, but after review, it turns out that they are."

"After review," Key said. "So you don't know yet."

"I do know," Genevieve replied, exasperated. "Kiana, I think you need to rest. Your disorientation is obviously causing you to be belligerent. Has Valerian filled in your blanks?"

"No." Key did her best not to sound surly. "We haven't had the time. She keeps putting me off. She says the storm outside is bad, so she wanted to get me home."

"That's a perfectly reasonable argument and I don't see why you should delay further, or why either of us should."

"You said you do know about the significance," Key said, not moving, holding doggedly onto her argument. "Does this mean that you're going to review what I brought in?"

"Kiana, even if I did, I couldn't share the results with you in case of adverse effects. You know the procedures. Significant or not, you're no longer working on this memory. This is your first time being reintegrated, so I understand that you're frustrated. Feel free to discuss the experience with Jing at your leisure. But enough is enough."

"Are you going to review it?" Key's voice grew louder with insistence.

"I have already reviewed it!" Genevieve snapped, sitting straight up on her chaise longue. Key took a step back, shocked. Genevieve had never spoken to her in anger.

What had happened? What had she said or done? "As no one else could, because of how far you dove. The memory is not significant and does not meet any of the criteria for significance. Pressing me further only convinces me more that Valerian had the right of it regarding your reintegration. And that is all the information I am going to give you. Go home. Because I've known you for years and know what dreams you have, I've humored your questions and answered as thoroughly as I can, which is more than any other hunter would get from me. And it's because of that relationship that I'll tell you that if you go home right now, I won't hold any of this entitled behavior against you. You're confused and you aren't acting yourself. You've had a long journey and you're physically drained because of the reintegration."

Key knew a dismissal when she heard one. She pivoted on the ball of her foot, stung, and opened the door.

Only to find Vale on the other side, her dark eyes wide.

Key startled and swore. "Blood in the mouth, Vale!"

"You were taking too long," Vale said softly. "I came to . . ."

"Valerian?" Key heard the rustle of Genevieve's clothes as she rose, the shushing of the carpet as she walked toward the door. "Take Kiana home immediately."

"Yes, ma'am," Vale said.

"Good night, Genevieve." She spoke the courtesy on instinct.

"Good night, Kiana. I'll see you next week. Until then, I recommend you schedule some appointments with whichever therapist is on call."

Alarmed, Key responded, "Next week?" She spun to look at Vale. "You said I hadn't missed much!"

“Yes,” Genevieve said before Vale could open her mouth. “You’re suspended from fieldwork because you were so tardy. I trust Valerian to fill you in on the rest. Leave my door open when you go; I’m just going to get my things.”

“Come on.” Vale grabbed Key’s hand and drew her toward the elevator.

“Is that true?” Suspicion wormed into her gut. “I’ve been suspended from fieldwork?”

Vale lowered her eyes, her lashes forming a silky black screen. “We both are. We were a week late because you wanted to stay and dive. You should remember that part.”

“Yes,” Key affirmed. The certainty she’d felt before her dive returned, lodging in her chest, solid and sure. The ancestors had a purpose in guiding her to Crystal Grove, and she would discover why, reintegration or no. “It was a good site. Is that where I got this cut?” She indicated the flexible mycelium bandage in the crook of her elbow.

“Uh-huh.” The elevator dinged, the doors clunking quietly as they opened. “What did you ask Genevieve?”

Key eyed her guardian, wary. “What did you hear?”

“Only her yelling at you. I’ve never heard her do that before.”

“I don’t know why she reacted that way. Vale, what did I do? Did something happen in the last two days?”

Vale shook her head. “Other than us being late and getting punished for it, no.”

“I don’t understand why she acted that way, then.” Key slumped against the side of the elevator car as it ascended, but as soon as she did, the elevator arrived at the lobby. “I didn’t ask her anything bad. I asked her if the memory I found was significant.”

Vale exited the elevator first. "You know she can't tell you about that."

"Well, she did. She said it was insignificant."

"Then it's insignificant, and you can stop thinking about it."

"I can't," Key said. "The saints want me to do something about it."

"Key, just once, can you listen to people when they tell you to do something for your own good?" Vale whirled to face Key, anger in her black eyes. "I was starting to think I was too harsh on you, that I shouldn't have listened to Burdock or Dr. Wilcroft. Now I realize I should have listened to them much earlier. I don't know and I don't care if the saints are telling you things. You've been told no by Dr. Wilcroft, and I had to call for a reintegration, and you're still being a . . . a barnacle about it!"

Jing and Cal each turned to listen to the conversation from where they stood in the foyer. Key steadfastly kept her eyes on Vale.

There was a loud silence, far too large and long for Key's comfort. Vale was right, from her perspective. Genevieve had said no, and Key should listen. But Key's desire to know was knotted tight in her and could not be unpicked. "I'm sorry," she said eventually.

"No, you're not," Vale replied, and stalked off toward Jing.

ELEVEN

May caught me drawing the same magnolia over and over during Lanelle's resifix induction. It's been decades since that dive, and I've had nothing intrusive in years. I've passed every test May gave me, yet the tree continues flowing from my pencil. Mershon noticed and is annoyed at me, as is his right as Lanelle's husband. He thinks I'm ashamed of my daughter because she did not follow me to the museum. The truth is it doesn't matter. I won't drive her away. I've already lost one child. I won't lose another.

—Journal of Aurissa Strade,
retired hunter for the Museum of Human Memory

THE STORM BLASTED THE CITY THROUGH THE NIGHT AND INTO the next morning, when Key awoke to a surly, mottled sky. Without the sun marking the time, she drifted in and out of sleep until finally, unable to lie prone any longer, she left the cocoon of her bed, sour in body and spirit.

Prayer would help. She went to the low altar beneath the windows of her room and dragged her kneeler out, settled her knees on it, and bowed her head, clasping her hands. But her rattled mind refused to focus, the standard prayer slipping from her grasp over and over.

Not significant. The thought dwelled, nestled beside the place where there should have been a skip in her memory. Her recollection of events remained unbroken, as smooth as the finest satin despite their incongruity. *Not significant.* That couldn't be true, even if Genevieve had verified the memory herself. Whatever Key had found at Crystal Grove could not be insignificant. The reintegration had not taken from her the gut feeling, her beaconlike certainty that the saints would guide her to a discovery. And her gut always pointed true north.

The empirical evidence supported her theory. In school, she was correct so often that some of her classmates jokingly called her an answer key. At temple, her visions were too clear and too vivid to be inaccurate. She was blessed, and that had been proven by the hundreds, if not thousands, of memories she had retrieved, selecting the correct one swiftly and without hesitation. If that was not the work of the ancestors, what was it? What else could explain her conviction, her lack of doubt?

But, like Key, Genevieve, too, was always right, and she did not have the saints to validate her.

They could not both be right on this, though Key understood as a student of history that truth in stories was an illusion, a trick of the light. There were as many truths as there were angles. Significance changed depending on the storyteller, which meant Key could call the memory significant if she couched it in the correct terms. But the museum had a rubric in place for just this situation.

Key had her faith on her side; Genevieve had facts and experience. Key was born into it as her mother and her mother's mother were, born to memory dive the way a fish is born to swim. She did not know how to do anything else. Genevieve was talented and hardworking, driven to succeed as if she were dogged by wolves. She was more disciplined than anyone else and had spent time honing her craft until it gleamed sharp and keen and incisive, capable of cutting through time to buried memories. But Genevieve had not been chosen by the saints. She was the one who had to be wrong. Had to be.

Because you're righteous and blessed and you've never been told no.

Discomfited at Jing's words and stung by her inability to pray, Key rose, telling herself the ancestors would prefer she not come to them with an empty stomach. She dragged herself into and out of the bathroom, then shuffled around her room, first hanging up her jumpsuit—there was a visiting card in the pocket from Rocket, and that she placed on the bureau—then dressing herself in soft, breathable trousers and a loose sleeveless shirt that accentuated the lines of her shoulders. She wrapped her hair with a colorblocked silk scarf of Terry's design and, after a moment spent inspecting herself in the mirror, added a pair of silver hoop earrings. A resifix, according to her mother, could not look sloppy, not even for a private, casual meal.

She went to her drafting table to get her journal and a pencil to occupy her as she ate, realizing only after searching for a minute that her journal was at the museum, confiscated as part of the reintegration process. Key picked up a half-used sketchpad instead, ignoring the sheets of paper beneath it, frowning at how it had been moved while she was gone. It must have been the cleaning staff, though they had instructions not to disturb her room when she was away.

The breakfast nook was deserted when she arrived, but the Strades' chef was in the kitchen, already preparing lunch. Key tiptoed in, poured herself coffee from the bottom of the pot, snagged the last pastry out of the basket, then returned to the nook, glancing at the barometer stationed outside as she took a seat. The mercury in it looked like how she felt: drained and shuddering, huddled in a tight heap at the bottom.

She drank slowly and massaged the bruises ringing her arms, each stab of pain a reminder of what she had lost. She must have fought the reintegration. There could be no other conclusion given the state of her body, given how fatigued and pale Vale looked last night as she sat in Key's room for the debrief, at some remove, lit by flickers of lightning. Logically, Key trusted Vale to do her job, to make the tough decisions even if Key herself did not agree. This was the pact hunters and guardians entered into, and until recently, Key thought it fairly reasonable.

But she was exceptional. An exception. She was chosen; she was blessed. The violence Vale and the other guardians kept sharpened and within easy reach would not be turned upon Key. She had thought mistakenly, hubristically, that she would listen to Vale when it counted. That she wouldn't ever need a reintegration because she was uniquely chosen by the ancestors and thus afforded special protections. Knowing she was incorrect on both assumptions was enough to make Key lose her footing and question what she knew about herself and her career.

Not significant. Her eyes stung. Key turned her attention outside before her composure broke, observing the wind tearing fractal edges into the clouds, listening to intermittent shocks of rain as she ate. All was still inside, but the air was charged and ready, full of potential like a pendulum hanging at the top of its swing. Key was glad for a house as large as hers, with space enough to separate many people, with enough old artifacts on display that the atmosphere had no choice but to take on the reverent hush of a museum.

She could be alone as the storm broke itself over the city. Key opened her sketchbook, flipping past pages of figure studies and five-minute sketches. One page was an ink doodle of Vale's face, drawn from memory. Key turned past it as quickly as she could, but it was too late. Her mind went back to the debrief in her room, Vale curled up tight as a pill bug on the drafting stool as she spoke, the wind screaming past the windows, expressing Key's horror at her reintegration in a way she could not. A resifix did not scream, and neither did a Strade.

Her sketchbook. Key refocused, flicking through pages until she found a fresh one, moving aside her coffee cup and empty plate to create room. Daily journaling and art therapy were staples at the academy, and Key was in the habit of practice. She picked up her pencil and stared at her paper, protecting her space as staff set down mini plantain frittatas, a dish of lightly dressed bitter greens, a small bowl of buttery cornmeal porridge, and a plate of cut papaya. *Don't think. Just draw.*

Her pencil hovered over the paper, the tip of it hesitant as if it, too, shared her lack of faith.

All it took to start, she reminded herself, was a single line.

Key swept her pencil across the bottom third of the page, and suddenly it was the edge of a wooden table. The image formed instantaneously, and the fear fell away. To give perspective, Key corralled the space with countertops, a stove with a hood on the left, a sink on the right, cabinets on either side. A window in front of the sink let in plenty of daylight.

Her hand moved fluidly as she laid long lines down, describing the slats of the hardwood floor, all converging at the far wall where there was a door. Back to the table she went to fill out details. A large knot in the wood, here. A chunky ceramic mug, hand thrown, glaze gathered into bumps on the handle, a spoon jutting from the surface of the tea like a branch in a stream, everything too hot to touch for now. The water had been boiling. Key's pencil traced the gauzy billows of steam as they rose.

The kitchen window hadn't been empty. Yes, there had been a stained-glass panel hanging there of a bull magnolia blossom in full bloom, snow-reflected sunlight shining green through the leaves. And, seated in front of her, a man old enough to be her grandfather, with hooded eyes and hair gone wispy and spectral, nasolabial folds pintucked down either side of his face. His mouth was set in a perpetual frown, though it was more from the effects of age than his actual temperament.

"Drink," he says.

Key reached for her coffee and slung a tepid mouthful back, then eyed the sketch. Her concentration broke at a clap of thunder, and the rain swelled with applause as she sat back in her chair, considering. Watercolors would match her vision perfectly.

Galvanized, she speared several chunks of papaya with a fork and crammed them into her mouth, then gathered her sketchbook and pencil and mug and hustled toward the grand staircase. As she passed by the open door of her mother's study, however, she heard her name.

Key stopped, her knee bending to absorb her forward momentum, and turned. "Yes, Mama?"

"The radio says the last of the storm bands are passing through, ancestors be thanked. We won't have to cancel Saintsday service. Go ready yourself. It's time you showed your face at temple."

"But—"

"No arguments." Her mother eyed her sternly from behind her desk, the way she used to when Key was a teenager. "I plan to leave soon, once I finish this administrative work and send the news station a gram. I have already notified Valerian. I expect both of you to be waiting by the car in fifteen minutes' time."

"I was about to start painting."

Lanelle shook her head. When she spoke, her tone was final. "When you return, you can. Fifteen minutes, Kiki."

Key went up the grand staircase and back to her room, her mouth pinched at the sudden change in plans. She approached her drafting table and set her mug beside it, then paused, gazing at the sheets of paper that had been under her sketchpad.

There were three pencil drawings of the exact same scene: a young magnolia growing next to a three-story house with a covered front porch. More buildings could be seen in the near distance. Key shivered, the skin of her arms tightening into goose bumps. She had no recollection of drawing any of these, yet they were unmistakably her drawings, her point of view, her style despite the sloppiness of the sketches, the lines of them wild and frenzied. She laid them next to one another for inspection, noting silvery-gray smudges strewn across each paper. With a sinking feeling, Key turned her right hand to look at the side. The light caught on a matching silvery-gray sheen.

She must have drawn the pictures overnight.

Her breath came faster, and her knees went weak, dropping her onto her drafting stool. Images poured through her mind by the thousands: faces and voices; sunrises and sunsets and bitter, starless nights; rivers and sands and bloated corpses; bloody, still babies and smoking pyres a dozen feet high. Each memory fragment whipped by as if propelled by the storm winds outside. Key pressed the heels of her palms against her eyes in an attempt to keep the deluge within, and, for a moment, as heat seared her eyeballs and wetness seeped from them, she feared her brain had melted and was leaking out.

The pieces assembled themselves one by one as she huddled, beset. Her last dive southeast of Crystal Grove. The abandoned compound with the fully mature magnolia. The sketch of that same magnolia, younger and still growing beside a freshly whitewashed house, a scene from the past. A woman, her throat opened by a knife, followed by a man with lank brown hair calling her a thief. Vale wiping her face clean of blood as she led the way to Crystal Grove Station.

It was not possible to remember things she had been forced to forget. The specimen used had been from three days ago. Memories swelled, overflowing their banks, flashes of recollection spreading like water around the bases of reeds. The man in the camouflage jacket, his heels scraping against the dirt. Vale's terrible beauty, her delicate features rendered harsh and stark under a heavy, merciless hand. Vale, her back to Key, trembling as Key undid her dress hook by hook. Key had almost leaned in, imagining her lips against the curve of Vale's neck, held in check only by the advice she'd given Cal yesterday not to push.

The reintegration, Key came to realize, had failed.

The shaking started as a tiny tremor, growing and growing until Key was shivering violently. It was all she could do to slip from her stool and curl into the fetal position on the floor as she tried, failed, tried again to process. The reintegration had *failed*. What did that mean? What was she to do?

For the first time, she did not know.

Saint Aurissa, Key begged. *Gramma, help me.* There had to be a mistake somewhere, or she was remembering a dream as reality. She flipped through her memories again, searching for where the reintegration had to have happened, where her brain would have smoothed over the hole of her missing time. In the academy, the instructors had likened memory loss to expertly mended rips in a piece of fabric rather than sequences with patches of static or stretches of nothing. What was unremembered simply did not exist. But there was no invisible seam made visible through the application of logic, no sudden transition from one memory to another. She could recall Genevieve's raised voice from last night with the same clarity as she could recall Vale's singing on the train from three days ago.

Neither was there any help from the ancestors. Ten heartbeats went by as Key waited for the perfect memory to surface, one that would answer all her questions. Then twenty. Then thirty, forty, fifty. And then she stopped counting.

Key turned her face into the floor once the clarifying vision refused to appear.

She, Kiana Strade, had undergone reintegration, a process guaranteed to succeed on anyone with the right sensitivity—and it had failed.

No one in history had ever failed to reintegrate. Or, Key corrected herself as the floor skewed and rolled beneath her, no one had ever recorded an instance of a failed reintegration. It was possible reintegration had failed on a hunter and a guardian had to do what was necessary to stop them. There were stories of hunters who needed reintegration and couldn't or didn't get it, whose personas had been eaten by retrieved memories or changed irrevocably by something in the dive. Ina had been fortunate not to end up like Merle Aviss, who was killed by his guardian, Meadowsweet III, after he'd poisoned her with deathcaps. She later died.

Key pushed herself upright, her hands trembling. Jing's words from the previous night rang in her ears. *If you need to keep it from Vale, keep it from Vale.* She could not know. If Key couldn't be reintegrated, all of Vale's choices would vanish and reappear as a single path ending in the termination of Key's life. Neither could her mother know. Lanelle would not hesitate to flex the power of her connections to pull Key from the museum and everything she'd always wanted to install her in the temple.

If you need to keep it from Vale . . .

Key grabbed for the edge of her desk and hauled herself upright, pausing for a second to let the dizziness pass. She scooped the top sketch off the pile and tore it in half, the sound as harsh and ragged as her breathing, lined the halves up and tore them again. She repeated the motion, tearing and tearing until pieces of the sketch drifted like snow from her hands. With a sob, Key dove for her trash can and swept the bits of paper off her table and into it, then fell to her knees to pick the stray bits off the floor.

She got up and was about to take the second drawing, but her sketchbook caught her attention. Key grabbed for it and opened it, almost ripping pages out of it in her haste to get to the drawing from breakfast. Her stomach tightened, knocking up against the bottom of her ribs. This, too, had to be from her dive.

Suddenly, the image of the kitchen popped into three dimensions, springing out of her sketchbook and in front of her eyes. Key slapped the sketchbook onto her other papers, covering her mouth with her hand, swallowing air between each sharp breath through her nose. Her heartbeat kicked, frenzied. On the kitchen table in front of her was the mug, steam snaking up in tendrils from the surface of the tea. Before her was her grandfather, his brown eyes growing a rheumy film that did nothing to lessen the intensity of his stare.

"Drink," he says.

The first cup had been awful. The powder her grandfather uses for the concoction forms clumps, and no matter how much she stirs, the insides remain dry.

"Key?"

"Nothing happened," she replies.

He pushes the cup toward her. "You just need more. The blessing does not come right away."

She ought to ask what the powder is. Her grandfather has never said, only that it's a secret formulation of his own making.

"Key!"

"Can't we do it later?" She'd rather be outside shoveling snow than here beneath her grandfather's deep-set, wild-rimmed eyes.

"Can't we do what later? Hello, Key?"

She startled at the touch on her shoulder, jolting so hard against the desk that a coffee can of colored pencils tipped over the edge. It crashed to the floor, sending pencils clattering and bouncing. Key turned, dread in her throat, to see Vale, her brow creased with worry.

"Whoa! Key, what's wrong?"

Key fumbled for the edge of the table, needing something, anything to hold on to before her knees failed her. Did Vale have a knife on her? She always had a knife on her. *If you have to keep it from Vale, keep it from Vale.* "Nothing."

Vale's disbelief was plain on her face.

"I was . . . wondering how many remembrance ceremonies I'll have to do at temple. You were right about how bad the storm is. And the houses in the department outside the city aren't built that well."

More silence.

"You just scared me, that's all."

Vale's brow went from creased to knitted. "You're *gray*. You look like you're ready to pass out. You know what, you shouldn't be up and around."

"I'm really—" Key swallowed, then flinched as Vale touched her arm, right on top of a bruise.

"Sorry," Vale muttered, dropping her eyes to the floor. She took Key's hand instead. "Sit on your bed, at least."

If she left the drafting table, Vale might find the sketches. Key shook her head and lowered herself onto her stool. "I'm okay where I am."

"I don't think you're okay. Clear skies or not, you should be resting at home." Vale let go, then kneeled to scoop up the pencils and deposit them in the can.

Key watched her, her stomach coiling tighter and tighter. Outside, the wind moaned. "I'm," she started, and then her mind blanked as the urge to run gripped her. She forced herself past it. Her thoughts returned, reticent. "I was thinking about last night."

Vale looked up, her fingers clutched around a handful of pencils. Her hair was braided but damp, and there was a glow about her, likely from a shower after morning training with Cal. He and Jing had stayed overnight once the weather worsened. "Did you want to talk about it?"

"Are you still mad at me?"

"Little bit, but Cal and I had a chat earlier and he told me to be gentle with you, since it's your first reintegration and you always acted like you were too holy to need one. He said I should be gentle with myself too." Vale snorted, her opinion on Cal's statement clear.

"He's right." If anyone deserved gentleness, it was Vale, even if she always misread Key's consideration of her as pity or condescension.

"Whatever. It ain't about me right now. Do you need to talk about last night?"

Key hesitated, her breath slowing as if her body were being squeezed. How much did her own life weigh when she had to hold it in front of her? "As a guardian or as a friend?"

Vale stood, putting the pencils into the can with a clatter, reaching past Key to place the can back on the desk. She smelled of the orange blossom soap the staff kept the house stocked with, but on her, the scent was enhanced somehow. Better. Alluring. What an awful time to be thinking about Vale that way.

"Both?" Vale said.

"Choose one." She'd let the decision rest with Vale. Key would tell Vale if she chose to be a friend. She would not if Vale chose to be a guardian.

Vale looked conflicted. She lifted a hand, hovered her fingers over the discolored skin of Key's arm. "My gut says friend," she murmured.

Key's heart leapt. "I need help—"

"But my mind says guardian."

Key bit her sentence in half, her teeth clicking together. Her chest wrenched with pain.

"What do you need help with?"

Dully, Key said, "Nothing."

Vale's demeanor shifted to closed, wariness etching a frown onto her face. "It'd be best for you to stay at home, but since I can't tell your mom no, it's a good thing you're headed to temple. You need to pray. You're really off."

"I'm off because I was reintegrated last night and I don't know what's going on."

"I'm not violating protocol by telling you. You're just gonna have to get over what Dr. Wilcroft said to you. You wanted me to choose between being a friend or a guardian, and I wanted to give you a chance as a friend. But, like I said, I'm still a little mad. You need a guardian."

"No, I need a friend." Key almost admitted it then. *Reintegration didn't work. Vale, help me. Help me, please.*

"You want a friend. You *need* a guardian. Be like Jing. Let go of what happened last night. You should get ready for service." Vale's eyes fell upon Key's open sketchbook. "What's that?"

Chills traveled up and down her spine. "Nothing. Just some . . . art therapy. Something new I thought I might work on. I was about to get some watercolors when you came in here."

Vale's expression told Key she didn't believe a single word. Yet she said, "Painting should help you, yeah. You'll have time for it after temple. Storm's leaving as fast as it came in."

Key tried for lightheartedness. "Is that your forecast, or the radio forecast? Mama says you should have been a meteorologist."

Vale softened, but only a touch. "Radio. Long waves. Are you sure you don't need help?"

"I'm sure." The help Key had wanted was a guarantee that Vale wouldn't immediately drive a knife into her upon revelation of her failure to reintegrate. She hadn't hesitated with Ina, even that close to the medical floor. She'd consigned Ina's life to the ancestors faster than she could draw breath.

No, asking for Vale's help was futile. There was only one thing to do. The answer to Key's questions was ever the same, regardless of the lack of clarity. She would turn to the ancestors. And she could do it at temple.

Vale folded her lips in, then said, "Okay. You should get ready to leave."

"You don't have to come. I know it's not your favorite place."

"Resifix's orders. And I just said you need a guardian. So I'm gonna be that for you." Vale moved toward the door. "Even if you'd rather me be a friend."

STRENGTHENING SUNLIGHT FILTERED in through the stained-glass triptychs set around the base of the temple dome, covering the aisles and pews with washes of tepid color. Though it was well into second service on a Saintsday, there would be few initial petitioners after a storm bold enough to force the river to rise and the trees to relinquish their branches to the rooftops below.

Reflexively, Key breathed in the scent of pine, then looked up at the stained-glass magnolia flower crowning the dome, surrounded by frescoes depicting the ancestors blessing the devout and granting them the miracle of memory diving. As a child, she'd loved gazing at the paintings, and when she hadn't been dreaming of attending the academy, she'd dreamed of becoming a fresco artist, traveling from temple to temple to paint her visions on the walls.

The familiarity of the temple brought her no comfort, only a burgeoning anxiety. Key walked down the wide central aisle of the nave, tension buzzing in her like two ends of an electrified wire about to touch. Vale walked beside her, her face blank, her demeanor gone neutral and stony.

As they approached the chancel, Vale detached herself from Key's side to slip into a pew, leaving Key to finish the walk alone, her mother in front, the coterie in back.

And though Key had not acted differently in any way, it still seemed that their eyes lingered a little too long on her, like the ancestors had whispered the truth in their ears and they were waiting patiently for Key's wavering faith to be exposed. If the fine hairs on the back of her neck wasn't already plastered to her skin from the humidity, they would have risen.

Her mother's main coterie was composed of three disciples: Zerua, androgynous and heavy-boned, their waist-length brown hair tied back simply, their small, wide-set eyes revealing nothing of their thoughts; Sima, the youngest of the group, an academy graduate from a few years past, though it was easy to mistake her for a student with her smooth, unblemished dark brown skin; and Wynne Jean, blocky and straw-haired, the longest in service, who should have been leading her own temple by now but was still assisting Lanelle with basic administrative work.

Her mother's coterie served her mother and only her mother, and a rivalry thick with resentment lay between them and Key, which only added to the distress she was trying to defer. She couldn't blame them. There was no question of who would be the next head resifix, and if Key were starting from the bottom, she would also dislike the heir presumptive for being a generational talent who felt called elsewhere.

Key halted at the head of the nave, training her gaze on the stone cartouche crowning the circular arch that stood sentinel behind the divination pool. The temple, shaped much like a blood chalice, belled out at the front of the nave, and along the curved stone walls, floor-to-ceiling relic shelves had been built. Every compartment had in it a knickknack or family keepsake, and at intervals in front of the shelves were altars set with matches and votive candles and shallow disks of charcoal atop slabs of rock. Small wooden boxes, plain and undecorated, held rocks of pine resin incense.

On either side of the raised divination pool occupying the chancel were large busts of Key's grandmother and great-aunt, their painted faces serene with devotion, circles drawn in pine ash over their foreheads. Larger altars with kneelers were placed in front of the busts. Key's mother struck a match and lit a votive on each altar, calling the ancestral spirits to come forth and bear witness as she did.

Key held herself tightly, head bowed and eyes closed, listening as her mother spoke the opening prayer. Footsteps shuffled, leading away from Key in all directions as the disciples made the high temple ready to receive its petitioners. The grand double doors would be opened wide; the incense refilled in boxes; the candles that had burned down to their bases replaced. Key remained where she was, her breathing shallow, then opened her eyes and looked to her grandmother's portrait for a measure of relief. The distress would no longer be deferred.

Prayer was the answer. Prayer was always the answer.

Key approached her grandmother's altar, then used a match to light a charcoal disk, gathering her thoughts. She blew on the disk to help it along, stirring it to yellow-orange life, then opened the wooden box of incense and selected a decent-sized chunk. Her muscles started to relax in anticipation of the ritual she had performed her entire life. Here, in front of her grandmother's face, charcoal sparking before her, jewel-bright patches of stained-glass light on the floor, her mother's voice echoing in the nave, she would find her answer.

She lowered herself to her knees in front of the shrine, waiting for the disk to be completely gray, drawing in deep breaths through her mouth and releasing them from her nose, unable to quell fully what was vibrating in her like a plucked string. When the charcoal was ready, Key put the resin on. Smoke curled up from the incense, and the smell of pine needles rose, underlaid with the faint fresh earth and acridity of the blood chalice. She bowed her head and rested her elbows on the upper surface of the kneeler, closing her eyes to better immerse herself.

"I am seen," she murmured, the prayer keeping her grounded as the world began to shift around her. "I am heard. I am remembered. I am sanctified."

She waited out the initial disorientation of the incense. Once the shifting stopped and her body was as the smoke around her, she slipped into the slow whirlpool of her combined memories, allowing herself to be carried with them on the current. The right memory would appear before her, and she wouldn't have to search. That's how it always had been.

Saints, show me your presence. Give me a sign that you're still with me.

Key squeezed her eyes shut tighter, reaching for the sense of rightness that would guide her unerringly to the answer. Yet nothing came.

This was not abnormal, she assured herself. It was common to seek and not find, and that's why there were penitents in the pews day after day in the temple. And the ancestors themselves were not all-knowing. The fault lay with her for not asking the right question.

She lifted her head to her grandmother's face, the painting's expression unchanging.

"... her devotions," her mother said.

Key put her forehead to her hands, the effect of the blood chalice–laden incense still swirling in her veins, the smoke of it suspended in the air of the temple. She had gotten no real answers. Even the smallest question merited a flash of memory, but Key hadn't seen anything.

What did it mean? What did the absence of the ancestors and her failed reintegration mean for both her and her work? What did Crystal Grove have to do with it, and why, despite the silence, did she continue to feel that she was right about the importance of what she'd found?

"Wynne Jean," Key heard her mother say, "please start divinations. I need to speak with Kiana."

The whisk of long robes against the stone floor grew louder as her mother approached. "Kiana, a moment."

Key shut her eyes tight, the world moving around her like she was suspended in water. Or perhaps it was tea, and she was being stirred in like the powder. "I'm praying, Mama."

"Are you all right? You seem troubled."

"Nothing that prayer can't fix."

"Come to my office." Lanelle's voice was perfectly smooth, as still as the surface of the divining pool. "I need to continue—"

"Miss Key?"

Key opened her eyes and twisted around. Elin Raymond stood behind Lanelle, partially leaned over to peer around Lanelle's body. He was the middle child of Amarene and

Lawson and had been a dutiful attendee at service for many years. He had matured since the last time Key had seen him, his body losing its lanky look and filling out, and a respectable beard covered his cheeks and jaw. His dark hair, once in braids, now was twisted into short locs. He held a tiny necklace of colorful beads cradled in his hands, and he offered them with a bow of his head.

"Wynne Jean is tasked with divinations today," Lanelle said.

"I'm so sorry, ma'am," Elin replied. "But I wanted—that is, I thought Miss Key would be the best match, and I prayed the storm would pass quick and she'd be here, and here she is!"

Key glanced at her mother, then Wynne Jean, whose thin lips were so compressed they'd turned white. She stood, gripping the kneeler, and faced Elin. "If the saints so decree, how can I do anything but listen to your request?"

"Thank you, Miss Key. I'm sorry if I've caused some trouble," he said.

Key donned her half smile easily. "That's all right, it's nothing we can't sort out. What do you ask of the ancestors?"

"Well, we just found out my big sister is in a family way," he said, and a grin broke across his face. He drew closer to Key and lowered his voice. "None of us can agree on any names. I want to be the one to give the best name. I was hoping you could intercede for me, give me some suggestions. And when it's time, have a Witnessing for the book."

"I'd be happy to intercede. The ancestors always give me an answer." She said it partly for Elin's ears and partly for her own, as if the statement was one of the affirmations

Genevieve would sometimes write for herself. Key was at temple. Of course she would receive answers. What caused the reintegration to fail? What was so significant—because it had to be—that it persisted through the procedure upon which Jing pinned his mental health, the procedure that allowed the memory hunting industry to endure?

"Your dedication is admirable, Elin," Lanelle said, then addressed Key. "Come see me once you've finished Elin's divination." She moved down the line that had formed to the next petitioner.

Wynne Jean placed herself next to Key, directing a half smile of her own at Elin. "That's a lovely idea, and very thoughtful of you. But Key has just gotten back from her trip, and she must be quite tired. I'd be happy to do the intercession on her behalf."

"Oh, no, thank you, ma'am," Elin said. "I appreciate it. I know Miss Key must be exhausted, but it's been a couple of days, and I was hoping she'd be the one to divine the names, since I wanted to go several generations back, not just to my grandparents."

Wynne Jean's smile went brittle.

"You cannot take from the chalice later."

"What?" Elin looked at Key, astonishment on his face.

"Just something . . ." Key cast about for an explanation, her skin flushing with sudden sweat. "It's something one of the ancestors used to say. Time is of the essence."

"Of course." Wynne Jean's voice had taken on a biting tone. "Miss Key, though she has yet to complete her novitiate, is the most blessed of us, and the ancestors speak through her."

"We are all blessed here. Even those of us who take years to complete our vows." Key kept her focus on Elin and took the necklace gently from him. Saints above, she had to get out of here. Having intrusive memories was one thing, but to have them in temple, in front of people, during service, would be a public relations nightmare for her mother. "I would be honored to divine names. To whom did this belong?"

Elin's gaze darted between Key and Wynne Jean for a second before he said, "It was my mother's baby necklace."

Key raised an eyebrow. "Did you get permission to bring this offering? I'd prefer not to be a dinner table discussion between your kin."

"Yes," Elin said quickly. "Ma knows I'm here."

"You'd best share the suggestions with her." Key kept her pleasant expression, though the thought of delving into Elin's ancestral memories sat poorly on her stomach. He was sweet natured, but the rest of his family was not. His great-uncle had been mean, his great-aunt not much better, and the two of them had thrown mean down the line. She hoped the memories retrieved from the necklace wouldn't be theirs. Many people had good folks in their families, but just as many had family members Key would cross a street to avoid, had she known them in their time.

"Thank you, Miss Key," Elin said, putting two fingers to his forehead.

"You are heard." Key touched her own forehead, swallowing saliva as a memory surfaced of Elin's great-aunt falling against a dining table, her cheek on fire, her heart swollen with rage. There was something cold and slim in her hand, a lance for her fury. "Elin," Key managed. "Why don't you schedule a Witnessing with Wynne Jean in the temple office? The calendar fills up fast, so it isn't a bad idea to set aside a date, even this early. I expect three days will be enough for the divination pool to return an answer for us, so please come back next week during divinations and see me."

Elin nodded. "Thank you, Miss Key."

Key pretended not to notice the glare Wynne Jean shot her once Elin's back was turned and called over Zerua. "Please record," she said to them, then gave the details before ascending the chancel and walking toward the divination pool. The scent of loamy earth greeted her, as did the instantly recognizable tang of the blood chalice. The pool was twice as wide as her father was tall, the perfect circle of it bordered almost completely with a planter, save for a notch where Key now knelt. Fruiting blood chalices in every stage covered the planter, taking on the look of bloody tumors, and between the chalices grew lumps of moss and sheaves of leafless needle orchids, their thin, pale stalks tipped in miniature petals of pink and purple. Each morning, a temple worker would soak up the guttation from the ripe chalices and prepare them for dives later in the day.

Key muttered a prayer to the ancestors as she moved the necklace in a circle three times over the water, then submerged it. In several days, new chalices would mature, bearing the memories of the relics she left today. That was slow compared to the museum's chalices, which had been bred to fruit overnight and yield higher concentrations of memory fragments.

And slower still were the chalices her grandfather had sown in the graveyard—

Her breath caught, and her hands burned, as if she'd wrapped them around a too-hot mug of tea.

Key bowed her head in her own prayer, her ears thundering with her rapid heartbeat, and asked once again for answers. For a guiding light. For reassurance.

Show me someone who has failed reintegration and lived.

Her knees were starting to go numb when a memory swam up, pausing in front of Key before enveloping her. She was in the compound with the magnolia and the house. Vale pricked her finger. And then there was a stretch of blackness, so blank and bleak that Key could not see anything in it.

This couldn't be correct. This wasn't what she wanted or needed. *Saint Aurissa, show me someone who has failed integration.*

Again, the memory presented itself to her. Key's concentration wavered, but she left the memory as quickly as she could and tried again. The memory returned a third time, and—

"Key?"

Her eyes snapped open, and when she turned to see who it was, her bloodless legs did not obey. Key grabbed for the edge of the planter before pushing herself up, wincing at the rush of pins and needles. Sima stood close by, her hands cupped around a tarnished spoon. "There's a line forming."

"Apologies. I was—having a strong experience." Key exhaled slowly, willing herself to calm down. "May they speak just as loudly to you as they did me."

She stepped away from the pool and toward the next penitent in line, her mind only half on her duty, bewildered and unsure of what to make of the messages the ancestors sent her. In response to her plea to show her their presence, there was emptiness. In response to the question about failing reintegration, there had only been her.

Perhaps that itself was the answer. Perhaps what she needed to do was reframe her point of view.

"Might I have a blessing, Miss Key?" the penitent said.

"Of course," Key replied. "You are seen."

"I rejoice in your sight."

"You are heard." Key had to go back to Crystal Grove to dive. She had to solve the mystery herself. She needed to return to the last place where her faith had sung in and through her, and it was there she would regain whatever she had lost. That was the message from the ancestors, loud and clear.

"My voice among many."

"You are remembered." Joyful energy surged through her. She knew what to do.

"I shall not want more."

"Be sanctified," Key said, lifting a hand to inscribe a circle in the air in front of the penitent's forehead. The next penitent—Lenny's sister-in-law—approached, wanting a benediction. Key granted it, but her mind was on the train schedule she and Vale had used to plan their trip to Crystal Grove. The trip lasted almost twenty-two hours; eighteen if taking the direct line between Asheburg and Sweetcreek. The direct left Asheburg only once a day and Key had already missed it. Calculations streamed through her head, each part of her itinerary flapping into place as if being displayed upon the arrivals board at the station. First, she'd have to check the radio to see if service was running on schedule. Second, to avoid arousing suspicion, she could not leave before dinner. It would take time to slip out one of the often-overlooked west wing entrances and walk to the station to purchase tickets, though, so Key would need to excuse herself early.

Another divination; another keepsake in her palm; another walk to the pool. Key's head whirled, and she looked up at the stained-glass magnolia set into the dome, thinking only of the kitchen and its cold winter light, the fresh snow beyond.

"Can't we do it later?"

No. She had to leave tonight. She'd pack once service was over, enough for a few days at most. The only problem with her plan was the guardian. Key couldn't take Vale, of course. Not after being forced into a reintegration, and not with their relationship already strained. And if Vale went with Key and Genevieve found out, she would terminate Vale's contract immediately and petition for an emergency revocation of Vale's guardian license. No, it was better to protect Vale by not bringing her. It was better to take this choice rather than the one that would endanger Vale's family finances.

Who would accompany her to the train station? All the staff answered to her mother and wouldn't keep a secret from her. But if she hired someone, someone unexpected but within the circle of her known contacts, who could hold privileged information—

Key, on her knees, lifted her head and looked at the portrait of her grandmother.

The imagine of a pristine white visiting card atop her bureau flashed into her mind's eye.

Cordelia. *Rocket.*

The ancestors had spoken.

Key would send a gram as soon as she could. Until then, she would occupy herself with the petitioners assembling in the temple. She would throw herself into her duties and pretend she was too busy to talk to her mother. And she would pretend that the searing touch of Vale's eyes upon her, watching her every move, wasn't the look of a hawk tracking its prey before the kill.

Three Years Ago

THE AUTUMN EQUINOX FESTIVAL IS VALE'S FAVORITE HOLIDAY, but she's missed it for the last seven years. No one in Asheburg really celebrates it except for those who've come from the eastern and southern coasts. In years past, Burdock has brought Vale to small gatherings where they light incense and sing and feast, but this year, when Vale knocks on his new office door, he opens it, his face drawn, eyes haggard, short hair unkempt.

"Burdock, are you okay?"

"Vale," he says, opening the door wider, gesturing for her to come in. He sounds exhausted, worn. "Had a long night and morning. I won't make it to the equinox."

On his desk, on top of an old, scratched-up blotter, is a container of spicy roasted groundnuts and a small bundle of sugarcane stalks tied together with twine. It's obvious Burdock had meant to bring the food to the party. Beside it is a newspaper, open to the middle section, where the stories of passing importance are printed. Black type corralled in small boxes crowds across the page, the headlines each vying for attention.

There are a few spots of dried water on the paper as well.

Vale scans the page, reading through headlines: LIGHTNING STRIKE BRINGS WILDFIRE; PRICES FOR GRAIN TO RISE; RACK AND RUIN. When she gets overwhelmed by the letters, she turns back to Burdock, who is standing in front of the massive map of the Spine on the wall, his hands clasped behind him, staring at a spot somewhere in the south.

"You should go without me," Burdock says to the map. "It's in the usual place."

"Won't be the same without you," Vale replies, settling herself into Burdock's creaky desk chair. She means it. The people at the potluck are from the coastal areas, and what brings them together is that they all celebrate the equinox—and they're all considered outsiders to Asheburg. Drifters. Even if that's not true of everyone because not everyone is from the south. But aside from broad traditions, like making sure to have a balance of salty and sweet food or singing ballads and entertaining late into the night, there's little they have in common.

Burdock's from a region nearest to the places Vale grew up, so he understands what the others do not. Building elaborate cairns, for example, or praying for lost spirits to be found, or playing round after round of stones. Back home, Vale's family would have brought a monetary donation and a keepsake to a resifix to have a binding ritual performed. The equinox is the best time to do it. Life and death are balanced, just like day and night.

"Appreciate you wanting to stay." When Burdock speaks, he lapses into his regional accent, his speech taking on the sway of a boat on the sea, the wideness of spaces scrubbed dead and bare by wind or fire or water. When he and Vale truly talk, they're nigh incomprehensible to most folks. Key has heard them do this once, and the amount of excitement she displayed convinced Burdock never to use his dialect around her again.

It's a private thing, he'd said. *Ain't for her and hers to have.*

He had meant, Vale understood, not Key specifically, but the people who would take a magnifying glass to their speech to inspect its construction, who would rip apart every stitch and seam until the language was in pieces and could no longer hold its own soul, then pin it up like a bug under glass and style themselves as experts. Burdock is a guardian at heart, same as Vale, and he wants to protect living things, not yield them to people or echoing hallways that would kill and dry and preserve. There's not much for him in Asheburg, so he's stingy with what he's got.

"Can't leave family." Vale pulls out a pocketknife. She slices through the twine holding the sugarcane together, picks one of the stalks, peels the end, and cuts it off. Then she pops it into her mouth and lets her teeth get to work, humming with happiness as sweetness cascades over her tongue. She's reminded instantly of herself and Bo and Elsie and Roland using the long stalks as swords until her father gently scolded them.

"So." Burdock finally comes over to the desk, grabbing a chair on the way, sitting catercorner from Vale. He groans as he slouches, like all his muscles have unionized and gone on strike. He reaches feebly for the container of groundnuts. Vale opens it, then slides it in his direction. "Last year at the academy. How are you feeling?"

"I don't know," Vale answers truthfully, whittling away more sugarcane stalk, cutting a piece for Burdock. "Like it's not real. Like I'll never get out of here. My classes are hard."

Burdock scoops a few nuts into his palm and tosses them into his mouth. "You're gonna finish," he says between crunches. "Admin already has their eye on you."

"I about failed history last year."

"And when I told you to forget the books, that history's the same as a family lay, you just gotta sing it—what happened after that?"

"I passed. Full marks."

"See?" Burdock scoffs. "Not your fault they don't know how your mind and culture work. Doesn't matter though; they won't let you fail, little sister. Got too much ridin' on your shoulders to let a student like you go. They can teach someone like Rocket everything in the book but they'll never teach her what you came with."

"Not being mean?"

Burdock barks a laugh, then covers his mouth, coughing. "Damn chili powder," he says once the fit has passed. "That too. I meant your instincts. Your willingness to fight. Your drive. Your principles."

"That's not gonna get me through the rest of the year," Vale says glumly, thinking of her practical psychiatric methods class.

"If you'd rather give up now, you can drop out and start taking contracts right away. Laurus would vouch for you. You could start small, take the easy ones."

"For the black market?" Vale shakes her head rapidly. "They got no insurance. Half of 'em look like stray dogs, anyway."

Burdock chuckles, though he sounds tired again. "That much is true. But if you did want to take off-book contracts, what would convince you?"

Vale throws him a narrow-eyed look. "Why you asking?"

"Call it curiosity."

"I dunno, steady hours? Insurance. A payout in case something happens to me. And a better reputation. Can't send money home what's ill-gotten, especially after the whole village knows I'm up here for guardian school."

"'Fraid the better reputation ain't happening." Burdock puts his piece of sugarcane in his mouth and chews, his hooded eyes thoughtful. "Guess I ought to help you get in the place with a sterling reputation."

"What, like the museum?"

"Exactly like the museum. You don't wanna shame your ma and ba? Wanna be the pride of your village? That'll be the place for you."

Vale sits up, extracts the chewed-up piece of sugarcane from her mouth, and drops it into the wastebin. "You can do that?"

"I can't guarantee that gig for you, no, but I can put in a hearty word. By the way, look under the desk."

Vale rolls the chair back and ducks her head low. She spots a woven bag, handles draping over something deep yellow, curved, hand sized. Recognition strikes her. "Are those—"

"Last of the season," Burdock says, affirming. "Mango harvest is done. That's what's left. Managed to wrangle some for you yesterday at the market."

Vale snatches the bag up and holds it to her chest, grinning. "Thank you so much!"

"You're welcome, little sister. Figured this is your last year, so this may be the last time I can do this for you. Let's eat, yeah?" Burdock smiles back. For a second, the exhaustion melts away and the shadows clear from his face, leaving nothing but sunshine.

Vale hands Burdock a mango. It's tradition, of a sort, for him to cut the fruit for her. He produces a thin blade from somewhere as he turns the mango in his hand, angling it just so. He's quiet as he works, and as Vale watches, his eyes grow suddenly bright with tears.

She's not sure what to do or what to say or whether even to acknowledge what's going on in front of her. It's the time of year, after all, to think about home and family, whatever those things even mean anymore to someone who's been so long away. It's the time of year to call out to ancestors, to hold on to the only things that cannot be taken by a wrathful earth. So Vale sits like she's at a vigil, keeping her eyes on Burdock's rough, calloused hands, being a witness to Burdock weeping silently in front of her. He finishes, placing the sides of the mango on the desk, keeping the pit for himself.

"You wanna learn a song?" Burdock says finally, then sniffles. "Ah, fuck."

"What kind of song?" Vale picks up her piece of mango and flips it inside out.

"You've been asking for years about village songs. Reckon why not, it's your last year. Might be my only chance to pass something on that ain't fightin' to you."

She sits up straight. It's an honor to learn someone else's history, to keep the small stories alive. "Really?"

Burdock nods, cleans off his hands and knife, then gets to his feet, walking over to the corner of his office to lift his guitar off its stand. "You make me a promise before I start. This is between you and me only. No one else gets these songs. Not other guardians, not your family, and especially not some scholar or museum."

Her eyes widen, and she nods solemnly. Oral traditions like hers and Burdock's exist to be passed from person to person, not put on a pedestal in the public square. "I promise."

He begins tuning the guitar. "Listen well, then. This one's a family lay from Fairlee."

TWELVE

I got matched with my guardian today. Her name is Valerian. I think she's fought everyone who's looked at her wrong at school. Mama doesn't like her, but Papa does. He thinks she'll be better for me than Rocket. Every princess needs a knight that's brave and true, he says, and she's the bravest and truest. I hope he's right about her. Saints, she's pretty. And terrifying.

—Diary of Kiana Strade, aged twenty-three

VALE FINISHED PINNING HER BUN AND TOOK THE END OF HER RIBbon out of her mouth, sliding its narrow, textured length between her thumb and forefinger. She'd chosen something plain but sturdy, a woven cotton ribbon dyed a deep black that would be camouflaged in her hair and could be used as a tool if needed. She wound it around the base of her bun, and as she did, her mind drifted away from chasing Key and toward the artisan who had woven the ribbon. What factory did she work at, and who was she? Maybe one of the coastal laborers who had no choice but to attach themselves to the southern textile farms that produced cotton and silk. Or maybe she was someone like Vale's mother, Phoebe, who would take temporary jobs for extra cash before festival season and come home with the odds and ends, pieces of colorful silk and satin that Vale's elder siblings would then fashion into bows and trims.

"Pay attention, Valerian," she muttered to herself.

The door to the train car opened, letting in the sound of rushing wind and clattering wheels, and the conductor leaned his body inside. "Crystal Grove Station! Next stop, Crystal Grove Station!"

Vale tied off the ribbon and exhaled. She bent and withdrew her vambraces from her rucksack's pursed mouth, sliding them on and tightening them down, then pulled on thin mycoleather gloves. After she set Burdock's sword on the empty seat beside her, she stood, adjusting her mycoleather-reinforced shirt. The routine of preparation crowded out her feelings, allowing her to be in the present and focus on a single thing at a time. She shook out her legs to get the circulation back into them, tapping the toes of her knee-high boots against the train floor, wiggling her feet against the soles to work out any wrinkles in her socks. She stretched her arms over her head, arched forward and back and from side to side, and did a set of hip circles.

With that done, she returned to her worries, which were as fresh and unspoiled as they'd been when she'd gathered them yesterday.

Key had to be here. Vale could not think of any other place Key would go.

She braced herself against the wall of the train as it began to slow, checking the placement of her knives in the process. The best-case scenario meant she wouldn't be forced to use any weapons, but considering the uproar Key had caused already by disappearing, Vale doubted there would be a scenario that could be categorized as best. After all, she and Key were outsiders returning to the scene of a murder, and news of strange faces traveled quicker than grams did in a village as small as Crystal Grove. Key was in an unknown state of mind and possibly a danger to herself and others, but, to Vale, that ranked below the danger of locals taking their revenge. Where Vale had come up, they'd called it natural justice.

She hung Burdock's sword on her belt and glanced around the train car. It was mostly empty but for a few passengers, which was to be expected on a line as lightly used as this one. A few rows down, a man was turning over the tab folder he'd just purchased from a vendor hawking a genuine Witnessing of a simple drifter building a puzzle cairn (proof of purchase good for 15 percent off an authentic miniature cairn at Chipburn Main Station).

A luxury, Vale thought, to feel secure enough to take a tab, however unauthenticated, unsafe, and fake the contents were, and drop into secondhand bliss. She'd do it if she could, but like a few of the people she'd met from the southern coasts, she was unaffected by whatever the tab contained. That inability, which Vale's eldest brother, Claude, believed was caused by a lack of faith, made the already-few resifixes that much more valuable when it came to accessing ancestral memories.

If Vale ever got to go home, she'd tell Claude how wrong he was. Most of the Asheburgian population could use a tab, and many had a small, insignificant amount of diving talent, but most of the population did not attend temple services devoutly. If diving ability were based on piety and piety alone, Claude would have been head resifix by now. But he wasn't. He was a field hand, his talent for storytelling bent first to entertaining his siblings, then his fellow workers, and then his children, and never to the paper and pen he once dreamed of using.

Thinking of Claude and his wasted potential only served to get her more upset, so she stopped thinking. Vale hoisted her rucksack onto her back and secured the chest strap, then went to the back door of the car to wait.

The white-hot fear from the day before had ebbed, leaving her with a smoldering, dark red anger—at Key, and at herself. She should have known. She should have seen something. She should have paid better mind to Key asking about what she'd retrieved at Crystal Grove, should have figured out that Key wanted to know more, not because she was half a mule and had an unwavering faith in her own correctness but because she somehow could not shake the memory. Vale should have put it together: the long smudge of graphite on Key's right hand, the wildness in her eyes, the way she tried to block Vale's view of the drafting table. Vale should have understood that Key's uncharacteristic fogginess at temple was because she was fighting off intrusive memories and not because she was in the middle of a holy experience. And Key, knowing how Vale could be, had taken advantage of her stupidity.

Pay attention, Valerian. She'd heard the mocking tone of the phrase in her head over and over for the past day. Except this time, it wasn't Rocket or her academy teachers or that petty sow Wynne Jean, but herself.

She'd come to a few conclusions while stewing on the train. First, Key was the stubbornest bitch Vale had ever met in her life, respected no authority but the saints', and was determined to retrieve the memory, no matter the cost. Second, there was a chance, however impossible—Vale tried to believe this notion was born of her tendency to catastrophize—that reintegration had not worked on Key.

Third, if Key wasn't already dead or kidnapped, she would be meeting her end at Vale's hands.

And that was why Vale had slunk out of the Garnet House during the morning chaos like a coward. She would not have been able to look at either Lanelle or Mershon and say to their faces that she might have to kill their only child.

The brakes sent up a protracted squeal, and Vale slid the back door open to stand by the coupler as the train arrived at the platform. Before it had come to a complete stop, Vale had leaped off, one hand on the sword to keep it from tangling in her legs. She drew in a deep breath of morning air, taking brief pleasure in it before angling herself toward the station house to freshen up.

"Come through again, girlie?" said the station attendant from behind her window once Vale emerged from the restroom.

Vale gave the woman a short nod before remembering her social niceties. "Yes, ma'am."

"You keep your eyes open," the station attendant said, beckoning for her to come closer. Worry laid sharp creases into her tanned, weathered face. "Been some uproar since you and your friend left. Got bodies in the woods and hunters everywhere, and then yesterday I seen your friend come back through."

Vale seized on the information. "By herself?"

The woman snorted. "No. But that's two city folk if I clocked them right."

"Two?"

"Your friend. And a redhead."

Betrayal reared and hissed, but Vale kept herself from profanity, just barely. Not only was Key acting foolhardy and erratic, she'd broken their contract and taken Rocket. "Thank you, ma'am. I'll be careful."

"Never told you to be careful." The station attendant grinned, showing crooked teeth. "Just said to keep watch. See me?"

"Seen and kept," Vale replied, then turned for the door.

There was a large area map on the outside of the station house, and it was here that she and Key had plotted their original course. Vale's mouth tightened as she studied it, tracing the route she would take with a finger before snagging one of the maps in the wall rack and shoving it into the side pocket of her rucksack.

A metallic rattle drew her attention. Vale cast a glance behind her to the boxcar of the train, where over a dozen people had gathered, including the conductor and a couple of porters. The conductor disappeared inside, motioning for others to follow, and soon, boxes marked with the familiar poison symbol found on the museum's antifungals were handed out and passed down the line. At the end of a line was a slender figure with a wide-brimmed hat and a sword riding her hip.

Vale squinted. Something about the person was familiar. At that moment, the woman began speaking to the person beside her, and pushed the hat back so that it dangled down her back by the chin ties, revealing honey-blond hair in a low chignon.

Shock pinned Vale's heart to the inside of her ribcage. She stood for what felt like an eternity, speared through with helplessness and fear as Dr. Wilcroft nodded, then bent to inspect the rucksack at her feet. *Turn around,* Vale told herself, but her body refused to move. *Turn around. Turn around.*

Vale sucked in a breath and began walking briskly toward the western exit of the train station, willing Dr. Wilcroft not to see her. Her pulse crashed into her eardrums like waves in a storm, relentless. Was it a coincidence that Dr. Wilcroft was here? She was rarely, if ever, in the field these days. Maybe there was another site in the same area. Or maybe there wasn't and Key really had found something significant, and Dr. Wilcroft had lied about it.

It didn't matter, Vale decided, breaking into a trot the second the sidewalk turned, cutting off line of sight to Dr. Wilcroft and her crew. It'd be the hook for both Vale and Key if they were found out. Ahead, there was a clump of three armed men standing at the edge of the road. One of them jerked his head toward her, and a second later, all of them had turned hard eyes on her.

"Hey," one of them called.

Vale didn't slow.

"Hey, *friend*," he called louder.

She stopped and pivoted to face them. If they wanted to start trouble, they'd need to come to her. "What do you want, friend?"

The man, who must have been the leader of the group, glanced at his companions before sauntering toward her, his hands on the pommels of the knives at his waist. "Where's your guardian?"

It had been a source of constant amusement to Key whenever Vale was mistakenly thought of as the hunter, and Key, because of her size and athletic build, the guardian. Vale played along, not wanting to waste time. Dr. Wilcroft would emerge from the station at any second, and Vale needed to stay unencumbered if she wanted to get to Key before anyone else. "Don't got one."

A smirk bloomed on the man's face. "Registered hunter like you? Hear it's dangerous out there," he said. "Best not go on your own."

"I hear you," Vale said. "You registered too?"

"Sure," the man said, his smirk widening as he approached. "The three of us would be more 'n enough to protect you, if you get our meaning. Seems like there's a monster in the woods."

Vale raised her eyebrows. "A monster?"

"Yeah, a savage one, from the looks of it. And you don't look too handy with that shiny new sword."

She had been underestimated too many times in her life to take offense. "I look like I need protecting?"

The other two men laughed as they drew closer, surrounding her.

"Not too close. Give her some space," the leader said.

Vale kept her stance relaxed, though she casually sized up the men on either side of her. If it came to it, she'd go left first and incapacitate the one most likely to become a nuisance. He was big, but she knew how to handle big, and there was no way any of these men could deliver to her what Burdock could.

"Like what you see?" the man said, leering.

Vale smiled, imagining how she'd attack him. It was unfortunate she couldn't preemptively solve her problem by killing all three men where they stood, but not even she could justify the use of guardian law when her hunter was a multi-hour hike away. "No. And I've got the protection I need already."

The men laughed again, patronizing. "That little stick?" said the big man, indicating Burdock's sword. "Looks like it'll break if I breathe on it. I'd do a better job."

She made a face. "Sorry, lemme say that again, but different. You think you're the right folks to protect me?"

The leader spoke. "Lots of hunters around here. Two from the city went out a few days ago and didn't come back. There's a search on."

"Might be they found something and decided to cut you out," Vale suggested. "You know how hunters do. City ones, 'specially."

"Might be the monster got them."

"Might be," Vale said.

"Or other folks, and now they're hog feed." The leader shrugged. "That's why you gotta be careful. You know how hunters do, you said so yourself. If it's another group that got them, there'll be hell to pay. Not one of us wants you to get caught up in that."

"That's real sweet of you to think of me when you ain't know me," Vale drawled, lapsing into her home accent. "Tell you what, though. Since you've been so kind with information, I'll return the favor. Just saw some city folks come off the train. You know the only reason why they come around here."

Another man spoke up. "For thieving, yeah."

As if these men weren't themselves thieves, ready to take memories from the ground or one another and sell them to the market. What little talent they had could have been better used for forensic work or the entertainment industry, but the black market's money held more temptation and excitement than a folder of porn tabs and a soft bed. "I counted six in total. Might be a good haul for you. Their swords looked shiny too."

The leader didn't take his gaze off her, but the other two hesitated.

"What are you waiting for? You're welcome." Vale stepped backward.

The leader shot out a hand and grabbed her upper arm. Vale gritted her teeth but didn't react, shucking off the desire to break the man's wrist. He drew her close, his eyes glinting. "No, I don't think you're going anywhere. You know more than you let on. And if you think you're gonna pit our numbers against theirs, you're out of your mind."

Vale exhaled, holding the edge of her calm. Whatever happened, she had to get to Key before Dr. Wilcroft could. "Okay," she said. "You wanna escort me, then escort me. I'll tell you where I'm headed. Long as we get going now."

"In a hurry?" the leader said, smirking.

"Yeah, I am," Vale retorted.

"You two." The leader indicated his companions. "See if what the little girl says is true. If so, rustle up the others."

"You gonna be okay?" the big man asked. "What about the monster?"

"Ain't no monster," the leader said. "And I think I can handle her."

Vale tried to look as unthreatening as possible despite the instinct that told her to bury a knife in her captor's guts. "Maybe there *is* a monster. I'm scared."

"She don't look scared," the other man said.

Vale tried her best to look scared and hoped she didn't look constipated.

"Scared or not," the leader said, "I think I can handle it. Get out of here."

The two walked off, leaving Vale, her anxiety over Key, and her captor. He started forward, still gripping her arm.

"West," Vale said, pointing down the main road at a faded signpost. The trail they needed was beyond the village limits. "You really think there's nothing in the woods?"

"No." There was a long moment of silence. "Real monster is other people."

"That's deep."

"It's just the truth."

"You sound like you got experience." Vale glanced demurely up at the man. That always seemed to disarm people, make them lower their guard. "So, what's your name?" *To remember you with once I kill you.*

"Silas." He eyed her, his hand tightening on her arm. "What's yours?"

"Call me . . ." If someone found Silas's body and took his blood to a forensic hunter, she'd be implicated if she gave her academy name. The monster in the woods could not be Vale. But she could be . . .

"Maris."

VALE TURNED ONTO the overgrown path leading to the compound, the air around her hanging heavy enough to strangle. The heat drew a clinging humidity from the ground just as it drew the scent of copper and iron from her clothes, where Silas's blood had splashed her. Present, too, was a thread of decay, likely from the location where Vale and Key had dragged the bodies of the hunters five days prior. If the wild hogs hadn't already gotten them, they would soon.

Vale unslung one of her water bottles and downed a large mouthful, then pulled a fan from a pocket in her rucksack and waved it at herself. Her sweat-soaked skin welcomed the chance to cool down, but it was at best weak relief—a bad sign. The heat index was rising, but there was no time to rest if she wanted to get Key out before Genevieve arrived. Vale squinted past the canopy of the trees at the sky, which was a blue mottled with white, hoping to see thunderheads forming.

Nothing yet. Midday was too soon for storms.

At least she was under the trees and not in full sunlight. Vale replaced her fan and water bottle, picking her way from shady patch to shady patch as the path grew more defined. Only days ago, when she and Key were covered in sweat and exhausted from the hike, Key had relayed a memory of a time before the Decade of Storms, before it was unbearably hot and heat waves came with death tolls, before the peaks of the mountains were bald and gray and wore instead white caps of snow in winter. And Vale swore she could feel herself cooling down and drying out as Key spoke, as if she were standing on one of those peaks during an early fall snow. A flurry, Key called it. Like tiny, cold kisses on your cheeks and forehead. Vale had smiled at the image.

She was not smiling now.

She approached the break in the growth that signaled the entrance to the compound, dead grass and leaves crackling beneath the soles of her boots. It was enough noise, Vale reasoned, to capture the attention of any guardian worth the price of the academy. When she and Key had arrived here initially, they hadn't bothered with bushwhacking. She observed that the trail had felt the tromp of feet since, as well as the bite of a machete—the underbrush had been freshly hacked away in spots, leaving clumps of greenery on the ground beside shorn grass and flushes of jewel-bright russulas.

Key's here.

Vale paused, took a long breath, and silently drew her sword.

She entered the compound to the naked silver gleam of Rocket's saber, held at the ready. But all Vale could see was Key crouched over the fruiting bodies of the blood chalice, white molars in the dark gums of the earth. In that instant, everything disappeared under the flash flood of her emotions, drowning her and carrying her away.

She was not aware of moving until after she heard the clash of swords and Rocket's shrill yelp. She was not aware that she was running full tilt at Key until their bodies crashed together and they tumbled onto the leaf-covered forest floor. *Why?* someone screamed, the animal sound of it tearing the air. It wasn't her. She wasn't giving voice to the pain and betrayal of Key's abandonment. Her throat was not tight and raw.

Vale pushed herself up and threw herself over Key, straddling her, both hands around her throat. She screamed at Key again, wordless.

"Vale." There was no sound, but she read it clear on Key's lips.

The anger crested. Vale unsheathed her dagger and let go of Key's throat, then gripped the handle of her knife in both hands and placed the flat of it against Key's neck. The blade moved subtly, telegraphing the frenzied beat of Key's heart through Vale's fingers and up her arms. If she turned the blade—if she cut now and put all her weight behind it—it would be fast and clean.

She inhaled, her muscles tensing, and looked into Key's soft brown eyes.

Vale dropped her knife, her fingers numb, and fell forward, catching herself on shaking arms, air rasping through her throat. She couldn't. She *couldn't.*

And yet she had to. She wrapped a trembling hand back around Key's neck, pushing the webbing between her thumb and forefinger firmly against the ridge of Key's voice box.

"Cochineal," Key whispered.

Vale went still. "I didn't tell you the word."

"I knew," Key said, then swallowed, the muscles of her throat shifting beneath Vale's palm, "you'd find me." Key swallowed again. "I hoped you wouldn't."

"I have a job to do."

"My name is Kiana Strade." Key stared up at Vale, her eyes clear and unclouded. "Hunter for the Museum of Human Memory. You're Valerian IV. Guardian."

"That doesn't prove you're still you."

"The day we came back, you hit Rocket in the face and gave her that bruise. Burdock punished you by giving you yours."

Vale's grip on Key loosened, and her chest heaved with the sawing of her breath. She had not been catastrophizing, then. It was not possible, but Key's reintegration hadn't—

"I gave you a new dress Terry made especially for you." Leaves rustled, and Key lifted a hand, touching the backs of her fingers to Vale's cheek. Vale froze so hard at the touch that her diaphragm ached. "I helped you put it on. I did your hair and makeup. Vale, you looked beautiful."

Key changed the position of her hand to cradle Vale's cheek, then applied gentle pressure downward. It was a simple ask, and Vale lowered her face toward Key in an immediate answer, captured completely by the touch, unable to break away even as she tightened her hold on Key's neck.

"I should have kissed you," Key murmured when they were a hair apart, the distance between them stretched thin and trembling, like water about to overflow a glass. "I almost did. If I'm dying by your hand, let me know what you taste like before I go."

Vale made a small, helpless sound, and then Key's lips angled across hers, and the tip of her tongue glided across the seam of Vale's lips, and she had no choice but to open and—

Time stopped.

"Can someone tell me what the *hell* is happening?!" Rocket shouted.

Vale broke from the kiss and gained her feet, snarling, "*Fuck off!*" But it was too late. Rocket's shout was like a slap to the face or an ice cube down the back of her shirt, shocking Vale back to her senses. Horror made her lightheaded for a second. "Key. We need to leave now."

"That explains nothing," Rocket hissed. Vale ignored her and stomped over to her fallen sword, inspecting it before returning it to its scabbard. "What are you doing here?"

The anger rekindled. "My *job.* The fuck else do you think I'm doing here?"

Rocket drew near with slow, measured steps, accompanied by the crackle of magnolia leaves underfoot, her eyes on Key and no one else. "Vale's job? The contract isn't up between you?"

Key got back up, only to hunch over the chalices. They were all too freshly bloomed, their plateau-like tops a pristine white. Only one was in the early stages of ripeness, a meager amount of liquid gathering in the deepening central divot. Key reached into her pocket, pulling out a crumpled myco-plastic bag with a single tab in it. She took it out and eased the corner of it into the guttation. "You didn't ask."

"I didn't think I had to ask," Rocket replied, her brows furrowing with a glare.

"I subcontracted you." Key sealed the tab back in the bag and shoved it into her pocket, then stood, squaring her shoulders. "One trip only. Vale is still my guardian."

The kiss, Vale decided, meant nothing. "Oh, *now* I'm your guardian? After you ditched me in the city and snuck out with someone else?"

"It was to protect you!"

"Protect me? I'm supposed to protect *you*. I don't know how other people will see what's going on, but they'd say this is fucking crazy behavior and if you think I'm going along with whatever you're trying to do here, you're wrong. Whatever you're doing, you're finished. We're leaving. Now."

"We can't," Key said. "The chalices aren't ready; you can see that for yourself."

"I don't fucking care," Vale said. "You have to leave now. Before you're found out. This isn't a forgivable mistake. This isn't coming back a week late or challenging Dr. Wilcroft, this is you going out against your orders and doing something that every single guardian in the institute would agree is dangerous to yourself and others. Pack up. We're leaving now and we'll deal with the rest on the train."

"You're really insistent on getting Key to leave," Rocket said. She turned to Vale, suspicion in her eyes. "What aren't you telling us?"

"You're right, I'm not telling you something, but it's real important that everyone packs up and leaves *now*. I can explain it on the way, but we don't have time to chat about it."

"No," Key said. "Tell us right now."

"You stubborn—" Vale's nostrils flared as she sucked in a breath. "Pack up first."

"I won't budge until you tell me."

"Blood in the *mouth*, can you do what I say just this once!" But arguing was useless. "Fine. I have bad news: Dr. Wilcroft is probably ten minutes behind me with a crew, and if she isn't, then it's a bunch of local hunters who are jumpy about two people going missing from earlier this week. We. Have. To. Leave."

Whatever color Key had remaining in her face disappeared, and she swayed on her feet. Vale tensed without thinking, leaning forward, readying herself to catch Key.

"Say that again?" Key whispered.

"Which part?!"

"Genevieve. She's here?"

"Yes, so you get why I want to be as far from here as possible, yeah?"

"With a crew?"

"That's what I said." Vale, satisfied Key was not going to pass out, stalked toward the front porch of the house where Key's belongings were. To Vale's annoyance, most of the site had been packed, but not all; it made for sloppy work and a delayed exit in a setting where anything and everything could happen, from bears descending upon them to disgruntled hunters and a boss who would fire her if she were caught.

"She said it wasn't . . ." Key covered her face with a hand, bowing her head, her shoulders drooping. Rocket moved toward her, an arm outstretched.

Vale did not have time for Key's emotional crisis. She spoke, snapping her words. "Rocket, no. Pack up."

The other guardian stopped, craning her head around to look at Vale. And then, ancestors be blessed, Rocket hustled near and began shoving items into bags.

"Vale," Rocket said, her voice pitched low. "I didn't know. I should have asked, and I didn't."

"Because you've been aiming for my job." Vale glared. "Whatever it is you're trying to say, don't. She lied to you, same as she lied to me, and that's that." Vale tossed the contents of Key's cup over the porch, gave it a vigorous shake, and shoved it into Key's rucksack. Would the smell of coffee linger inside for days? Yes. Did Vale care? No. "All that matters is us getting out of here without being seen, so the faster we move, the—"

Dr. Wilcroft stepped through the break in the overgrowth.

"Fuck," Vale finished.

"Blood in the mouth," Rocket whispered.

Vale got to her feet and went to Key, whose posture had changed, every line of her body corded out with tension.

Dr. Wilcroft walked, deliberate and unhurried, toward Key. Vale had expected to see surprise, but all she got was a curated blankness, a stillness mirroring the weighty hush before a storm. In Vale's family, whenever her mother got that look, it meant someone was getting the switch. Vale wasn't sure how to read it on Dr. Wilcroft.

"What are you doing here?" Key demanded, moving forward, intercepting Dr. Wilcroft.

"Kiana." Dr. Wilcroft spoke softly. "What are *you* doing here?"

Oh, shit.

"What are you doing here?" Key was half yelling now. "You told me it wasn't significant! You said—you said—"

"I know what I said, and if you could lower your voice, that would be appreciated. You need to answer me: How did you know to come here?" Dr. Wilcroft's eyes landed on Vale. "Valerian? I thought you were better than this. I see Rocket is here as well."

Vale bristled even as shame surged, but said nothing. Dr. Wilcroft could not know the truth about Key.

"They don't have anything to do with this," Key snapped, gesturing between herself and Dr. Wilcroft. "This is between you and me. You lied to me! What are you doing here?"

"What am I doing here?" Dr. Wilcroft said levelly. Finally, her composure cracked, showing irritation. "You're suspended from fieldwork. You had a reintegration but broke protocol and somehow looked at documents you know you're forbidden to access for fear of this exact situation happening. You have two guardians and are at a site I distinctly do not remember sending you to, and you're asking what *I'm* doing here?"

"What. Are. You. Doing. Here." Key leaned forward, the gesture aggressive. "Why do you have a crew?"

"I'll ask the questions, thank you." Even in the wilderness, Dr. Wilcroft had a presence, and it was hard to ignore the command in her voice. "You have no right when you are supposed to be at home."

"I have no right? Are you trying to steal this from me?" Key demanded.

Vale moved up slowly beside Key, keeping her hand away from the hilt of her sword, assessing the crew members shuffling in one by one, each laden with stuffed rucksacks and equipped with shovels. One carried a sledgehammer.

"Answer me!" Key grew shriller. "Are you trying to steal this from me? You told me this memory was worthless! That it was insignificant!"

"You're repeating yourself," Dr. Wilcroft said coolly.

"Key has a point," Vale said. "You're here with a crew. If you aren't trying to steal from Key, you might want to articulate your reasons."

"I'm speaking to Kiana," Dr. Wilcroft said, not taking her eyes off Key. "Although if you'd like to give a report, Valerian, by all means, go ahead. What's happening?"

Key shot her a look. Vale shut her mouth.

Dr. Wilcroft cracked her voice like a whip. "Report, Valerian, if you'd like to stay employed."

"Please don't," Key said in an undertone. "I'll make it up to you, I swear, just—"

"Valerian, immediately."

She kept silent.

Dr. Wilcroft's eyes narrowed, glittering a pale green. "I'll reinstate your pay grade and double the next paycheck for your loyalty."

"That's bribery!" Key exclaimed. "How dare you!"

Vale dropped her gaze to the ground. Out of the corner of her eye, she saw Key's hand lift a fraction, the tendons in it starkly defined as if drawn. On her own, Vale would never bare her throat and kneel for the museum or for the curator, not after two years of being looked down upon and dismissed by her. If Dr. Wilcroft believed that the museum meant anything other than a paycheck to Vale, she was a worse judge of character than Vale thought.

But would Vale bare her throat for Key? Was Key worth sacrificing for?

Vale thought of the kiss and how she'd wanted to sink into it forever. She thought of days and nights alone with Key and the single touch against the skin of her back that had sent goose bumps rippling over her like wind over the grass. Of all the time spent in silent companionship, working together so seamlessly that it bordered on precognizant. Of trekking to rocky lookout points and breathing in the fresh air under the bowl of the sky. Of laughing from the sheer delight of being together.

And then Vale thought of Dina's baby, and the house repairs, and the next installment of Bo's tuition. She thought of the shirt in the seconds bin and her empty, aching stomach. Her loyalty was to her family. Never anything or anyone else. If she had no one else to provide for, maybe she'd keep her mouth shut. Maybe she'd put her faith in Key's word and not Dr. Wilcroft's.

"Key subcontracted Rocket as a guardian in order to come back to Crystal Grove and did not tell me," Vale said, trying not to see how Key had closed her eyes and turned away. "I found out and went after her for her safety."

"Is there anything else you'd like to add? Your part in the matter, perhaps?"

Vale set her feet to withstand the weight of Dr. Wilcroft's

glare and returned the look. She had done what Dr. Wilcroft asked and would do nothing further. "No."

"I see." Dr. Wilcroft's mouth became a line, razor straight and just as sharp. "Kiana. You disobeyed my orders."

"You *lied* to me!" Key cut in.

"And you thought you knew better than I did. You broke museum protocol and risked yourself and those around you. You abandoned your guardian to go on a wild goose chase. What sort of behavior is that?" Dr. Wilcroft drew herself up, imperious. "I'll tell you what. It's the unacceptable sort."

"Keep trying to evade questions, then," Key said through teeth ground closed. "You're trying to divert me. I found something big, and you knew it. You wanted the recognition all for yourself. So you lied to me and said it wasn't good, and the second my back was turned, you went to get it so you could take the credit! Would you have you mentioned me in your work at all? Or would you have made my name disappear, the way you did Burdock's? How many people have you done this to?"

"You are raving. Do you hear yourself right now?" Dr. Wilcroft scoffed. "I would never steal someone else's work and claim it as mine."

"Jing was right about you!" Key spat. "You're a liar, and all you want to do is keep your own position."

"Jing is wasted talent who is jealous of others but doesn't have the guts to do the work," Dr. Wilcroft snapped back. "It's only because there was no one else better than he that year that he got that position. As for my job, I do intend to keep it. You fought me and lost. You fancy yourself ready to take on a curatorial role? Far from it. You think this work is granted to you by the ancestors. You've known nothing but success your whole life. I will teach you otherwise. To let you know what the real world is like."

"You're my boss, not my mother," Key growled.

"I am neither." Dr. Wilcroft smirked. "Kiana Strade. You're fired."

Vale's knees went weak. Despite knowing that the firing would in all likelihood happen, it was another thing entirely to hear it realized, to have it spoken out loud and heard and witnessed.

"What?" Key said, aghast.

"You cannot *believe* I'd keep you in your position. You're fired. Right now. This instant. I will request that you be stripped of your license so that you cannot do this job at any other institution. I will not have my subordinates actively disregarding their orders and breaking safety rules. It puts their lives and the lives of others at risk. You've questioned my competence—"

"You've questioned *my* competence!" Key threw back. "You lied to me!"

"—and though I've been patient with you, even granting you leniency on an infraction that would have resulted in any another hunter being let go from the museum, there is no way you can continue working under me." Dr. Wilcroft cast her eyes on Vale. "And you were deceitful toward your guardian. I expected better of you, Kiana. All that talent, but no sense. If you were going to be foolish, you should have thought of Valerian."

"Nothing here is Vale's fault," Key said. "She wasn't even supposed to be involved—"

"Valerian, I appreciate your willingness to tell me the truth, despite the consequences it would have for you."

"Despite . . . ?" Vale mouthed, confused.

Dr. Wilcroft went on. "You should have notified me the second Kiana asked you to look at her files. You should have notified me the second you realized what she had done. Because you didn't, I consider your inaction a dereliction of duty."

"Wait," Vale said, alarm jangling up and down her nerves, as shrill and dissonant as a station bell. She began breathing faster. "I did what you asked. Just now."

"You did the bare minimum, which wasn't enough. Unfortunately, Valerian, I'm terminating your employment as well as recommending your guardian license be revoked immediately."

"No!" Key cried.

Vale's knees finally failed and deposited her onto the ground. The pommel of her sword jabbed her mercilessly in her side, but she ignored the pain as pins and needles rolled from her head to her toes, her heartbeat like crashing waves in her ears.

A mile or so from her village, on an eroding spit, were the remains of a lighthouse, the top broken off and a side caved in. Year after year it stood fast, its foundation part of the earth, unyielding. During storms, the sea would reach up and smash it, and the only things that could withstand the force were the barnacles.

Vale was no barnacle. She was a weak, soft-tissued thing trapped between the lighthouse and the sea, the winds screaming over her head, the water harder and more solid than a stone wall. Hit after hit she took, leaving her reeling. Her hands shook; her jaw shook.

Then she realized all of her was shaking.

"You can't fire Vale!" Key was shouting. "You just promised to give her money back! None of this is her fault! Don't take it out on her!"

Dr. Wilcroft's voice came to Vale's ears from far away. "You and your guardian are one entity when you are paired, or did you forget?"

"You can assign Vale to another hunter. She needs this job more than I do. You're being unfair!"

"You should have taken Valerian's situation into account before leaping into action." If Dr. Wilcroft was looking at her, she had no idea. All Vale could see were the wide, brown magnolia leaves on the ground. "Escort these two from the area. Rocket can stay on if she so wishes. There's always opportunity for new guardians."

Vale's vision swam, and heat stung her eyes. *Are these tears?* she wondered, reaching up a hand to touch them. She hadn't cried in years, hadn't since the first night she arrived at the academy and realized she was alone and wholly out of her depth. She'd soaked the pillow with tears, then vowed from then on not to show weakness in front of these strange city folk, these people who wore their climate privilege like their own skins, who stood upon an invisible support of money, power, and knowledge, who shamed her because she had none of those things yet stole into their hallowed spaces and had the temerity to stay. She wouldn't cry until she could go home.

Rough hands grabbed her arms and hauled her up, and Vale went limp as two of Dr. Wilcroft's crew dragged her bodily from the compound and dropped her onto the overgrown dirt road. She landed on her front in the grass and didn't move. Tears rolled hot off her face and disappeared beneath thin stalks of green.

In that moment, Vale hated herself.

"Vale?" Key put a hand on her shoulder.

"Don't touch me!" Vale slapped Key's hand away and scrabbled to her feet, sweat breaking out anew over her entire body, her face and neck hot with shame. "Don't look at me, get away!"

She had to leave. She had to go somewhere, anywhere that wasn't here, anywhere that wasn't a stage where she was exposed. Vale swiped at her eyes with her sleeve, dashing the tears away, but they came back, insistent. The world narrowed to herself and the trees as she ran down the path like a rabbit or squirrel, a prey animal fleeing with no awareness of where they were going, only that it was away. It was this panic Vale had counted on when she had hunted with her father as a child; it was this panic that would take the animal straight into a waiting trap or snare.

Mud turned under her foot as she stepped on an extra-deep pile of magnolia leaves. She slipped and went to one knee. Behind her, she heard someone calling her name, but she didn't care. Vale had to go. She got up and kept running, her breath on fire in her chest, her mind whirling. What would she do now for money? How would she support her parents and her family at home? Where would she live, what would she do?

She didn't see the root that tripped her, only knew that she was face down on the ground, her wrist and nose smarting with pain. Groaning, Vale curled into a ball and sobbed, and only when she tasted copper did she understand she was bleeding.

The wildness drained from her all at once, leaving her as hollow as a bored-out log, ready to crumble into the earth.

Vale stopped crying, unable to muster the energy to do even that. She lay on her left side and watched the ants marching over the forest floor. A breeze caressed the trees, and a branch rustled, followed by the flapping of wings. Birdsong near and far rang out in an uncaring chorus.

Footsteps crunched toward her, the cadence familiar. Vale didn't have to look to know it was Key.

"Are you okay, Vale?" came Key's soft voice. "You're bleeding."

No, she was not okay. She turned her face toward the earth.

"Vale?"

"I don't want to talk to you," she said, and that was that.

THIRTEEN

Although usage of the blood chalice (*C. diabolum*) is well documented in official temple history, scientists have not yet determined why or how it has evolved to take up memories through its mycelial network. A small but significant portion of the Spinal population is unable to experience the memories locked in the chalice's guttation, leading some to hypothesize that there is an undiscovered step in the translation process.

—Jethro Gorley, *Field Guide to the Mushrooms of the Southern Spine*

KEY SAT SLUMPED IN HER SEAT, LISTENING TO THE WORDS OF occasional conversation from the other passengers in the car. Ahead, a middle-aged person slept deeply, knocked out from the memory tab they'd purchased earlier from the shifty vendor trawling the rows for a sale, their snores a dissonant grumbling against the clatter of the train rolling over the jointed tracks.

Across the aisle was Vale, drawn tight against the window, her head turned steadfastly to the outside, one hand clutching the sheath of her sword. Dusk had pulled itself over the forest and tucked itself around the trees, and beneath Key, the train swayed and rocked, a steel bassinet bearing them north on the overnight line. Once more, as she had been doing over the last several hours, Key stretched her ears, trying to catch Vale humming, since she often did so on long trips. But there was only a block of silence between them, as transparent as glass and just as impenetrable.

Key could not—would not—be soothed by the approach of night or the monotony of the train. In her dives she'd lived through amputations, some of them traumatic, and no matter the anesthetic or the preparation, the body was not equipped to have a limb severed so suddenly. Despite the evidence, the mind still believed the limb was attached, still tried to gesture with it or reach with it, meeting with failure and frustration each time. Key surfaced from those dives aching, the ghosts of those phantom limbs so acute that she was convinced, before she was fully lucid, that she once had a third arm or leg.

Despite the evidence, she was still convinced that she had a partner.

She pressed her hand to her chest as if something had spilled from it and swallowed the knot in her throat, then worked her fingers into her pocket, touching the bag containing the specimen from the compound. The material of it was crinkled, and undoubtedly the tab inside would be crinkled as well. Key took it from her pocket again and held it up, observing the smears of liquid that had been squeezed out of the paper, the rusty redness refracting orange under the jaundiced overhead light.

At what cost had she won her prize? As an only child of a wealthy family, she'd been called spoiled; she reframed it as determined. Her desire to get what she wanted had never been seen as anything but positive by her parents. And even if they disapproved, she could always find justification from the ancestors. In this case, she believed it was the ancestors who urged her to return.

Doubt ate at her again, as it had done many times over the past half day. What did it mean if the saints had led her astray? Had she gone to Crystal Grove out of selfishness, or dogged righteousness? If Genevieve hadn't arrived, what then?

Vale shifted, and Key automatically looked at her. Their eyes connected. Dirt-laden blood had caked into a mask over Vale's left cheek and had spread in rivulets down her neck before drying. Her nose was purple and swollen, her eyes red and puffy. Not even the tab vendor had wanted to interact with her.

Key put the specimen bag away and reached for her handkerchief. She held up the cloth, offering for a third time.

Vale said nothing.

It wasn't a full rejection. Key took up her water pouch and crossed the aisle, pushing against the weight of Vale's silent accusations with each step. Vale's hand moved to the grip of her sword, the knuckles showing white as Key broached the space, but Key nudged the weapon out of the way. She sat, placing the pouch between them, then took the scabbard in hand. Key had always taken comfort in being right. And there was no room for fear in the conviction of the heart.

She slid the scabbard off the sword. The light played across its silvery width as she laid its edge over her jugular, resting it just so on her shoulder.

The corners of Vale's mouth began quivering. The skin of Key's neck stung, the length of the blade amplifying the shakes of Vale's hand.

Key didn't so much as tense as she unscrewed the top of her water pouch and tipped some of its contents onto the handkerchief. Slowly, she raised the cloth to Vale's face and pressed it to her cheek.

Vale lowered her head on a sob. The flat of the sword rattled on Key's shoulder.

"I'm sorry," Key whispered. Vale continued to cry, and Key kept cleaning, bearing holy witness as she was meant from birth to do. She swept the handkerchief over Vale's cheek, leaving a smear of blood; she wet the cloth again and, with tender fingertips, turned Vale's face to begin removing the crusted blood from her nose.

Key didn't notice the absence of the sword on her shoulder until after she finished cleaning Vale's face. The weapon chimed as Vale rested the point of it on the floor of the car. Key gave it a cursory glance before returning to her task but found herself blocked when Vale moved her hand in front of her own neck. Wordlessly, Key handed the damp kerchief over, watching as Vale swiped aggressively at the blood on her skin.

She gestured at Key and pointed when she was done. Key put two fingers to her neck, blinking when they came away with fresh blood. She looked at the dirtied handkerchief, still in Vale's hand, then at Vale. It was frowned upon for hunters to mix blood and taboo for them to taste it because of the immediate effects; that went double for a resifix, whose mental state and psyche had to be preserved, who, without a current specimen, could not be brought back if that equilibrium were upset.

She plucked the kerchief from Vale's hand. Vale stared back, her eyes immense, as deep and black as mystery itself. Key pressed the kerchief to her own neck and held still as Vale gasped, her lips parting.

"I don't understand," Vale said. Tears welled, and Key

felt the pricking of them as if they were her own. "I don't get any of this."

Key answered the unspoken question. "Because you're my friend and I care about you, and I've wronged you in many, many ways, and I'm so sorry. I should have told you about the intrusive memories, and I didn't. I should have told you when I realized the reintegration didn't work, but I was afraid of what you'd do, so I didn't. I should have asked for your input so that we could present a united front. Together, as we should have been from the start."

The train went around a curve, and that motion was enough to send a tear down Vale's cheek. "You were afraid I was going to kill you?"

"I was," Key admitted.

Another tear fell. "I was too."

Key took the cloth from her neck; the cut would be clotted by now. "But now I know I shouldn't have been."

"It's my job," Vale whispered.

"Not anymore," Key replied.

Vale's face crumpled.

"And I'm glad," Key went on as gently as she could, "because I know your heart just a little better." An image unshrouded itself: Vale in a cream-and-red dress, her hair in braids crowning her head, black eyes wide, breathtakingly beautiful. Key had her finger on the enticing fullness of Vale's lower lip. She had stared at that lip and that perfect red and entertained for a second the thought of pulling her finger to the side, smearing that lipstick, and kissing Vale. There was vulnerability in her still, a precious softness that had yet to be stamped out by the merciless demands of survival, and Key wanted to hold that in her hands.

No, she wanted to kiss Vale again, to finish what Rocket had interrupted, to find out in a room of their own how far they might go. But that was in a fast-dwindling future, a perhaps-scenario fading as quickly as an apparition.

Key continued speaking, aware of the growing weight of her silence. "I'm glad you won't have to kill me."

"That's not better!" Vale tipped her head back and thumbed her eyes, then winced. "That's not the whole thing! Easy for you because you have the temple. Your family has money and respect. What am I good for? The black market? Fighting in some production that'll get made into a Witness tab?"

"You're more than your fighting ability." Vale was ferocity and loyalty, a moonbeam song, a delightfully scattered mind. She was the love beneath the grit, the laughter on the breeze, a singular devotion made physical. Key should have given voice to this long ago, but she hadn't. For someone as correct as she was, not doing so had been a huge mistake. "And now you don't have to choose between supporting your family and taking someone's life."

Vale gave a short, bitter laugh, then sniffled. "It was an easy choice until you. What're you gonna do with that specimen? It's not your job anymore either."

"I don't know." Key leaned down to pick up the scabbard, angled it for Vale to slide her sword home. "I want to leave it. Wash my hands of it. Look what I did because of it."

They listened to the *k-thunk k-thunk* of the train.

"But?" Vale said finally.

"The ancestors called me here. And I'm always right." Key retrieved the specimen bag from her pocket, cradling it in her hands. She exhaled. "I'm *always* right. I knew this was significant. Why else would Genevieve bring a crew? She's going to set up for an excavation, and I . . ."

"That wasn't digging equipment she brought," Vale said.

Key straightened. "What?"

"I didn't put it together until just now. Her crew brought antifungals and plenty of shovels, but I didn't see any sifters or specimen bags."

"She was going to . . . destroy the site?" Unease in her gut lent the guess the heft of truth. "What did we turn up?"

Vale's head tilted, and after a moment, she said, "You're going to dive, aren't you?"

"What else can I do?" What else was there for Key to do but search for the truth, as demanded by her ancestors? To take hold of the past and bring it to the present and link them together to provide comfort for those who had questions? To ensure people could be seen and heard and remembered, even if the lens was turned on herself, even if what came under the glass was ugly and malformed. That was the burden of history and truth. Without that burden, Key would be a storyteller, dealing in myths and parables. And people—communities, societies—could easily be led astray with fairy tales.

That was the burden she had also shouldered when she joined the museum as an associate hunter, though at the time, her excitement and enthusiasm over realizing her dream had eclipsed the solemnity of public history. The truth could be unkind, but the duty of the anthropologist or the historian meant she had to stand in front of it, unflinching. Genevieve, Key realized, had illuminated the museum and all inside it with the brightest light, and only now did Key notice that there were no shadows and no way to tell they had been blinded.

The sense of *right* in her strengthened, intensified. It began transforming, the doubt from earlier burning away to reveal something pure. Key's holy directive was not to provide comfort, as she had long suspected. Neither was it her mission to walk in her grandmother's footsteps. No, Key's holy directive was to provide *answers*.

"Genevieve is scared of whatever's in here. This is the only specimen I have. There's a strong chance I won't find anything. But I'd rather try and fail than never try at all."

Vale looked at her for a minute, staying quiet long enough that Key thought it might be the end of the conversation. Eventually, she said, "You know there's no coming back from this. The thing you've wanted your whole life, it's already gone. I don't know what'll happen if you dive again. You're going back to the same memory that caused you trouble. Is it worth it? Wouldn't you rather walk away? I know you don't want to hear it, but go to the temple. Become—"

"No." Key steeled herself. Holding back would mean that what she said to Vale only minutes ago would be all lies. "The reintegration didn't work. I still have intrusive memories. Nothing changes for me whether I do it or not. I have to know what she's afraid of. I have to know why I did all this."

"You might be able to overcome the intrusions right now. But if you dive again, if you come out with less of your mind, you're dead the second any guardian susses you out. Guaranteed."

Key wasn't so sure a run-of-the-mill guardian would be willing to mercy kill the only child of Lanelle and Mershon Strade, but Vale had the right of it. "I know."

"So you need me to help you?"

"I want you to help me." Key swallowed. "But no. I don't need you to help me."

"Who will sing you out?"

Key shrugged. "Genevieve has been diving on her own, somehow. It stands to reason that I can too."

Vale considered her. "It's dangerous."

"Which is why I'm not asking you to help me. I'll wake up. I'll deal with it."

"I can't . . ." Vale sighed. "I'll watch you."

Key's mouth twitched. "I don't know what else to say but thank you. I know it's not easy being generous."

Vale's dark eyes were unreadable.

"One last dive, then?"

Vale set her sword point-down on the floor, wedging its length between the wall and the seat to secure it. She reached for the seat back in front of her and hauled herself to standing. "There's no good place to dive, but maybe you can lie across two seats. Use your rucksack as a pillow."

"Okay." Key got up, dragged her rucksack down from the overhead rack, and plopped it onto the window seat. She then took the specimen out of her pocket and sat in the aisle seat. "This is the only one I have," she said. "It feels like there should be something . . . bigger than this. Like I should say some words before we pray."

Vale scoffed, coming to stand beside her. "You've been at temple too long."

Key lowered herself, wiggling until she was marginally more comfortable. She opened the bag and reached in, pinching the tab with her fingers and pulling it out. She exhaled, then opened her mouth.

"Cochineal," Vale said softly.

Key paused, then blinked at the sudden, furious needling of tears. "It smells awful."

There was a responding shine in Vale's eyes. "You complained so much."

"Cochineal." She placed the tab on her tongue, holding Vale's gaze. Bitterness and spice filled her mouth, and her salivary glands went into overdrive, sending an ache into her jaw. She closed her eyes.

Saint Aurissa, guide me.

Key felt the touch of Vale's hand on hers before she fell backward, sinking into memory.

Diving experiences vary among individuals, which makes sense when one thinks of it. The blood chalice and how it takes up memories is still not fully understood, and the key to its cultivation, the food that makes the spores morph into hyphae and tangle into mycelium, was discovered as a fluke. Key's instructors at the academy couldn't answer questions about why the fungus did what it did, what role it played in its natural environment, or why humans had developed the ability to read memories from it.

Key's sense of self balloons out, stretching joyfully past the limits of her body. So too do her senses, expanding in filaments that branch and converge and branch again, seeking the greater unknown. She—whatever constitutes her, whatever parts of her soul live in the liminal spaces between her brain and the electric impulses that form her mind—seeps into the world around her, connecting to thousands of points, plugging into the universe. It is she, and she is it.

She can't stay in this spiritual, euphoric state for long; she has been called, and she must answer. Reluctantly, she picks one of the many branches, operating on instinct, knowing somehow which one will take her to the memory she seeks. She enters it, and the world shrinks until she's floating again, corporeal again, her self delineated sharply from the stuff surrounding her.

It's likely the blood chalice has drawn into it new material along with the old, but Key won't know until she does, the same way she knows anything when she's diving. Things are not until they are. Memories don't exist until they do. In one moment, it's dark, and in the next, the memories flutter and snap, vivid streamers of color. She picks the one she already knows, the one that tastes of salt and pepper and butter.

She plunges through time, passing the lean years, the storms one after another, the melancholy winds blowing past erased coastal towns. Key drops back, fades further from the present, neck-deep in memory but not yet at her destination. The years press in on her, and like before, it grows more and more difficult to dive; she pushes through year after year like she's encased in gelatin.

Finally, bitter metal coats her tongue, and she knows she's found the correct memory. Once again she deforms herself, shaping herself to fit. It's so much easier this time to shave off what doesn't belong. Here she is in the kitchen with her grandfather and his white-rimmed eyes, the mug before her, the wood of the kitchen table rough beneath her hand.

"Can't we do it later?" she asks.

"You cannot take from the chalice later. There is a timeline for it." Her grandfather spoons honey into the tea and holds the spoon over the mug, and she watches the slow ooze of it thin out to a thread. The honey doesn't help. The tea, if it can be called tea, retains a sludgy, gritty mouthfeel and a coppery tang that no sweetness or thickness can mask.

Her grandfather finishes stirring and pushes the mug toward her, leaning across the table until he's close enough for her to see the rheum at the edges of his irises. She swallows and backs up in her chair, unsure now what to do, hoping that her father will return soon. Lately, her grandfather has been erratic, more erratic than usual, and it's getting to a point where she feels uneasy around him.

"You must drink this. You will be anointed. You will know the truth."

The truth is that she doesn't want to do it. Not anymore. "I think I'm all right not being anointed."

"You don't know what you're turning away. I'm offering you a chance. You've had one drink, but it takes two or more. If it isn't meant to be, then nothing will happen. Either you wake up blessed tomorrow, or you stay as you are. What's wrong with that?"

"Can I have something to eat as I drink it?" She eyes the cup. The powder is forming on the top, gray bits clumping together, looking much like the scum boiled out of the hog bones they use to make stock.

"No. Better to get it over with now."

She exhales, hesitant, and brings the mug to her lips. The first sip scalds her tongue, and she jerks away, avoiding splashing the tea out of the mug.

"More honey, please," she says, grimacing. The front of her tongue is a crackling numbness. Her grandfather puts more honey in, stirs, and sits back.

The next sip is an improvement, though it's like saying a blizzard is an improvement over a nor'easter. She inhales through her nose and drinks, ignoring the cutting heat in her throat and chest, just wanting to get as much of it down as possible without throwing up. She'd almost done it yesterday.

Movement catches her attention from outside. It's her father, his head and shoulders dusted with snow, with a rabbit in one hand and a bundle of firewood in the other. She gets up so quickly that her chair falls over, bounding for the door to open it. Heat sloshes in her belly. "Papa!"

He hands the wood over without a sound, grips the doorframe, knocks the snow loose from each boot before he steps inside. Her grandfather turns, those blue eyes piercing.

"What's this?" her father says, looking at the unlabeled container of what was once chicory coffee on the counter. "What are you doing?"

"Just having some tea," her grandfather says.

Her father drops the rabbit onto the counter and pries the lid off the container. His eyes widen, and his face, the medium brown skin already ruddy and glowing from the cold, gains an undertone of lurid, angry red. "What did you do to her?"

"We're just having tea!" Her grandfather stands and faces her father.

"You gave it to her!" Her father slams the lid on the counter hard enough to send vibrations through the floor. "I told you not to!"

The sloshing heat in her stomach putrefies.

"She wanted to do it."

"Did you?" Her father fixes her with his deep brown eyes.

She clutches the firewood to her chest, shakes her head rapidly. "No. But Grandpa said I would be blessed."

The rage increases on her father's face until it's as bright as the sun. She flinches from him, but he's no longer looking at her. "I told you never to bring this shit in here again!" he shouts, seizing the container, twisting the tap water on with such force that water bursts, surprised, from the faucet. He upends the container into the sink.

Her grandfather leaps toward the kitchen, but it's too late. Her father is already sending the dust into the pipes. "No!" her grandfather howls. "She must be made to see!"

"You're insane!" her father shouts back, shaking the tin in her grandfather's face. "What were you thinking, giving this to her?" He throws it into the sink with a clang. "Bad enough you give it to the believers. Not to your granddaughter! Not to my daughter!"

"You deny our ancestors. Why do you want to be closed to them?" her grandfather demands. There are tears brimming in his eyes, and she can't tell if it's because he's arguing with her father, or because he's mourning the powder that's gone down the drain. What had he given her?

"I am not closed to them. But what you do is blasphemy. It's sin." Her father shuts the water off, grabs her grandfather's arm. "You're to leave now. You and all who follow you. I've tolerated your fanaticism and your experiments, but that stops now. Keep it to yourself, I said. Don't force it on someone who doesn't know what you're doing."

The nausea returns, building in her, rising in degrees up her throat. "What did I drink?"

"Nothing," her grandfather says quickly, just as her father says, "Hog brains. Dried and ground up."

She puts a hand to her mouth; she puts two hands to her mouth, dropping the bundle of wood. Her stomach squeezes and the tea spills up and out. She gags, scrambling to the sink, coppery bile and honey and blobby gray brain spewing from her mouth and nose, hitting the tin, splashing onto the faucet, the counter, the floor. Between each heave she hears snippets of the argument happening.

"You don't know—"

"You're right, I don't know—"

"You've never been willing to take risks. Your whole life you've been like this—"

"This isn't a risk, it's insanity! You're killing these animals—"

Her grandfather begins laughing, a wild, shrill sound she's never heard in her life. She clings to the counter, dizzy and shaking and swaying on her feet, hoping she's purged everything from her system. She hasn't had time for it to be digested, she hopes.

Except she had some yesterday.

"Animals? You think this is hog brain? We take of the blessed for the blessed, my son. The flesh of the Progenitor consecrates the willing. Your daughter will be a voice among many."

"You're sick," her father breathes.

She has no idea what it means and doesn't have time to wonder as her father yanks on her arm, spinning her, and jams a thumb into the hollow of her collarbone. She gags and swallows, then retches onto the floor.

"Get out!" her father shouts at her grandfather, but her grandfather continues laughing. Her father hauls the kitchen door open, grabs fistfuls of her grandfather's shirt. "Get out, and never come back!"

The memory frays, wearing thin like an over-loved blanket. Key pops out the other side of it, molded in the shape of the nameless girl. Other memories branch from her, so many that they form a tangled mat. One of them is thicker and stronger than the rest, so she moves toward it. She fits it easily, the memory enveloping her, becoming her skin.

She's with her grandfather again. It's been months since she's seen him. After he left, she'd been ill for a week, lying abed consumed with fever and hallucinations. They'd taken the form of her grandmother, who'd died years ago, and it was that holy vision that convinced her to seek her grandfather out, that vision which has driven her to be here today. She's sitting by his bedside.

He has deteriorated. There is no other word for it. He moves rarely, and when he does, he shakes. It's a shocking development since the last time she saw him, when he could split lumber and tend his garden with ease. He speaks just as rarely, and often the only sign he's paying attention is the movement of his eyes, the whites of them as deadened and wilted as old parchment.

His followers are gathered outside, chanting, their voices rising and falling in melodious waves. They fracture in and out of harmony; let it not be said the faithful cannot sing. It's the voice that links everything, her grandfather used to say. We use our voices to exalt. We speak for those who cannot. And we are the voices of those who came before us, who continue to guide us. We are the blessed.

"Grandpa," she says, touching his hand. Her father doesn't know she's here. He hasn't seen the note her grandfather snuck into her room during her times of delirium. But her father suspects something has happened. He might be searching for her now. She has to finish the rite quickly.

Her grandfather's hand flexes, and she takes it in hers, squeezes it. He squeezes back, his strength a distant echo of hers. He's aware she's here. His eyes sharpen, and he turns his head to her, his lips seaming open and shut.

She hums the song from outside. It's an old tune, widely known, but the words have been adapted by her grandfather and the others from the first crop into a hymn for their humble temples. He squeezes her hand again, and she takes it as permission to sing. She fills the small room with her voice. Her grandfather draws in a tremulous breath, air escaping from his throat as he tries to sing with her.

Nothing but a soft moan comes out, but she understands his intent. He's ready to join the ancestors, and the rite is how she will inherit all he knows. "Do you see me?" he mouths when the song is over. "Do you see me?"

"You are seen, Grandpa." She's holding a needle in her other hand. "You are seen and heard. And you are remembered."

He trembles with the effort of lifting his hand, so she eases his way and lifts it for him. His other arm jerks, so she waits for the spasm to pass in order to perform the rite safely. It won't do to stab herself by accident. When his arm stills, she takes the needle and pricks his finger, the tip of the needle slipping through layers of papery skin. A meager amount of blood appears, a red so dark it's black in the low light.

"Go in peace, Grandpa," she says, bowing her head. "I will become you, as you and all the others became the Progenitor. You are sanctified."

She puts her grandfather's finger between her lips, and iron and copper flood her mouth. The blessing of the ancestors takes effect immediately, yanking her from consciousness. She tumbles onto her grandfather's body, her eyes open and unfocused as she's pulled into the current of ancestral memory. She sees, now, understands what it is her grandfather has been doing. The procedure to extract her grandfather's brain is stomach-turning, and it will bring her no joy to defile his corpse, but the flesh is temporary. He has made the final sacrifice for the future. The blessing he can provide them will last through generations.

His memories will become hers the way his predecessor's memories became his; his memories will become the common ground for all the believers. They will be sanctified.

FOURTEEN

AFFIRMATIONS

I, Genevieve Clarinda Wilcroft, am the best memory hunter of the entire Spine. I make wonderful, thrilling, unique, impossible discoveries that benefit all humankind. I am the first Wilcroft to become head curator at the Museum of Human Memory, the youngest ever to do it, and the first Wilcroft to become director of the Institute of Human Memory. I am a cornerstone scholar in my chosen fields and I never want for funding. I am known outside my field of study. I am known to the general public. A permanent collection is named after me. I do not let anyone or anything stand in my way, and I SUCCEED at everything I decide to do.

—Journal of Genevieve Wilcroft, aged twenty

HER MOTHER'S LULLABY WOVE THROUGH HER, CARRIED ON THE silver thread of a voice. She opened her eyes to the back of what looked like a bus seat—no, a train. Her head was on someone's lap. She turned herself, her body a chorus of groans, and wetness rolled over the bridge of her nose. Above her was a woman with a freshly bruised face and concerned, dark eyes, her black hair bound back. A thin ribbon served as a headband.

"Key?" the woman whispered. "You're crying."

She blinked, and more wetness ran down the sides of her face. She *was* crying. She lifted a hand, scraped away tears with her fingers.

"Here, let me help you up," the woman said. "My legs are gonna fall asleep and you should go to the toilet. I let you stay in for double."

She sat up, putting a hand to her head. "Where . . . ?"

The woman narrowed her eyes, then indicated the door of the train car. "Behind there."

She stood, grabbing one of the safety rails to keep her balance, and took the few steps needed to get to the door. She wrestled it open, then the bathroom door, finding herself in a dingy stall with a filthy toilet and meager sink. After relieving herself, she washed her hands with a dirt-streaked sliver of soap, waiting for the thin stream of water to rinse the gray bubbles away.

A glance in the mirror made her stop and stare, the water continuing to snake in small rivulets over her hands. Her face was familiar and not, like a favorite cousin seen only once a year, or an old classmate who'd fallen out of touch. She reached for her reflection, touching her cheeks, her fingers leaving teardrops of water on the glass.

Who am I?

"I am blessed," she muttered, and then began laughing. She clutched the sink and leaned helplessly against it, tasting iron and honeyed tea, bile pressing upward in her throat in an inexorable crawl. She gagged and dry heaved, laugh-sobbed herself out of breath and sank into a squat, gagged again and stood too swiftly and had to lean on the sink once more, sparks swimming in her vision.

"Key?" The woman from before pushed her way into the bathroom, coming closer with the manner of someone approaching a cornered animal.

Key. Was that who she was? Her arm muscles bunched as she forced herself upright, her breathing erratic. The other woman's name came to her without effort. "Vale."

"Are you okay? What the hell happened on the dive?" Vale held the door open for her, and Key staggered back to her seat, her legs suddenly unsteady.

She landed without grace on the seat and put her hands over her face, leaning her elbows on her knees.

Vale sat beside her. "What's our word?"

This, too, came to her effortlessly. "Cochineal."

"Who are you?"

"I," she began. Her voice rasped, as if she hadn't used it in days. She cleared her throat. "I don't know."

The woman swore. "Who am I?"

"Vale."

"What's the last thing you remember?"

"My grandfather," she said. "He was . . . dying. I gave him the last words. I took his blood."

"Anything else?"

"There were people outside. Standing vigil. I didn't know all of them, but they all came to learn from him. To build a new faith and a new temple. They were singing." She watched the woman's lips purse while thinking.

"What song was it?"

"Old tune," she replied immediately. "New words."

"Can you sing it for me?"

She nodded, sat straighter, and began. Her voice was low, the timbre husky and compelling, with the sheen of brushed copper. But that wasn't right. Her voice was supposed to be higher, breathier, weaker as it climbed. She faltered, unsure.

"Go on," Vale urged her softly. "A circle unbroken. And then?"

"It's not right." She frowned.

"It sounded right to me."

"No. My voice. It's not right." She placed a hand on her throat, swallowing. "I don't feel . . . right."

"Sometimes you can unlace when you come back." The term meant nothing to her, except she understood instinctively what it meant. "I might be able to help. Do you know this song?"

Vale hummed for a few seconds.

"It sounds familiar," she allowed. "The melody is nice. Is there more?"

"Yes," Vale said. "It's the lullaby your mother used to sing to you when you were a child." Vale took a breath, and this time she *sang*, and her voice was silver and moonlight, the chime of a crystal wineglass, the running of snowmelt beneath a strong sun. As she sang, bits and pieces of memory flashed, fragments of images passing by too quickly for her to comprehend, streaking through her mind like a radio dial being turned from the lowest frequency to the highest. A circular pool. *Acusdactylus caliceum*, the needle orchid. Static. A revolver on a shelf. A stately woman with medium brown skin and hoops in her ears and webs of mycelium filigreed over her bicep. An older man, pale, laughing wildly.

The song stopped, and someone took her hand, uncurled her fingers, and squeezed. "Key, look at me," said Vale. But she couldn't, hunching into herself, covering her face with her elbow. *Who am I? Who am I?*

An answer key. Mean throwing mean, all the way down the line. Stained glass, stained glass, stained glass. Shelves of brown paper folders in a stifling, windowless room. Falling snow and hymns and a skull cracked open as delicately as a soft-boiled egg.

Who am I?

A pinch of pain made her head snap up.

Vale leaned in and kissed her cheek, hard and swift, then pulled away, her eyes intense. "Who are you?"

Shock made several memories rattle back into their correct spots. ". . . Key?"

"Damn," Vale muttered. "Okay, then." She leaned in once more, slower this time, her eyelids lowering.

Key parted her lips, expectant.

"No," Vale whispered when she was achingly close. "I'll get blood in your . . ." Instead, she placed her fingers across Key's mouth, then lowered herself to Key's neck.

The first touch of Vale's lips on her pulse made her gasp, the air hissing through the spaces between Vale's fingers. Vale's tongue flickered, then pressed over the skin of Key's neck; Key moaned, arching, desire unshackling itself from its hidden places. Over the last year, she'd had a recurring dream where a mysterious someone had laid claim to her just like this, but it would always end before she could see who it was. Key knew now, as heat spiraled through her, that it was Vale.

The kiss broke off abruptly; Key's eyes snapped open to see Vale widening the gap between them, high color in her cheeks. Key stared at Vale and the fresh, bright blood welling in a string of tiny beads at the corner of her lip, where it was split.

"Who are you?" Vale demanded.

"Kiana Strade," she replied immediately.

"Details."

"I'm a hunter—was a hunter. For the Museum of Human Memory."

"And who am I?"

"Vale."

"The full name I was given."

"Valerian IV. Guardian. Former guardian."

Vale's jaw flexed. "It worked. You back all the way now, Key?"

"Yes." Saints, was what Vale had done an escalation of the grounding techniques taught at the academy? Or had Vale given in to the feelings Key was increasingly sure were there? She resisted touching her neck, where the ghostly imprint of Vale's lips lingered. It was better by far than the edge of Vale's knife.

"Did you get anything?"

Key scraped her tongue against her molars, then swallowed. Her head was starting to ache. "I saw a lot."

"Was it worth the dive?"

She closed her eyes, letting her head fall against the wall of the train car. What, precisely, had she witnessed? "I think I saw . . . Vale, I think I saw the creation of our ancestor worship customs."

"I thought we had been doing that for centuries."

Key rolled her head back and forth against the wall, then opened her eyes. "Yes, us as a whole, but in this region. It's different for you, right? In the south."

Vale shrugged. "We definitely don't do it your way, and neither do Jing and Cal."

"Yes. Our records point to the first temples being established around the end of the Decade of Storms. What if . . ." She trailed off. "No. I know. I think I must have witnessed the beginnings of the temple."

Vale gave her a frankly skeptical look, all traces of her blush gone. "How would you know that?"

"Because," Key answered, "the ritual was performed. Whoever I was inhabiting, she knew what to do."

"The ritual, like 'see me'?"

"You are seen," Key said automatically. "Yes. That one. And at the end, she pricked her grandfather's finger and"—her face twisted with disgust—"licked the blood off it."

"Ew," Vale said.

"Oh, saints." Key put a hand to her head, swooning as she recalled the scene in the kitchen. A teaspoon clinked, and on the backs of her eyelids, an image of the kitchen table formed. "I—think I saw— I'm—"

"What did you see?"

She opened her eyes, but the vision of the table refused to fade. The memory of the powder in the tea was so vivid Key almost spat to get the taste out of her mouth. "Can't we do it later?" she muttered.

Vale put a hand on her shoulder, and that simple act was enough to bring Key's awareness back to the present. She was on the train, not in the kitchen. There was no grandfather, only Vale and her bruised face and mirrorlike black eyes.

"What did you see?" Vale said.

Key tried to respond, but her thoughts were swarming, in disarray. If the girl had drunk the tea and gained the ability, even after throwing it up . . . "I saw the same scene I told you about before. With the grandfather and the powder he put in the tea. I found out what it was, and . . . Do you remember saying, a few days ago, that people can get diseases from brains?"

"Yeah. Why are you asking?"

Key swallowed. "Because that's what this person's grandfather put in her tea. Dried, ground-up brain. Said it'd turn her into one of the blessed."

"Blessed like you?"

Vale didn't have to put it so bluntly, but her words made it all too clear. "Yes. Blessed like me. Able to be a voice for the ancestors. Her grandfather was the leader of the group, but . . . I think there was more than one group."

Key slipped easily into the recollection. "I didn't want it. It's gross. And then my father came back, and I threw up, and my father and grandfather had an argument, and—"

"What? What's wrong?"

"They argued about my grandfather feeding me pig brains. And then my grandfather laughed and said the flesh of the Progenitor consecrates the willing."

Silence.

"Okay." Vale said. "Okay, first, that's disgusting. Second, that's not a religion, that's a cult. You're telling me all of this is based on some guy two hundred forty years ago eating a man's brain and learning how to dive?"

Key shook her head, unable to speak.

Vale pressed her fingertips to her forehead, her eyes going wide. "Blood in the mouth, I can't— Did you really find the start of all this? Is that possible? A lot of people can use memory tabs made with the mushroom juice. There's . . . Key, what do you call it? The thing. Everyone has it."

"A baseline ability," Key said, tilting her head back. "But you don't have it."

"No, I don't. The tabs just give me a weird trip."

Key focused on breathing in through her nose and out through her mouth. What she couldn't calm were the storm of thoughts in her head. "We all—except you and a few others—are capable of experiencing these memories, if we have the right circumstances."

"Yeah. Some combination of genetic material and mushroom juice, right? Okay, so if everyone can do it, it's got to have been something we could do for a long time. Someone like Jing wouldn't have been able to suddenly develop that ability on his own. Then what you saw must have been, like . . . a boost?"

"Whatever happened, it enhanced the ability." Key closed her eyes, unable to bear the sight of the ceiling. The space around her wheeled, leaving her reeling. Saints, she wasn't blessed. She was cursed. Unclean. How could the world go on unperturbed after what she'd learned? "We don't have records in the temple about its beginnings. It's as if the temple sprang out of nowhere, with resifixes already in place. There was a schism early on, where some resifixes left because they thought they needed to be watched over, but . . . Vale, I can't. Everything is ruined. I can't."

Softly, Vale said, "You can't what?"

"Can't go back to the temple. It's all a lie. It's always been a lie. We're not blessed at all. This is a *disease*. All those times I was told I could dive farther because I was blessed—that I knew things because I was born righteous, that I could trust in my connection to the saints—none of that is true.

None of this ever existed! We've been making it up all along, lying to people who put their trust in us, who really think we can speak with the ancestors. And the worst thing is, I don't know if my family knows we've been lying! Is this why my grandmother left? Is it— Does my mother—"

She felt a hand on her knee. Vale's warmth seeped through the cloth of Key's pants. Key pressed fists to her eyes, her body bowing in defeat. "What have I been doing? How can I reconcile what I know with what I've done? The saints *ate* each other. Infected who knows how many others. My family is tainted. How can I continue, knowing this? How many problems have I created because I believed falsely? How many people have I led astray?"

"Hey," Vale said. There were brief touches on Key's shoulder, her back, her head, as if Vale was trying to be soothing and couldn't figure out how to do it. "I'm no good at this cheering up thing. But none of this is your fault. This is how you were brought up. If I raised a chicken with a flock of ducks, it would think it's a duck. You've always been passionate about what you do. Whatever it is you've decided on, you give it your all. So I don't think you've led people astray, or failed them."

"It's all a lie," Key whispered. "And they should know about it. But I can't just . . . turn on the temple."

"I can't make that decision for you." Vale withdrew her hand and settled back into her seat; the bench creaked. Key's body tightened for want of comfort. "There's no good way out these brambles. But this is all on you. So let me ask you: What do you want to do?"

But there couldn't be any comfort. Not from the saints, and not from Vale. "I can't go back to the temple." Key put her hands down and opened her eyes. "And I can't go back to the museum either."

Vale's head tilted. "You think this is what Dr. Wilcroft came to get? You thought she was trying to steal the memory from you. This would be a big one."

"That doesn't make sense. Why would she put herself in direct conflict with the temple?" Key massaged the sides of her head, where throbbing aches had started. "Jing said Genevieve had her own agenda. That she wouldn't publicize something we found if it went against her principles. That she likes where she is, and she likes her power."

"Okay," Vale said. "He's always right about someone's character. Takes the bad in you to see the bad in someone else, he says. If he's clocked Dr. Wilcroft, I'd trust it. But tell me, when did he give you this free advice?"

"I didn't say it was free."

"You didn't have to. Something this serious always has a price. Jing doesn't do anything for free, unless it's for Cal."

"Not even for you?"

Vale laughed, but it had no joy. "Especially not for me. Nothing's free, where he comes from. That cute little bread-breaking custom they have out west, that equivalent exchange thing they give each other in greeting and stuff? That's not just for show. It evens the scales for them. So if he's given you advice and you haven't paid, you owe him."

"He said it was free."

"And you trusted him?" Vale laughed again, the sound cutting.

"I don't know what I can give him. I don't know if I'll get the chance to ask. I don't know what to do after this. I don't know if I can go home and look my parents in the face. I can't go to the temple. I don't want anyone seeing me. I don't know what anyone's doing here! Genevieve—"

There was a flash of clarity. Perhaps her ability to dive wasn't divinely granted by the saints, but her intuition had to be. It hadn't failed her yet. She could take heart from that.

With talent like that, you're bound to come across unsettling things, Jing had said. Did *he* know? Did Cal? "She already knows what's there. She had to be one of the hunters the villagers talked about. The records must have been expunged. And Jing has to know, too, he must have been the other hunter mentioned. He and Cal lied when they said they hadn't been here. He said Genevieve wants to preserve the status quo. She likes where she is. She especially likes her career and how far she's come. She can't have this information getting out and undermining the museum and the temple. She'd rather cover it up than let it out."

"I got fired because she was gonna play dirty, huh?" Vale snorted.

"You got fired because my head's too big for my shoulders." Key looked at Vale and waited until Vale made eye contact. "It's my direct actions that got you fired. I'm still sorry about it. I want to make it up to you however you want. In whatever way I can."

The narrowing of Vale's eyes told Key the apology had not been accepted. "I don't know why I'm gonna ask. It's not like I'm getting my job back." Vale sighed. "So, again, what do you want to do?"

Key rubbed her temples again, then scraped her tongue over her top teeth. The taste of the tea lingered. "Do you think anything would change if this information went public?"

Vale shook her head. "I don't know. People are a mess. Some of them would care, I think. And some of them wouldn't. It's in the past, what's it got to do with them?"

"I want to believe that they would."

"But then what would happen after? People would quit going to the temple because of something that happened hundreds of years ago? Might be nothing happens at all. This is a big city. Lots of people, lots of opinions. There'll be people who feel like you. And there'll be people out there who won't give a shit."

"The truth is important," Key murmured. "That's what I was always taught. This is a moral and ethical obligation. I was given this . . . gift . . . to be a voice, to speak the truth. That gift is rotten, and everything built on it is rotten, but I still believe in the saints. The ancestors were real, and their experiences are what guide us. The people who come to see me have to take it on faith that the saints were real. They choose to believe in my connection. But I have no choice. The memories I hold are from those who came before us. I'm obligated to tell the truth; what would be the point of anything if I lied? No. I was called to this mission."

"Are you going to stand in the center of the city and yell? Hand out pamphlets?"

"Maybe?" Key knuckled her forehead. "Maybe if I preach at the next service . . ."

"I think that'd be dangerous for you. You're going to be blaspheming in the eyes of the ancestors. Half the city goes to the temple, and they all know who you are and what you stand for. You can't just drop into town and start saying the exact opposite without proof."

"So we have to go back to the museum." Key groaned. "For an extraction. I can't be the only one holding this memory. We'll need to refine and duplicate it, and the lab is the only place that can do that."

"And the only place where you can be reintegrated," Vale added.

"I don't want to forget—" Key started but faltered at the expression on Vale's face. *I don't want to forget the taste of you.*

Vale's mouth thinned. "It's for the best. We have to try. It's not safe otherwise."

"Okay." Key owed that much to her. "I'll do it. I promise. I'll listen to you."

"I'm not your guardian anymore," Vale said quietly.

"I did prefer you as my friend." And she would have wanted Vale as a lover.

Vale swallowed. "To be honest, I'm not sure if I'm your friend anymore either."

Key blinked back sudden tears, her chest going tight, as if Vale had taken her sword and eased it between the chambers of her heart. She deserved it. This. To feel the consequences of her actions. To know what lay between them could never bloom fully. "I'd like you to be."

"What can you do for me now, Key? After everything you've done? You can't fix it with money or a new job as your personal guard—" Vale's voice caught. "No. I was—" Her voice caught again. "For old times' sake. I'll go with you to the museum."

"And after?"

Vale stood and went across the aisle to her rucksack. From it, she fished out a new journal and a pencil and thrust it at Key. "Do your thing. Write. We got some time before we're back in the city."

Key's hand trembled as she took the notebook, her vision blurring as tears welled and spilled down her cheeks. Across the aisle, Vale resumed her seat, her sword in her lap, her face turned away.

FIFTEEN

The Museum of Human Memory has been a leader in memory sciences since its founding. The museum, a marvel of architecture located on the slopes of Ashe's Peak, is funded by the Asheburg Council for Public History and boasts the longest continuously running research and field retrieval program in the Spine and one of the largest collections of memories in the world. Experience memories firsthand through highly detailed historical memory tabs while resting in the softest recliners in the city, all custom-designed for patron comfort. Visit the museum from Firstday to Fifthday to see how the museum carries out its mission of benefiting society. Of special note is the Strade Collection, located on the fourth floor, and the Curator's Corner, located on the second floor.

—"Asheburg, Jewel of the Spine," a travel brochure

VALE FOLLOWED ON KEY'S HEELS AS SHE SWEPT INTO THE FRONT entrance of the Museum of Human Memory, her carriage straight, chin held at a slight upward tilt, the butt of her staff tapping sharp and severe against the sandstone floor. Though she was wearing a set of plain travel clothes and her hair was a frizzy, uneven halo around her head, she had gathered about her an air of importance that wouldn't be out of place at one of her father's city council dinners. For the afternoon, Key had eschewed her approachable, saintlike exterior in favor of her mother's demeanor, transforming into a woman on a holy mission, shot unerringly at her destination as an arrow from a bow.

Not a bit of the turmoil Vale had witnessed on the train—the crying, the praying, the crying and praying—showed in Key's appearance, despite the exhaustion shadowing her eyes. Petitioners were received with sincere warmth and generosity, but dispatched quickly, and all questions regarding Vale's appearance were deflected.

Key lifted a hand in brief greeting to Alec, whose head came up sharply with surprise, then banked to the right, toward the elevators. She was remarkably serene, unlike Vale, who had traded her previous calm for a twitchy anxiety. She was full of so many thoughts dashing in different directions that she was sure passersby could catch them. She'd need to move in with Jing and Cal. Which meant she had to explain her new lack of employment to them. Should she say anything about the brains? Was Jing infected like Key, or did something else allow him to dive because he was from the west? It would be weird to ask. Would she have to tell Jing about Key kissing her? Would she have to tell him that she kissed Key back? More than once? That probably counted as cheating. She shouldn't say anything.

Key cast a quick look at Vale before pressing the down button for the elevator. "Almost there," she whispered, then lifted her gaze to the row of numbers above the elevator doors.

The sound of soles tapping against the polished floor caught Vale's attention. She turned to see Alec walking up, his floppy brown hair tousled as if he'd pushed his fingers through it repeatedly. He stopped in front of her, shifting his weight from foot to foot, his hands flexing and unflexing as his mouth opened and closed.

Vale said flatly, "What?"

"Hi?" Alec's face started to get pinker.

"Hi, Alec," Key said, giving him a brief smile. "Is something the matter?"

"I'm sorry, Miss Key," he stammered, "you and . . . Miss Vale aren't allowed to go down there."

Vale's stomach plummeted.

Key smiled pleasantly, seemingly unaffected. "I'm not sure what you're talking about. Vale and I have some important business to attend to."

"I'm sure," he replied, his face attaining a glow usually granted to the most determined of drunks. Vale was worried he'd burst a blood vessel, which would be a pain for her to deal with, seeing as the academy hadn't trained her on anything other than field medicine and first aid. Aneurysms were out of the question. "B-but Dr. Wilcroft sent a gram this morning and . . ." He trailed off, then gulped.

"Vale," Key murmured, touching her shoulder. "You're frightening him."

"Am I?" Vale responded, then realized she was leaning forward and glaring.

"I'm sorry," Alec said again. "I can't let you go down there. Please don't kill me. I'm just the messenger. It's what Dr. Wilcroft said."

Vale tried not to glare further and failed. "Did she tell you why?"

"Because you're no longer employees at the museum," Alec said so softly Vale could hardly hear it. "She didn't say anything else."

"We can at least go down to get our things, right?" Key settled into her temple voice. "Surely Genevieve would let us clean out our desks, as it were."

Alec shook his head rapidly. "No. I mean, no, ma'am! I'm sorry. She said, in her own words, that under no circumstances were you to be permitted back in the offices or the labs, and you were to be confined to the lobby."

Vale broke in. "We can't even look at the exhibits?"

"I don't know!" Alec said, backing up a step, his eyes darting downward. With effort, Vale took her hand off the pommel of her sword. "She didn't say anything else!"

"That's just not fair." Key sounded level, but she took on a gently chiding tone, as if Alec were a youth and she were rather disappointed that he'd taken cookies away from a sibling. "My family is responsible for multiple items and experiences in the museum. We can't be barred from enjoying our own work."

"That's what she said!" The elevator dinged, and the doors slid open. Alec scuttled in front of the doors and flung his arms wide, barring entry. "My job's on the line if I don't do this! I'm sorry. I really need this job."

Vale took a breath.

"You said just the lobby," Key said, interrupting her. "We can stay in the lobby. If you could be so kind as to call Dr. Arman and ask him to come up, we'd like to say goodbye to him."

Alec shook his head again, his eyes showing white all around. "You have to leave. I'm so sorry. Dr. Wilcroft's orders."

"Vale." Key tugged on her hand as the elevator doors closed.

She almost snatched her hand out of Key's grip but thought better of it. "Get Dr. Arman, Alec. It's the least you could do. We won't even be breaking any rules if we stay in the foyer."

"If I could do it, I would, I swear!"

The tromp of boots on the floor echoed through the open space of the museum, and Vale followed the turn of Alec's head toward the lobby.

"What the fuck?" she spat. "You called security on us?" She lunged for the down button to the elevator, dragging Key behind her, but Alec was faster than she gave him credit for, throwing himself in front of her, causing their bodies to crash together. Vale swore, wrenched her hand free from Key's, and dealt Alec a full-armed slap across the face that sent him stumbling to the side.

"Vale!" Key exclaimed.

But Vale's blood was up as she stared at Alec, who was huddled against the wall. The only specimen they had to re-integrate Key with was downstairs, and Vale was not about to let a coward get in her way. Mad as she was at Key, she could not leave her with half a mind and no escape plan. "I'm giving you this one chance to let us by. Or it's gonna be your guts on the floor."

"You can't do that!" Alec protested.

"You're right," Vale admitted. "It'll be your blood on the floor instead. You can bleed lots and not die."

"Vale!" Key snapped, grabbing her by the arm before she could fully draw her sword. "We're—"

Three security guards arrived, all men, and arranged themselves in the doorway to the lobby.

Vale gritted her teeth, taking stock of the situation. Three against one—four, if she counted Alec—was bad odds, but not impossible if she took the correct sequence of actions. Burdock would categorize it as a challenge. "Too late."

"We'll go quietly and won't cause you any trouble," Key said, stepping in front of Vale, her back straightening, her shoulders leveling. "It wouldn't do to harm a resifix and her guardian, would it?"

One of the guards, a man of medium height who was built as solid as a ham hock, responded, "The head curator gave us license to deal with you and your feral cat in case you caused a fuss."

Key's voice firmed. "I will not tolerate your disrespect of me or my guardian. You will not lay hands on me. Let us by."

No one moved.

"I have an eidetic memory." Key drew herself up, gripping her staff as she did so. "You understand what that means, don't you? Of course you do. The ancestors gifted me with the ability to never forget anything. A face or a name, or a book I have read, or a memory I've retrieved. I remember it all."

Key inclined her head at the guard on the left, a taller, thinner man with a shaved head and an uncertain expression. He was also Vale's pick to be the first culled from the herd. "Lenny. You've always been kind to me. The first day I started here, you let me in early. Your wife came to service this past Saintsday. We've known each other for years, so you understand that I don't want to cause a conflict here."

Vale came to Key's side slowly, holding her breath as she watched the guards for signs of attack.

Lenny faltered.

"The saints bear witness." Key's tone grew soft. "It doesn't seem like it, but they do. They see each of you—all of us—at our best and worst. They see me right now, and they know you don't want to hurt me. You don't want to silence their voice. If you do, think about what consequences that will have—not just for you, or me, or my mother and father, but for the rest of the good people who come to temple services looking to reconnect to the past. To hear the wisdom of all those who came before them. To link forward and back and keep the circle unbroken."

Key closed her eyes briefly, sighing. "I know you don't want my blood on your hands. All we'd like to do is go in peace. But if you are ready to act regardless, then that's the will of the saints, and I'll kneel in front of you and bare my neck."

The three guards glanced at each other uneasily. Lenny stepped forward, bowing to Key, drawing a circle on his forehead. "No need, Miss Kiana. You can go. See me?"

"You are seen."

"Hear me."

"You are heard."

"Remember me."

"You are remembered." Key started toward the door, but Lenny stayed in his bow.

"Sanctify me."

She paused in front of him. The silence drew taut, and it seemed to Vale that even the sunlight held weight. Finally, after heartbeats upon heartbeats, Key spoke. "I'll see you at temple for service."

Then she turned on the ball of her foot and looked each

of the other security guards in the eye, as well as Alec, holding their gazes. "I hope to see you *all* at service."

"Yes, ma'am," one of the other security guards said, but Key was already gliding toward the front doors.

Vale congratulated herself for not kicking the nearest guard in the crotch and hurried after Key, whose long legs carried her farther per step. They passed through the pneumatic doors and into the humidity of the afternoon, hooking toward the incline.

Vale waited until they were almost there before speaking. "You've never done something like that before."

"I had to. You can't fight your way out of every situation, tempting as it is to let you, sometimes." Key slowed, glancing at an alleyway between two commercial buildings, then ducked into it. She put her face in her hands, drawing a loud breath through her fingers before exhaling and looking at the strip of sky overhead. The set of her shoulders softened and drooped, and the illusion diminished and bled away, leaving only a vulnerable, exhausted young woman. "Where do we go from here, Vale? Everything we need is at the museum."

"I don't know." Vale leaned against the wall opposite from Key and let her head fall back against the brick, breathing slow and deep to calm the adrenaline shakes. "Your house?"

"My mother can't know I got fired. Not yet. Or if she already does, I don't dare show my face." Key shuddered. "No. Not home. Any other suggestions?"

"The academy? There's a lab, right? It's set up for extractions."

"Yes," Key replied, "but it's not as advanced as the lab in the museum. It's for students and those who can't dive as deep as I can. And before you say something, yes, reintegrations are done there. But we don't . . . have a specimen. Vale, what are we going to do?"

"I don't know," she said, helpless. Short of breaking into the museum, there was nothing they could do. She poked at her forehead fruitlessly. She wasn't a solutions person.

But she knew someone who was.

She retreated to habit, her mind going to the one person who always had the answers, who, in all their years of knowing each other, had never let her down. "We should go see Burdock."

"What's he going to do, help you fight the guards?" Key turned her head to look at her, and Vale saw the long hours of travel showing plain on Key's face—purpling shadows beneath her eyes, an ashen cast to her skin. Vale's own face was probably the stuff of Alec's nightmares.

"No? I don't know. Maybe he knows a back way into the museum. He used to work there. He also has a lot of connections. Or maybe he knows of another place where we could—" Vale froze. "Wait."

"Wait what?"

"I bet he does," Vale breathed, an idea sparking in her head, one so ridiculous and counter to her beliefs that she could hardly believe she was suggesting it. "Key . . . what if we went to the black market for this?"

"I don't understand."

"What if," Vale said slowly, her mind turning over, "we solved our problems by going to the black market hunters? You have something they'll never get. They already know who you are and what you can do and have lost two of their people to get at you. Our problem is getting the word out.

You offer them the memory, and in return they distribute it for you. They got their own lab, their own radio operation, so I bet they have their own shipping, or whatever. Maybe you can get a cut of the money they'll make."

Key straightened. "Vale."

"It's not as stupid as it sounds!" For Vale, the puzzle pieces had already clicked together. The plan would work. It was perfect. As long as Burdock had a contact, they could make a deal. And if Burdock didn't, well . . . she could always bait the hook with herself somehow. The black market would pay a lot for her, Burdock had said. There was proof enough in all the offers that had come her way after her black-flag fights.

"It's not stupid." Key looked pensive as she spoke. "It's risky, but not stupid."

"Risky is all we got."

"What about my specimen?"

"We talk to Jing and Cal. They'll understand. They can get it for you fast."

"And what do we give Jing to get such a huge favor from him? Vale, he already knows the truth; he has to. And he hasn't done a thing about it."

Vale's forehead wrinkled as she tried to understand what Key was saying. "You don't know that for sure. And he likes money. Give him enough and he'll do most anything."

"I do know. And it's not going to work. But let's play the what-if game and assume I can get what he wants, which may not be money, and he agrees to the deal, and everything goes according to plan. I get reintegrated and it actually works. The black market takes us up on the offer, and the tab is made and goes into distribution. What then? Is truth-telling finished when the truth is made public and the teller can't remember the story? What do I do in the meantime? What do I do after?" Key slumped against the far wall, defeat in the lines of her shoulders, her grip around her staff slackening. "Do I continue as normal? But there won't be a normal after this. Do I talk to my mother? My father? Hold sermons at the temple? I don't know!"

For Vale, the answer was simple: Leave. Go somewhere else. "I don't know either," she said finally. "But I do know one thing. You'll do what you want, and this time you don't have to think about what everyone else is thinking. You'll get to make the choice for yourself."

"I'm going to need money." Key groaned. "But everything I have is at home or at the bank. And the banks are closing soon, if they aren't already. Alec is probably sending a gram back to Genevieve as we speak."

"Maybe you can't get to the bank, and maybe we can't ask Jing or Cal," Vale said, "but there's enough cash in the envelope you gave me to cover train fare up and down the Spine. Wherever you want to go next, you can do that. Set up a new life somewhere with what's left over. Hire out your skills. Won't be long before you'll be working steady, I promise. I'll take what I need for a one-way home. The rest is yours."

Vale watched the bob of Key's throat as she swallowed.

"You're not coming." It wasn't a question.

No, Vale was not going with Key. Maybe Burdock could recommend her for a post somewhere or take her on as a recruiter, and she could make enough money to stay on with Jing for a while as long as Cal was okay with having a second roommate. That sounded doable. Vale wouldn't have to worry about Key and her city girl tendencies, wouldn't be waiting to see broad shoulders, wouldn't feel soft fingers on her lips, wouldn't worry about getting expensive dresses dirty. Vale wouldn't think about the way Key's skin smelled or tasted. Jing would be enough. Was enough.

Or Vale could go home to the family she hadn't seen in a decade and spend with them the time she owed. Her nose stung. Vale had already cried once, and that was plenty. But then her eyes stung, too, as if her previous crying session had primed her, and through a haze of tears that she refused to let fall, she thought about being at home. Of eating her mother's food, and the smell of the sea air, and being an aunt to the nieces and nephews she'd never met. Of reconciling her nostalgia with reality and learning what was new, what had changed. Of spending half a day walking the shore until one of her brothers or sisters would come find her, shouting, *Maris! Dinner!*

No one alive had called her that name in a long time. Vale hadn't told anyone in Asheburg, wanting to keep for herself the last bit she had of home. The only person who knew was Burdock, who had recruited her.

She was tired, she decided, of being Valerian IV. She was ready to be Maris again as soon as this was over. Maybe she'd even convince Jing to go south with her to meet her parents.

"No," Vale replied. "I'm not."

Key nodded tightly. "Okay. I deserve that. I . . ." She paused, her jaw flaring, and for a second Vale thought Key would lose her composure, would crack and spill like a dam broken. For a single, hopeful second, Vale thought Key would close the distance between them, pin her against the wall, and tell her vehemently and passionately why Vale should not go. There was a sudden, ferocious light in Key's eyes, and Vale readied herself to hear what Key might say: that she wanted more than a friend. That she wanted to see whether their next kiss would be better than the last. And Vale, with her foolish head and even more foolish heart, might listen.

"Thank you," Key said, and Vale's chest constricted, pain knifing its way up to her throat. She didn't know why she expected Key to turn onto the untrodden road, to stray from habits twenty-five years ingrained. Key had a divine calling, and Vale wasn't anywhere near a saint. "For everything. I could not have asked for a better guardian. I only regret I wasn't a better friend. I'm sorry I caused everything to go wrong for you."

She hesitated, her voice taking on a halting, quivering tone. "Do something with your life that isn't fighting. I've seen from the beginning who you are, and you're so much more than a body to put in front of someone else. Tell yourself every day the things you hated hearing from me. You're determined and brave and principled, and you're wise in ways no one in this city understands. You deserve good things, Vale, and I'll believe it for you even when you don't. Treat yourself like the precious soul you are."

Words hovered unrealized on the edge of Vale's hearing. She strained her ears, ready and waiting, wondering what they were. But Key only said, "I wish you the very best."

A hot tear escaped and slid down Vale's cheek, followed by another, and another. The silence between them grew unbearable, weighed down with grief for things that were ending and things that would never be.

"You too," Vale said eventually. If she gave in to the prickling heat of failure, if she gave in to the need to fall to her knees and sob into her hands, all would be lost. She'd had enough taken from her in the last two days. She would hold on to the last scraps of her dignity. "We should get to the academy before it's too late."

"You're right." Key dashed her own tears away. "Give me a minute to compose myself. Can't have citizen reporters sending scoops to the dailies."

"Yeah," Vale agreed. She could use that minute too.

SIXTEEN

THIEVES THWARTED
Security System Success

ASHEBURG.—The quiet of a sleepy Fifthday evening was shattered when burglars attempted to break into the Museum of Human Memory, triggering the new state-of-the-art security system installed after the last break-in. A stout chase ensued, but the would-be memory thieves eluded the guards and escaped empty-handed. "We remain vigilant against outside agitators who would rob Asheburg and her people of their stories," said Dr. Genevieve Wilcroft, head curator of the museum. "Protecting our cultural heritage is our top priority. We plan to ask the council for more funding to increase our security measures."

—Candace Cooper, *Asheburg Gazette*

THE GYM WAS DORMANT AND EMPTY, AND WITHOUT BODIES IN the space, the scrape of the door opening echoed up to the rafters. Vale stepped in, waited for Key to enter, then shut the door, taking a moment to look around at the weapons resting tidy in their racks, the pads hanging on hooks, the helmets heaped in their bins. When she was a student, the gym was only quiet at night after Burdock left, and Vale had spent many of those late hours listening to sheets of rain passing overhead, cocooned in a blanket on an uncomfortable cot in his office.

She almost felt like a student again, stealing into the gym after dark, toeing off her boots, padding across the floor toward the watery golden beacon of Burdock's office light, watching his warped silhouette flash across the window like a fish beneath the waves. The door opened, and before Vale could stop herself, she was sprinting toward him, her feet thumping over the mats, tears brimming in her eyes.

"Burdock!" she cried, throwing herself at him.

"Vale?!" Burdock caught her with one arm, the air whuffing from him, and suddenly she was a slip of a girl again, fourteen years old with no friends, fresh from the country, deliriously homesick. Burdock's other arm moved like he was tossing something; the something clattered onto his desk. A knife, probably.

Vale clutched him tighter, unable to speak, and wailed.

"What is going on?" Burdock exclaimed, concern coloring his voice, then returned the hug, squeezing her until the breath left her, murmuring *it's okay* and *don't cry*. Vale crumpled against him, grinding her forehead into his shirt, her chest heaving. She wasn't supposed to cry anymore, but this was Burdock. He was safe. He was the closest thing to home she had and didn't count as an audience.

"Key?" Burdock spoke above Vale's head. "Did Jing do this? Because if he did—"

"No," Key replied quickly. "It was me."

Burdock's arms tightened around Vale. "You?"

"I don't know where to start," Key said, "but—"

"She fired me!" Vale sobbed. Burdock moved, and after some shuffling, she found herself dropped into a chair. She put her face in her hands, a sharp gasp escaping her.

"Okay, calm down, Vale. Who fired you? Key?"

Vale curled into herself, her words coming out shaky and uneven. "Dr. Wilcroft, and it's Key's fault!"

"It is," Key said, her voice subdued as she lowered herself into Burdock's office chair. "Genevieve fired me too."

"What the . . ." Burdock drew a breath. "Explain."

Vale tried, but the words poured from her mouth without making sense. "The reintegration didn't work and Key wouldn't listen to me and the temple is cannibals and Key needs more reintegration but we can't get to it and it's so gross, it's brain eating!"

Burdock sighed. "Okay."

"But Dr. Wilcroft found us and had a whole crew and wouldn't answer questions and she lied to Key about whether the memory she found was good—" Vale paused, her breath sawing in-out, in-out. "That bitch!"

She waited for Burdock to defend Dr. Wilcroft as he usually did or turn the subject away. Instead, he said, "I'm not entirely sure what the story is, but the last part definitely sounds like Gen."

"The bitch part?" Vale hiccupped, then sniffled.

"She's always had nothing but kind things to say about you," Key countered. "I thought you were at least still cordial."

"Cordial?" Burdock snorted. "I haven't spoken to her or seen her in years. If she's got even you believing she's got a standing invite to Saintsday dinner, I wonder what else has been rolling off her forked tongue."

A stillness came over Vale, as sudden and shocking as the eye of a storm. She'd been right that something had happened between Burdock and Dr. Wilcroft. It was as if a spotlight had been turned on him, throwing his reluctance from five days ago into sharp relief. "What do you mean?"

Key echoed the question.

Burdock half shrugged, turning his palms up. "She built her career on lies and betrayal. Don't you ever wonder who she stepped on to get where she is? I'm not surprised she'd do the same to you."

Key shifted, sitting forward. "Genevieve has always been open about her research and her methodology. If you're insinuating she didn't earn her spot—"

"Don't," Burdock said. "Do you hear yourself? You sound like institute propaganda. Knock it off."

Key blinked, startled, then said, "You're right. I'm sorry."

Burdock cast a dark look at Key. "Genevieve has always been good at showing you what she wants you to see."

"What are you talking about?" Vale spluttered, her frustration rising. She had to get words out before she couldn't anymore. "You've never told me anything! How am I supposed to know anything about her?"

"Genevieve said your split was amicable and that you were still friends," Key said.

Burdock threw his head back and laughed. "Is that so? And you bought it, the whole hog? Key. I thought you were smarter than this."

Vale curled her fingers into claws for lack of something better to do. "Burdock, just tell us what we're missing!"

"You hear this, you won't be able to go back, even if you wanted to."

"Well, I don't, so just say it!"

"I didn't want to disillusion you. This job was important to you and your family, and I didn't want you to doubt that.

That's why I've never said a negative word about Gen, the museum, the institute. You had to be the guardian the academy promised you'd be. Without question, in full support of their goals. You understand why I said nothing?"

Vale scowled.

"Key?"

She nodded. "You thought Vale could be what you couldn't."

"What a story she'd be, yeah? What a—how do you folks on the mountain say it?—a credit to her people. Proof that someone like Vale could lift herself out of her circumstances and become a respected member of high society. And if she could do it, then that'd provide opportunity to all the other kids in the country who wouldn't have had a chance."

Key spoke. "What happened to you, Burdock?"

"Gen betrayed me," he said quietly. "Not the same way she did to you, but a betrayal nonetheless. The discovery she used for her doctorate, that first wonderfully reconstructed view of an unknown village's life . . . that was a sister village to mine."

"I don't understand," Key said.

"I wouldn't expect you to. You've lived here your whole life. Your family and the other rich families have been here for generations. Sure, there are hurricanes and the New River floods, and the unfortunate lose everything. But the whole city isn't at risk of being destroyed. Where Vale and I come from—we don't even know where we come from. Right, Vale?"

Burdock continued without waiting for a response. "When you move that often, the connection to land is lost. All we have is what we bring with us. Our communities. Our heirlooms. Our ancestral memories, our songs. Those are the most valuable. It's proof of who we are. It's our own museum, to put it in terms you'll understand."

"So," Key said slowly, her brows furrowed in thought. "Your sister village . . . ?"

"Chamuna. You recognize the name, don't you? We'd lost track of it decades ago. We had aunts and uncles there, probably a crop of cousins. Long story short, village history has it that a storm roared out the sea without warning, and they weren't prepared. This was before Aurissa Strade brought back radio blueprints that allowed long-range weather broadcasts. Many people died. The rest, disappeared. Fled, or scattered, or were separated. Gen and I . . . I'd brought her to meet my kin. They told the story once they knew what she was. So we started chasing after ghosts. Thought it'd be a noble thing to lay the wandering to rest. To remember them and fix them in our memories."

Burdock's shoulders sagged. "We went to the right spot, or as right as we could make it, since the land is now salt marsh. I tried to find something in the water. At low tide, structures emerge—posts, walls, other things. I took specimens for her. Gen set up and dove in. She came out breathless with wonder, grinning. I'll never forget it. She'd found something, she said. Something she thought I'd be interested in.

"And then she said a name. No one but my family and my village would have known that name. I was stunned. We had to go home, I said. And then I begged her to let me have the memories first, to get them duplicated so I could bring them back to my village."

"What did she do?" Key broke in.

Burdock inhaled, looking suddenly agitated, and began pacing a short track in front of them. "Do you know how much of a privilege it is to know who came before you? To be able to know where you came from, to trace them through years of history. To have someone like you, Key, link the present and the past so you can have just a minute, a second of their time. To see through your mother's and your mother's mother's eyes and know what they knew?"

"Yes," Key replied, her voice hushed. "I do. I understand."

"Each of us is the sum of those who came before. But this world, it erases us, sweeps us out to sea, forces us to leave everything behind to survive. Branches of family trees snap off. We can regrow, but it's not the same as what we lost. If we had what Gen found—if we could have the wisdom of our families and communities—"

Vale's heart ached. Here she was, a cutting of her family transplanted to Asheburg without even a few grains of soil or mycelium to help her grow, and she was expected to put down roots and flourish. How could she do that without a system to feed her? If she had a single family member with her, life would have been much different.

Key spoke, her voice soft and warm, soothing. "What did Genevieve do, Burdock?"

"She said yes, of course. Something this important should go to the community first, especially since they were still alive. It's living history. And it belongs to those with the greatest claim on it. But I want to study it as well, she said." He pressed his fingers to his eyes, blew out a breath, and continued. "We went back to the village. She presented her initial findings. Only later did I realize she gave us scraps.

She promised to bring the memories back. And that held until we got back to the museum, when she decided she'd keep them for the greater good. Because my people were incapable of storing and protecting those memories. It'd be unethical to keep them outside the museum."

Key made a noise in her throat.

"We argued. I told her she'd find something just as wonderful, something more important to Asheburg and the Spine than some lost southern village that my community thought the ocean had taken. We had a home for the lost spirits. We could anchor them. Reunite them with our ancestors."

He fell silent. Vale prodded him on. "And then?"

"We came to a compromise." Burdock scoffed. "I didn't realize how little of that word she understood. We'd return to Asheburg with the specimen, she'd duplicate it, and she'd give that copy to me to bring home. I agreed to it, since I figured she'd be busy recording and doing all the paperwork while I was away. Instead, she stonewalled me. I never got the specimen, or even a copy. We fought over it. Then I quit and never spoke to her again. Later on, she sent me an invite to the exhibit's grand opening, can you believe it? The audacity of that woman. Tell me, Key. You're her protégé, same way Vale is mine. Who tells your story? Whose story do you decide to tell, and what right do you have to tell it?"

Vale glanced at Key, then scrambled to her feet. "Key?"

She didn't answer. Vale took three steps to Burdock's desk, an oily, sick feeling spreading in her gut at the sight of Key's eyes, open and vacant, unfocused.

"Key!" Vale put her hands on Key's face, cradling her jaw in her palms. "Look at me."

She blinked slowly and took in the room. "Where am I?"

Vale almost laughed at the timing of it; she'd cry otherwise. The urge to kiss Key rose, ludicrous as it was. But it had worked to ground Key. It could work again.

"Vale. You said the memory was strong?" Burdock joined her, frowning slightly as Vale grabbed Key's hand and squeezed hard.

"What's that got to do with anything right now?"

"Is this her first lapse?"

"I don't know!" Vale slapped Key across the cheek gently, then shook her.

Key startled and gasped.

"Key. Who am I?"

"Vale," Key replied, but her eyes met Vale's for only a second before they slid away. "Where are . . . Burdock?"

"She needs reintegration," Burdock said.

"No shit," Vale snapped. "But we can't get to the museum, where her last specimen is."

"Why are you here and not the school lab, then?"

"Lab won't work, Key said so." Vale squeezed Key's hand again. "Stay with me."

"I don't . . ." Key sagged in the chair.

"That doesn't answer my question," Burdock said. "Why are you *here*?"

Because I couldn't think of anyone else, Vale almost said. *Because you're my brother and you always have the answers.* "The black market hunters. Take us."

Burdock shook his head. "Vale, you've brain-jumped too far. Back up for me."

"We need their lab. For an extraction."

"And not a reintegration?"

"That too. Then we want to make a trade."

"Of? For?"

"Key found the origins of the temple's practices," Vale explained again, frustrated. "Didn't you hear me? It's disgusting! They ate each other's brains and no one knows how many people they infected with their disease."

"Ah. That's what you meant earlier." Burdock said nothing else.

"You *knew*?" Vale backed away from Burdock. "You knew and you never said anything?"

"What would that have accomplished?" Burdock barked a laugh. "It was centuries ago. Gen thought about bringing it to the head curator back then, but decided she'd track it first. She came to believe the practice died out. The ability is within the population now. And then she considered what consequences might stem from bringing the information to light. She decided her career was more important. What am I supposed to do about that? I don't have a stake in hiding the truth, not like Gen. I'm an outsider like you, little sister. I do what I need to in this damned city in order to survive."

There was silence. Vale stared at Burdock. "You *knew*."

"And it's not my business to interfere. It's not my place to say what the temple does with its own history." A sigh poured out of him, the sound weary and torn, stained with exhaustion. "Is it what I believe in? No. It's not what you believe in either. But you and me, we don't have the power here. She does." Burdock hiked a thumb in Key's direction. "I'm curious about you now that you no longer believe."

"But I do," Key replied softly.

"That makes no sense."

"It doesn't have to make sense." She looked up at Burdock, a faint smile on her lips. "My ability may not be granted by the saints. That's something I'm going to wrestle with on my own time. But the ancestors are real. Their memories are real. What they experienced is real, and what I know is real. That can't be taken from me. And I'm sorry Genevieve stole that from you. I'm sorry the museum stole that from you. It had no right."

Burdock's jaw flexed. "So you want to make a trade. For what?"

"Why didn't you just go home, Burdock?" Vale watched him, observing the vulnerable set of his shoulders. She had never known his history, and briefly, she wondered what else she didn't know about him. "There's nothing for you here."

He stiffened, then flung his hand in the direction of his wall map, where a newspaper clipping was pinned on one side. The headline read RACK AND RUIN. "Ain't no home to go to. No folks to miss me. The trade. What're the terms?"

"That was you?" Now Vale remembered: Burdock, weeping while cutting a mango; the family lays and village songs taught to her over the last three years. He hadn't been crying because he was sad Vale was going to graduate. He'd been mourning the loss of his entire family.

Burdock repeated, his voice half a growl, "The terms, little sister."

She wanted to be soft in the moment. Wanted to go to Burdock and mourn with him three years too late. Wanted to build a cairn with him and tell him she was sorry and offer her sympathies and try to keep him company in his hurt. But he had hardened himself and wouldn't take kindly to pity.

Vale met iron with iron, as she'd been taught. "We offer the black market hunters this memory to sell, and they let us use their lab to reintegrate Key."

"With what specimen?"

Vale threw her hands up in exasperation. "I don't know! I'll figure it out, even if it means breaking into the museum."

"You serious about that?"

Vale gestured sharply at Key. "I mean! If I have to! Either way, it's a good deal for the hunters. They've been after Key. They can take everything she has if they wanted."

"And you think that I have a direct line to them?"

"More than I do! You actually know where to go."

"You know what you're asking, right?" Burdock frowned, looking between her and Key. "You do this, you sell out the temple. You can't turn back."

Key straightened, her posture firming. "Did you think I could ignore what I learned? I can't be part of either institution. Genevieve wronged you. Who knows how many more are like you, still split from their kin? Going back to the museum means agreeing with its methods. I can't do that. At the temple, we don't keep the memories. They aren't ours to hold. I know now that I'm not blessed. But I can still be a voice for the ancestors, with or without the temple."

"I have no job," Vale said. "What else do I have left but to get out of here?"

Burdock folded his arms across his chest and bowed his head. "I might be able to get you in. But they may not want what you have."

"Bullshit! They were willing to kill her for what she has. They just want her for free."

Burdock laughed, the sound grim. "That much is true."

"And how do you know what they want, anyway?"

"I'm just guessing. But these are incredibly huge asks of an organization that doesn't know you except as Key's guardian, one who killed three of their own."

Three? How did Burdock know it was three? No one had marked her leaving with Silas but for the other two hunters, and she'd hidden the body off the trail. "It wasn't—"

"And now you have no hunter to guard. You can't invoke the law."

"They don't know that," Key spoke up.

"It's true," Vale said. "They don't know that, and none of us here will say a word about it, right?" She looked first at Key, who nodded, then Burdock, who gave the slightest movement of his head. "We're desperate. Please help us, Burdock."

He drew in a breath, then let it out noisily. "Okay. I'll see what I can do. Wait outside the gym. I'll meet you in a few minutes."

She gave him a suspicious look.

"Go." He opened the door.

They crossed the darkened gym and exited, standing in front of the doors as dusk settled and began shading into evening. Minutes later, Vale heard the crackle of tires against dirt and saw the twin beams of headlights from around the side of the building. An electric car rounded the corner, Burdock behind the wheel.

The car was, Vale recognized, a model from one of the western cities beyond the Spine. It was somewhat boxy, painted a sleek black all over. Key's family had several of the same brand, though the model their butler drove was larger, more capable of handling multiple passengers.

He reached across the front passenger seat to roll down the window. "Get in. Vale in the front. Key, you can have the back. I'm sure you're used to it."

Vale suppressed the instinct to snipe at Burdock, instead yanking on the door and climbing in. The interior had a woodsy, new smell to it, but she got the sense that the car had belonged to Burdock for some time, given how comfortably he rested his hands on the wheel.

"I didn't know you had a car." She shoved her rucksack into the space in front of her, adjusted the weapons on her belt so as not to get poked by them, then pulled the seatbelt over her body and clicked it into place.

"There's a lot you don't know about me, little sister." Burdock gave her a faint smile.

"Well, there's a lot you don't know about *me*," she fired back.

"That so?" He grinned at her as Key opened the rear passenger door and slid into the back seat. "I'll wager I know everything about you."

Vale scowled. "I didn't know you could afford a car." Just like she didn't know he could afford all those sweet weapons in his armory.

Burdock's smile grew feral, stirring unease in the pit of Vale's stomach. Discomfited, she stared at him, unsure how to handle what her gut was telling her. Over the last decade, Burdock had been at first a teacher, then a mentor, and finally, a friend. Someone with a common background who knew more than anyone else at the academy what sort of values Vale had, what she held dearest. He could be mean and callous, and intractable sometimes, but not . . . suspect.

Her gut, she decided, was not reliable after emotional distress and hours of no food. This was Burdock. Vale trusted him with her life.

"Again, there's a lot you don't know about me. Key, are you buckled in back there?"

"Yes," she replied. "Where are we going?"

"Edge of the city. Not too far." Burdock depressed a button, locking the doors, and took his foot off the brake. "We'll be there soon."

SEVENTEEN

The papers are reporting that Ginseng II is dead—*dismembered*, saints protect him—and that Chauncey snapped and killed him, then himself. I don't believe it. I don't! I just saw them last week. They were fine. They talked about building a cabin for themselves in the mountains and creating a waystation for other travelers. The story must be a plant. I'm going to find them. When May and I finish here, I'm going to hunt them down.

—Journal of Aurissa Strade

ASHEBURG SHONE IN THE EARLY EVENING SUN, ITS CLUSTERED buildings reflecting the strong, searing light as the car wended its way past the neat houses of the middle-class district, then the increasingly ramshackle houses of the working-class district, and finally the industrial warehouses and docks crowded cheek by jowl on the river. Vale had not seen the city from this angle since she'd begun working at the museum, but there was no time to take in the sights, not when Key's lapses were occurring with increasing frequency. A quick glance over her shoulder showed Key slumped against the door, her head against the window, her hand curled loosely around the staff angled diagonally across the space.

"Burdock," Vale said, "I gotta sit in the back."

Burdock's eyes flicked up to the rearview mirror. "She'll be fine. And you stay put. We need to talk."

"I don't want to talk. I want to sit in the back."

"Saints' sake, Vale, *listen*. You need a job, right? What I said before still applies. There's always a contract waiting for you if you want it."

"How am I even supposed to think about that right now?" she asked, her tone rising with agitation. "You want me to put my life down for who? Those black market assholes? They don't give a shit about anything! They were gonna kill Key!"

"Things have changed a lot in the last few years, and after what you saw Gen do to Key, you should rethink who the actual assholes are. Back when I took you to the ring, the black market was neutral toward the museums. Museums had their own territories and the black market stayed out of 'em. That's no longer the case. Black market's openly hostile now."

Vale recalled the northern museum guardian who had turned up dead in the forest and the museum hunter who still had not been found, and wondered how many more the black market had claimed. "What happened?"

"Change of leadership about three years ago." Burdock paused to look around an intersection before making a turn. "And that's led to a lot of new faces and new attitudes."

Vale thought back to the black market hunter she'd killed, how green he was, how he hadn't recognized her. He'd accused Key of theft. She'd told Key on the train that what they did wasn't stealing. That still held true for their specific situation, but now, after learning of what Dr. Wilcroft had done to Burdock, Vale could understand why the man felt that way. The museum was supposed to champion public history, but the vast majority of the information there was stored in the archive, where the public could not access it.

Nor was there any public record of what the museum and institute had in storage. In effect, the museum held memories captive and could do it for so long that even the curators and archivists themselves could forget the memories existed, rendering history forgotten yet again.

Small wonder Burdock was the way he was, with no love for the museum. It must have been unbearable to be adrift and alone for years, knowing his community's memories were so close but unable to retrieve them for his people. Vale knew they shared a core of injustice-fueled anger, but the injustices done to Burdock far outstripped hers.

"You're being too quiet," Burdock said.

"Just thinking, is all."

"While you're thinking, let me ask you: When we walk into the building, will you be with me or with Key?"

"Why wouldn't I be with both of you?"

She practically heard Burdock grinding his teeth. "No. I mean you need to choose before we go inside. Are you with me, or are you with Key?"

Normally, Vale wouldn't balk at sticking by Burdock's side. He was family, and she was loyal to family. "What happens to Key if I walk in with you?"

"You'll be safe. She'll need to plead her case alone."

"I don't think she can do that."

Burdock gave a quick shrug. "Then the hunters will harvest what they want from her."

Vale shuddered, unable to bear with stoicism the idea of her memories being taken from her and sold to random buyers, let alone Key's, who held her penitents' memories along with her own. "And if I walk in with her?"

Vale caught Burdock's sidelong glance. "Why choose her, little sister?"

"She needs help," Vale replied immediately.

"That's it? She needs help? You'd choose her over me?"

From the back, as softly as trees exhaling mist on the mountainside, Key said, "He hits you in the *face*."

Alarmed, Burdock said, "Who? Jing?"

"No, she means you," Vale replied.

"That was for your own good. You're meaner than a catamount when you want to be. Why protect Key? After all I told you, why do all this for her when she represents everything rotten in this city?"

Because Key was the only person to tell Vale that she did not deserve Burdock's treatment. Key paid attention to and cared about the things Vale found important not because she was personally invested, but simply because Vale cared about them. Key knew the names of all of Vale's siblings, remembered what Vale's family was up to, tolerated Vale's quirks, and apologized after wronging her.

No one had ever apologized to her before.

Vale didn't answer immediately, deliberating on whether she should reveal her weakness to Burdock. Eventually, she decided on reciprocating the honesty. "I had . . . chances. Two weeks ago, Ina showed signs and I acted exactly the way a guardian should. I could have killed her. Was close to it. But with Key . . . I had so many chances to just, you know. Finish it." Vale lowered her head. "I couldn't. She's my friend. Maybe the best one I have. I can't kill her. If I walk in there with you, she's dead. I go in there at her side, might be she has a chance."

He huffed quietly, the sound final. “I see. No convincing you, then?”

“To let the black market hunters kill her? No.”

“Never mind, then,” Burdock said. “Let’s talk about the plan.”

“What plan?” Vale glanced back again, trying to figure out whether Key was resting or in the grip of a memory. The longer a hunter stayed in the intrusive memory, the harder it would be to get them out. Key was strong, but Vale wasn’t sure how much of that strength was left.

“Do you think we can just show up? We’ve got a Strade. You’re an academy guardian they don’t want running loose. We have to have a plausible story.”

“Is the truth not plausible?”

“Vale, please.” Burdock heaved a sigh. “Quit looking at Key. Fifteen minutes in a memory isn’t going to harm her permanently.”

“What crawled up *your* ass today?”

“You and Key did, and if we want to make it so the three of us aren’t bodies floating in the New River later tonight, you’ll focus up and listen to my plan.”

Vale crossed her arms over her chest. “Fine. Tell me.”

“You’ve got to promise me to play along, okay? You gotta keep pretending.”

“Pretending what?”

Burdock slowed briefly to turn a corner. The wheels of the car bumped over streetcar tracks, rattling Vale in her seat. In the back, Key sat up with a sharp intake of breath.

“Pretending that I caught you and am bringing you in.”

“I don’t get it.”

"Okay. I am going to pretend to be a black market hunter who has caught both you and Key and is bringing you in to get my reward. You are going to pretend that you actually are caught. That means I take your weapons and tie your hands up, like real prisoners."

Vale didn't like that one bit. "Is that why you asked if I'd be with you or with Key? I don't want my hands tied up."

"Yes. It's plain you're on her side right now. Hopefully, you won't have to stay tied up. I'll make it so you can escape if you have to."

"I don't like this plan."

Burdock signaled, then turned left. "You got a better one?"

No, she didn't. Vale didn't even have a plan to start with. "Fine. But you gotta promise to let me out so I can negotiate."

"Of course."

Vale returned to watching Key. After a series of turns, Burdock drove onto a straight stretch of road, dotted here and there with the occasional car parked on the street. The neighborhood they were in was composed mostly of industrial buildings, some with bamboo scaffolding clinging to the facades, all crowded together in clumps of four and five. Various pipes spat runoff into the river below. Burdock pulled in front of a squat, three-story warehouse with a meager number of blacked-out windows and a hipped roof topped with the same ocher shingles that marked so many of the working-class district's houses. Tacked onto the front over the door was a sign that read PAPER SURPLUS. Vale eyed it as Burdock drove into a side alley and parked in a covered spot attached to the building.

"Remember," Burdock said as he set the emergency

brake, "these people are more likely to listen if they know you can't be a threat. You've gotta be convincing. Pretend that your life depends on it."

"So I gotta pretend to be your prisoner in a convincing way and also pretend that my life depends on my pretending?"

Burdock paused, sighed, and lowered his face to his hand. "Yes."

"Okay." Vale got out of the passenger side and went to Key's door, opening it. "Key. Key?"

Key turned her head and blinked slowly at her, the set of her gaze on something beyond Vale's shoulder.

Vale reached out and took Key's hand, squeezing firmly. "Look at me. I need you here right now. You need to know what we're doing."

"Didn't want it," Key murmured.

"I know." Vale let go of Key's hand to grab her legs and swing them out of the car, forcing Key to face her. She took Key's wrists in each hand, curling her fingers in so her nails dug into Key's skin. It would have been easier to kiss her, but something told her not to. "Tell me what you're feeling."

"Sad."

Wrong answer. Vale squeezed harder.

"What are you doing?"

That sounded more like her. "Tell me something you feel with your body."

"Your nails."

"Good. Tell me something you hear."

"Your voice," Key said. "And—a car door shutting? Footsteps."

"That was the trunk, but yes. Tell me something you see."

"I'm sitting in the back seat of a car. There's a door

to a warehouse. I see you." Key blinked again and leaned forward, shaking her wrist free of Vale's grip. "Vale, your eye—"

"Don't worry about it." Vale exhaled slowly, a small bit of relief relaxing the tension in her shoulders. "Welcome back."

"I don't know how long I can fight it off." Key closed her eyes briefly. "But I think I got the gist of Burdock's plan. Do you really think you can do this?"

"I don't know," Vale replied. "But you gotta keep your head on. I need it."

"If you can hold my hand, I think I can stay grounded enough to—"

"No holding hands," Burdock interrupted.

Vale immediately said, "Burdock, you know that—"

"No holding hands," he repeated, then showed Vale two coils of rope. "And it's time to take your weapons."

Vale swallowed her discomfort. Burdock knew how to manage hunters; he had to understand why Vale would want to keep a hold on Key. But Vale stepped away from the car regardless, then put her hands behind her back and turned away from Burdock. He looped the rope around her wrists, tying the knot with quick, efficient movements.

"Ow," Vale said. "You're hurting me. It's too tight. I won't be able to get out."

"Sorry about that. You'll be able to get it off soon. Like I said, we have to convince them you aren't a threat."

"Just *tell* them we're not a threat. Everyone knows you. They'll listen."

"I told you, there's been a change of leadership. Things aren't the same as you remember. If I'm pretending to be one of them, then I gotta be hostile to both of you."

Vale ground her teeth and turned around, watching as Key exited the car and was tied the same way. "Hey," she said in warning when Key winced.

"She's fine." Burdock tugged on the rope, tightening the knot.

Key glanced at her. "I'm all right. This is good, actually. It'll help me stay here."

Then Burdock drew close to Vale, his fingers finding the buckles keeping her borrowed sword attached to her belt. A few yanks, and the weight of it fell away from her hips. Vale trained her eyes on the weapon as Burdock belted it on himself. "I liked that sword."

"I bet you did," he replied. "Did you get to use it?"

"Not as much as I should have."

"A good thing, considering the people on the other end of your sword have a high chance of injury or death." Burdock grinned, but Vale found herself unable to smile back as he patted her down and removed the stiletto strapped to her thigh. "This one's mine, so I hope you don't mind me taking it back. These"—he unclipped the two knives she kept on her tactical belt and the one on the side of her boot—"I'll just borrow for a while." He then took the pouch on her right side and pulled out the brass knuckles. "These are mine too. Got any more, little sister?"

"No," she said, watching him arrange the weapons on his belt.

"I've gotta admit, I'm surprised. Thought you'd be keeping a punch dagger around your neck."

"You told me it was useless."

"That I did. Good on you for listening to me."

"You aren't going to check Key?" Vale looked at Key, observing the slight pucker of her left cheek. She must be chewing on it in order to keep herself in the present.

"I'm not worried about her," Burdock said pleasantly. Then he went back to the car to retrieve two lengths of cloth.

"Is gagging us really necessary?" Key said.

"You had that in your car the whole time?" Vale said once Burdock didn't reply. "You kidnapping people on the side or what?"

Burdock snorted. "Open." Vale dropped her jaw obediently, then grunted as Burdock rammed the gag in. He tied it as efficiently as he'd tied the rope around her wrists, then did the same to Key. He took Vale's elbow with his left hand and Key's with his right, walking them up to the back door, which had only a peephole in it. To Vale's right, toward the front of the building, was a single window, its curtain drawn, and to Vale's left, the alley ended in a bamboo fence, blocking the view, if not the smell, of the river beyond.

Burdock knocked on the door. "Remember," he said to Vale under his breath, "you have to keep pretending no matter what."

The sound of bolts unlocking followed. Vale counted three, as well as a chain. She glanced at Burdock beside her, his face stony and impassive, unreadable. Finally, the door opened, and behind it stood a thin, bearded man of middling height, dressed in a loose gray shirt and black slacks. He gestured, and Burdock guided them inside, nodding to the doorman as they walked past.

"That was easy," Vale muttered, or tried to.

"Hush," Burdock said.

The murmur of voices came to her, as well as the faint, distinctive smell of blood chalices. Vale craned her neck to give Key a meaningful look, but Burdock shook Vale roughly, and she subsided, reminding herself that she was supposed to be a prisoner. She settled for observing her surroundings instead. The inside of the warehouse was packed with open shelving units on the first floor, rows of them creating narrow aisles. Vale noted a small elevator on the far side of the room, a ramp to her left, and a disconcerting lack of available exits except for the one she and Key had just gone through. Burdock, however, directed them up the ramp to the second floor, the murmur of the voices growing louder, the smell of people and blood chalices strengthening.

Having a gag in her mouth put a crimp in the plan to negotiate with the black market hunters; she wasn't sure how to get their attention. But as they approached the top of the ramp and came within sight of the people gathered on the second floor, it became apparent to Vale that there would be no need. Though the room was divided into sections—Vale recognized paper presses in one corner, a large planter of blood chalices in another, and a long apparatus made of vats and tubing along the wall—there was no way to hide except in what looked like a repurposed cargo car on the far right side below a lofted area. One by one, the people in the room fell silent, each of them turning from whatever they were doing to watch Burdock and Key proceed through the room to a short stage on the other end.

And then the silence was broken by someone shouting, "Thief!"

More people took up the call, chanting "Thief! Thief! Thief!" as Burdock propelled Vale and Key toward the stage.

Boos and hisses followed until Vale felt compelled to duck her head. Key, however, walked with a straight back, her face displaying nothing but grace.

"Up we go," Burdock said, pushing Vale and Key onto the stage first, then stepping on behind them. He turned Vale to face the crowd that had gathered. Flutters rose in her stomach as she looked over the black market hunters. What Burdock had said was true: Things had changed. Most of the faces were unfamiliar, but there were a few she thought she recognized vaguely from her time in the academy. Beside her, Key tensed, and Vale followed Key's line of sight to a face she definitely recognized as a classmate from school. Shock jolted her, followed by dismay. Logically, it made sense. What better place to recruit from than the academy, whose graduates didn't always find jobs?

Burdock is here. Instead of feeling reassured, however, Vale's anxiety only grew.

Burdock gestured at two men standing at the fore of the raucous crowd, beckoning them closer. "Hold them," he said.

Rough hands clamped down on her arms. Vale growled through her gag and glared at the man touching her.

"What'd you haul in, Arvensis?" a woman called from the crowd.

Arvensis? Why did the name sound familiar? Vale wriggled, but the man holding her tightened his grip. Next to her, Key stood still, with only her head turning on her neck as she took in the room, still outwardly calm but for her slightly wide eyes.

Burdock ignored Vale, facing the crowd, spreading his arms wide until the people stopped speaking. "Friends," he said, his voice carrying clearly across the room. "I know many of you wanted that reward, but I think it's going to come to me."

Several people in the crowd laughed.

Friends? That didn't make any sense either, unless . . .

Arvensis, also called bindweed. Vale had asked the black market hunters who sent them. *Arvensis*, the woman said. Vale had thought the name a mockery of the academy.

Because it was. The world spun and dimmed. Burdock was Arvensis, and of course he knew Key's alias because Vale had told him, and so that meant he'd sent those hunters after Key to kill her, knowing that if they succeeded, Vale would be the next guardian left cold and unremembered in the forest.

"No doubt you already know who this is, but for those who don't, today I bring you Kiana Strade, the next head resifix of the temple and a former hunter for the museum, and her guardian, Valerian IV."

Vale drew a labored breath through the gag, then another and another. Breath after breath came faster as the realization crested and broke on her, and she swayed on her feet, lightheaded. Pretend? Ancestors, she was so stupid. Burdock had never meant for Key to go free. Key was going to be a prisoner here, a living farm of memories, or she'd be murdered after the hunters took her blood, and Vale—well, she was less than useless.

Betrayal, Vale was learning, hurt more than any wound Burdock had ever given her. What had she meant to him, exactly, after all their time together? How did he go from the big brother who sheltered her from harm and taught her his family lays to someone who saw her as a necessary sacrifice?

All it took was the sight of the terror on Key's face to ignite Vale's rage, lying thick and oily beneath the confusion and hurt. "You *liar*!" she shrieked at Burdock through her gag, hurling her weight forward and down. She broke free from her captor, stumbling before regaining her balance. "You *liar*!"

With a primal scream, she threw herself at Burdock, not caring that her arms were bound, not caring that he could easily sidestep her.

His eyes were the pitiless black of a storm at night as he unleashed a fierce kick, driving a foot into her stomach. In the past, during practice, she'd gotten several of those to the gut, but the force of his kicks had always been blunted with a mat or protective equipment. There was no such protection here, and Burdock was wearing combat boots. Vale crumpled with pain around his foot, the breath leaving her as she fell to the stage floor on her side, boneless.

"Wait," Burdock said.

Vale coughed and gagged, her eyes streaming with tears, the rhythm of her breathing beaten from her. Her body spasmed, and she dry heaved once before she threw up for real, bile streaming out her nose and around the gag in her mouth, soaking into it, splashing back down her throat. Her stomach and throat contracted again.

"Get that off her before she chokes to death." Someone seized the back of the gag and some of the hair in her braid, and Vale whimpered as cloth and hair were torn away from her head. The crowd was shouting again, but the words were unintelligible through the pounding of the blood in her ears. Vale lay on the stage, her cheek in a puddle of her own vomit, and didn't move except to curl her hands tight enough to pop the small knuckles of her fingers. Slowly, too slowly, she regained control of her body, though there was a sharp, throbbing pain in her middle. Vale hoped Burdock hadn't ruptured anything.

Because she was going to need the full strength and speed of her body. Because she was going to wring every bit of venom from herself and use it to kill him.

She rolled herself up to her knees. "You betrayed us," she said, softly at first, but her voice grew louder with each fresh, restoring breath she took. "You never cared for me. You *tricked* me. You *lied*, I hate you, I fucking *hate* you—"

She looked up, murderous intent spreading heady and acidic through her, burning in her veins in a way she knew she would pay for later. Burdock remained impassive, and like this he was a stranger and not the man she'd relied on for wisdom and advice from her childhood through her adulthood. This was not the Burdock she knew, the one who'd drop food off in front of her door, who'd toss her a pair of used, perfectly fitting shoes from the lost and found, the one who let her sleep on a cot in his office when she was homesick and ostracized and couldn't bear being around the other students any longer. This was not the Burdock who spent hours training her outside of school, not the man she saw as more of a brother to her than her actual family.

Maybe that Burdock had never existed. Maybe she had been too grateful for her scraps of kindness to see his faults. Maybe she was just too stupid, too uneducated to put together the clues. The words he spoke in the car came to her then: *There's a lot you don't know about me, little sister.* He was right. He'd said it plain. And then all the other things he'd said over the years came flooding back, assembling into a fuller picture, as if the words in the car were a keystone holding the shape of him together. How everyone knew him at the ring. His occasional absences and unexplained injuries. His map full of pins. The ledgers and the numbers in his office. The weapons in his personal armory. His car.

Her image of him collapsed, then rebuilt itself into the face of her enemy. *Die*, she thought, the word ricocheting in her head, amplifying until she could hear nothing else. Her muscles tightened with want.

"Don't," he said.

"You don't tell me what the fuck to do," she growled back. "Traitor. I loved you. And now I want your fucking *head*. You lied to me this whole time? For what? Because you hate Dr. Wilcroft?"

"No, Vale," Burdock said, "I didn't lie. I gave you chances to see me, and you never took them. I loved you, too, until you chose her over me."

"How is this *my fucking fault*? *Fuck* you, how does this—how does using me and Key make you any better than the museum?"

Vale saw her rage mirrored suddenly on Burdock's face. But then footsteps thunked on the stage as someone approached—probably her captor from before—and Vale somersaulted to the side, gaining her feet. She spun to face him, dodging his arm as he tried to grab her, and lashed out with a snap kick that caught him right under the chin, cracking his teeth together hard enough to ring his head like a bell. The man fell, boneless, instantly knocked out.

Vale bared her teeth, seeking Burdock, but he wasn't there.

"Stop."

She turned, ice shivering through her as she saw Burdock standing next to Key, a knife gleaming against her throat.

"Genevieve and I are nothing alike. If you think we are, you're too far astray for help."

"Coward. Cut me free and fight me," Vale spat. "I'll take the fucking blood price off you, I swear it."

"And why would I do that?" Burdock laughed. "You fight dirty. No thanks. You're staying like that, though if you're going to remain as spicy as you are, I'll break your leg and tie you to a chair for good measure."

The man on the ground stirred, and without a second thought, Vale kicked him in the face. He went limp again, blood oozing from his nose. "I dare you."

Burdock tsked and pressed the knife into the flesh of Key's throat. She inhaled loudly, her eyes wide with fear. "Keep your head on. You came here to bargain, not to take Key's life. Or so you said." He raised his voice. "The guardian has a proposal for us. Shall we hear it?"

There was silence from the crowd.

Burdock pulled away from Key and flicked his knife shut. "Tell them, Vale."

Vale clamped her lips together, her diaphragm clenching with a suppressed scream. Bargaining was the last thing she wanted to do. She wanted to fight. She wanted to douse herself in violence and go up in flames until she'd hurt Burdock the way he'd hurt her. But Key could not reliably hold her condition, and Vale was still, for reasons she couldn't explain, trying to save her. Trying to protect her. Even though Vale could walk away right now.

She *should* walk away.

She took a breath, then another, overwhelmed by emotion. She squeezed her eyes shut, dragging air through her mouth, willing herself not to regress into the explosive shrieking or rage hitting that had so worried her parents when she was little. Eventually, she opened her eyes and spoke. "I want you to extract a memory from Key and put it on the market."

"This sounds like a demand, not a bargain." An older woman emerged from the crowd, her stone-gray hair bound in a long braid that draped over her shoulder.

"It's a gift. We don't want any money in exchange. Just use of your lab and a guarantee that Key will stay alive and unhurt. I know what you'd do to her otherwise." The black market hunters did not have a reputation for being merciful, and Key, with her perfect memory, would remember where the hunters were located, how to get there, and the faces of every single person she saw. There was only one clean solution.

"And why would we take this . . . gift?"

Vale flexed her fingers behind her back, making sure there was still good circulation to her hands. "Because it's about the origins of the temple and the reason why the resifixes can dive so deep."

The older woman raised an eyebrow. "And what might we do with that?"

"Sell it. Distribute it, earn the money. I just want access to your lab. You can tell your buyers that you know exactly how the resifixes developed the ability to voice the will of the ancestors. What they had to do to get it. Sex sells, right? So does blasphemy."

The older woman laughed. "All we have is blasphemy. You'll have to do better than that."

"Not this kind." Vale walked over to Key and placed herself beside her. "It'll prove that the temple is false, and the resifixes have never been blessed. There's no such thing. There's only an illness."

"An illness?" The woman tilted her head. "What sort?"

"You'll have to find out yourself when you extract and purify the memory, then let us go."

"That's all well and good," Burdock said, "but I think I can ask for more."

Vale glared at him. "You know damn well I don't have *shit*."

"You have Key. And seeing as she's not wholly there right now, maybe we can take more than one memory from her."

"No!" Vale burst out. She tugged uselessly at her bonds, but they wouldn't budge. "You can't! The deal is for one!"

"You're not really in a position to say no." He was right. "But maybe you can bear the rest of the exchange if you're this determined to protect her."

Vale wanted to look away, but she straightened, settled her shoulders, and stared him dead in the eyes. "What do you want?"

"You said you'd break into the museum if you had to. I want you to break into the museum with me so I can take back what's rightfully mine." He lifted an eyebrow. "Don't look at me like that. You need to go there anyway if you have any hope of saving Key. Gen has what I want in the archives. Where, I don't know. My knowledge is outdated. Yours, however, is not. Get that master for me. Because you're my little sister, I'll do what you want, extract the memory from Key, set up distribution for it, and instead of sending your bodies down the river, I'll send you on your way to whatever place you want to go next." Burdock extended a hand. "Is that a deal?"

Key spoke suddenly, her voice strong, if distorted, through the gag. She took a step forward, pulling against her captor, her lips moving around garbled words.

"Take that off," Burdock commanded the man holding her.

Key worked her jaw once the gag was gone, then looked directly at Vale. "I'm coming too," she said. "I know the archives best. I know Genevieve's system. I know exactly the file you're talking about and I'll get it fast."

"Key—" Vale began.

"No. I have to go with you."

"You'll stay here," Burdock said. "As collateral."

"So your lackeys can drain me while you're gone?" Key's voice gained a steely quality. "Vale has no way of knowing whether I'm safe if we're split up, and from the way she's looking at you, I'd be scared to be alone for even a second with her."

Burdock scoffed. "She's welcome to claim my life if I don't claim hers first. Fine, then." He cast a glance at Vale. "Don't you make a move. We've just come to an agreement, and you don't want to upset the balance." Burdock waved a hand in the air, and a woman with blond hair braided close to her scalp and a hard expression stepped onto the stage, taking Vale roughly by the arm.

"Laurus?" Vale said.

She inclined her head. "You remember me."

"Quit talking," Burdock ordered. "You and Key stay separated until we leave. We'll go an hour after sunset. Most of the guards should be gone by then. In the meanwhile, eat and rest. We'll want to be prepared before we go in."

"Wow, you were ready," Vale said, caustic.

"You wanna wait? Look at Key and tell me she can give me eight full hours without her brain melting. No? Didn't think so. End of discussion."

With that, the crowd dispersed, leaving the group on the stage alone. Burdock pointed at a set of stairs leading to a lofted area, and Laurus shoved Vale toward them hard enough to make her stumble.

Vale ascended the steps, keeping her eyes trained on Key and only Key, who was in front. "Key. Are you okay?"

Key looked over her shoulder, pausing with a foot on the next stair. In the dim light, it was hard to see much, but her smile was unmistakable.

"How can you smile right now?" Vale demanded.

"Because I'm okay. I'll be okay. As long as I'm with you. I have faith in you."

It was like being kicked in the gut all over again. Vale pressed on, ashamed and wordless, her eyes burning with salt.

EIGHTEEN

Sayre,
I wanted to keep my promise, but after your constant haranguing and the disrespectful, hurtful language you've resorted to, I feel I have no choice but to hold these discoveries at the museum. This isn't a new issue between you and me, and you know it. You should have thought more carefully about how you talked to me.
—Unsent note from Dr. Genevieve Wilcroft to Burdock III

THE ROOM TO WHERE VALE HAD BEEN USHERED WAS SMALL BUT adequate, at least to her standards. For Key, it likely would rank as a hardship. Vale looked around from her place in front of the door, noting the mismatched, patchwork décor and the flickering overhead light, which, when combined with the clash of the floral pinstripe wallpaper against the small jute rug in the center of the room, was liable to give Vale a headache.

Against the right-hand wall was a small chest of drawers that had likely been rescued from the curb. Also on the right-hand side was a water closet, its door standing half open, the dusky shadows within hinting at a toilet and a sink. Set against the far wall was a twin bed with plain white sheets and a frayed, thin-looking duvet.

Vale paced out the space to orient herself, then took a seat on the bed, having nothing else to do. Rest, Burdock had said, but rest was the furthest thing on her mind, especially when the mattress beneath her felt like it had been chiseled directly out of Ashe's Peak. She exhaled, her shoulders lowering. Then the rest of her lowered as well until she had her head in her hands and her elbows on her knees. The sound of her own breathing was the loudest thing she heard.

Footsteps thumped outside the door, and a second later, a key grated in and out of the lock. The doorknob turned, and as Vale lifted herself up, straightening her back, Laurus entered the room, weaponless, holding a glass of water and a bowl with a spoon already in it. Vale watched, suspicious, as Laurus approached and held out the food.

"Tempeh with bulgur and some long beans," she said. "Can't have your stomach giving you away during the job."

Vale eyed her.

"All right," Laurus said, and walked the food over to the chest of drawers, setting the bowl and glass down with soft clunks. "I'll leave this here for when you're ready."

"Why are you really here?"

"To talk." Laurus glanced around, muttered something, then shifted her weight to one leg, jutting out her hip, putting her hands on her waist. "It's not too late to join us. You're free of the Strade girl now and free of the museum."

Vale had to admit that she admired Laurus's nerve. It took a certain audacity to punch someone in the mouth, then immediately kiss it. "Now why would I throw in with you after what was done to me?"

"Because you've got few options and Sayre still cares for you. He wants you with him."

Vale's forehead wrinkled. "Who?"

Laurus hesitated, then opened her mouth. "Burdock."

Reflexively, Vale cried, "You know his name?!"

"Don't you?"

Vale put a hand to her chest, pressing it against the knot of pain growing there. She swallowed, blinking hard as her eyes began to sting. No, Burdock had never told her. That had been the unspoken rule between them—not to give anyone in Asheburg the knowledge of their names, to keep one last thing of home for themselves.

"No," Vale choked out. Goose bumps broke over her skin, cascading down her arms and legs, and were followed by the glow of sweat. Laurus was not one of them, she was sure of it. The students at the academy came from well-to-do families that didn't need scholarships. They had houses on the mountain or in the most beautiful sections of the city and had no idea what kind of mettle was needed to survive on the coasts. Laurus might have renounced her family and her connections, but she'd never be clocked as a drifter. How could Burdock tell her?

"Hmm." Laurus tilted her head, then pursed her lips. "Well, you can call me Oryana, then."

Familiarity was not given where Vale and Burdock came from; it was earned. Laurus should have understood that. To assume that Vale would return the gesture with her own name was the height of arrogance. *I ain't know you like that*, she almost replied, but Laurus didn't deserve the honor of being spoken to like someone from back home. Vale straightened up her speech, righted what leaned and leaned hard, scrubbed away the sea salt and country dirt until the vowels were right and proper and the consonants were shiny and bright.

I'm not close enough to you for you to be this informal with me.

"Is that what he calls you?" she said instead.

"At times."

Vale narrowed her eyes. "Are you *fucking* him?"

"That's none of your business and not what I came to talk to you about," Laurus responded, her tone even. "Sayre knows you're too angry to be in the same room with him, so he sent me to have the discussion you should have had."

"That's a yes, then." Vale looked at Laurus's light but muscled form, her blond hair, her slate-blue eyes, and noted the similarities to a different powerful woman in Burdock's life. There wasn't a bit of her given to mercy or softness, not after all the years under a black flag in the ring. That was what Asheburg produced. Strength without tempering. People who mirrored each other, reflecting violence and pain without cease. Whatever had been done to Burdock and Dr. Wilcroft, whatever they had done to each other, was now coming to Vale and Key with the expectation that they would continue it. Burdock must have wanted Vale to be like Laurus so she could join him in his hatred of Dr. Wilcroft and the museum. Vale being unable to kill Key must have stung him incredibly.

There was nothing for Vale to do but be mad and stay mad. At herself, at Key, at the black market, at Dr. Wilcroft, and especially at Burdock. Her classes at the academy had taught her that anger was a reactive emotion, a protective one that covered the feelings beneath and needed to be bypassed to address the real issues. If Vale looked at the underneath, she'd crumble. Anger had taught her to survive, and anger would have to do until there was, if there ever could be, time and space to let go of it.

"He wanted to tell you that he never gave instructions to hurt you. The job was only for Key."

"Same thing," Vale said, bitter. "They'd have to go through me to get to her."

"It wasn't meant to happen all the way out there." Laurus sighed. "Be that as it may, Sayre wanted to explain himself, give you one last chance."

"One last chance for what? Is every word out of your mouth supposed to be rude?"

Laurus huffed a short laugh. "He wanted to know if you'd join us if he gave you everything you wanted."

"What's that mean?"

"A ticket back south, money for your family, a steady job that wouldn't keep you away from home. We even have insurance now, thanks to your suggestion. Pay in a little each cycle, and we use the pooled funds if one of us falls or is injured."

"All while murdering hunters and their guardians in the woods and selling off their parts on the market. Sounds cozy, if you can ignore the blood prices stacked on your heads."

Laurus frowned. "This is a serious offer. Sayre does care for you, you know. He wants you to achieve your goals."

Ancestors curse her, but Vale considered it for a moment. What would happen if she gave Key up to the black market, then took a place among their ranks to fatten her pockets? She had no loyalty to the museum, no moral obligation to the Strades or the temple. She could make good money, and quickly. Enough to move her family to an inland town where they could have a chance to grow roots.

Two years ago, on her final day at the academy, Vale had received a telegram from her mother, a rarity among rarities.

I trust you to do the right thing always, it said in footed black type. Was it the right thing to compromise herself and her morals for the benefit of her loved ones?

Vale returned Laurus's frown with one of her own. "By helping him achieve his goals? I help him steal his memories back from the museum, and he's going to give me a paycheck forever?"

"No," Laurus said. "You join us for as long as we can make it work. The memories are an unexpected opportunity he's been waiting years for, but they're a small part of the bigger picture."

"Which is?"

"Warren should be alive right now. You understand? My hunter should have had a short career and a long life. I warned the director about how much work there was. I knew it was going to happen. And it did."

Small wonder Laurus had looked haunted at her ceremony. "So you turned to the black market. How is that better? Killing hunters and guardians who've done nothing to you? Selling their memories, like that's better than the museum or a university claiming them for authenticity?"

"Kill enough of them, and maybe the museums will change their practices." Laurus shrugged. "What did you think I would do, petition the council? Ask the institute and museum nicely to create a steering committee that would oversee a subcommittee on new rules to protect hunters, only to have them ignore me? Ancestors, no."

"If you want me to be mad at the museum along with you, I can't be. Not the same way you are." Vale couldn't spare any more anger for Laurus. She was spending enough on herself.

"I don't want a repeat of us," Laurus said softly. "No one deserves that. But there's no other way to make that happen but to destroy the whole thing."

"If I join," Vale challenged her, "how do you guarantee I won't end up just like you? Or Burdock?"

Laurus put her hands on her hips, exhaling. "I can't guarantee that. But I do know something about you, Valerian. I've watched your fights in the ring. I've seen for myself how much you love combat. You go home to your community, maybe you take a farming job, maybe you find factory work. You'll never need to fight again. Could you give that up?" She gave Vale a searching look. "No, I don't think you could."

Vale might, out of contrariness. "Say you assigned me a diver. Say we go out and we run into other black market hunters and they attack my diver. You expect me to provide the same service for that person that I did for Key?"

"Yes," Laurus said. "That's what we're looking for in our hires."

"And should that diver get pulled under like Key, would you expect me to kill them too?"

"We don't push for discovery like the museum does, and we don't need our divers to go that far. It's fairly low-risk for them."

"But if that did happen, if reintegration couldn't save the diver. What are my choices? Leave them to fend for themselves or put my knife in their throat?"

Laurus's face grew stormy. "I see where you're going. I'll answer in good faith. It's the knife in the throat."

"Now, how the *fuck* is that different? You got the same system here that already exists in the city. I ain't staying for that."

"You don't need to stay for Key either," Laurus responded. "You've done more than enough for her."

Vale glowered. "I'm saying no for myself, not her. Burdock doesn't want the museum to steal more memories. You don't want other people to break the way you did after you killed your hunter. I don't want to kill the first real friend I ever had. You know what the actual problem is?" She bulled on without waiting for a response. "It's the diving. All of this, because some people can dive and a lot of people can't and the people who can't want what the divers have. The black market isn't better. Maybe tell the city or the council or whoever that diving should be outlawed and that we don't need a museum for memories anymore. There are other ways of keeping history other than drinking mushroom juice and hallucinating."

"The family lays," Laurus said. "I know."

Doubtful, Vale replied, "How?"

"Sayre taught me his."

Vale's heart, taxed as it already was, stopped.

Burdock had taught Laurus the songs from his village. His family lays. The ones he made Vale swear never to teach anyone else, the ones he said would bind only the two of them.

"You should join us, for his sake. He wants you with him, Maris. You're family."

Vale lifted her eyes millimeter by millimeter to Laurus's, then inhaled slowly through her nose. On the shore, on the days when the ocean was calm and the water was clean enough and Vale could wade into the surf, she used to stand and stare at the horizon for minutes at a time, her feet sinking into sand as the water moved and shifted the grains around her. This was how she felt now, sinking into the earth with every wash of the tide, seafoam applause echoing in her ears.

"What did you call me?"

"Maris. That is your name, isn't it?"

Betrayed by her brother over a rich city woman. *Never forget where you're from, little sister*. How many times had he said that to her over the years? Vale would laugh at the irony if she weren't so wounded.

"He shouldn't have told you."

Vale exploded off the bed, propelled by rage, and tackled Laurus around the thighs. They fell to the floor with a thud; Laurus gave a shout. Vale was up instantly, gaining enough space to set her feet and throw herself atop Laurus, rearing back far enough to deliver a headbutt so fierce the sound of it cracked like thunder through her brain, making her teeth ache. "Don't you *ever*," Vale screamed through hazy, blue-sparked vision, forming a fist, every muscle in her tightening for a punch, "fucking call me that!"

Someone flung the door open with a crash, and an instant later there were hands on her body, hauling her off Laurus. Vale hurled invective as her arm was wrenched behind her with enough force to send lightning up her shoulders.

The person holding her cuffed her across the temple. Vale swayed but stayed standing. Still incensed, she breathed through flared nostrils, her heartbeat charging through her, and watched Laurus.

Laurus got to her feet, murder in her eyes, and touched a finger to her purpling nose, where blood was trickling.

"You'll never be her," Vale spat, not caring if what she said was true, wanting only to hurt the other woman. The fire in Laurus's eyes quenched instantly and was replaced with ice. "He'll fuck you and call you Genevieve and you'll take it, but you'll never be *her*."

"You hellacious *bitch*," Laurus snarled back.

"What should we do?" said the man holding Vale. "Arvensis needs her alive."

"Tie her up." Laurus wiped more blood away from her nose before turning for the door. "Leave the food. Enjoy your meal, you fucking animal."

NINETEEN

ASHEBURG.—Protestors have gathered in front of the Museum of Human Memory on day one of the Memory Stewardship Colloquium, chanting slogans and demanding the museum return allegedly stolen memories. The colloquium is the largest yearly gathering of Spinal memory curators and archivists. "These people do not represent Asheburg," said Dr. Genevieve Wilcroft, head curator of the Museum of Human Memory. "These are outside agitators. We will not let paid disruptors keep us from our mission of education and archiving, which benefits not only the Spine, but all humankind. This critical work cannot be done by people without training, and the museum will not release any material. No further comment."

—Candace Cooper, *Spinal Tap Daily*

THE MUSEUM LOOMED OVERHEAD, ITS SHADOWED, SHALE-CLAD sides blending in with the steep rock face of Ashe's Peak. Incandescent lights glowed drowsily through its windows, lending warmth to the sleeping building, a contrast to the otherworldly green foxfire lining the curbs some distance away. Vale glanced around as she approached one of the service entrances in the back, Key's footsteps sounding behind her. Ahead, Burdock's lean, lithe form slipped from shadow to shadow, melding into them as if he'd been born one himself.

"Take this." Once at the door, Burdock shoved the slim sword in its mycoleather scabbard at her, then added Vale's knife. "If things go sideways, I can at least depend on you to use these."

Vale trapped the sword and dagger against her chest, her lips flattening. "What about Key?"

"What about her? You were her guardian. Guard her."

"She should have something too."

"Not in her state. You think I want to be the next Meadowsweet? Look at her. We shouldn't have brought her."

He would have preferred to bring Laurus, Vale guessed, but after their altercation, he'd sent her offsite, out of the radius of Vale's fury. Vale had yet to experience Burdock's retribution, but it was coming, she was sure of it. "Key, you with me?"

Key breathed in slowly through her nose, then exhaled just as slowly. "For now."

"You let me know as soon as you have issues. I'm going to get you out of this, I promise."

Key nodded.

"You done?" Burdock drawled, his accent showing.

Vale winced. Hearing him talk like he did back home only served to drive the betrayal deeper into her back. No interaction between them remained untainted. During the rest period, after she had thrown all dregs of her dignity aside to eat from the bowl, she'd found herself questioning every single aspect of their relationship, starting with their first meeting eleven years ago, when she'd stopped him on the road and demanded to know, her walking stick pointed at his head, why he'd come to her village. Had Burdock ever cared about her? Was she some kind of long project to him, an experiment? Or had she been used as an excuse or alibi for when he'd been out handling black market business?

"We're done." Vale shifted the weapons to one arm and took Key's hand in hers, though Key didn't need it at the moment. It was nice to have the comfort, though, and Key squeezed Vale's hand in return.

Burdock drew a mask over the lower half of his face, leaving only his eyes visible, and pulled lockpicks out of a pouch on his belt.

Vale buckled the sword and knife to her belt. "You know there's a security system, right?"

Burdock paused long enough to give her a flat look. "Yes."

"And there are guards."

At this, Burdock only scoffed.

"Thought about this a lot?"

"More than you know," Burdock replied, turning his pick. "Had a little practice too." The deadbolt to the door slid open, and Burdock withdrew his tools and set to work on the second lock.

"You planning to teach that at the academy? Hand-to-hand combat, breaking and entering, betrayal, and how not to ask simple questions like 'Vale, can you get something for me from the archives? It's culturally important to me, and by the way, did you know that the temple is a cannibal cult?' "

"Vale, hush," Key said, her voice low. She'd screwed her eyes shut, her head bowing as if in pain. "It's like you want to get us caught."

"I never asked," Burdock half whispered, twisting open the lock on the door handle, "because you and yours needed the money and the security. You also belonged to *her*"—he tilted his head at Key—"as much as you belonged to the academy, and the museum, and all the lies they made you believe." He straightened and put his tools away. "Now shut up and listen. The second I open the door, the alarm trips. They're coming here first, but they don't know what we're after. We take the back stairs down to the archive as quickly as we can and will be done before they figure out what's happening."

Burdock shouldered the door open before Vale could argue. She braced herself for a screaming alarm, but the service hallway remained dim and silent.

"Move your ass!" Burdock hissed, then took off at a brisk jog in the direction of the stairwell.

Key grabbed Vale's hand tightly. "Vale, *help*."

"Are you—" she started to say.

Bells shrilled, and Vale jumped. Key, too, flinched and cried out.

"Go!" Burdock shouted from down the hallway, all pretense of secrecy gone. Vale broke into a run, Key loping beside her as they raced through the back hallways of the museum toward the nearest stairwell down.

They reached the door, the pounding of their feet keeping pace with the frenetic pounding of Vale's heart in her chest. The alarm continued to ring, the sound of it scraping along her nerves until she felt like a jangly guitar string being tuned, unsteady and dissonant with the world.

Burdock threw himself against the door to open it, and the three of them sped down the first flight of stairs, which ended at the locked door to subfloor one.

"I don't have my—" Vale began to say.

"I have mine." Key fished out a small ring of keys, found the correct one, and fitted it into the lock. The door clicked open, and Vale wriggled past, assuming the forward position, hustling down two more flights of stairs. The alarm was louder in the stairwell, the sound waves bouncing around and crashing into each other, buffeting her head, making her dizzy. She gritted her teeth and kept going, her feet moving in a controlled fall toward the fourth subfloor door.

Vale burst out of the stairwell, her eyes adjusting to the difference in light levels, and looked around. Seeing nothing, she opened the stairwell door and motioned the other two to follow her, then trotted toward the archive, navigating the featureless halls with the sureness of habit and experience.

A turn here, another turn there; a sprint down a long hallway followed by a quick peek around the corner to check for guards—there: the wood-framed, wired-glass double door to the archives. Vale jogged past it to the other end of the U-shaped corridor, ensured no one was coming, then returned to the archive and took up a position next to the door, her hand on the pommel of the sword, glancing from one end of the hall to the other.

"Here. An extra." Burdock detached a sheathed knife from his utility belt and held it out. Vale took it, her mouth settling into a grimace as she strapped it into its rightful place on her belt. Burdock then picked the lock on the door, frowning as he maneuvered his tools. The look of satisfaction on his face was all Vale needed to affirm his success.

The alarm shut off suddenly, leaving a ringing silence.

In the absence of noise, Burdock said, "They'll have locked down all entrances. Let's make this quick before the sweeps reach us. You know the file, right, Key?"

"Yes," she said. "But there are multiple folders."

"Okay. Vale, you stay out here. I'm going with Key," Burdock declared. "For insurance. I know Gen's handwriting, and I know the date it was made. She was always meticulous in her recordkeeping." His hand moved, and a knife appeared in it, the overhead lights flashing off its short, shiny length. "Key. Go in now."

Key looked at Vale, the hesitation clear in her eyes.

Vale's nostrils flared. "I'll be okay out here. They don't know what our objective is, after all. They'll probably search the other levels first, and it'll take time."

"Okay." Key reached out but, at a glare from Burdock, retracted her hand. She and Burdock then slipped into the room, their forms fading as they left the meager pool of light from the hall, transforming into ghosts haunting the stacks.

Vale breathed deep and exhaled, measuring out her air the way she'd measure out a line on the boat with her brothers and sisters. On calmer days they'd go sailing, navigating the shallows by the shore in their little boat, tacking left and right to catch the wind, or sometimes rowing when the air was dead. Anything could happen on the sea, and Vale had seen that for herself, when one second the sky was blue, the clouds fluffy and bright, and the next, hard and angry and gray with a squall forming, a dark smudge growing darker.

It didn't help to panic in that situation, and it didn't help to panic now. She might go down fighting; she accepted that. Had accepted it since signing that contract to put her body before Key's in every way possible. Had known that her end might be filled with blood and pain, but a righteous pain served with adrenaline, burning her impurities away and leaving her clean and at peace.

It was Key who worried her, Key and her fragile mental state, with Burdock near. Before tonight, Vale would have trusted Burdock with Key's life, but . . .

Vale pulled her knife from its sheath and passed it from hand to hand to warm up, then followed the exercise by shaking out her increasingly tense arms and legs. Burdock had been a guardian, and one of the best. He would know what to do if Key fell back into the clutches of her memories. And besides, Vale reasoned, Burdock and the hunters still needed Key for the secrets living in her. There was no reason to harm her before the hunters got their end of the bargain.

Afterward, though . . .

Vale refused to think about it and kept herself from peeking through the archive doors to check. Though, now that she was contemplating her options, it might be a better idea to hide inside the archive. She could lure the guards in, maybe.

No, the glass doors presented too much of a problem. The situation required more strategy than standing in the dark, hoping people wouldn't see her through the door before she engaged them. Having her there, in addition, would mark clearly what she was guarding. Where would Dr. Wilcroft expect thieves to go? The laboratories, probably, where hundreds of specialized blood chalices were grown, or the artifact archives, which held some valuable items. Or even the armory, where there was an impressive collection of weapons and gear.

Time passed heartbeat by heartbeat, and the silence grew stifling. Vale willed herself not to fidget, but the compulsion to move was there, an itch made worse by the interminable wait. The more she thought about it, the more she regretted not splitting up. She could run interference while Key and Burdock looked for Dr. Wilcroft's stolen research. But it was too late now. She had a job to do and no time to prepare the field. Not like an empty hallway was a good place to lay a tripwire anyway. There was nothing to be done but stand guard, though she could change which door she guarded.

Better than nothing. Burdock would, she was sure, have come up with a plan. Perhaps he'd break into the registrar's office at the corner of the hallway and turn the light on to lure guards in. Maybe he'd make some noise to draw the guards into a trap. But Vale wasn't Burdock and lacked the brute force necessary to fight opponents who were ready and squared up. She had only two things, surprise and viciousness, and she was going to wield them as deftly as the knife in her hand.

Silently, Vale padded diagonally across the hall to a solid door with a square pane of frosted glass and took her place there, noting her new sight lines.

She waited.

The faint sound of shoes echoed down the hall, but Vale knew that the labyrinthine sublevels of the museum easily amplified any and all noises. She stayed where she was until she could pinpoint from which direction the people were coming. *Here we go*, Vale thought, crossing the hall to the corner, risking a peek around it.

It was a pair of security guards she didn't recognize, one shorter and slimmer, another taller and stouter, older than the first. The younger guard, a woman, looked to be fresh out of whatever training was given to guards; her face was drawn, apprehensive. The older one moved steadily but not quickly, a hand on the pommel of his sword.

She pulled back before they noticed her, then took a deep breath and let it out. The calm of a fight began to settle upon her as she set her intentions, warming her like the searing purity of afternoon sunshine, the kind that caused an immediate smile because, in that moment, life was good. Vale changed her knife to her left hand, drawing her sword with her right. It hissed in soft warning.

She would live. They would die.

Except she couldn't invoke guardian law anymore to protect herself.

Vale gritted her teeth, her lips moving in a silent swear.

The pair approached the corner. The second they came into view, Vale sprinted into action, charging the woman without hesitation. The woman screamed, but it was too late for her. Vale swept her sword in an arc, the blade parting the arm of the guard's uniform easily and cutting deep into the flesh beneath. Before she could react, Vale drove her shoulder into the woman and shoved, slamming both guards into the wall. Vale's left arm came up and around, her muscles bunching as she drove her knife into the woman's back and tore it out. She then disengaged, sliding out of the reach of the other guard, and extended her sword arm in a thrust so quick even Burdock would be impressed by it. The tip of her sword whipped forward and plunged into the other guard's thigh.

He bellowed and grabbed for her, but she was too far away and too fast for him. The woman crumpled to the floor in slow motion, a hand on her torn arm, blood spilling from between her fingers and smearing across the linoleum floor. Vale put distance between herself and the mess at her feet, and as she did so, Burdock's voice came unbidden to her mind. *Always be aware of your surroundings. The worst is stepping on something and losing your balance.*

The other guard drew his sword, rushing her in a limping shamble. Without further thought she parried, side-stepped, and kicked his knee in. He bellowed again as the joint cracked backward and he fell with a thump, clutching his leg.

"Shut up!" Vale snapped, sheathing her sword and dagger. What a nuisance to have to leave people alive and making noise. She looked for the radio transceiver all the guards carried—there, on the woman's belt. Vale picked her way over gingerly so as not to get her boots bloodied and worked it off the guard's belt, then examined it, trying to figure out at a glance what buttons did what. She stood after a second, intending to reestablish her position at the supply closet door.

But to her surprise, the older guard pushed himself to standing, using the wall for leverage, and launched himself at her, a knife in his hand. At his speed, with both legs injured, it would be easy to dodge. Vale took a step—and nearly stumbled as a hand clamped around her ankle.

I should have just killed both of them.

There was nothing fancy in the way she fought, and there never had been. Burdock's training had been thorough, the final lesson unchanging in all the years she'd known him: Win at any cost. With no other options, Vale faced the guard, bracing herself to block his strike. She caught his arm with hers but couldn't avoid his weight and momentum as he fell atop her.

The transceiver skipped away as Vale landed hard on the floor, half the wind knocked out of her. Somehow, the guard stabbed toward her face. She dodged, her stomach muscles clenching as her body jackknifed like a fish on a line. The weapon's tip hit the floor and scraped across it, the force of the blow enough to send the blade skittering straight into the back left side of her neck. Pain lanced through her, but along with it came the kick of adrenaline, and as the guard lifted his hand to try again, Vale brought her arms up, blocked him, then jabbed her thumbs at his eyes. He reared back on a swear.

Use their hips, little sister, Burdock had told her in training, lying atop her in the same position. *Control their center of gravity. You might be small, but no one can fight the natural laws of the earth.*

Vale got a foot on the floor and thrust her hips up, sending the guard's body sliding to the side. It was enough. She wrenched her ankle free from its snare, then drove the heel of her palm into the guard's injured thigh. He screamed, his body contorting. Vale wriggled out from underneath him when his weight left her, grabbed his knife hand, and gained her feet. As soon as she had the superior position, she stomped on the back of his shoulder.

He screamed again.

"It's just a dislocated shoulder!" She leaned over for a second, bracing her hands on her knees, sucking in air. "You stabbed me in the neck, you fuck. And *you*"—Vale straightened, then kicked the first guard in her injured arm—"should be grateful I didn't give your life to the spirits. Best pray for help and hope they're listening." She plucked the second guard's transceiver off his belt and chucked it down the hall, then glanced around for the one that had escaped. Finding it, she snatched it off the ground and held it to her ear to hear what the other guards were saying as she took her place in front of the closet door.

"Team two, report in." A man's voice, crackly and distorted, came over the line.

That had to mean the pair who were groaning on the floor. Wincing, Vale felt the side of her neck, probing the skin to feel how deep of a cut there was. She'd been lucky. The knife had missed all the major blood vessels, slicing shallowly across the back of her neck instead. She wiped her hand on her trousers, then squeezed the button on the transceiver. "Nothing on sub four."

"Who's that?" the man demanded. "I sent you to—"

Vale put the transceiver on the floor and crushed it with her heel.

There was no time left to waste. "They better have it," she muttered, because memory in hand or not, she was going to need to hurry Key out of there. Vale entered the archive, grimacing at the bloody fingerprints she left on the door. "Key? Burdock?" she called.

Burdock appeared a few breaths later, his trademark calm in place. "Trouble?"

"Two down, more coming. I hope you found the right thing."

"Key says she just needs a second more."

Vale darted around Burdock, going down the stacks the way he came, squinting as the dark enveloped her. "Key?"

"Here!" With so many shelves and boxes in the way, Key's voice was muffled. There was the soft sound of something sliding, and Key popped out of one of the stacks, almost colliding with Vale.

"Do you have it?" Vale looked at the file folder in Key's hand; the red string holding the flap of it shut was frayed and worn, obviously used many times. "Is that it?"

"I couldn't find it," Key said, desperation in her low voice. "I looked for it all over, it's not here—" She jumped suddenly and shrieked, dropping the folder, and threw herself against one of the shelves, huddling against it.

"Key! What's wrong?"

"It's not here," Key gasped, waving her arm in the air like she was scattering a cloud of gnats. "That's not real—that's not here, that's not you—"

Another intrusion. Vale forced away the chitter of fear and reached out, pinching Key's inner arm hard enough to bruise. Her skin was tacky with sweat. "Key, look at me. It's just you and me in the archive right now."

"Okay. Vale. I'm with you in the archive." Key swallowed. "What'd you . . . What was the question?"

"What's not here? What were you holding?"

Key shot an arm out and snatched up the folder, then pushed herself up to standing. "This is what Burdock wants. I'm talking about my blood, the specimen we took last week. For the reintegration. The registrar was supposed to file it, but it's not here, I've looked everywhere I could, I don't know where it could be—"

"Key." Burdock interrupted them softly, his footsteps sounding behind Vale. Vaguely, she recalled hearing the archive door open and shut. "Is that it?"

Key stared at him, the lines of her body hardening. "Yes."

"Then we're leaving. Let's go. Vale's made a mess outside and it's only going to get messier."

Burdock shepherded them toward the archive doors, opening one, and stepped into the hall before nodding, a signal to come out. The two guards Vale had incapacitated earlier were eerily, oddly still, with more blood than should be possible pooled around them.

She looked at Burdock, and her skin tightened into goose bumps at the dispassionate blankness in his eyes. To kill in a fight was one thing, but to murder people who were already down and not a threat was another. "What did you do?" Vale kept her voice quiet and level.

"What I had to." Burdock stuck his hand out to Key. "Give me the file."

"No." Key hugged it closer to herself.

"Now is not the time—"

Vale bared her teeth at Burdock in a snarl. "You don't get it until we're safe."

Burdock's jaw flexed. "Fine. We're leaving."

Vale followed Burdock, glancing at Key as she did so. "I didn't kill them, I swear."

"May they be remembered," Key murmured, looking over her shoulder, sorrow on her face. "I believe you, Vale. You're bleeding. That means you gave them a chance. Are you okay?" She lifted a hand.

Vale flinched away. "Don't touch it. I'm fine. You?"

"I don't know. I'm trying. Easier when the alarm—"

"We're not here to chitchat, girls." Burdock flexed his fingers, and light flashed off the brass knuckles he'd put on.

They exited into a different stairwell and climbed, the tromps of their footfalls echoing. At the third sublevel, Vale veered and reached for the door, but Burdock laid the flat of his sword whistling across her wrist, and she cried out, pain crackling up her arm. She cradled her wrist to her chest, the pain changing from flashfire to something deeper and slower, building upon itself.

"No," he said simply.

Tears sprang to her eyes, and she had to unlock her jaw to speak. "We need Key's specimen. It's probably in Dr. Arman's office—I just need a second, we need to get in there—"

Burdock's voice was cold, the pitiless blue of a sky after a storm, inured to the death and destruction it had dealt. "We don't have the time."

"But—" Vale looked at Key as the pain in her wrist continued to roll on. Suddenly, as if a levee had broken, emotion came pouring out, and the tears she'd tried to hold back spilled over. *No*, she thought as she curled into herself, her admonishment useless. She turned her face away from Burdock and gave voice to the wave of anguish with a choked, reedy wail.

As Vale's cry dissipated into the stairwell, Key whispered, her voice tiny and frightened. "Vale, *help me*."

Vale lifted her head. Then: "Key, no!"

Key blinked, the emptiness on her face yielding to confusion. She turned this way and that, looking at her surroundings before dropping her gaze to the folder in her arms. When she spoke, her accent was one Vale had never heard before.

"What's this? Who are you?"

Fear rang through her, panic in its echo. The academy's teachings, so abstract to her when she'd been taught, concretized in a flash.

> Reintegration is essential to a hunter's health and the best tool for prevention a guardian has. If the guardian fails to initiate reintegration at the correct time, the hunter will suffer. There are few actions that can be taken by the time a hunter manifests aspects of a strong memory or rogue personality. In the event that manifestation occurs, the following mitigation measures are recommended:

"Burdock," Vale said through her tears, "please, you gotta let me go to Dr. Arman's office, look how bad she needs a reintegration! I bet the sample's in there, I swear, it's probably on his desk or something. It'll take just a second—"

"No." Burdock leveled his sword at Vale, putting the tip of it right under her chin. Key gasped, the sound sharper than his blade. "We leave now. We'll figure out what to do with Key later."

Vale went still, but not still enough. The tip of Burdock's sword dug into her skin as she shook with suppressed cries, her chest heaving erratically. She wanted to scream. She wanted to tear out her hair, or rip herself in two with frustration, or surge forward and impale herself on the sword as long as she could put a knife through Burdock's heart and guarantee the ascent of both their spirits. But the pressure Burdock put on the sword tip pierced through those desires, shredding them like wet paper. She held her breath, gulping, as Burdock guided her to the stairs, indicating she should keep climbing to the ground floor.

"Who are you?" Key demanded. "What have you done with my grandfather?"

Vale moved on instinct, but Burdock only tightened his grip, the point of the sword describing a line of fire against her skin, and shook his head once. He then extended his hand toward Key.

"Give me your hand," Burdock said gently to her, and at that, Vale did sob, just once, at the familiar cadence of the man she'd once called a brother. "But keep that folder safe for me, all right? You can call me Burdock."

The sword point disappeared from her neck. Vale summoned the last of her willpower, grinding her sorrow back into the pit in her chest, and climbed. She clung to the railing like it was a life preserver, hauling herself up the stairs, each step feeling like the toll of Asheburg's clock tower bell, rung only for state funerals.

Once at the top, she opened the door and, hearing nothing, held it for Burdock and Key.

"Vale?" An instantly recognizable voice echoed across the polished floor of the lobby, and whatever was left of Vale's composure shattered into pieces on the stone. Jing stood in the center of the semi-darkened space, the long banners overhead reaching downward in shadowed tendrils, the banks of windows behind him showing herself, Key, and Burdock in their mirrored planes. A naked sword dangled loose in Jing's hand. Beside him was Cal, as stoic as Ashe's Peak itself, an axe haft resting on his shoulder.

For the second time in a day, Vale hurled herself into a man's embrace, relief pouring from her. Here, at last, was someone who could help. "Jing!" she cried, throwing her arms around him.

Jing staggered, exclaiming, then pried her off, pulling back, a hand going to her face, his expression changing to one of concern. Vale bit back a sob at his soft touch, the gesture of care almost too much for her.

"What is going on?" Cal said. "Key? Are you okay?"

"Vale," Jing murmured. "You look like shit."

She would laugh if she could. Of course. "Help us get out of here. Please. We don't have time."

"You don't have time?" Jing glanced at Cal, then took a step back from her. Gently, he said, "So it was you?"

"We were prepping in the armory when the alarm went off." Cal cast narrowed eyes at both Key and Burdock. The axe haft did not move from its position on his shoulder. "Genevieve gave us a new last-minute assignment earlier today. We saw some guards when we came out. Thought there was a break-in."

"Yeah, that was us." Saints, there was no time to explain anything. "I need you to create a distraction for the guards so we can get out."

"What's wrong with Key?" Cal's voice was level, wary, and Vale followed his gaze to where Key stood hunched around the accordion folder. Her mouth hung open, and her shoulders rose and fell rapidly. "Didn't we reintegrate her?"

"Yes," Vale said, "but—"

Cal strode forward past Vale, his arm outstretched. "Key!"

She scuttled away from him as if repelled. "Get away from me!"

Cal froze mid-stride. "Vale. Her accent."

There was a moment of stillness, of equilibrium. A moment where, once again, Vale had to look at the circumstances of her life and reassess what was true. Five heartbeats ago, Vale believed Jing to be her lover and Cal to be a dear friend to both her and Key. She was sure they would, based on sentimentality, help her and Key escape. Now, her storm sense told her that change was coming, and what had been certain—fair weather, clear skies—would turn as suddenly and decisively as a light switch flicking from on to off, and cease to be.

It seemed to Vale that her feet grew heavier, the air pressed down stronger upon her shoulders, and the yellow security lights dimmed and flickered. Even her sword, the grip of it appearing in her hand, felt unbalanced, clumsy. Vale observed the others as if watching a game of checkers, detached from emotion as Jing grabbed her, his fingers digging into her arms, and Cal settled both hands on the haft of his axe to lift it off his shoulder.

"I'm sorry, Key," Cal said. "This should have been Vale's job."

He took a step forward.

"No!" Vale screamed.

Jing spat a cuss, but all she knew was her fear raging white-hot through her, moving her body before she could think to do it. The emotions of the past days crashed into her with hurricane force, deluging her, almost tearing her from the last thing she had held on to: protecting Key. How many times had Burdock told her it was necessary to train her old habits out, to work at it until her reaction was the correct one each time? When she was sixteen, she had flinched at violence until she'd watched enough of it to be bored by it; Burdock had her desensitized in months. Vale had been Key's shield for two years. And Vale had only stopped being Key's shield for a day. Scant hours ago, she'd learned of Genevieve's transgressions. Burdock's betrayal? That was still fresh.

Faster than rational thought, at the speed of habit, the fear and abandonment compressed and compressed, collapsing into a pinhole that wouldn't have been out of place on Burdock's map. It was into that hole that Vale poured herself, the gravity of it stripping away everything but her sublime, radiant wrath.

Steel clashed, and Cal gave a shout, and Vale was standing in front of Key to protect her, her sword bared and thirsty. "*I will kill you if you touch her!*"

Cal stared at her, hurt written across the planes of his face. His axe clattered to the floor, and he put his left hand on his right forearm. Liquid welled between his fingers, red-black against the warm summer night of his skin.

The realization of what she'd done struck her. Cal had been one of her only friends. "I'm sorry," Vale wept. But her sword stayed steady. "I'm sorry, Cal, I'm so sorry, I'm so, so sorry—"

"Enough." Burdock's voice cut through her litany like a slap to the face. She looked up to find Burdock with an arm around Jing's neck, a knife point positioned under his jaw.

Jing stood still, and there was nothing but animosity in his eyes as he looked at her.

Cal spun around. "Jing!"

Burdock jerked his head. "Vale, take Key to the entrance we came in. Calamus, is it? Move, and your hunter will be dead before you take two steps."

Cal stopped. Vale sheathed her sword and took Key's hand tightly.

"I understand that there's a reciprocal system where you come from," Burdock drawled, addressing Cal. He began backing himself and Jing toward the far wall of the museum, where a corridor led to a service hallway. "Well, maybe not you, since you came here fairly young. But Jing, he likes a good exchange. Here's my offer. I let Jing live, and you don't bother Key, Vale, or me. This ain't your business to start with now that Key and Vale ain't part of the museum. You've got no obligation."

"Let him go," Cal said.

"Vale, get your ass out of here," Burdock snapped. "I'll join you soon."

She took one last look at Cal and Jing, mouthing *I'm sorry*. A tangible silence was her answer.

She deserved it. Vale turned, tugging Key behind her, and ran.

TWENTY

RECEIVED
M-I TRUST YOU TO DO THE RIGHT THING ALWAYS STOP
LOVE M+B CDTERB STOP

—Telegram addressed to Valerian IV

Vale fidgeted in the car, giving physical outlet to her emotions. Whatever the word was for the wasps in her chest, the ants crawling over and through her fingers, the desire to throw every object within reach, or wanting to eat a stick of dynamite just to feel better—she didn't know. She bounced her leg and dug her nails into her palms. She banged her forehead against the passenger-side dashboard. She wiped tears from her face. She drummed her fingers against the window, the arm rest, against the fingers of her other hand, against the hilt of her dagger, against—

"Quit it," Burdock said tersely. "You're making me nervous."

"Fuck off," Vale spat at him. She turned to check on Key in the back seat, but aside from lying down, Key hadn't moved after Vale and Burdock had maneuvered her into the car. Her head was draped over the edge of the seat, causing her curls to flop over, obscuring her eyes. Burdock's precious folder was on the floor.

"She catatonic already?" Burdock decelerated, taking a turn. "You could just leave her, you know. I can drop you off at the station."

Not without Key. "Don't fucking talk to me," Vale responded. She twisted in her seat, the gash in her neck pulling painfully, and prodded Key hard in the shoulder.

"Stop." Key's voice was soft, muffled by the car seat. "Hurts."

They spent the rest of the drive in silence, and the second Burdock pulled up in front of the building, Vale was out of the car as if fired from a sling, the slam of the car door echoing down the empty alley. She hauled open the back door, climbing in, shaking Key. "Hey, wake up."

Key did nothing.

Sweat broke out along Vale's skin, and a wave of radio static rolled through her. She took Key's arm in her hands, her wrist complaining again, and backed carefully out of the car, dragging Key upright. Her head lolled to the side, limp, and Vale had to catch her before she fell out. She cradled Key, then pushed her against the seat. "Key," Vale said, brushing the hair out of Key's eyes. "Key?"

Key had nothing but a dull stare and a slow blink. Her mouth sagged at the corners, and her usual alertness was missing, locked into whatever protective state her mind needed to keep from fracturing more with the unwanted memories. "Burdock, help!"

His footsteps scuffed behind her. "She's too far gone. She'll need to be carried. You were supposed to prevent this."

This time, when Vale whipped her head around, the cut in her neck opened completely. Blood leaked out, running warm down her skin. "How the fuck could I do that when you wouldn't let me get the sample? You wouldn't even let me sit with her. You stopping me from doing my job doesn't mean I—" Vale curled her hands into claws, the urge to explode rising again. Key wasn't her job any longer, and Vale should have walked away. If she had, she might still have a mentor, a lover, and a friend.

Burdock went around to the other rear door and opened it. Vale followed his line of sight to the file folder and lunged for it, but Key was deadweight against her, and she was too late. Casually, Burdock picked the file folder off the car floor and held it in front of him, gazing at it. A bright smile lit his face, appearing as suddenly as the moon from behind a veil of clouds scoured away by wind.

Just as quickly, the smile disappeared. "Well, I suppose it doesn't matter anyway. Long as we have her, we're all right."

"You wouldn't!" Vale punched the back of the chair. Key moved in her arms, groaning. Vale looked at her, then at Burdock's retreating back, unable to come to a decision on what to do as Burdock knocked on the hideout door and waited. After a moment, it opened wide and two people filed out.

"Get the doctor," Vale said as they surrounded her, her voice sounding unnaturally shrill to her ears. She tightened her hold, but they tore her from Key, throwing her roughly aside. Vale fell, tripping over the curb, and landed hard on her back.

She hauled herself up, willing to allow the insult to pass, watching as the two people lifted Key out of the car as if she were a heavy flour sack. "Please," Vale said. "Where's the doctor? Key needs the lab. Right now."

"You don't give the orders here, girl," one of the men said to her, and she recognized him as the one who'd held Key earlier in the night.

Vale bared her teeth at him in a soundless snarl but kept herself from stabbing him. That wouldn't do as long as he had Key.

"Animal," he muttered as he shuffled past, and Vale immediately regretted not stabbing him.

"You two, take the Strade girl up the elevator and get the doctor. Vale and I will meet you at the lab." Burdock locked the car, the file folder tucked under his arm, then gestured for Vale to go inside.

Vale refused to move.

Burdock clamped a hand over the back of her neck, and Vale yelped through gritted teeth at the flash of pain. He shoved her forward, directing her with the hand on her neck. "You always were stubborn."

She almost threw a retort out but thought better of it when she caught sight of the knife at Burdock's side. They entered the building, taking the ramp to the second floor, which had emptied of hunters except for a few standing watch and the two holding Key's limp, unmoving body. Under the lofted area was the repurposed cargo car, its broad side marred by a door so poorly installed that light escaped around it in a halo. That had to be the lab. It was the only space that could house the extraction machinery needed.

The woman with the iron braid came bustling out of the door. "Get her in, and quickly."

But when Vale tried to follow Key, one of the men stopped her with a palm to her chest.

"She's my friend," Vale said, trying to bull past. "Let me go! She's my friend, she needs me! I'm supposed to be there when she wakes up!"

The doctor gave her a quick, meaningless smile. "I'll let you know when she's ready."

"You don't know where to look!" Vale sidestepped, still trying to enter, to follow on Key's heels as she was borne away. "You don't know how far back to go!"

"Two days, max," Burdock said gruffly.

"Traitor!" Vale screamed, launching herself at him. She was caught midair by one of Burdock's underlings and hauled back, her arms and legs flailing. She struck out wildly, hoping to connect. "She needs me! Traitor!"

"You watch your mouth, or else," the underling said, depositing her away from the door. "Be a good little girl and—"

Vale drew her knife with a roar.

Burdock materialized out of nowhere, seizing Vale's already-sore wrist, disarming her, and wrenching her hand away with enough force for her to feel her bones twist and pop. The pain was paralyzing. "Control yourself!" he ordered her, his dark eyes afire.

Vale fought through the agony and went for the sword at her hip. But once again, the underling grabbed her from behind, pinning her arms to her sides, and all Vale could do, small as she was, was struggle against him.

Burdock stepped up to her, reared back, and dealt her a slap across the face that left her with stars in her eyes and a ringing in her ears. "Quit it."

She kicked at him instead. Burdock scowled and slapped her with his other hand, harder this time. Her vision blanked for a split second before she registered the fiery sting of her cheek. She tasted blood in her mouth; her neck was sore; her cheekbone throbbed. He must have hit her with his brass knuckles still on.

Then a wave of dizziness swamped her, and her fight lit out like it had to go home. Vale sagged in the underling's arms, tears and snot running freely down her face.

"You broke her, boss," the underling said.

"She's too cussed for that." Burdock bent to remove the sword and knives from Vale's belt. "And now I have my sword back. You couldn't die owing me, you said, and now you won't."

"If you're going to kill me, then kill me," Vale said, slow and thick. She sniffled, an ugly sound.

"We had a deal, and I don't go back on those. Though it's tempting to, right now." Burdock put a finger under Vale's chin and tipped it up to look her in the eyes. "You wanna come for me later, you're welcome to. The only reasons why I'm not dumping your skinny ass in the river are because you've held up your end of the bargain and you're too dangerous to be left unsupervised."

He then addressed the man holding her. "Put her back in the room. And don't go near her. She's spite and choler made flesh."

"Yes, boss," the underling said. "Should I collar her?"

"She's not an animal. But if you do anything, Vale, Key will bear the consequences, not you." Burdock gestured to the underling.

He lifted Vale, crushing her arms against her body, and began walking toward the stairs leading to the loft area. He deposited her back in the room from before, locking the door behind him. No doubt he was also standing guard in case she decided to kick the door down, a distinct possibility, and try to escape, which was not a possibility. Not without Key. And even if Vale could escape, there wasn't enough in her pockets to buy a fare home. She'd be easy pickings if she decided to hitchhike in her state.

There was nothing to do but wait it out and be ready for whatever happened next.

Vale looked around the bedroom, debating between cleaning herself up or lying on the bed to rest. If she lay down, she'd never want to get up, and that wouldn't help Key at all. She dragged herself to the bathroom and washed her face and neck, taking a clinical interest in her injuries—split lip and cheek, both starting to swell to match her other cheek and bruised nose from the day before; her bruised forehead, a lump arisen from the blow she'd dealt Laurus; the knife wound on her neck, still oozing—then rinsed her mouth, wincing at the sting on the inside of her lips, spitting out rust-tinged water.

That done, she set about finding something to stabilize her wrist with. Cleaning herself up had been an exercise in awkwardness, and her wrist had complained with every movement. Burdock had been anything but gentle, and the joint was clearly injured, the accumulated fluid around it impacting her ability to make a solid fist. Her wrist throbbed with each squeeze of her heart, and as Vale ran it under cool water, she grimaced at the thought of the exercises she'd need to do to keep the joint strong and limber.

She checked the chest of drawers for spare bed linens and was rewarded with a pillowcase. In short order, she'd torn it into strips and tied a makeshift bandage on her wrist. She'd need to get arnica on it, but that was a wish begged of stars and spirits. No one here was about to give her anything but violence.

Finally, Vale took a seat on the bed, a groan escaping her as her body sent up a cascade of aches and pains. The exhaustion hit her suddenly, and the next thing she knew, she was jolting out of sleep on the bed as the henchman loomed over her. Adrenaline surged, and her training took over. In a second, Vale had drawn the henchman's knife from his belt, grabbed his wrist and pinned it, and laid the knife against the inside of the man's elbow. "What do you want?" she snarled.

"You said you wouldn't do anything!" the underling whined.

"I didn't say that. And I'm not doing anything."

"The Strade girl is all done," the underling said, gulping.

"Will I be allowed to see her?"

"Yes, if you give my knife back."

This was how Vale knew Burdock hadn't taught him shit. *Leave no room for disagreement or misinterpretation*, Burdock would always tell her. *Give them only the choice to run or the choice to die.* "You'll take me to her, and I'm keeping the knife." She tugged sharply on his arm, unbalancing him, and kissed his throat with the point of the dagger. "Hear me?"

"I can't—"

Vale flicked the knife against the skin of the man's neck, laying the first layers open. He gasped, but she held him firmly, watching the cut fill with tiny, bright red seeds. "Oops," she said blandly. "Now I'm doing something. I only understand the word yes."

The man looked at her, and his muscles bunched as if he were preparing to fight. Vale moved the point of the knife to the cluster of lymph nodes beneath his jaw and grinned, putting into it all her rage. "Your choice. A knife in your brain, or you take me to Key. I'll give you a hint. You ain't faster than me."

"I hear you."

The doctor was waiting for her in front of the laboratory door, her face carefully composed. Her expression did not change when Vale held up the stolen knife and motioned for the henchman to move away. The area was still mostly empty, but there were sounds of movement coming from downstairs. Burdock was nowhere to be seen.

"Your name is Vale?" the doctor said.

She nodded once. "That's me."

"I'm afraid I have bad news," the doctor continued.

Vale flipped her grip on her knife.

"She's not dead," the doctor said quickly, holding her hands out. "She's very much alive right now. But she's in serious trouble." The doctor shuddered. "Key wouldn't wake up. She should have gotten a reintegration long before she got to her current state. I don't know what else to do but pray that she comes out, and comes out herself."

The unspoken words were clear: or else she would need to die.

"I'm sorry." It was empty coming from the doctor, and she knew it. "There's nothing I can do."

There was no grace left, not for anything; Vale lacked it to begin with, and grace was Key's domain. Vale shouted and kept shouting, her fury rising higher until she was nothing but a living pillar of it. "You planned this from the beginning! You never cared about the deal or about her! She's nothing but a tool to use now that Burdock has what he wants!"

"No," came Burdock's voice from behind her. Vale whirled, her fingers curling into claws, and went for his throat. He blocked her, but this time she'd learned her lesson, and she threw herself forward, her uninjured hand pressed against his arms to lock him down. She clutched the stolen knife as hard as she could, pain lancing through her wrist and up her arm, and shoved it into his stomach as far as it would go.

"You little bitch!" he gasped, staggering back.

Vale unhinged her jaw and screamed at him.

"Arvensis!" the doctor cried, moving toward him, but Vale swept her leg, tripping her. As she fell, Vale grabbed the woman's long braid and yanked.

The doctor shrieked, the sound high and thin, her hands going to her head. Vale put her knife to the woman's neck, staring directly at Burdock, an idea formulating. Her anger coalesced into a single sharp point, like the gleam of sunlight on the tip of a sword, sparkling and cold.

"Move," she said calmly, "and your doctor gets a new smile."

Wisely, Burdock didn't move.

"I'm amending our deal." Vale increased the pressure on the woman's neck, the point of her knife sinking into the soft flesh, a muscle twitch away from the carotid artery. "You said you'd let us go and I'm holding you to it. But I need my things, as does Key. You're going to get our rucksacks out from your car, along with Key's staff and my guitar, and you'll bring them here. I will go into the room with Key, and you won't bother me until we both come out."

Burdock said nothing.

"It's not much of an ask," Vale said. "I've played by your rules. I've been nice enough to keep your underlings alive and your building clean. You've gotten what you needed. But I can and will become a problem if you don't let us leave. I could kill this woman right now. And I'll sleep so good tonight if I do. You know it."

Footsteps came trampling up from downstairs, and more of the black market hunters emerged, stopping when Burdock lifted a hand from his position on the floor. The other hand covered his stomach. If only she'd had time to yank her knife across his body and open him like a pea pod.

"Smart move," Vale said to them without looking. "What do you say, Burdock?"

"What are you planning to do after you come out that door?" His voice was tight with pain.

"Walk out of here unscathed, both of us, and never see any of you again." Vale smiled at everyone in her vicinity. "Because if I do, you're dead."

"So you want me to get your stuff out of my car," Burdock said, "bring it up here, leave you alone while you get Key lucid somehow, then let both of you walk out?"

"That's exactly it."

"For the doctor's life?"

"If you wanna add some more lives to the bill, I'm game. I could also snitch on you to Key's ma and ba and the city council. Wouldn't that be fun?" Vale showed her teeth in a rictus grin. "Think of it this way. For all the trouble we just went through for that precious folder of yours, if you let the doctor die, you won't get to profit from Key's misfortune. You won't get to destroy the system you hate so much. It's a wildly uneven exchange. All I'm asking is for you to leave Key and me alone."

Burdock nodded. "Agreed as long as you don't run and snitch immediately."

"You heard all that, right?" Vale addressed the other hunters. "That means all of you too. No one lays a finger on us." She paused, then narrowed her eyes. "See me."

"You are seen," some of the black market hunters said in response. Burdock sat, refusing to speak, his eyes flinty and hard, blood leaking from between his fingers.

"Hear me!"

"You are heard." This time, more of the hunters chimed in.

"Remember me!" Vale shouted, pulling the knife away from the doctor's neck and holding it aloft.

"You are remembered!" the hunters chorused back.

"You're coming with me." Vale tugged on the doctor's braid, forcing her to stand. "Open the door."

The woman did so.

"Get our things, Burdock. You've been witnessed." Vale backed into the room, keeping the doctor in front of her as her shield.

Once inside, Vale shut the door and locked it. "Sit," she said.

If looks could kill, the doctor would have made a decent attempt on Vale's life. "Where?"

"I don't care. You stay in one spot and you be quiet." Vale approached Key where she was lying on a hospital bed, one of her sleeves rolled up, a piece of wadded mycobandage jutting out from underneath medical tape. She was breathing on her own and seemed asleep.

"Did you sedate her?"

The doctor didn't answer.

Vale growled. "Tell me."

"No. She's too far gone to need it." The doctor made a face as if she was going to spit but didn't. "You're a real piece of work."

She'd learned from the best. "Unless you want those to be your last words, you oughta fuckin' shut up." Vale ignored her, focusing on Key.

> Reintegration is essential to a hunter's health and the best tool for prevention a guardian has. If the guardian fails to initiate reintegration at the correct time, the hunter will suffer. There are few actions that can be taken by the time a hunter manifests aspects of a strong memory or rogue personality. In the event that manifestation occurs, the following mitigation measures are recommended:
>
> - Reintegration with a specimen at twenty-five times the standard concentration
> - Neutralization of the hunter
>
> Blood integration is not recommended and should be avoided even during emergencies, as the results are unpredictable for both hunter and guardian. For examples, see "Pioneers," 6; "Historical Cases," 34; and "Adverse Effects," 79.

Vale turned her knife on herself, bracing as she placed the tip of it against her finger. She could never explain it, but larger injuries seemed to hurt less, weren't as frightening as this small, insignificant pinprick. Vale closed her eyes and pressed in until the skin popped. She hissed with pain.

"What are you doing?" From the corner of Vale's eye, she saw the doctor rise.

"Key, I know you can hear me," Vale murmured, putting her knife down. Blood coalesced into a bead on her skin, began oozing down her skin in a dark red slide. "I'm only doing this because I have no other choice. I'm sorry. I hope you can forgive me."

"What are you doing?" the doctor demanded again.

Vale peeled open Key's lips and drew a red smear over her teeth, then squeezed her fingertip to drip blood over and into her mouth.

"You can't do that!" The doctor's voice rose with alarm. "You're going to ruin her!"

Key's eyes began to move beneath her eyelids.

There's iron and copper in her mouth again.

She's sucked into blinding light. Immediately, she begins freefalling, tumbling through infinite space alongside a bright, colorful ribbon-twist of memories. She expands, limitless, becoming all things, existing all places. Joy overflows within her, addictive in its headiness. This must be what paradise is like. She could stay here forever; here, she is forever. This is the elusive perfection she's been searching for, the promise given by the ancestors every time she dives, now fulfilled.

There's no scheme to the space, just colors of every type and every kind of ribbon. Some are edged with lace, and some are smooth and satiny; some are thin, and others are thick. They look a lot like the ribbons Vale keeps for herself, the ribbons she keeps trying to put in her hair.

Vale.

The space narrows into a bottleneck, and the joy dims. She chases it, expelling the concept of Vale, and briefly, infinity returns. If she is to stay here, she must rid of herself of all connections.

Vale.

No. Not Vale. Vale isn't her name, even though the memories from the last ten years all have that taste. Vale, or Valerian IV, exists only for a length of those ribbons, and the ribbons themselves wind and stretch back and back. She reaches out and touches a wide, pale green ribbon made of a light, transparent fabric—organza, the memory tells her—best suited to little girls going to big temple functions. She's seen these before, tied around waists, forming perfect bows in the back.

The memory pulls at her. She drops in, and she's at the academy graduation, uncomfortable and prickly with shame at her threadbare uniform, the same one she's worn for two years, the one she's grown out of. Around her, the academy students are dressed in their finest, or, barring that, their freshest, newest uniforms. Some of them, mostly boys, have purchased dress uniforms, wearing brown and beige slacks and shirts. They're shiny with pride, the graduates, each of them turning to find their families in the audience, beaming.

Not her. Not Valerian, as she's had to call herself for the last eight years. She's done her best to get away from the name assigned to her. "Vale" doesn't sound close to "valerian" at all, and that's just fine; valerian's a sleep aid, a calming herb, and none of that describes her. She could have been a pepper instead, something prettier like Solanaceae or nightshade, spicy or deadly.

Solana is seated two rows in front of her, however, and though she loves to gossip and snipe at other the guardians in the class, she's mid-rank at best, able to hold her own in a refereed weapons match but unlikely to survive a street brawl.

It's the biggest day for an academy graduate, because not only will they be assigned a partner, they'll get to spend time with their families. Vale would, if she could have scraped the money together to pay for train tickets. But she didn't bring income in, and she would sooner eat pine resin before asking Burdock for a loan, not even for the price of a single fare for her mother. Not when it was summer and field hands were in demand and children needed to be watched and money had to be hoarded.

The trouble with large families was that money flowed out of their hands like seawater, and with two parents, six siblings, and nieces and nephews, there was never enough of it. A single fare wouldn't work, anyway. No one went by themselves anywhere in her family. It wouldn't be two or three tickets, but five or six. No matter how many times she and her brothers and sisters had fought, they'd always have each other's backs, although Vale had missed the giant, all-out brawl in the village square from a couple of years back. She'd volunteered to return, even if her return would be several months too late, but her mother had told her to remain in school.

All Vale has is a piece of paper, folded and refolded and secured like a handkerchief in her uniform pocket, with congratulations from her entire family. She'd been the scholarship kid, the mountain ruby Burdock had dug out and tumbled and cut into shape. Now she's poised to give back to her family, to start sending money home for the repairs they always need. They never say much to her, but Vale knows how things go: There's always a bill somewhere.

She has no new uniform because she can't afford one. The knees have been patched, the cuffs and hems of her trousers repaired with neat little stitches, though nothing can hide how her ankles stick out from her pants. She's small to start with, like a doll, she's heard, and her clothes are even smaller. Her shoes are held together with wood glue and hope. The thinned soles, she tells herself, give her the ability to sense the ground, and therefore give her an advantage in a fight.

She reaches up to touch the handful of colorful ribbons wound around the base of her ponytail. They're her own, a mess of color that sets her apart from the drabness of the audience. She's collected as many as she could find, purchased with her few coins the others, and has spent much time tying them just so. She's proud of herself for that.

Or she is until Lanelle Strade shows up and calls her a ragged country bumpkin. "I'm a ragged country *bitch*," Vale spits, squaring up, ready to fight.

Sadness overwhelms Key, and she retracts herself from the pale green ribbon, already knowing what's next, unable to watch through Vale's eyes. Another ribbon beckons to her, and this one is a lovely, satiny dark pink, edged with lace. Key slips in before she can stop herself. It's too easy.

She's walking along the thin shore, where seagulls cry overhead. In the distance, she spots the white belly and black wings of an osprey as it surveys the ocean and the few roofs of submerged houses that poke up at low tide. Rampikes pierce through the surface of the sea, dead monuments to the marshes once lining the coast. Sandpipers scuttle down the beach in the wake of the waves, poking their beaks into the sandy silt, hunting their prey. She's supposed to be at home doing chores, but it's finally clear out and the ocean isn't ready to kill her, and she's going to take advantage of it, even if that'll cost her when she gets back.

"Maris!" a young-sounding voice shouts.

She turns to see her little brother running full tilt at her, determination on his face. "Maris, you're in trouble!"

"Then you're in trouble with me!" Maris laughs and takes off down the beach, her muscles bunching in her legs as she powers through the clam-dotted sand. She sprints past dying jellyfish and stinking clumps of seaweed, hurdles chunks of concrete and broken timbers, sends the sandpipers fleeing and squawking before her. Later, it'll get hot and the clouds will build again, and maybe tonight they'll have storms. Tomorrow, for sure, there will be, and Maris will be trapped inside, or in the mud ringing their house, unable to do anything but grump at the weather (but not too much, because the spirits might be cruel and send a hurricane) and be glad for the break from her family.

Maris.

Vale's never said anything about her name. It's an old-sounding one, evoking the sea, which fits her so much better than Valerian. Vale—Maris—can be as mercurial as the ocean, soft in one moment, hard and gray in the next, unyielding in her determination. Water erodes everything, and so too will the sea claim the land, and whether through flood or encroachment, the sea gets what it wants.

She gets what she wants. She, Vale. Maris. Kiana.

Another ribbon. Another memory. She's in the training gym, sparring with a boy who is half again her size. It's wet out, but the sun has appeared, and to escape the mugginess and a history paper, she's come to train, hoping Burdock will make another excuse for her and get her teacher to grant an extension. She's mid-match when the door opens, and usually she pays no attention to distractions, but for some reason, this time she looks.

A girl walks through the doors, broad-shouldered and brown-skinned, sunlight catching in the dark coils of her hair and creating a halo around her face. She's heard of angels before, or spirits that show themselves in beams of sun and in curtains of rain, and this girl—this athletic, hourglass-figured girl with the wide-tipped, slightly upturned nose and those brown eyes—this gorgeous girl must be one of them.

But that can't be, because Maris has seen her in the halls. They've never talked, but she knows this girl is a celebrity, the top student in their class except for combat training. She's a Strade, Maris remembers suddenly. The girl is out of Maris's reach. Everyone at the academy is, but this girl is so far out of Maris's reach that she might as well exist on a different continent. Maris is about to avert her gaze when the girl looks at her, their eyes connecting.

She freezes, shivers fracturing along her skin, her bones. The world stops. Noises deaden. She can't breathe. The girl freezes, too, surprise widening her eyes, a light flush making her freckles—ancestors, she has freckles—stand out against her cheeks and the bridge of her nose.

A fist crashes into Maris's face. She's rocked back on her heels, the spots where her opponent's knuckles connected stinging furiously. She's supposed to be sparring, she recalls, but she has no idea who this boy is in front of her, what move he'll make next, or whether she should be attacking or defending. The Strade girl has disconnected her from reality, snapped her right off and sent her into a place free of time.

"You let me land that one," her opponent complains.

"What?" Maris says, her attention still on the Strade girl. She's approaching.

"Oh, screw you." He slides toward her.

Maris meets his body with hers, cradles his head to her shoulder, pivots, and shoves herself forward. The boy pitches to the floor right before her hand closes around his throat. She grins at how loudly he slaps the mat, then scrambles to her feet. She has to meet this girl. Even if they can't be friends. Just once, Maris wants to say hello.

It's odd looking at herself through someone else's eyes, to sit in someone else's memories of herself and experience their feelings. Key leaves that memory, too, and gets tangled in yet another one. She can't stay long; it's a violation of Vale's privacy, and though Key has been her partner for two years, she still doesn't know much of her. She's so curious about who Vale is, who Maris is, and without thinking Key catches hold of a black ribbon, a black the same color as Vale's eyes, wraps her hand in it, and slides down its length into the memory.

It's recent, and a more complete recollection of what's happened in the last forty-eight hours. Key has holes in her memory, and she patches them with Vale, takes all of Vale's ribbons and plasters them to herself until they can't be removed, until the shock of Burdock's betrayal and the sawdust despair of Jing and Cal aligned against Vale are Key's as well. There were, until this point, a handful of people who had earned Vale's trust, and having them turn away from her is a pain she can't express in words.

All she has is violence. All she's ever been able to do is be physical about it. She needs the comfort of touch, the surety of movement. It's been a blessing growing up between the sea and the forest, where the sand could soothe the jitters in her legs, where climbing the ancient live oaks could order her mind and grant her calm. In Asheburg, Vale is bound by the city, by decorum and expectation and rules. She isn't book smart the way Key is; she has no money; she has no friends. She's a foreigner, a cutting and not a transplant, left to fail or thrive with the minimum of care.

And that's why Burdock's betrayal hurts so much more than the sprained wrist and the bruised face, why severing him and Jing and Cal from her life feels much like losing a limb. Maybe it was naïve of her to believe Jing could be someone permanent. He was her first, and she'd hoped he'd be her last, though deep down she knew he wouldn't be.

Key is the only one left, and even then, the knots holding them together have been unraveled. If Key could cry, she would. Vale is excellent at hiding her feelings, at subsuming those parts of her that have nothing to do with her job.

Except they have everything to do with Key and how she feels about Vale. The infinite joy from before fades, replaced with a glowing warmth. She realizes, as she begins rising through space toward a silver shimmer above her, that she's less interested in Vale as a guardian and more interested in Maris as a person. She's tried reaching out to Vale, but

Vale is so prickly and so good at being angry that it's easier to relent. She should try harder, because underneath Vale is Maris, and Key wants to know what expression will be on Maris's face when she sees the ocean again.

Key should try harder because she's hurt Vale. Jing's assessment was correct. Key is self-assured to the point of arrogance, and that has almost broken her relationship with Vale. She can't let Vale finish the job. That hurt is part of Key, now; she knows it as well as Vale does, and she also knows how to heal it.

The shimmer solidifies. Vale is singing, though it isn't Key's recall song. It's a song from her village, a song about the ocean, which is fitting. Key stretches toward her voice, willing herself out of the dive. Infinity will have to wait.

She opens her eyes.

TWENTY-ONE

It was like looking into a mirror. Her face—no, Vale's face—hovered over her, black eyes wide with hope, though the effect was marred by the crusted blood and purpling skin over both her cheeks. *That's right*, Key thought. *Burdock hit me twice.*

No. Burdock had hit Vale twice.

"Who am I?" Vale whispered.

Key grabbed on to the routine. She knew this for certain. "Maris."

Vale gasped, a hand flying up to her mouth, tears starting in her eyes. Key looked at her, wanting to pull Vale's hand away so she could see those rosebud lips. She hadn't been imagining things. Vale really did feel—

"She's awake?" came a woman's voice, which Key recognized as the doctor's.

Vale ignored her, grasping Key's hand. "Who are you?"

"I'm Key," she said. "Kiana." She gripped Vale's hand tightly in return, anchoring herself.

Vale exhaled, relief clear on her face. Key held on, unwilling to release her. "We gotta get out of here. Come on." Muscles bunched as Vale took a step back and hauled, helping Key sit up.

But once she was upright, Key tugged on Vale's hand, drawing her close.

Vale's eyes widened right before Key kissed her.

The third time, Key vowed, would be proper, without interruptions, without ulterior motives. The one time she'd tasted Vale had not been enough. Key had kissed other girls, dated them at the academy, and thought she knew what desire was: a pressing need between her legs, a craving for release that, if it went unfulfilled, would drive her mad. But with Vale—how was it possible to yearn for her even when their mouths were joined and her soft moans were vibrating into Key's lips?

Key slid her arms around Vale's lithe figure and held her, marveling at their closeness. Silvery thoughts flashed in and out of her mind. To be here with her, with no past and no future—that was happiness. To know it was the two of them again. To want Vale in body and spirit and be one with her until they could wear each other like clothing. For a second, Key couldn't help but think about what Vale had been like with Jing, who'd only wanted it to be fun. Did he know how much fire lived inside Vale? Did he know she kissed like she was dying and only Key could give her breath? Did he know how Vale would have committed her life to him if he'd asked it of her?

But maybe Vale wouldn't have because she'd been in love with Key the whole time. Ancestors, Key had ignored all the signs, had ignored the lingering glances, the extra time spent together, the telltale flush in Vale's cheeks as Key had applied her makeup. She'd ignored Vale's leniency with her and had let herself be fooled by the anger and prickliness Vale wore around her like armor.

"Maris," Key said, breaking off the kiss to look at her. Blood was smeared over Vale's lip; the wound Burdock gave her had reopened. Key leaned forward and licked it from Vale, took in the tang of bright metal as she claimed Vale's mouth, then gave it all back to her. And it was a claim, because Key had tasted Vale's blood, had incorporated Vale's essence into her own body in a way no one else could.

Vale moaned and shivered delightfully under Key's hands, and the action was like the twisting open of the valve on a burner, desire flaming up, uncontrollable. It was surprising and gleeful how unfettered she felt with Vale, how light and joyful it was to have Vale's scent in her nose, to have had her mouth. Key wasn't driven by emotion the way Vale was, didn't operate like she had a thousand things to do and only a week to do them in. Key was the steady one, even-keeled for her penitents, and her feelings weren't allowed to be hers. But she would hold all of Vale for herself and herself alone. Here, right this moment, united in a single point of time and space, with no road behind and no road ahead.

"Call me Vale for now," Vale said softly, shifting so she broke contact with Key.

Time restarted, and as Key looked at Vale, she had the sensation of chrysanthemums opening, of a sunrise washing the land in light and clarity, of filaments branching and branching. A kaleidoscope turning on itself. Fractals birthing fractals. Infinity and joy in all things.

Vale pulled Key forward so their lips could meet again, and this time Key swore she felt the presence of the saints like a shock of rain across windows. Senses sharpened, and the filaments pruned themselves back until they were numerous but orderly, connected and networked. Key kept kissing Vale just for the euphoria, for the anticipation of having Vale to herself and teaching her the meaning of patience over the course of a night.

Later. All of that for later.

"How are you not in a dive?" Vale asked, breathless, before she turned toward a woman Key recognized as the doctor.

"I'm not sure." Key slid off the bed and landed on the floor. Her legs were steady; she felt strong. "I can only guess, but maybe it's because . . . I've already dived, and I can't do it again."

From outside came the sound of raised voices and general commotion. Vale glared at the doctor. "What was that?"

"I don't know," the doctor replied.

Vale strode toward her, a bloody knife somehow in her hand, and jerked the woman upright by her collar. "Doesn't matter. We're leaving. Burdock better have all our stuff. I'm more than ready to get the fuck out of here. I have—"

"—a train to catch," Key finished for her.

Vale grinned. "Exactly."

Key reached for the door, but Vale beat her to it. Key shook her head. "You don't have to go first anymore."

"Habit," Vale replied. "Let's hold on to that until we're safe. Then we can figure out things from there. Besides, the doctor's going first anyway." With that, Vale opened the door and kicked the doctor in the rear, sending her sprawling through the doorway. Vale barreled through immediately after, knife at the ready—and one of the two guards facing the door slapped her arm away, trapped her in a bear hug, and lifted her, legs kicking, off the floor.

Flashfire anger seized Key. The rucksacks, guitar, and staff lay nearby; Key dove for them, eluding the other guard, grabbing her staff off the floor. She came back up—

"Are we done yet?" Vale leans on her staff, the bruises along her ribs throbbing, sweat dripping off her chin. It's dark o'clock and she'd only gotten a few hours of sleep before Burdock prodded her awake for training. He stands in front of her, implacable and immovable and immune to her whining.

"I'll let you rest when the sequence is in your body. It's not yet. Again!"

Vale straightens, wincing, but settles her hands on her staff. She's grateful Burdock gives her extra time, pushing her harder and further than any other student, allowing full-contact, no-holds-barred sparring. Pain is the best teacher. She's had a dozen lessons tonight.

She sinks into her stance, then whips her staff in an overhead strike, steps back for the poke, winds up to stir the pot—

"Key!"

She gasped. Her staff was still in her hands, but both guards were on the floor, out cold. Vale was staring at her, eyes wide, mouth open in shock.

Always be aware of your surroundings, Burdock had said. Key glanced around, but the doctor had disappeared in the melee.

"Key, what the *fuck*? When did you learn to move like that?"

"I . . ." She looked at her hands, then at the guards. "I think I just did. From you."

"What?" Vale slung her rucksack over her shoulders, as well as her guitar, then dragged Key's rucksack over.

She became aware of the raised voices on the floor below, unintelligible shouts that still conveyed alarm and fury. Key donned her rucksack and did the arithmetic: a mostly empty upper floor, Burdock injured, multiple voices below. The fight to get out would test her limits, but she could not flag. Vale had already done so much and was hurt. It was Key's turn to be the vanguard.

"Hello, Key? What the *fuck* does that mean?"

"It means I learned how to fight. From you. From your memories." Key took a deep breath, then reached out, cupping her hand around Vale's less injured cheek. "And Burdock. Vale, you had that in you this whole time?"

Vale gave her a dark smile. "Takes a lot to be the best. While everyone else was sleeping, I—" She tensed, head and shoulders turning to the back of the area, where several hunters had come boiling up a hidden stairwell.

To Key's surprise, they ignored her, going instead to the tab-making apparatuses at the side of the room, their hands moving swiftly over glass tubes of rusty-red liquid.

"Don't question it," Vale muttered. "Let's go, now." She turned for the ramp, hustling across the floor before Key could take point. Key followed two paces behind on Vale's heels, bracing herself for a fight as she descended the ramp.

But there was no need. From her vantage point at the top of the ramp, Key saw Burdock standing, flanked by a handful of subordinates, speaking to—

Genevieve.

Key broke out in a sudden sweat, her rage igniting. "You *bitch*!"

Genevieve turned cool eyes toward her. In the dim lighting, their green depths were gray and unreadable. "I thought I'd find you here. Valerian's doing, I bet."

"You don't get to fucking talk to us," Vale growled, stepping forward. "We've got nothing to do with you anymore. We're leaving. Get out of our way."

"On the contrary. You're coming with me. Unless you'd prefer a scandal in the papers." Key had thought Genevieve would lose the icy composure she wore for the museum when she was off work, but it was out in full effect, enhanced by the sleek black clothes she wore, the outfit much the same as Burdock's: a black long-sleeved shirt tucked into black slacks, the hems of which ended in high-top combat boots. A sword at rest hung off her left hip, and on the other side, she wore a dagger.

"You have something that belongs to me. I am here to retrieve it. I looked the other way from this operation for years; the market has its uses. But you've overstepped your bounds for the last time."

"That something never belonged to you," Burdock said. "It was my community's. What right do you have over any of it? And you come in here and make demands of me? You built your career on theft."

"Is it thievery if the house you are taking from is empty? Is it robbing if the people have abandoned their homes?"

"Theft is theft. It's only justice that the memories return to me by the same route."

"You let me have them."

"Only because you promised to return them. I should have realized what your word was worth."

"All you had to do was ask," Genevieve said, looking at Burdock, her iciness melting into anguish. "But there was never a good time to reach out after you left me. I had a copy of it ready for you. You kept your distance, even after everything we shared. You hurt me, Burdock."

"I hurt *you*? You should teach swordplay with those deflection skills. You stole what was mine. You hurt *me*. You had your chances to return the memories, but you didn't because you never intended to."

"If I returned the memories, as you allege, that would set a precedent for all the other museums. What should they do, allow the public to raid their archives?"

Burdock laughed, pain flashing across his face. "Yes, actually. Open the vault. Let us see what you're hoarding, whose stories you've erased because you love having something special and unique above all else. Make public history public."

"No. It cannot be done. There aren't enough trained workers to care for things that are so precious. The museum is where the memories belong."

"This is exactly the pretentious bullshit that sickened me when I worked with you. You have no respect for any method but your own and won't believe there are other methods that work as well as, if not better than, yours. Key's right, you know." Burdock scoffed. "You're a bitch. The master specimen is staying with me. I'm sure I'll find something to do with it."

"Still trying to go home, are you?" Genevieve replied. The ice returned. Her smile held a touch of nastiness. "They never respected you anyway. You're delusional to think this will restore your reputation. If they wanted you back, they'd have said so."

Beside her, Vale made a strangled sound, tensing so hard that she leaned forward from it. Genevieve did not know, Key realized. She had no understanding of what the memories meant to Burdock, how desperately he'd fight for them.

"And if you wanted to give me the master as you promised, you would have done so." Burdock kept his voice even. "This comes down to you and me, Gen. I gave my word that Key and Vale could go, and I make good on my promises. Step aside, and once they're out that door, let's have that fight we always meant to have."

"With all your people behind you? I doubt it."

Burdock laughed. "As if you didn't bring people yourself. I'll give you credit where it's due. You walked in here on your own and left your backup outside. That's admirable. No one's got more brass. But I know *you*. And you haven't changed." He spoke to one of his subordinates. "Go, open the door. Let's see the curator's hidden hand."

"You never lacked for brass either." Genevieve smiled faintly, stepping aside to allow Burdock's subordinate to pass. The sound of the door opening funneled down the hallway, as well as the sound of footsteps. At least three people, Key figured. "All right, fine. Kiana, Valerian, you may go. Burdock is right about this being between the two of us."

Vale's lip curled in a snarl as she took a step toward Burdock.

"No." Burdock's voice was sharp with command. "Vale, get out of here. This is not your fight."

"The hell it isn't." Vale kept moving forward.

"*Valerian.*" Something in his tone made Vale stop, one foot in the air. He stared hard at Vale. "Leave now, with Key. I know you don't want to hear it, but this is my last lesson. Survive. As you always do."

Key reached out, grasped Vale's hand, and found it as tense as a constricting snake. Wordlessly, with effort, Key towed Vale and her heavy feet past Genevieve and the four guardians arrayed behind her, their faces masked, all of them dressed in black, but the curator held still and didn't move. Key refused to look at her as she walked by, wanting her heart to fill with her emotions for Vale, not wanting any piece of it to remain for the woman she once admired and aspired to be.

Vale unlocked the door and hauled on it, letting in humid summer air and cricket song and the hint of smoke. She then exited in front, the vanguard as always. The door began swinging shut, slow on its hinges, like a coffin being lowered into the earth.

Genevieve's raised voice was a beacon in the night. "You must be crazy to think I'd fight you. I invoke guardian law. I claim the blood price from you, Arvensis, and every single person associated with you."

"No—" Vale twisted around, too many paces away from the door, panic transforming her face. Key pivoted as well, but the door was already well into its trajectory.

Genevieve reached behind her, pulled something from her belt, lifted her hand. The scene slowed before Key's eyes. She heard the scrape of Vale's shoes against the pavement as the overhead lights caught on what Genevieve held: a revolver, the same one she kept on the bookshelf by the chaise longue.

The scream burst from Vale's lips, but Genevieve had already fired. The sound was deafening.

Far away, beyond the other side of the door, Burdock crumpled into the arms of his subordinates as around him, silver swords flashed like rain.

Vale's next scream tore through the night, so loud that the crickets went silent. She rammed her shoulder against the door, jerking on the handle, tears streaming down her face.

There was a second gunshot, muffled. Then a third.

"It's locked!" Vale slammed her hand against the door, her distress rising from her, infectious. "Let me in! *Fuck you*, let me in!"

Key almost joined her, her shock and grief over Burdock expressing itself as a moment of stillness and detachment as Genevieve fired three more times, emptying the chamber, the sounds of gunshots visceral, punching Key in the chest, vibrating through her like a bell tolling death.

The combat instructor, Burdock, is looking at her keenly. The only reason why she remembers his name is that he'd introduced himself when he recruited her. Maris takes a seat on one of the benches in the gym to put on her shoes, though she doesn't know what she's going to do now that class is over. Dinner, if she can make herself walk into the cafeteria. Although it's the first day of school, it feels like everyone already has friends, and she smells too foreign, too country, to be allowed near the others.

She takes her time, and the gym empties until it's the two of them. Burdock saunters over, and Maris tenses. "I'm just getting my shoes on."

"Don't worry about it." Burdock tilts his head, that keen look back in his eye. "What name did they give you again?"

"Valerian." There's a hint of sullenness in her tone.

Burdock laughs. "The fourth. Big name for someone so small, and a mismatch too. Nettle would have been better. Not a fan of it, I take it?"

Maris shakes her head.

"There's no rule in the academy that says you can't shorten your given name," he says. "Valerian II went by Val. Valerian III went by, believe it or not, Riri. They may call you by the full name, but you can choose something that's more you. Sound good?"

Maris says nothing.

"Well, think on it while you're at dinner."

She pauses in the middle of tying her shoe. "I'm not hungry."

As if on cue, her stomach rumbles.

Burdock laughs again. "I've got mangoes in the office I was going to cut up. Want some?"

Mangoes. They're expensive here because they're shipped up from the south. Maris nods once, wary of kindness, then takes her shoes off and follows him into the office. Burdock chatters as he wields his knife, shearing the sides of the mango away from the pit, scoring the golden flesh. "I'll introduce you to some of the kitchen staff after this. Some of them are from the south too. It'll be like back home, everyone knowing everyone. They'll look after you."

He hands her a piece; he's got the pit held between his teeth. The first bite is sweet sunshine and happiness. Tears spring to her eyes. Ancestors, she wants to go home.

"I've got an idea," he says, watching her with sympathy on his face. "How about Vale?"

"Vale," she repeats, trying the name in her mouth. It tastes like mango. "Okay."

She had loved Burdock like a brother, even after everything.

"Burdock!" Vale's voice cracked.

Key gasped, coming back to herself like a freshly wound watch. There were tears running down her face, and the weight of sorrow in her body was almost too much to bear. Genevieve had claimed her prize. What more unique and special an item could she have than the entirety of Burdock's life? There would be no greater joy for her than to make Burdock property of the state, to be exploited and distributed as the council saw fit.

Genevieve would do the same to Vale, given the opportunity. The woman was thorough.

Key could not give her that chance.

"Vale, we can't be here, we have to leave!"

"Burdock!" Vale shouted again, kicking the door. Key pulled Vale away and into an embrace, squeezing when Vale fought her, squeezing tighter when Vale's knees went weak and a wounded cry poured out of her mouth. It was heartless to force Vale to keep moving, cruel to hold her close and drag her bodily away from the door. But Burdock's final lesson had to be learned. It had to be internalized, same as all the other lessons he'd taught.

Key picked Vale up, her tears a mirror to Vale's, and staggered away from the building, rounding the corner, her ears ringing from Vale's screams.

"I know. I know, I'm sorry, I'm so sorry." She didn't bother saying anything else. There was nothing to say. Genevieve's aim had been true, and Vale hadn't lacked for conviction when she'd driven a knife into Burdock. That memory was fresh, blazing blue-white in Key's head. "Vale, we have to leave, we—"

Vale strained against the circle of Key's arms, her eyes so wild that the whites showed all the way around. "I'll fucking kill her, I swear it, for everything she's done, *she's dead*, she's fucking *dead*—"

Key swung Vale around, slamming her back against the side of a building. They had been so close to getting what they'd wanted, and as each second passed, receding irretrievably from them, Key realized that the new path onto which their feet had been set would end only in violence. Vale would not be given the chance to be the person she deserved to be, outside the shadow of the museum.

And neither would Key.

Nonetheless, Key had been given an order. "He told you to survive!" Key hissed in Vale's face.

"I don't want to!" Vale shrieked back. "Let me go, the blood price is mine—"

"Maris!" Key shouted so loudly that Vale jolted and

went still. "Survive and *live*, dammit! Not just because he told you to, but because I want you to. Because—" Key, realizing her volume, dropped her voice to a whisper. "You're more than a sacrifice. You deserve a whole fucking life. You deserve to teach others your songs. I will not bring you home just to build your cairn in front of your family's house!"

Vale stared at her, chest and shoulders heaving.

Key kissed Vale fiercely. Their rucksacks thumped to the ground; Vale's guitar emitted a quiet complaint. Vale fought, then yielded, her mouth softening beneath Key's, her tears smearing against Key's cheeks.

"Vale," Key murmured once she pulled away, her lips brushing against Vale's ear, her voice low, calm, controlled. "Maris. Please. We have to leave."

She tightened her free arm around Vale in an embrace, tucking herself around her. Vale had taken care of Key for so long. It was only natural for Key to take care of Vale in return, to act when her partner couldn't, to step in front of her and shield her in her most vulnerable moments.

Vale drove her palms into Key's chest, shoving her back, then stooped to grab her belongings, swiping at her face with her hand, another choked wail pressing itself from her like water through the cracks of a dam. Beyond them, around the corner, there was a commotion of heavy footsteps and slamming car doors.

Vale straightened, her shoulders hitching with suppressed cries, and said nothing. The crickets began singing again, a backdrop to the chaos blooming nearby.

"We have a train to catch," Key said firmly, taking Vale's hand in her own. "Quickly, before someone spots us."

Vale swallowed, then slung her rucksack onto her back, followed by her guitar case. "I'm coming back."

"I know. I won't stop you."

"You owe me fare."

Key kept her hold on Vale. "I owe you a lot more than fare."

Vale's shoulders slumped, her vitality snuffed out as if blown, leaving nothing but gray smoke curling despondent over the wick. "Let's go, then."

Six Weeks Later

If it weren't for the storms thrashing the coast with frightening regularity, Key could get used to living here.

She glanced overhead at the position of the sun. The sky was the clear, endless blue of a calm, deep breath, without a single strip of cloud. The storm from the night before had stolen them all away, and for a couple of days, there would be enough peace in Maris's village to patch holes and fix the broken things, to get electricity up and running again, and to shuffle families from neighbor to neighbor until repairs and inspections could be finished.

Seagulls called to each other as they flew, and below her concrete perch, fiddler crabs scuttled in and out of tide pools left by the retreating waves. At high tide, Key could almost believe she was on the true coast, that there weren't countless towns and villages lying dead and smothered beneath the water, that only sand and rock and deep ocean awaited her if she swam out. Maris had cautioned against it, regardless; the slack was best for swimming, but because no one could tell what gifts or curses the ocean would bring, it was best not to get in at all.

She remembered it vividly: that spring when she was ten and Elsie and Roland were twelve, and how Trey had taunted the twins, dared them to go swimming.

No, that was Maris's memory. She was Key, whose childhood was spent passing in and out of the gates at temple, running around the west wing of her huge, empty house. Key pressed two fingers against her forehead, trying to ground herself, but it was harder without Maris.

None of them know about the rip current beneath the waves, and when Roland gets sucked down, it's Nadine who jumps in and saves him and drags him out the water. The second Roland coughs up water and wakes, Dina screams at Trey for what feels like hours. Maris doesn't know what to do other than hold on to Elsie and tremble. The next day, Dina and the twins get sick and need the doctor, and there goes all the money Mama has been saving for the temple, to ask a resifix to dive for new memories before the autumn equinox festival. It's one of Maris's favorites, full of sticky, sweet food and recollections and rituals where they bind their ancestral spirits to the family to ensure they won't get lost and turn into wandering ghosts.

That was the job Key should have been doing all along. She should have been traveling the coastline, using her money and her abilities to relink the past and the present for those who needed it the most. There were so many lost spirits who needed a guide back to their loved ones, who needed to be forged back into the chain of wisdom. But without a supply of chalice spores, the work could not be done. Wild-grown chalices were practically extinct, and if they could still be found, they weren't half as strong as the temple's, and those in turn weren't half as strong as chalices bred at the institute.

She had spent a week in thought over what Burdock had said, doing nothing but staring at the ocean in the day and lying awake at night. She'd kneeled in prayer, asking for wisdom from Saint Aurissa. She'd meditated and fasted. If Burdock's story had been known—if Burdock could have spoken of the wrongs Genevieve had done to him without fear of reprisal from the museum, the institute, the academy, and the press—would Key have pursued her dream so ardently? Could there exist any other obstacle to force Key from her path to the museum, and what was her path now?

Distressingly, she'd gotten no answers from the saints other than a growing certainty that her mission had changed and thus become more difficult. What the ancestors wanted her to do remained in doubt, and weeks passed without a sign.

In the meanwhile, it was not bad, Key reminded herself, rubbing the fresh calluses that had formed on her hands and fingers, to put the knowledge in her head into practical, real-world use. The precision and clarity of her recollection had improved since arriving in Jesdon, and she had tapped ruthlessly into the memories of all the tradespeople she had stored in her mind. Some buildings in town already sported structural improvements, and if the weather and the ancestors and the supply chain were kind, more and more buildings would gain upgrades.

Footsteps approached, but Key didn't bother turning, knowing that cadence as well as she knew her own. It was only when they'd stopped that Key looked up to see Maris staring out at the horizon, joy in her freshly tanned face. Dangerous as it was, Maris had always loved the sea and took strength from it.

Key stood, patting off the grains of sand, then mirrored Maris's stance. For a moment, she was lightheaded, her vision pulsing in time with the heartbeat rushing in her ears. She put a hand to her head, but the lightheadedness only worsened when her reflection didn't do the same thing.

"Who are you?" It sounded like she was speaking aloud, but it was Maris who'd spoken, Maris who gripped her hand, Maris who held her gaze.

Key blinked, hard. "Key. Kiana Strade."

"Who am I?"

Vale. Valerian IV. "Maris."

"Good." Maris peered at Key but didn't let go of her hand. "I didn't even need to kiss you this time."

"You could, though." Key smiled, but it was halfhearted.

"Your differentiation speed keeps improving." Maris continued as if she hadn't heard Key, but the corners of her lips turned up anyway. A burst of salt-laden wind came off the sea, blowing strands of Maris's hair into her face. "Ugh!" she exclaimed, using both hands to push the locks away. "Should have put my fucking hair up."

"I like it better down," Key said, and let her eyes linger on Maris's mouth.

"Key."

"I do," Key protested, helping Maris tuck a ribbon of hair away from her face. And since they were already close, Key leaned in and kissed her. Maris wavered and softened, her lips parting.

"You know we shouldn't," Maris said once the kiss ended, but the protest was weak. "It's too soon to tell if what you feel is real or not."

"What *you* feel is real. What you do for me, that's real too." Maris remained concerned over how much of her personality had been absorbed into Key's and whether the affections they traded were genuine. After Jing, Key understood why Maris was worried. She'd already had a relationship with a mirror. She didn't need another. "I stay me when I'm with you. I'm not sneaking into your room in the middle of the night because a year ago, you thought about doing that. I'm doing it because I want to."

And because, truthfully, Key needed to. It was easiest to hold on to herself when she was entangled with Maris and had so much physical sensation to swim in. To have all five senses activated and humming, keeping her present in the moment so she could maintain the boundary of her mind.

There was also a sixth sense born of generational experience, one that told her that the best way to approach Maris would be slow and deliberate. Even though they woke beside each other and kissed sweetly until they ached; even though Key helped Maris notate and practice the lays composed during her absence; even though Key learned the names of Maris's nieces and nephews and was woven day by day into the fabric of Maris's family, Key still had to wait for Maris's signal.

Key touched Maris's face again, brushing the backs of her fingers over Maris's cheek. A trio of sandpipers hustled past, and suddenly a new memory appeared in her mind. A small one, harmless. Thank the saints. She couldn't predict what triggers set off hidden memories, both the ones that had supposedly been erased during reintegration and those of other people, and neither could she predict how deeply she'd be drawn into them.

Without warning, Maris threw an uppercut.

Key could only fling herself back enough to turn it into a glancing blow; her teeth clicked together nevertheless. She lashed out with a straight punch, but Maris moved like water, slipping to the side, reappearing inside Key's guard. Key flung her arms around Maris, trapping her, then froze.

"What's next, Key?" Maris breathed. "You know it. I've done this hundreds of times. Thousands."

"I can't—" Key released her, the specter of Burdock hanging around them. Maris had stopped saying his name, but he was as present as they were, appending himself to Maris's sentences, appearing so clearly in her movements that it looked at times that she was possessed by his spirit. This was no surprise. Burdock had no one left to build him a cairn.

"I'm not a fighter. I know you don't want me to be helpless. But it's all different. You're always the smaller one. The angrier one." And despite having all of Vale's fighting knowledge, actively wearing the parts of her persona that were so dissimilar to Key's, as opposed to riding the memories passively, felt wrong.

A quick smile lit Maris's face. She tilted her head to the side, those black eyes gentle.

"Finish it," Key whispered.

Maris pressed her thumb into the hollow of Key's collarbone, kept pressing until Key swallowed, faintly nauseous. "This is you," Maris said. With anyone else, it would be a threat. With Maris, it was assurance.

Key stepped back, breaking contact.

"Have I, um . . ." Maris's no-nonsense guardian demeanor disappeared, replaced by a shyness. Key waited, patient. "I just . . . wanted to say that . . . you've been getting bigger. As in, your muscles."

Key flexed her right arm, noting the glow rising in Maris's cheeks. She'd always worn her blush pretty. "I feel stronger after doing so much construction work."

"And I think the haircut looks . . ." Maris swallowed, visibly uncomfortable, but she gestured to Key regardless, indicating the new hairstyle, cut short on the sides with longer curls left on top. "Good." Before Key could do anything but grin, Maris said, "Break's over. We gotta get back."

"Thank you. Mind if I have one more minute?"

Maris turned back to the ocean, then muttered, "I can't believe how different it all is."

Key changed her grip, interlacing her fingers with Maris's. When they'd first hauled themselves off the train, Maris hadn't been able to figure out where she was. The entire area had changed in the ten years she'd been gone. Jesdon, previously a small village on a distant barrier island, had grown and become a town. The center of it had moved, leaving Maris's family far enough on the outskirts that their community could be thought of as a separate village.

In Maris's memory, her family's house had sat beside a balding salt marsh dotted with rotting timber and seaworn foundations. Now, the house sat on a hill, facing others to create a small neighborhood. The salt marsh was thriving, and a maze of growing oyster reefs could be seen at low tide, built upon salvaged concrete blocks.

"Did the mail come in yet?"

Maris shook her head and began walking back toward the village. "I haven't checked, but I haven't heard anything."

Key sighed, relieved. News arrived seldomly from the Spine cities, and the only changes Maris's village were interested in were the shifting demands for their produce and labor. What Key did know from listening to the long waves was that the museum had reported another break-in, blaming it on black market hunters, and that Asheburg was abuzz with rumors of her disappearance. Of note was the death of Burdock III, former advanced combat instructor for the Asheburg Academy, now known as Arvensis, a black market leader. Also of note was Dr. Genevieve Wilcroft, a would-be hero who had tracked down Kiana Strade's last whereabouts, confronting the traitor, Burdock, and mounting an almost-successful rescue.

The temple's equilibrium, too, had been disrupted, but try as Key might to find out more, there was only silence.

Not for the first time, Maris said, "Now might be a good time to go."

"This again?"

"We can't stay here," Maris said. "I love my family, but everything's too different. *We're* different. I've missed home, but I was missing a version of home from my childhood a decade ago. I'm not a child anymore, and that version is gone. I can't get that back, and I shouldn't try."

"We just got here."

Maris sighed. "I know."

Also not for the first time, Key said, "You've been uprooted so much that you don't know what it's like to stay in one place anymore. Don't let your old habits keep you from what matters the most to you."

"Temple voicing me again," Maris muttered.

"How about a cabin in the woods?" Key suggested. "Close enough to see your family, but not so close that we'll always have houseguests."

"I'll think about it."

They ascended the steps of the embankment hand in hand, the sun's rays searing the back of Key's neck, and walked toward the construction area down the street from Maris's house. As they passed Maris's front door, Phoebe came bustling out. "Maris!" she exclaimed. "Key!"

Maris stopped. "Yes, Mama?"

"Come inside, come inside. We've got a visitor." Phoebe's black eyes sparkled, and Key saw the strong resemblance between mother and daughter.

"I told Claude I'd bring Key right back," Maris said.

"Don't you worry about him. I'll set him straight. Our visitor's too important to keep her waiting."

"Okay," Key said slowly, her pulse rising with warning. Around her, at a volume only she could hear, the ancestors began whispering.

Maris tensed.

"Inside." Phoebe hustled them in, where Key took off her shoes, then stepped onto the raised floor of the house. "In the living room. Oh, I wish she had sent word ahead. I'm so ashamed at the state of this place! Right after a storm too."

"There's no need to worry," came a warm, pleasing voice that froze Key in the doorway to the living room. In the spindle-backed chair in the corner was a woman with skin the same shade as Key's, her hair in elaborate cornrows threaded through with gray.

Memories unlocked, lifting as a cloud of particles, and swarmed.

> "You wanted to know if we needed to be at the temple. I suppose for this, we don't have to be." Lanelle pushes the loose sleeve of her dress up, baring her arm to the shoulder. Thin bangles clink against each other as she tilts her arm, turning it until the light catches the inside of her bicep. There, growing a soft cream against her medium brown skin, is a branching tangle of filaments about an inch in diameter.

"What the . . ." Maris said.

Key felt sick.

Lanelle Strade stood, the bangles on her wrists chiming, her long sleeves falling all the way to her knuckles. Despite the heat of the day, she wore a high-necked, floor-length robe. "Kiki," she said warmly, opening her arms. Her eyes shone, fever-bright. "I've missed you so much."

ACKNOWLEDGMENTS

IT'S PROBABLY CLICHÉ TO SAY IT BY NOW, BUT NO BOOK MAKES IT into the world on its own. All books are group efforts, and this one is no exception. The process for *The Memory Hunters*, which was referred to as Key & Vale for many years, involved many places and people. The Appalachians, which I've had the privilege of going through for over a decade, are some of the oldest mountains in the world, and seeing the forests of the Great Smoky Mountains exhaling mist always excites me. This book could not have existed without the Alleghenies, the Smokies, the Blue Ridge, and the rivers winding through them. Neither could this book have existed without the hills and rivers of Pittsburgh, the magnolias of the Deep South, or the red clay of Georgia. I arrived in Atlanta many years ago as an ignorant Yankee, not understanding how the South would humble me. I have since gained enormous respect for the people, who have an indomitable will, and the land. America as we know her now was made here.

To the Atlanta Botanical Garden, especially the people at the Fuqua Orchid Center and the Orchid Research Library, thank you for being an endless source of inspiration. I can't wait to get back there on a regular basis.

To my agent, Anne Tibbets, thank you for being the first person to give me the go-ahead when I pitch a wild idea and for always having faith that I'm going to make it work. To my editor and champion, Viengsamai Fetters, thank you; I'm delighted we have the same brain on so many things. Thank you to Sarah Guan for also believing in me. I still have to pinch myself, sometimes, to believe I've been noticed. To the rest of Erewhon Books: Marty, Cassandra, Leah, Kelsy, Diana, Quinn, Alice, Rayne, Ari, a huge thank-you. Thank you to my cover designer, Kristine Mills.

Thank you to Beth, whose incessant earworm helped plant the seed for this story. To Johan, who has been a wonderful cheerleader, thank you. I've been so fortunate to have so many other cheerleaders: Jen, Lauren, Leanne, Phoebe, Manu, Larissa, Brent, and Yoon. Thank you to my pub siblings Cee and Victor for the words of encouragement and the Loon Slack for using the rolled-up newspaper emoji on me when I say something that deserves it. Thank you to Carrie Feldman of the Smithsonian Institute, who I met by chance at a con and who had the museum know-how and enthusiasm to read through a draft of this book and tell me exactly where I went wrong; thank you to Matt DeAngelis for the academia gut check.

Thank you especially to Mel Blue and Grace Wynter, whose knowledge I treasure. Thank you to Adina Langer for the multiple conversations and the museum visit that helped create the foundation for this book. To Gabriella and Faye, who I've been so blessed to walk alongside on our publishing journeys, thank you. I can't imagine doing this without you. And my hugest thanks go to Casey Berger, whose feedback is worth more than its weight in gold.

Finally, thanks go to my family, especially my kids, who continue to be patient with me as I adapt to author life while also handling the many other aspects of life, and who also want to fight the people leaving bad reviews on Amazon. I love your spirit. Thank you to the animals who've reminded me to take a break and kept me company as I wrote: Gremlin and Pooka, I miss you so much; Portia, the best round; Puddles, who never wants to be where she is. And thank you so much, thank you forever, to my husband Brian, who has been tireless in his support, who has a never-ending well of excitement for my ideas, who grounds me and who also helps me work through the tough questions that come up when I'm writing. I fuckin' love you.

REFERENCE LIST

PERIODICALS

Braga, Luciana Lorens, Marcelo Feijó Mello, and José Paulo Fiks. "Transgenerational Transmission of Trauma and Resilience: A Qualitative Study with Brazilian Offspring of Holocaust Survivors." *BMC Psychiatry* 12 (September 3, 2012): 134. https://doi.org/10.1186/1471-244X-12-134.

Hampton, Jeff. "Massive Magnolia Tree in Manteo Could Be Largest and Oldest in North Carolina." The Virginian-Pilot (blog), February 8, 2019. https://www.pilotonline.com/2019/02/08/massive-magnolia-tree-in-manteo-could-be-largest-and-oldest-in-north-carolina/.

Karp, Ivan, Corinne A. Kratz, Lynn Szwaja, and Tomas Ybarra-Frausto, eds. "DOCUMENT: Declaration on the Importance and Value of Universal Museums." *Museum Frictions: Public Cultures/Global Transformations* (2006): 247–249. https://doi.org/10.1515/9780822388296-015.

Nizhnikov, Anton A., Tatyana A. Rzhova, Kirill V. Volkov, et al. "Interaction of Prions Causes Heritable Traits in *Saccharomyces cerevisiae*," *PLOS Genetics* 12 (2016): e1006504. https://doi.org/10.1371/journal.pgen.1006504.

Taylor, B. Kim. "Clothing Made of Mushrooms Might Just Be the Future—And It's Actually Pretty Cool."

Bustle (March 21, 2018). https://www.bustle.com/p/clothing-made-of-mushrooms-might-just-be-the-future-its-actually-pretty-cool-8018663.

BOOKS AND ESSAYS

Agnew, Vijay, ed. *Diaspora, Memory, and Identity: A Search for Home*. University of Toronto Press, 2005. https://doi.org/10.3138/9781442673878.

Dolin, Eric Jay. *A Furious Sky: The Five-Hundred-Year History of America's Hurricanes*. Liveright, 2021.

Edson, Gary. *Museum Ethics in Practice*. Routledge, 2016.

Elliott, Todd F. and Steven L. Stephenson. *Mushrooms of the Southeast*. A Timber Press Field Guide. Timber Press, 2018.

Fry, Carolyn. *The Plant Hunters: The Adventures of the World's Greatest Botanical Explorers*. Andre Deutsch, 2017.

George, Adrian. *The Curator's Handbook*. Thames & Hudson, 2015.

Golding, Vivien, and Wayne Modest, eds. *Museums and Communities: Curators, Collections and Collaboration*. Bloomsbury, 2013.

Higgins, David M. *Reverse Colonization: Science Fiction, Imperial Fantasy, and Alt-Victimhood*. The New American Canon: The Iowa Series in Contemporary Literature and Culture. University of Iowa Press, 2021. https://doi.org/10.2307/j.ctv1wdvx4q.

Hildebrand, Caz. *Herbarium*. Thames & Hudson, 2016.

Langer, Adina, ed. *Storytelling in Museums*. American Alliance of Museums. Rowman & Littlefield, 2022.

Mayblin, Lucy, and Joe Turner. *Migration Studies and Colonialism*. Polity Press, 2021.

Osterholz, Anna J., ed. *Theoretical Approaches to Analysis and Interpretation of Commingled Human Remains*. Bioarchaeology and Social Theory. Springer, 2015. https://doi.org/10.1007/978-3-319-22554-8.

Rush, Elizabeth. *Rising: Dispatches from the New American Shore*. Milkweed Editions, 2019.

Sheldrake, Merlin. *Entangled Life: How Fungi Make Our Worlds, Change Our Minds & Shape Our Futures*. Random House, 2020.

Spaid, Sue. *The Philosophy of Curatorial Practice: Between Work and World*. Bloomsbury, 2020. https://doi.org/10.5040/9781350115361.

Ulehla, Julia. "The Memory of the Body: Folk Song as Key for Releasing Cultural Memory." In *From Folklore to World Music: On Memory*, edited by Irena Přibylová and Lucie Uhlíková. Municipal Culture Centre in Náměšť nad Oslavou, 2018. http://image.folkoveprazdniny.cz/2018/kolokvium2018/sbornik2018_14_Ulehla_en.pdf.

Zimmer, Carl. *She Has Her Mother's Laugh: The Powers, Perversions, and Potential of Heredity*. Dutton, 2018.

MUSIC AND POETRY

Johnson, Emily Pauline. "Through Time and Bitter Distance." *Flint and Feather*. Musson Book Co., 1912. https://poets.org/poem/through-time-and-bitter-distance.

Rajat Subhra Karmakar. "আমি যে রিকশাওয়ালা । Ami je Rikshawala - An Indo Taiwanese Cover." Posted September 23, 2023. YouTube video, 3:15. https://youtu.be/I4-ZZtVY-XA.

Rajat Subhra Karmakar. "Jag Ghumeya - A Simple Cover with Taiwan Yueqin." Posted September 29, 2018. YouTube video, 4:13. https://youtu.be/T8kyVBpnyiw.

潮台灣Trending Taiwan. "【叁獎】Ballad of the Moon Guitar / 月兒圓圓思想起 -《2016潮台灣》." Posted Mar 24, 2017. YouTube video, 3:00. https://youtu.be/xcbYpGB6oNA.

twdavid10000. "(月琴之友Yueqin Friends) 恆春民謠阿嬤陳英 月琴彈唱: 思想起." Posted Sep 7, 2011. YouTube video, 5:10. https://youtu.be/8zOoTNcmKdE.

yourhighness336. "Ali Shan De Gu Niang - Chinese Mountain Song (Acoustic Cover)." Posted on April 16, 2011. YouTube video, 2:01. https://youtu.be/MKKkOwv1hAU.

WEBSITES

MycoWorks. "Our Heritage." Accessed August 19, 2024. https://www.mycoworks.com/our-heritage.

U.S. Forest Service. "What Are Mycotrophic Wildflowers?" https://web.archive.org/web/20220525190717/https://www.fs.fed.us/wildflowers/beauty/mycotrophic/whatarethey.shtml.

NOAA. Sea Level Rise Viewer, n.d. https://coast.noaa.gov/slr/.

Wayne's Word. "Fungus Flowers: Flowering Plants That Resemble Fungi." https://web.archive.org/web/20181113165746/https://www2.palomar.edu/users/warmstrong/pljune97.htm.

Woodrow Instrument Company. https://www.thewoodrow.com.